POSSESSING THE SEASONS

THE PLANTING LOGS OF LINKUM REGARDS

CHARLES PROWELL

This book is a work of fiction. Names, characters, places, and incidents are the product of the author's imagination or are used fictitiously. Any resemblance to actual events, locales, or persons, living or dead, is coincidental.

©2025 Charles Prowell
Cover ©2025 Robyn Leigh Lear
Interior Design ©2025 Sydney Bozeman

-First Edition

All rights reserved. No part of this publication may be reproduced or transmitted in any form or by any means, electronic or mechanical, including photocopy, recording, or any information storage or retrieval system, without permission in writing from the publisher.

Publisher's Cataloguing-in-Publication Data

Prowell, Charles
Possessing the seasons: The planting logs of linkum regards / written by Charles Prowell
ISBN: 978-1-953932-31-0

1. Fiction - General 2. Fiction - Literary 3. Fiction - Coming of Age I. Title II. Author

Library of Congress Control Number: 2024949065

To Mother, Anne, Sarah, and Mary.

To Sallie and Janie.

To Pearl.

ONE

I lean back away from the little desk set against the attic dormer beside her drawing board that hasn't been moved since it was first displaced by my own desk some seventy years ago. A desk built by True Pond and dragged from the darkest vestiges of the attic to where I could look out over the lawn and lower pasture and the river and ultimately, with the arriving light, the thin lines of the ridge in the distance. Built, I imagine, not long before True was caught up in the thresher, losing that arm and no one but his father Wrestling present to watch a son only twenty-eight years old bleed to death. But before that, before his accident, it was with both arms in tact that he fashioned the tenons and splines and tapered profiles of a walnut drawn from the west field hollow in an act that was nothing if not spiritual. You don't create from nothing, something so lasting and inspiring without the presence of a lofted spirit.

The earliest light lifts and filters through the crevices of the ridge and I massage my old fingers and run my hand over the page as if smoothing the notebook away from the present and back into the past. Noises, sleeping murmurs from the corner where little Henry and I camped in the great featherbed in the great attic as an adventure. An adventure with Poppa. Checked on by his mother Dominate, tucking us in like schoolboys and again the sound of her soft footsteps up the winding stairs in the middle of the night repeatedly and it was a mistake, giving in to everyone's insistence that the stories be committed to paper. Reliving a life already lived that somehow alters the life being lived on any given day. But lives, their lives, everyone's lives, are now lived with an ongoing daily account posted to the internet without the discipline or sovereignty of a life less examined. Less scrutinized. And how the very act of scrutiny itself impacts the authenticity of anyone's life. Gradually over the past months I no longer make my way to the barnyard with the anticipation and optimism of what every single day brings, but rather with the baggage of recollections and reflections drawn from a past being put to words in what they insist is my contribution to the Pond Planting Logs. A contribution, I'll add, no longer concerned with a fixation on crop rotations, planting schematics, and weather…… or worse, my father's abbreviated and annotated gibberish studded with the algorithms of genetic mutations.. But, moreover, a narrative bumping between what I know and what I've imagined I know through those eighteen months so long ago when everything changed.

The words come easy. They always come easy. The words and sentences pouring forth and when I pause to gather the accuracy of a past, they keep spilling forth, impatient, ambitiously breaching the dam of my aging mind like a log jam and yet mindful of the protocol, the disciplined importance of a desk that faces a river whose current chugs along seamlessly. I'm mindful of purpose and structure, the detective novelist, or the master craftsman who replicates a centuries- old bureau, the order that gives way every morning to something more, to music and imagination. They find their place, the words, sidling up to one another on the page with the solidarity of something greater than the sum of their unselfish selves. They cooperate. They allow themselves the dalliance of a suffix or a mutated phonetic that would have Mrs. Hall turning in her grave. They bend and stretch and abuse the rules of who witnessed what for the sake of music and imagination. Of telling the story.

Do they know, do the words and my sons and daughters-in-law even care that I made up the description of my aunts Elizabeth and Madeline wearing matching patterned dresses to sit in their Plymouth with its matching patterned upholstery or how I write of a bloodhound that never existed or when Scooter's mom Ruby went away, I failed to mention the Home for the Mentally Insane over in Anna and how there was so much mental illness. How the generations of inbreeding had come to accept as normal this quirkiness better known to a learned mind as schizophrenia and manic depression and the chronic stupors of delusional psychosis?

Do they know I make things up? How I freely and frequently trespass into the sovereign moods and conversations beyond my actual purview? How Verity and Mariah are not present to insist on my accuracy or truthfulness?

For the longest time it was only my sisters and I who noticed the subtle changes in our mother's behavior. Although it was never mentioned, not even to one another. We were less than adults and distracted, like everyone, by the slow culmination of events beyond anyone's control. Tip-toeing, circumventing direct confrontations in lieu of indirect insinuations. Straining to maintain a pretense of normalcy, as if everything was fine at a time when it was not fine. Our culture was being threatened on so many fronts that we simply dug in, adhered to our rituals and routines as if the good life would continue forever. And it worked. All things considered, it worked.

Late in that third drought-stricken summer we would sit on the back porch of our sprawling old farmhouse, fanning ourselves, talking. Mother standing over a chair with bobby pins pursed between her lips, setting Mariah's curlers with Aunt Dee and Verity occupying the far swing and Aunt Bim and myself on the opposite swing and if it was a Saturday night, the twins, Aunt Elizabeth and Aunt Madeline, sharing the living room couch in matching floral frocks, yelling at the radio, at the ref for allowing an infraction, an illegal full nelson by a wrestler known for his cowboy hat.

Countless evenings passed like this. Father standing at the screen, his trousers hiked up over his boots, staring into the changing light as the sun dropped down behind Kickapoo Ridge a mile off and every so often flicking the screen to send a fat clinging june bug somersaulting back toward the yard. Back where it belongs with the fireflies and the mosquitoes and those black flies big enough to choke on.

Uneventful is what mostly comes to mind. The sound of the chains riding against the ceiling hooks while from the barn Horse talking to Cow and Cow responding, followed by Sow One and Sow Two and for a few moments a flurry of snorts and whinnies coupled with a thousand crickets in a cricket symphony along the river punctuated by a holler from the living room and Aunt Bim making funny sounds to mimic a good scalp rubbing while running her fingers through my hair as I leafed through a photo book of Civil War battles. And from the opposite swing Aunt Dee grazing her open palm along Verity's arm as Verity leafed through one of her horse books and when she found something she liked Dee would nod and because Dee ran the Alterations shop in town, yet another likeness of yet another horse photo would show up embroidered on yet another one of Verity's identical white blouses.

At some point, we would be rewarded with a breeze. It would come up slowly once the sky had gone from blue to blood red to a fluctuating purple hanging off the horizon over the ridge like a changing kaleidoscope. Working its way down off the gorge and along the river to carry over the lower dell and up the rise of the lawn and onto the screened-in back porch to graze our cheeks with the relief of a swamp cooler. We would turn collectively toward the canopy of cottonwoods along the river, turn head-on toward the breeze as darkness settled in and as a lone car might approach the bridge from Snead's Corner, creeping up onto the elevated bridegboards and then the clap of the loose oak planks before dipping back down onto the roadbed with the headlights bobbing to the sound of shifting gravel and if I remember any one of those hundreds of identical summer evenings, it would be when we first heard proof of the albino's voice. Singing up off the river, lifting out from the cover of the thicket and the river canopy to wend its way up over the lower pasture like the Messiah. A clear, sustained medley of alternating octaves that silenced the crickets and the bullfrogs and had us all on our feet, pressed to the screen, knowing for the first time how it was more than a mere rumor, more than fanciful exaggerations appearing sporadically over the past

185 years in the hand-written planting logs stashed in the attics of every single one of the forty-seven farms situated along southern Illinois' Salt Fork River.

We stood to the screen, all of us, quiet, listening, as I imagined running down to the river, in the dark, barefoot over Slave Hill and through the cool basketgrass below and along a riverbank pocked with snakeholes to rout the legend from the thicket and lock it into a full nelson and drag it up into civilization, into the light of the moon and thereby, at eleven years old, accomplishing something magnificent. Something legendary.

The following day, or any day for that matter, I would make my way from the house to cross the lawn and the barnyard and enter the sanctuary of the Annex where Father sat hunched over his logbooks. A room where the temperature and humidity were constant through the winter freezes and the summer melts and where I arrived sent from the kitchen by Clare with news that lunch was ready. I took my place along the bench wearing the wool Yankee Great Coat and kepi and oversized boots culled from the chest in the attic and sat quietly, sweating, making my announcement while gazing upon the hundreds of potted plants and grafted stems of a tropical jungle: string beans the size of sausages; fat plump tomatoes as red as fresh paint. The shelves along the common barn wall stacked with those logbooks coded in a language of formulaic notations. I sat, waiting, sweating in a room where the air was as thick as gelatin.

"I be reckonin lunch's ready, Dad."

Silence. I pondered my options. With Clare's communiqué successfully delivered I could wait for a response, risking death by dehydration, or exit unnoticed and make my way back across the barnyard to the house, back to Clare's kitchen with the Great Coat dragging in the dust and return with a plate of sliced fruit and chopped vegetables and opt yet again for the stifling heat of the barnyard over the unbreathable air of the Annex and return yet again to see the plate untouched and take a seat.

"Clare says eat or starve or otherwise nothin till dinner."

He reached for a wedge of sliced pear and studied it, holding it up to the light, twirling its mutations across his fingertips, taking a bite, and another bite, and reached for one of the logbooks off the shelf to begin making notes and when he was finished, he looked up as if I were a fencepost and a moment later, "What are you wearing?"

"Clothes, I reckon." To which I had added our ancestral saber clattering awkwardly off my hip.

"Whose clothes?"

"Someone's."

"Someone who?"

"I don't rightly know. Granddad or someone."

"Justus, it's a hundred degrees today. Take those off. And stop talking like some Appalachian hillbilly."

"Civil war, Dad. Civil war."

"Whatever. It's my fault. Mine and your mother's. To the girls we read nice little bedtime stories, but you…to you we read the encyclopedia. And look where it's led? There's already no more room in your brain. It's full."

"You don't understand the brain, Dad. It's something else. For instance, the reason Burnside was so late in defending the bridge was…"

But he's not listening. Watching, but not actually listening.

14

TWO

I had learned to anticipate that hour just before dawn when my parents woke. The sound of them shuffling in their room off the library at the bottom of the stairs as I lay on my side staring into the darkness of my window facing the lawn below, the lower pasture and the faint shadows of the rusting trellis over the bridge, watching him rounding the corner of the house and making his way up the barnyard where the bloodhound, Bo, might appear and the two of them disappearing into that jungle Annex as Mother's footsteps could be heard, climbing first the stairs off the library to cross the dayroom outside my bedroom and then up the winding stairs to the attic as her drawing-board chair scraped the floorboards over my head. If I wanted either one of them to myself, without the interference of sisters, or before Clare woke rattling dishes in the kitchen, or the hands living seasonally in the old slave's quarters off the barn, or the certainty of any one of my aunts arriving from town, or the neighbor Dolores who either walked the half mile to our house or Mother walked the half mile to her house every single day of their lives…if I wanted them to myself, however briefly, I slipped from bed not to wake Verity still sleeping below a shelf lined with her collection of plastic horses and tiptoed up the winding stairs to stand at

15

the landing, adjusting my eyes to the faint light off the drawing board beside the dormer. I went first to the old featherbed along that half of the sprawling attic cluttered with the antiques of dead Ponds for that sensation of sinking, or floating, on a mattress that billowed up around me as I lay listening to the scratching of her pencil. The intermittent creaking and moaning of the overhead timbers breathing, adjusting to the coming heat of the day. And if I was late and the sun had already surfaced from beyond Kickapoo Ridge, I might pull one of the planting logs off the shelf, any of which read like an encyclopedia of living history, studded with the superstitions and embellished claims of a cheap novel.

There were bookmarks, as I recall. Torn pieces of paper where I had marked those entries for quick access to the written proof. The written word, as a recurring reference to the myth or legend or belief in an ageless giant albino living for one-hundred-fifty years in the tupelo woods between the Point where the river drew south and the gorge, where the river narrowed to the limestone canyons of Kickapoo Ridge. Wrestling Pond, with his entry in 1832 of a *strange whitish creature affrighting to the riverbank*, penned not long after he and Chastity broke from southern New Hampshire in an exchange of strict Puritanism to settle the Salt Fork Valley as a lenient colony of Anabaptists and Amish. Or by Experience Pond in 1873 with a *singing white black'n*. Or by the repeated anonymous entries during Reconstruction when Dust Pond threshed his arm and bled to death, spoiling any thoughts of his father Experience retiring and because Dust's only heir was just eight, the logs are inconsistent and likely penned by one of the learned hands who repeatedly claimed to have associated, even befriended, an albino gifted with the '...*critters and posessun a hypnust's qual'ty.*'

But eventually I shuffled toward the dormer to crouch soundlessly on the floor and lean against the side of her chair where now and again the sensation of her fingers ran through my scalp. The world beyond the attic paused. Time itself stopped as the reservoir slowly filled and I scampered away, disappearing down the winding steps and down the second steps and through the library and down the hall adjacent to the long kitchen where Clare would be up, humming her whispering hymns as I made out the back door and over the fence rails and up the barnyard and into the tropical air of the Annex where he sat at the bench. Father, scribbling in his logbooks in a language no one but Father read or understood as I stretched out on the floorboards washed by Bo's sloppy tongue. If I wanted either of my parents to myself, before the competition of everyone else, I had to be awake before dawn.

THREE

The hands were seasonal. No different today than when I was eleven but for an efficiency of spreadsheets and databases adopted by my youngest son Conquer and his wife Dominate that provides health care and proper payrolls and investment mandates while the premise itself, the willingness to work and the need for field hands, has not changed.

They migrated up from Cairo in April. Walked, back then, all the way from Cairo. The regulars would come straight to the old Quarters and find their own personal cot and the others would get situated beneath the bridge, living there with their campfires to stand along Pond Road every morning, hoping to be plucked by us or Givens Marsh or Guy Faller or Liberty Snead, but never Mr. and Mrs. Arthur of the Amish farm abutting our east field. The Arthurs plowed with draft horses and lived in an unpainted house without electricity.

The Quarters itself was once a chicken coop, repurposed long ago as a safe house still embedded with the initials and markings carved into the framing and girders by slaves breaking for the Promised Land, the Land of Milk 'n Honey if compared to deep Mississippi. Coming up by a system of transports and underground sympathizers to that holy state where the Emancipator was born. The Land of Linkum, and walking from Cairo to the Salt Fork Valley where they were put to work and fed and housed and although they were never paid, they were free from whippings and the cruelty of indentured servitude.

❊ ❊ ❊

Aside from the Javitts-from-Kentucky who swapped flourishing crops for goat breeding, Father alone was not born from the stale continuum of inbreeding. Forty-seven farms propagating among ourselves, ending on the day he arrived. An outsider, marrying his way into the fertile valley as a pragmatist, a non-believer, a scientist who had developed an early hybrid corn seed while a graduate student in upstate Urbana.

They were naturally distrustful, the others, of anyone who for seventeen years had failed to appear for a single service. All those Sundays when my mother and great grandparents and aunts and essentially everyone would gather at the Fall Ridge Church to hear the still youngish Brother Reeves ranting and raving of doctrines and dogmas followed by a young Mercy May Jenkins striking a few chords as a prelude to the hymns drifting and wafting down across the north field and the following foot procession along Pond Road for an afternoon Sunday supper at one of the three farms between the church and river. Givens and Vivian Marsh or Guy and Dolores Faller or the Pond farm of the aging Dust and Obedience Pond someday and forever more to be the Roe farm. Everyone gathering on the sprawling front lawn then as they have throughout much of my own life with the women dancing between the kitchen and the lawn, commiserating like songbirds, and the men target shooting tin cans off the back of the barn and the kids stripped near naked diving off the trellis bridge and this often extending to early evening when the chairs and benches were lined along the top of the rise to overlook the lower pasture and the river as an opportunity for everyone to make their own amends. A meditation of sorts to the backdrop of a sky going pink purple and a deep blood red as the sun drifted down beyond

POSSESSING THE SEASONS

the rising peaks of Kickapoo Ridge, marking daylight from dusk when
as if on cue the crickets woke with a symphony of white noise to awaken
the Herefords braying like bass drums and the banshees squawking and
all those sitting along the rise chatting and chuckling and wondering
if possibly, on this evening, there may be evidence of that voice from
down along the river somewhere, rising and falling from the registers of
a mythical beast.

20

FOUR

We by routine would come to town on Saturday mornings. All of us, released to the spoils of town and all that town had to offer. Aunt Bim Bim's *Gazette*, where I had a job now and again cleaning ink from the press rollers but had yet to be paid and where Aunt Dee's shop *Pond Alterations* was located across the street where Mariah spent time honing her passion for fashion and Dr. Stayer the Vet where Verity went as if it were a public zoo, hoping for a job doing something, anything, and the Depot at the end of the block next to the *Gazette*, where the one-o'clock from Centralia was of a passing interest, the residual proof of a world beyond our world.

Father and I in the truck and later Mother and the girls in the car and because Buddy Faller often spent Saturday mornings, as he put it, 'blowin out the carbons,' parading his customized Ford around town, Mother would have for the umpteenth time reminded Mariah that at fifteen she was *not* allowed inside that car.

We took the back route through old Mr. Arthur's south field along the narrow wagon path tamped by a century of draft horses and we talked of the new crop. The drought-resistant barley and alfalfa making its debut in the east and north fields. Cell walls bred like succulents, insulated from the heat and holding moisture against dehydration and yet it needed a little rain.

"How much, Dad?"

"Half inch. Half inch Sport is all we need."

"Half inch is a half inch, Dad."

The previous winter had passed without a single measurable snowfall. With no spring snowmelt or mudholes. Cold, with plenty of days below zero and good skating on the river, but no real weather. No icicles slung like daggers off the eaves and fencerails.

Town's past was as much a part of our lives as the present. How we do what we do today is built upon how we did what we did long ago. Modern history, beginning with the Reconstruction years, was marked by bored veterans who built Town Hall, desperate for something to do that had nothing to do with a proximity to bayonets and blood. Timber framers and bricklayers and cabinetmakers whose roles in the war—as Anabaptists—were relegated to cooks and quartermasters. They chose the southeast corner fronted on one side by a muddy Main Street grooved and furrowed with wagon wheel ruts and on the other by the sharp defile of a creek someone should have known would flood most every spring, rising up and oozing through the masonry basement walls and receding to leave a foot of mud and silt most every spring that had to be scraped clean with snow shovels and hosed down and aired out with scented bouquets of blooming elderberries and purple coneflowers. But they didn't think. They were in a hurry to get started, get building, and put the past behind them. They were starved for progress after years of endless marching under a succession of endless officers so inept it was a wonder they won the war. So, they marched down Main Street, retrofitting everything that existed or building anew and by and by the great Fall Ridge revitalization ended eight years later with the overly elaborate millwork for the gabled portico on the face of the new bank and it was the sort of deranged progress and productivity that defined a droopy drowsy farm town with elements of prideful pizzazz. Which would describe us perfectly: droopy quirky God-fearing folk who farmed like poets. Farming as an art form.

FIVE

We occupied the booth along the elevated window of Davis' Café on a Saturday morning two and half years into the drought. As the weekend waitress, Acceptance Davis took our order in her slipover cotton dress and as I recall, to this day, with her brother's belt at the waist dangling against her hip in a way I'd always found attractive. The air was stolid, thick with the scent of sausages and smoke. Talk of rain. Lots of talk about rain without mentioning rain. But that was also about to change. It was early May and I was a month from turning twelve. The crops were in, and what was required, what was the object of everyone's prayers, was enough precipitation to give the seeds a chance of breaking ground and avoiding a third consecutive starved harvest that would to some, more than who let on, present a series of options and choices no one discussed.

"I'll say this, we don't get some weather and soon and some folks'll do what they have to do."

That was Diligence Wiseman whose farm was south of the Point, where the river banked off our west field. Diligence was also a self-taught hydrologist with a second-hand drilling rig worth more as scrap iron than that of a functional rig.

"Do what, Dill?" It was Guy Faller's voice, left to hang in the smoky air like an omen. He sat wedged in a booth built for smaller men, shared with his son Bump and myself and Father. Bump and I next to the window where we watched a group of hands gathered at the outdoor tables, playing dominoes.

"You know. You know what, Guy. What Sapp's done did."

The Sapp farm of only 125 acres had always been a marginal harvest. Set on the foothills with shallow soil, the Sapps were poor by the poorest standards, hunting muskrat, squirrel, and pheasant for food. But rumor was that it had been offered up through an agency in Evansville. Just rumor, but with the exception of the Javitts-from-Kentucky, it would mark the first spread in the valley's history to be sold to an outsider.

Acceptance arrived with our breakfast and I thought how without her and it was just a crowded room of farmers smoking their pipes and cigars. She lingered for a moment too long and both Guy and Father glanced at her and then me and smiled and she left and Bump's foot tapped my shin.

From an adjoining booth Listen Allerton said, "It ain't just the Sapps. "Pears the only crop breaking ground is over to the Ponds."

A subtle slight, when for the past seventeen years and forever more it was the Roe Farm. He turned to look at Father and added, "What is that you got going over there, Hank?"

Listen Allerton owned and operated Allerton Feed and Grain and if there was a renegade crop in the works, it would be Listen who fixed the market value come September[1].

Father shrugged and suddenly everyone was watching our booth.

"Tell us, Hank," Givens Marsh added, leaning against the far counter, "Cause it don't appear like soybeans or corn."

---

1. *It should also be noted that all of Listen's ancestors were named Listen and it was that heritage, starved for affection, for companionship, for love, who kidnapped or eloped with Chastity Pond for ten days back in the 1790s. The Allerton men had a history of dying wives. Even the current Listen, whose wife died from consumption before I was born. I wondered if Father knew all this. As if Father had actually read all the planting logs with all their stories.*

But Father was silent, watching out the window where the hands were arguing with one another when Tip Rawley of the Leven place suddenly swept the dominoes off the tabletop and walked back to lean against the Levin truck parked along the curb.

They watched us a moment more, those in the Café, waiting for Father's answer, when through the corner of the window Buddy Faller's Ford appeared, coming from beyond the school and down Sycamore Street to a rolling stop before Mercy May Jenkin's little cornerstone home built across the creek from Town Hall. It sat idling against the curb like shucked corn vibrating in the bed of a gravity wagon. Mariah squirmed out of the passenger window of a passenger door that had been welded shut for no good reason. She stood on the curb leaning into the open window, raising her voice over the efforts of the idling engine and the conflicting din of Mercy May practicing her violin for Sunday's service and Mariah started off down the walk toward the corner. The Ford rolled along behind her, Buddy leaning, talking to her through the open window and Mariah walking, carrying a satchel of fabric she'd brought to town this morning to pattern off at Aunt Dee's shop and as she crossed the street, her rhythm changed, flinging her hips out with each step in that exaggerated march of what Clare called the Queen of Sheba when Tip Rawley from across Main Street whistled and Mariah hollered something back. At that point, Buddy forgot Mariah, revving the engine as if the guttural roar of his engine alone was a weapon and he lurched across Main Street and braked directly across the street from our window in the Café to throw a straight arm at Tip still leaning against the truck. Calling out. Tip turned away and Buddy roared on up Sycamore Street as Mother appeared, walking down toward Main Street and I thought there's no one she visits living up that way except old Dr. Steadfast Stewart, who delivered my sisters and I and my mother and her five sisters. She glanced at Bump and I and waved as she passed directly below us before disappearing around the corner toward Aunt Bim Bim's *Gazette*.

We turned back to the ongoing smoky talk in the Café and the sound of Givens' voice. "Would to God wish I knew what you's up to, Roe."

I watched Father as he watched my pancakes and he said, "How's the cakes, Sport?"

I made a face, uncomfortable with the talk in the Café, pushing things around the plate and not wanting to abandon Father but glancing at Bump and to Father a moment more and making to leave I said, "We'll be at the depot, or Bim's."

Leaving the Café, we headed up Main Street, Bump and I, pausing at the benches in front of the bank to watch the elders chewing tobacco and spitting like target practice into corroded spittoons surrounded by puddles of black goo. They were talking horses. Reins and bridles and the smell of horsehide before tractors and gas engines and the smell of horseshit piled along Main Street as if it were something other than horseshit. As if it were a meadow of gladiolas.

We turned into the *Gazette*. My workplace. An apprentice, a proud laborer. Bim and Mother were sitting at the layout table, talking, and we went straight for the press without a word and set out the solvent and the brushes and I said to Bump, "Not too much. Don't splash it on the plates." For the next fifteen minutes we inhaled the solvents and the ink and made faces as if we were drunk while Mother and Bim sat watching, rolling their eyes. Waiting for Aunt Dee, they spoke in whispers about Dr. Stewart. Dr. Steadfast Stewart's concern for Mother's headaches when Bump and I put away the solvents and cleaned the brushes, and on the way out I said to Bim Bim, "Quarter hour, boss. On the clock." And Bim, bent in close to Mother, whispering, nodded and waved us off. Out on the walk we staggered, laughing like drunks drunk on fumes.

Carl's *Wabash* was expected to arrive at one sharp on Saturdays, which meant anywhere from eleven to two. The depot was empty but for the napping stationmaster Lester, and Scooter, who stood waiting behind the coal bin. He pulled from his shirt pocket a crooked rolled cigarette pilfered from his mother Ruby's dresser drawer. He stood leaning against the back wall of the *Gazette*, smoke rings lingering and drifting and whisking off in the breeze above the bin.

Bump said, "They don't like what they don't know," referring to the Café talk.

"They're idiots. They don't know dung from doo-doo."

"They'll know all right when it's knee-high. They'll know it ain't soybeans or corn."

"Know what? What ain't corn?" Scooter asked.

Bump and Scooter stood sharing the wrinkled cigarette rolled from Ruby's tobacco tin, waiting for the whistle when Verity appeared, looking at Bump and a moment later they're gone, Bump and Verity, walking toward Dr. Stayer's and I'm left with Scooter who made his way to the tracks to stand on his hands as if Verity were still around, walking along the rail upside down as the whistle carried from Bonnel Road two miles off. But Verity, who had rarely even acknowledged Scooter's existence, had crossed the tracks at Main Street and she and Bump had paused to watch Buddy's Ford as I moved over to the tracks beside Scooter and the second whistle sounded.

"Hey, Carl's coming."

But Scooter wasn't right. He had never been right. He spread his legs scissor-like, laughing, and I glanced at the crossing where Buddy sat idling, the front of his grill painted flat black and surrounded by bright yellow tiger teeth and he waited, talking to his brother, to Bump. I glanced up the tracks and then at the window of the *Gazette* where Mother and Aunt Bim Bim were watching, drawn by Carl's whistle and Buddy's familiar game and Bim was silently shaking her fist at the crossing and Lester appeared, rubbing his eyes as Carl made the turn, black as a gun, sounding his whistle and leaning out, angrily shaking his fist as the Ford accelerated and lunged for a running start into the crossing to just clear the lowering crossarms. Carl rolled to a steaming hissing stop at the depot. Thick white clouds lingered and hung without the hint of a breeze as Scooter danced and skipped and moved to retrieve his string of metal scraps flattened and fused together in a way that had always fascinated him.

I didn't understand Scooter. He lived with his mom Ruby in the small house near Dr. Stewart's house on Sycamore. I knew like everyone knew that she and Dilligence Wiseman the well-driller had been sneaking around for years until his wife Violet drove that dilapidated drilling rig onto Ruby's front lawn and up the front steps to crush the porchboards like kindling.

Ruby. Ruby made the rest of us seem normal. She was a splotch of red, dulling the rest of Fall Fork to a gray sameness. And although we were never just the two of us in conversation, I can see and hear her now as well as my own sisters. Ruby Morrow wore bright colors and long bright scarves that hung to the back of her knees and when she drove her scratched and dented little MG around town, her scarf flared out in the wind to flap against the trunk and it once caught the rear tire and nearly broke her neck. She'd gone away to Anna a few times 'to get fixed,' as Scooter would say, and in her absence, Scooter managed alone, cooking and cleaning as if he were grown. But he was only eleven. People looked in on him and made room in spare bedrooms as if he belonged to everyone, but no one kept him for long; for the most part he lived alone, waiting for his mom to return and when she did, he cooked for them both.

Carl had come down from the cab to lean against the tender. He lit his pipe and talked to Lester while eyeing Scooter. He took a step toward us, just a slight motion, and quickly we turned and jogged toward the alley behind the *Gazette*, laughing, carry on down to the back of the Café and back up Main Street and eventually we ducked into Aunt Dee's alterations shop as if we'd slipped a manhunt.

There was an adjustment; we caught our breath, cooled by the breeze from several floor fans situated around the shop, circulating a current that fed through hundreds of bolts of fabric shelved upright floor-to-ceiling from one end of the shop to another. Dee had the Widow Drew on the fitting pedestal, pinning a loose thingamajingie when she looked at us with several loose pins pursed between her lips; her raised eyebrows were as good as words.

"It's nothin, Dee. We've just been running some."

"Exercising," Scooter added. "They say it's good for you…and maybe I might play track next season, though Coach Plenty thinks a scholarship—"

I stopped him. Shoved him onto his heels. Scooter just wasn't right. He'd just go on and on with each lie bigger than the one before.

From the back pattern table Mariah looked up and turned to Dee who tugged lightly on the Widow's hem, smoothing wrinkles from a fabric that belonged on a sofa. Dee straightened and pressed a palm against the small of her back with a grimace as she stood back to view the Widow and motioned her toward the changing room. The Widow stepped down from the pedestal and glanced at Mariah in her svelte black stretch pants and red leather flats and said, "Honey, you're like a fashion model. Like paris france right here in Fall Ridge."

Mariah smiled without actually looking at the Widow as Dee moved to the back pattern table, studying the pattern as she held Mariah's hand and Mariah explained, "I want it on the bias," and the Widow added, "It must be nice having a rich Daddy who can afford…"

"Go change, Loretta," Dee said, and at us she added, "You two hooligans sit down and behave yourselves."

Mother and Bim arrived carrying the teapot and the three of them settled around the front table to have their tea and sweetcakes and over the others Mother said, "I believe Carl's looking for you two." Bim and Dee turned toward Scooter and I sitting on the front bench and I shrugged and Scooter said, "Oh, he's prob'ly lookin about my help. He said he would hire—"

But the others had turned away, back to their conversation and their Saturday tea break as the Sheriff entered, standing for a moment, taking us in, and then took a seat on the empty stool beside Dee with a kiss on her cheek as Bim poured his tea and in their whispers a moment later Bim spoke, "The ole coot has given her something new."

"He's fishin," Dee added.

Sheriff held the pills close and set them down and ran his open hand along Dee's sore back and muttered, "More pills."

"Exactly," Bim said. "Exactly my thinking."

Mother said, "They're to help sleep is all."

"Exactly," Bim repeated. "Doc's fishin and time we make inquiries up north."

The Sheriff smoothed Dee's back and Dee ran her fingers along his arm. Sheriff had been Dee's beau for all *my* life, maybe longer. He had returned from the war with metal in his head and Town had pitched in for a uniform and a badge and a red light he kept behind the seat in the cab of his truck. No one had ever been arrested. There was no jail. There's still no jail, seventy years later. There were no laws anyone was aware of, nor even a stationhouse. Just Sheriff's house he was born in over on Oak Street. To Sheriff, policing was about calming people. Settling minor disputes.

Carl pulled away from the depot in a fit of steam, catching me in the shop window and pointing a lazy finger out the cab as Bump and Verity skipped across the tracks, holding hands as they approached Main Street to turn in the shop and instantly they separated. Verity moved to the front table to kiss Mother on the cheek and then to the back beside Mariah who explained, her hands sweeping over the pattern table as if conducting an overture, when Widow Drew appeared from the changing room with her new dress folded over one arm and to Bump, Scooter said, "So, is she yer girlfriend?"

Bump slapped him hard enough to bring the Sheriff from his stool to fold his arms around Bump as if he were a puppy and Scooter stood poised, standing on the front bench bouncing like a shadow boxer as Dee called out, *"Lewelyn Morrow,"* and she pointed to the door.

A moment later Scooter stood alone on the walk outside the window, still bouncing, shadowboxing, but no one was watching except Father, who appeared up the sidewalk from the Café to pause for a moment as he studied Scooter as if he were an alien. He ruffled his hair and smiled and forgot him altogether as he entered the shop and leaned in to kiss Mother and wandered back to watch Mariah and Verity and then back, giving the Widow Drew a wide berth as he seated himself at the table with the others.

"Whiskey straight."

Bim poured his tea and offered the plate of sweetcakes and Father sat. He considered the prescription pills set on the table like a flowering centerpiece. He fingered the bottle. He twirled it across one palm and he looked back at Mother and Mother smiled and he kissed her on the eyelid as he rested his hand on hers and said, "Let's go to Chicago."

People in Fall Ridge don't just *go to Chicago*. Chicago is Mars. Technically the same state but because none of us had ever been to Chicago, it was figured to be full of aliens—from Mars.

But Bim and Dee and the Sheriff both nodded their approval and a moment later Father added, "On the train and a nice hotel and we'll see who we need to see and—"

"When," Mother asked.

"Soon. Right away."

"The kids'll stay in town," Dee offered. I perked up, when from back near the fitting room, the Widow declared, "The Beast is back."

There was a short silence. The hum of the fans carried her voice through the shop and it lingered like a drizzle as Dee left the front table to arrive at the fitting room where the Widow had been forgotten, left standing all alone with her new dress draped over one arm waiting for Dee, for something.

Dee took the dress and folded it and set it on a shelf against the wall and to the Widow she said, "How bout Tuesday, honey? Will that work?"

The Widow offered a faint smile. A lost smile as Dee guided her by the elbow toward the front door and at the door the Widow declared again, to Dee and to anyone else who was listening, "I heard from your sister. From Elizabeth. The Beast is back."

SIX

I didn't understand, as an eleven-year-old, how Father could have a normal name like Henry and register at a hotel in Chicago and no one would know he's from Salt Fork County. My mother had not been beyond the county since she returned from school at Champaign with a normal man named Henry. She had never stayed in a hotel nor had she ever been to Chicago and had never taken Carl's *Wabash* beyond a few trips home during her school year in Champaign.

Why did Dolores and Guy Faller across the road have normal names, and for that matter within our own family the twins Elizabeth and Madeline, while Aunt Harriet, the oldest of the six Pond sisters, went from Fortuna to Harriet when she moved to St. Louis. Who decided? Their parents, my grandparents, were dead and unavailable for such inquiries and my great grandparents Ma and Dad Pond, were also unavailable and who decided on Elizabeth and Madeline that allowed them to peddle their bibles in Carbondale while my mother's Gracious was like a signpost, or my own Justus, or Verity's Verity—like tattoos across our foreheads if we ever left the county. People would know, I was told. They'll know the minute you introduce yourself that you were… that you were from *that county.*

33

POSSESSING THE SEASONS

My oldest sister Mariah would leave someday. Everyone knew that. She knew it. And although Mariah wasn't Dolores, it was normal enough for her to be a fashion designer in St. Louis or paris france and not have everyone knowing she was from a place where they believed in beasts that live for two-hundred years in the tupelos along the river. And recently, according to the Widow Drew and Aunt Elizabeth, that stretch of river fronting only our farm, the Roe farm, and no others and somehow they associated it with Mother's health. Her up and down health as a child and then as a teenager and now again as a grown woman. They made that assumption and connection because my mother was Gracious Pond, Baby Grace, of the Chastity Pond legacy and it's that legacy, that heritage that was as defining as the soil every other farmer in every other county on earth would give up everything to own.

SEVEN

With the head of their bed to the window and the sash open to a sliver of crisp air, I can still hear their voices whispering from within their bedroom door. Here, now, while I wallow in the past, I not only hear them, but I can close my eyes and see them. Picture them, like watching a movie, as Mother considered the idea of Chicago, which to her was as indefinable as paris france.

"I don't understand how long we'll be there…and where will we sleep?"

"A week, as I understand it. And we'll sleep in a bed. They sleep in beds just like we do. We have a hotel. A nice hotel."

Mother was quiet, organizing the idea of a hotel to fit somewhere within a mind that had never experienced a hotel. And as Father endured the silence, he considered for a moment how she seemed less concerned with all the probing and the poking and the invasive procedures that would account for most of that week than with the peripherals—where they would sleep and where they would eat. Mother had never been inside a hospital, and the train to Chicago would mark six and a half hours confined to the restrictive parameters of a moving boxcar, with windows.

35

"How will we get from the hotel to the doctor?"

"A taxi."

And again, there was a silence as she considered the idea of a taxi. Something yellow, honking its way through traffic along narrow streets lined with tall buildings.

"They'll laugh at me."

"Who? Who will laugh?"

"Everyone. The person driving the taxi and the person who owns the hotel."

"Why would they laugh?"

"Because I'm not like them."

Father pulled her in close and she molded to him like warm sculpting clay. From their pillow he could look up into the side-yard elm. The moonlight as it struck the thinning canopy and filtering down through the limbs and branches like navigating a maze. The same light sprinkled onto the foot of the bed linens, and when the breeze ruffled the elm leaves, the bedsheet danced and twinkled and Mother said, "Jussie's growing up wild."

The comment lingered. The symphony of crickets and assorted insects had gone silent. From the barn, not a murmur. The banshees all in their roosting nests. The birdsongs not yet returned, mass quantities of them somewhere en route. Father folded his hands behind his head and made a sound that passed for a response, or the lack of a response.

"And I'm worried about Verity, who's not so tough as she lets on, and about Buddy and that part of Mariah that's drawn to Buddy and—"

EIGHT

That following morning early before light, five-thousand geese, woodthrush, and hummingbirds approached an end to their annual migration that had found them leaving their wintering climes of Costa Rica, Guatemala, and the high desert of Mexico to gather somewhere over Nebraska for an approach into southern Illinois that would impact their arrival over Kickapoo Ridge with an annual re-entry Ruby Morrow never missed. In part, as she often admitted, she simply loved driving the gravel roads flanked by the scent of chuck-wills-widows and in part because, almost apologetically, she loved the sound of her scarf, flapping and whipping like muted fireworks. The best spot was just over the bridge adjacent to our farm, along the turn-a-round Givens Marsh had carved so his tractor could make the pivot down one furrow and up another. From this vantage she could watch the ridge over six or seven unobstructed miles of the valley with its early stunted corn and soybeans sprouting from topsoil as black as coal and interrupted only once by the stands of sycamores and cottonwoods along where the river dog-legged back toward the ridge from where it began.

We had watched her often enough, from our front lawn or the barnyard as she parked on Pond Road to kick off her shoes and make

37

herself comfortable. That morning, early, with the arriving songbirds and a blackening sky, Verity and myself were barebacking Horse with the hound lolloping ahead, on the supposition of the Legend's voice off the back porch the other night and of the Widow's reminding rumors. It was Bo's territory, all three-hundred acres, at the top of a food chain infested with muskrat, rabbit, raccoon, squirrel, water moccasins, and a feast of grouse and pheasant. Beyond the occasional bone Clare might toss out the kitchen window, Bo was left to his century-old instincts.

While Mother and Father packed for Carl's northbound and Clare was making up a traveling lunch, we walked Horse along to the edge of the barnyard and paused at the vantage of Slave Hill. A good moon but low in the sky and we stared tentatively for a moment, adjusting to the distance while standing most certainly on someone's decomposed remains marked by a scattering of crooked listing old markers circling a long-ago dead bottle tree. Not in anyone's lifetime had anyone seen a single leaf on this tree. What you saw were old bottles. Blue- and brown- and green-colored bottles strung off the naked branches that caught the sunlight at certain angles of the day and according to the hands, and mentioned here and there in the Planting Logs, the bottles were evil-absorbers.

The countryside below furled out with the faint lines of the ridge in the far distance, interrupted by the river bramble as nothing but a broad black swath. We had no real intention of actually penetrating that thicket.

"Sing," I said in a low whisper.

"What?"

"Do your singing. See if He responds."

"Who? If *who* responds?"

"You know…"

"…"

Verity whispered to Horse and we mounted, proceeding slowly along the edge of the fencerails separating the front lawn from the lower pasture and onto the graveled Pond Road to face the bridge where

Ruby, with her view from the rise of Pond Road behind us, claimed to have followed a set of headlights some several miles beyond Billing's Corner. Tracking those lights, at this sneaky hour, of what could be land speculators who would have knowingly taken the wrong turn onto Route 10 to leave the county seat that set their descent down Moingwena Rise to another wrong turn at the graveled Bonnel Road and yet anothern onto the earthen Deere Road to put them, ultimately, where they didn't belong. Where they were now: smack dab in the heart of the heart of milk and honey. Of opportunity.

Ruby dangled her bare feet over the passenger door, pleased with her ability to stay focused on the arriving migration. Pleased as well with how the hem of her skirt rose up her legs primarily because they were very nice legs—according to a particular gentleman whose opinion she valued. She gathered the scarf and maneuvered it down the side of the driver's door so that it gathered in folds to rest over Givens' field dust while reminding herself for gawd's sake don't forget to pull it up and away from that rear wheel when she leaves cause nearly choking to death once was enough for anyone.

The speculators themselves, the opportunists, were traveling along Bonnel Road like little boys in the throes of a minor infraction, their smug expressions revealing a confidence in the success of a stupid plan worked out the night before that had them in an old borrowed car with a long jagged crack in the windshield and balding tires and layers of dust all in a silly attempt to appear local, to appear as something other than what they were.

They were normal men, from St. Louis, freelancing a hard-scrabble existence with ambitions of someday becoming rich. Although themselves they had no wealth to speak of, they did have ambition. Enough ambition to have concocted this plan of infiltrating the Salt Fork Valley like carpetbagging carnies with no more notice than, say, a bird migrating home. Enough ambition to have convinced truly wealthy men to consider the investments of a coal-rich depository said or suspected to have been said to link directly to this valley whose topsoil was as black as, well...as black as coal. They hoped, beyond hope, to engage a local or two into conversation, explaining their geographical loss with a wrong turn here, and there, and knowing the plight of crop failures as per rain failures, they had in the trunk a suitcase of Chicago-backed cash. A cash offer here and now, one time only, whataya say?

The road itself was distinguished from the fields by what was left of the moonlight and the scattering waves of overhead birds as the hound moved ahead, halfway to the bridge and then down off the elevated roadbed and through the selvedge to disappear into the black holiday of the riverbanks.

"Just do what you do with the Sows and Horse and Cow. Yer critter-talk."

"It's not an animal, Jussie."

"It could be. Could be a bit animal and a bit human and a bit beast who eats newborn babies like ripe cherries[2]."

"It's a myth, Jussie. The planting logs are full of them."

Verity was ruled by a mind like our father's, rooted in science and logic, but unlike Father, she was spiritual. And like myself, she had read every word of every handscripted page of every one of the Pond Planting Logs and most of the Faller Logs and the Marsh Logs and you can't read those without an open mind to the spiritual concoctions of living history. We trod across the bridge planks and down to where the road flanked the east field that in years past, every year but for the past three, would by now be a foot under water. And with mention of newborn babies, I thought of those accounts by our founders arriving from New Hampshire and in their little cabins all fronting the river. Puritan rebels with an itch to start propagating, to shock the restrictions of their former church by doing what the Moingwena and Kickapoo woman did.

---

2. *Did I mention cherries? He fed on newborns as if they were fresh plump cherries. That's a fact.*

Whence the new moon seeth the nakidity of our women, wrote Wrestling in 1791.

Making their way across the river to strip naked and lie face down in that soil as rich as baking dough to press themselves and their special parts against that soil. Wallowing naked under the full moon...*to filleth their wombs and bideth by the immaclate conception of the Lord's will,* in the same year by the script of Helpless Faller.

We left the macadam to carry through the dry gully to follow the cow path that was once an Indian foot trail heading away from the east field and into the highland foothills of Kickapoo Ridge and I said, "He probably didn't even chew 'em. Swallowed 'em whole."

We paused a hundred yards above the road and sat Horse for a moment and watched the set of faint headlights bobbing along toward Billing's Corner visible by the absence of what would normally by now be a field of knee-high corn. From the river a hundred yards off, the tree frogs were singing like a chorus and a pair of bob whites nested in the tupelos were singing their same notes over and over and the arriving songbird express was deafening. The first hint of light sifted through the peaks. It was warm, already. A thin breeze carried off the higher ground unobstructed by trees or the whorled milkweed of the lowlands and Verity said, "There's nothing about cherries, Jussie. Or about swallowing cherries."

"If it's as big as they say, newborns would be like a cherry."

"You make things up, Jussie. You're a liar, basically. You and Aunt Bim tell stories because they sound good."

"That's because they're *stories,* Verdi. *Stor-ies.*"

The songbirds, over Cape Girardeau, Missouri in the formation of some genetic geometry, banked twenty miles south and five miles east and twenty miles back north to skirt a mountainous geological plate that ceased to exist ten-thousand years ago. Flanked on the left by the hummingbirds and on the right by the woodthrushes, sensing the landmark Mississippi River as an approach to home. They would have begun to anticipate those nesting spots, converging to share the trades toward the sycamores and cottonwoods and flowering dogwood along the Salt Fork River. Settling in, making babies in that ancestral valley where water and food were plentiful.

As far as Ruby knew, she was the only one to consider the impact of the returning birdlife as something more than an unofficial turn of the seasons. No one else anticipated the event. No one else dressed for the event. No one else rested the expectations of a turning leaf on the event. No one else weighed their past against their present against their future with the same prescient anticipation of this woman trapped between the confines of Salt Fork Valley and a bipolar diagnosis of unlimited expectations.

It was her unfortunate fate, as I believe she expressed it…her unfortunate fate to have been born into an out-of-the-way valley peopled by brilliant farmers farming a gifted soil. Inhabited with the exclusivity of birth rights and ancestral privileges unavailable to anyone outside this sphere beyond the rare mixed marriage or a widow capable of stepping beyond the known world.

Ruby was just such a widow. Her dowry was the valley. Access to a legal residency within the valley. But where were the suitors? Women with linen skirts exposing pretty legs and colorful silk scarves fluttering off the trunk of an aging MG sports car were, to the few local candidates in their bib overalls, more of a sideshow attraction, as in the spectacle of a sinful imagination.

Horse trod along the open meadowplain onto an understory of basketgrass nibbled short by the grazing stock, gradually working higher into the foothills and then into the dale of mimosas and suddenly we were at the edge of the high-ground tupelos and mulberries studying a thin dark trail into the womb of the gorge and ultimately along that upper run of the river where the banks were narrow and the current had purpose. The forbidden stretch, pressed through high limestone walls and not at all like the sluggish river below.

We heard it, the Gorge where the beast slept when not feasting on babies, the stone caves and the precipice ledges and the solid canopy of this place where the sun never shined. This place for a pale giant to live like a king for two hundred years and as we contemplated things, Bo sounded off and Verity sang back and a long suspended whining howl carried up from the depths of the gorge and suddenly we were riding off away from the thicket, back along the selfsame cow trail at a full gallop screaming like banshees across the highland meadows with the morning sun at our back while in the distance old Mister Arthur was harnessing his draft horses and in our own east field a few early hands were arriving to begin culling pebbles and arrowheads from the furrows between short almost luminescent rows of green barley. I pressed tight to Horse's flanks, laughing, gripping Verity's waist and as her pigtails bullwhipped my cheeks, I slapped at them like batting black flies, yelling nonsense, screaming under a sky that had awakened to a deep cerulean blue. Verity sang to Horse and Horse cleared the roadside draw in a weightless flight that sent me hollering like a little bellowing cricket with Verity's chanting cappella sitting on the upper registers of an octave as Mr. Arthur's draft horses broke free, spooked by the three men who had parked their car and honked their horn before climbing the Arthur fence, calling out friendly like, waving their arms like speculating vultures. Idiots.

Ruby watched, her eyes now on the road beyond the bridge as the first light gleamed through the highest crevices of the ridge, watching the old man struggling with the reins against the strength of horses the size of buffalo. And watching Verity and I, no doubt, as we pulled up and dismounted and where, from our own elevation, we followed the same strangers and their continued trespass deeper into the Arthur field waving their arms and scattering as if to corral the excited horses as Father appeared, just yards from Ruby's windshield, jogging down Pond Road, pausing to consider Ruby and her little car as if registering a spectacle before making his way down to the bridge and along his east field with the early hands turning, all of them, like a synchronized chorus. He jogged to the unfamiliar parked car, leaped the fence toward the old man tangled in the reins. It took only a moment, reaching them, yanking the harness and freeing our neighbor and brushing him off, brushing that beard as thick as a pillow, as the first of the songbirds cleared Kickapoo Ridge.

Ruby always spoke of that day as if she alone witnessed the sky clouding over, so many fluttering wings passing above the limestone ravine of the river gorge to create the mosaic of a partial eclipse permeated by slivers of light fluttering through the migrating mass as it swept down off the highlands and over the bridge giddy with the scent of home to the sudden accompaniment of the beast's choral call. His voice rose and fell like octaves on an oboe from deep within the river womb, while another voice settled on a progressive register where Verity braced herself, spreading her feet as if to summon the range of her voice from their higher plain down to the bridge and the river and the duet lasted only a moment or two as they traded octaves in a language of incantations, and then silence. A palpable silence. Every last one of the songbirds were adjoined in the living canopy now, stretching along the lower river from the bridge to The Point, where the river broke north with the coloring and current of molasses.

We reached the bridge, Verity and Horse and myself, slowing to a trot then a walk with the planks clapping under Horse's step as Hound appeared up through the roadside hem of mimosa and milkweed and we continued to the house and up the drive. We dismounted and quietly entered the back door to stand barefoot at the foot of the long hall, sweat-streaked, coated in dust, studying the two bags set against the wall.

Stiff-shouldered satchels of a thick heavy fabric with leather lashings and small turnbuckles. Suitcases. We fingered the buckles as Clare appeared with bagged lunches. She looked at us, as if we were two june bugs, and disappeared as Mother entered the hall looking vacant and unsure, wearing her Sunday dress. Father arrived out of breath; his one pair of town trousers were dusted from the Arthur field. He glanced at Verity and myself, paused, frowned, then motioned to the bags and I followed him out to the Sheriff's truck. We set the bags in the truckbed and he looked at me and said, "Where you been?"

"Ride'n. Out ride'n."

Studying the lying eyes, he slowly ran his fingers through my hair and said, "Stay away from the Gorge. You know that."

I nodded.

Max'll see to the stock. I've asked him to stay over, so Clare's not alone[3]. Guy will look in on the hands. That's about it. Mind your aunts."

"Sure, Dad."

And then suddenly Clare and Aunt Dee were standing at the back door and Mariah and Verity and I at the foot of the drive as the Sheriff backed out onto Pond Road with Father's arm out the window brushing

---

[3]. *Max, the journeyman bull breeder and admired horseman, arrives on his prized steed most Sundays after church to spend the afternoon holding Clare's hand and Clare becomes someone else, melting against him like silly putty as they stroll through the barnyard and on out toward the isolated west field where, years later, they would raise a family in a smart little house built by the competent hand Septimus to overlook the river. The whole south side of the house windows, framing the river and the groundcover blooms like a painting.*

POSSESSING THE SEASONS

our open hands and Mother sitting between him and Sheriff, smiling, looking frightened and vulnerable. We stood silent, at the foot of the driveway, watching. Watching until the last of the road dust has settled.

NINE

Aunt Bim Bim said, "Just a little something on the weather maybe. It's called a sidebar."

So, I wrote: *It was clear and hot yesterday. I reckon more tomorrow.*

"I reckon?"

What I was thinking but not writing was, *The week opened with skies dull and colorless and somewhere in Missoura or K'tucky they have skies with purpose. They have our skies belonging here with fat black clouds and raindrops the size of tomatoes.*

But I was learning to set type and locating each letter in those trays and setting them one at a time to the layout plate and then aligning the magnets and it seemed best to avoid long words and unnecessary words. Aunt Bim Bim sensed what I was thinking.

"If you're avoiding setting type, then pretty soon you'll have a paper that says nothing. Just blank pages."

I thought about that for a moment, a newspaper with blank empty pages.

"You write and then you edit and then you proofread for mistakes and then you set your type. There's no shortcut, Wonder Boy. It's work."

"When do I get paid?"

"Paid?"

47

"Paid."

"You're an apprentice. Apprentices are privileged to have the opportunity. They are housed and fed is all."

"When do I stop being that and start being paid?"

"When you've learned what you need to know. When you write a sentence that is more interesting than, *It was clear and hot yesterday.*"

"I can do that now."

"So, do it."

"Do what?"

She looked at me without expression. The hint of a frown maybe, and eventually pinched my chin between her finger and thumb and as she shook my head from side to side, I watched the loose skin under her arm swaying like a water balloon.

"And no hillbilly talk," she added. "No Civil War talk or anything about the Civil War. People don't want to read about war. Tell them something that catches and holds their attention and leaves them wanting more."

And so by and by my week in town passed at the *Gazette* spent either cleaning the press and getting drunk on the fumes of ink and solvent or hunched over the back composition table mixing some truth with some lies.

"People like to read about themselves," my mentor continued, leaning over my shoulder, "but not exactly."

"Huh?"

"They want to see themselves from a different perspective. Something that represents themselves but from a different angle. Like your mother's drawings, or a novel."

I honestly had no idea what Bim was getting at, but the words were damming up and time was wasting.

On Thursday the Widow Drew at 326 Elm made a complaint to Sheriff Sam Ditmar that her neighbor Redeemed 'Dee' Pond was firing buckshot from her front porch in broad daylight.

The Sheriff arrived and tried to talk Dee into putting down her weapon, a Winchester 12-gauge pump, which she refused to do and kept firing until the last of the crows had been flushed from her elm and several branches had been blasted away to fall on the electric lines and knock out power for most of Fall Ridge until Bobbie Ray and his crew could come over from Karber's Ridge to repair the broken lines. The Sheriff threatened to arrest Dee and Dee threatened to fill the Sheriff's trousers with shot and they haven't spoken for a week.

TEN

Our west field was a lost hollow situated off the back of the barn halfway to The Point, where the river turned south toward town. A hidden holiday between three gentle rises benefitting from good drainage, excellent exposure to both partial light and the casting shade of a stand of spindly cottonwood. The west field was visually inaccessible to anyone who wasn't trespassing. Just under two acres of what Father called an alluvial smorgasbord.

We walked out that Sunday afternoon to pause off the crest between the east field, with its carpet of alfalfa groundcover, and the west field with its carpet of mutant vegetables, and for a moment, several moments, we stood catching our breath. Dollops of color scattered among the leafage like new marbles. Splotches of bright red yellow green and orange shapes cast against the morning light and eventually Father broke the silence, "It might be time for an early garden sale."

"Two months early, Dad."

From where we stood, both the Arthurs' field straight off toward Billings Corner, and the Fallers' south field just across Pond Road, were like billboards to the state of the same stunted crops everywhere. Soybeans parched and wilting and corn barely ankle-high in late July and the closest front was working up three hours southeast in Casey County, Kentucky. A small weak pattern not worth mentioning in anyone's conversation.

Our barley and alfalfa had the fool's coloring of a false success. The coloring that was furthering suspicion and raising a few eyebrows but both crops, although harbored against evaporation and as Father explained, able to withstand the drier conditions of a succulent, were nevertheless doomed to the same fate as Guy Faller's corn and Mr. Arthur's soybeans. Rain was required.

It was the west field, however, unexposed to everyone, with its minimal two acres harboring the precious commodities of a mad scientist that had been marginally irrigated with buckets hauled up from one of Dad Pond's ill-favored trickling wells. But that west field crop—chemical mutants, synthetic imposters, aliens from Titan—appeared impervious to irrigation or sunlight or soil substrate. The suspicious magical wand of a test tube accompanied by the needled injections of a psychedelic?

Meanwhile, the watertable itself was dropping, lowered with each passing week to expose a riverbank pocked with snakeholes and isolated pools dense with suffocating carp that could be fished by hand, if you were so inclined. Within a month, the others would be turning to bought feed to sustain the stock for a mass run at the slaughterhouse market in September. A last resort and left with a credit line at Listen Allerton's Feed and Grain and with everyone doing the same, just how solvent was Listen himself?

The barley and alfalfa may not survive as a harvested crop, but the stunted leafage alone would be enough to avoid store-bought feed. Turning the stock loose in August on those two fields would be like opening the pantry door to a herd that had begun nibbling on the thorny brake of blackberry and mulberry growth along the river.

I knew this, all of this, the way a descendant of cobblers knew leather, hides, and dyes.

"What was it like?" I asked, finally.

But his mind was elsewhere. From the house came the faint sound of those voices gathering on the lawn. Clare and Aunt Dee and Aunt Bim Bim and Dolores Faller and possibly Mother moving between the kitchen and the lawn. Chairs had been set out under the shade of the twin elms. The Sheriff and Max were in the barn, cleaning and arranging the rifles for rounds of target shooting.

"Noisy? Crowded? What was it like, Dad?"

He lowered himself to sit on the wild grass of the hillside and I followed and he said, "All that, sure, Sport. All that."

"And Mom took care of things and all?"

"I'm thinking definitely an early garden sale," he said. "Several. Three Saturdays in a row."

I turned back to the splotches of color below us, the freaky mutants, watermelons the size of hot air balloons, and with a shrug, I said, "So, we'll make some money, I guess."

Approaching the bridge from Snead's Corner was Ruby Morrow, sputtering and coughing and backfiring. Her yellow scarf whipping off the back trunk. Father made a sound, chuckling to himself.

"We stopped off in Champaign on the way back."

"Champaign?"

"I showed them some samples. They're coming down to have a look."

"A look? A look at what? Who?"

"The University, Sport. Big schools support research. They'll look at the logs and the interim studies in the Annex and eventually the live studies in the field. *This* field. Tangible results. This and the east and north fields with the alfalfa and barley cell structures. They pay for research."

My father's life before my life was as blurred as the lives of my ancestors. The details, the stolen patents and the school's subsequent riches belonged to another era and although we would never know everything, it would be a long long time before I knew what I know now. The early hybrid as a graduate student, patented under the school's autonomy, boasted a cell structure that could redefine American agriculture, capturing the attention of the Roosevelt administration looking to buy time, to stall their entry into the war with a Lend-Lease agreement offering Father's quick harvests as a herculean package of grain. And later, the postwar Marshal Plan with ships anchored off the British coast boasting the weighty hulls of that magical grain intent on feeding a starving postwar continent. Both endeavors spearheaded by Averel Harriman, who muscled his appointed role into the boughs of ground zero by coddling and harboring the prodigal botanist with a purpose unknown to the general public. The hypothesis and early patented trials of that seed perhaps sustaining the starving Red Army along the eastern front and shifting the balance of an alliance with Stalin, thus relegating France and England to a declining role while stalling America's commitment, or readiness, as allies to a continent half a world away.

The young student with the unruly head of hair, seemingly disassociated and unnerved by the attention, was suddenly compromised in a race against time and results. Classified. Top Secret. Protected and harbored by both Washington and the University's Board of Regents until the venerable old Natural History Building on the Quad swarmed with young obedient soldiers camouflaged as students. Students with shoulder holsters.

There were no bedtime stories. Not from him nor my mother nor our aunts. To my sisters and I, our father was simply someone who enjoyed tinkering with plants. A farmer's farmer. We knew Ma and Dad Pond had allowed Mother one year at the school as an art major, that she was there, living with Aunt Bim Bim who was serving her apprenticeship at the *News Gazette*. That Bim had interviewed Father for the paper and had introduced them to one another. That the subject of Salt Fork Valley surely came up, with its fertile promises and protected obscurity. And that they left Champaign together, Father vanishing from his lab on Matthews Street and how it was seventeen years later before he resurfaced with those early garden sales. I was eleven, going on twelve, standing in the west field and listening now to this calculated crazy plan that would expose his genetically tampered secrets to the world as a coming-out party, a marketing campaign that elevated generations of farming to something far beyond just farming.

Still on the west field hill, considering the options, Father continued, "I never figured the barley would make it to harvest. Not without some rain. But with the initial hand-watering, it broke ground and it's enough to show them. To show them field studies of that and the vegetables."

He waved an arm lazily down toward the brightly colored west field.

"So, they'll pay us to experiment?"

"Hopefully."

I sat for a moment, a little confused.

"So, they'll own us?"

"*We* own us. I took care of that paperwork in Chicago. A lot of paperwork, filed and registered. If the school pays, they'll pay for certain rights and certain rights will be ours."

"So, we'll have a garden sale, then," I said. "Three of them."

"Three of them."

We sat a moment longer, watching from the rise of the west field across the lower pasture as Elizabeth and Madeline's old Plymouth came to a rolling stop on the bridge behind Ruby Morrow's MG. They waited, the twins, rolling the windows down in hopes of a breeze, both of them in their identical floral dresses patterned by Dee to match the Plymouth's upholstery, also patterned by Dee. Ruby left her car and was standing at the trellis, staring down into the shaded canopy of the river. Elizabeth stepped from the driver's side and approached Ruby and Ruby pointed and a moment later Verity appeared, riding Horse bareback up from the riverbank onto the Fallers' lower dell and along the tractor path at a full gallop to jump the wash and onto the elevated roadbed. Ruby stood watching, spreading her arms in wonder as Elizabeth impatiently returned to the Plymouth and Ruby returned to her MG and slowly both cars continued over the bridge toward the house. Elizabeth, with both hands no doubt gripped to the wheel, elevated by her small pillow that allowed her to see over the dash and through the windshield clear to the listing crooked hood ornament while waving to those already out on the lawn.

I turned back to Father.

"Chicago was pretty good, then. Mom's good, right?"

"We never got that far, Jussie. Your mother, well…there was State Street and all that State Street is and the elevator in the hotel and the room being on the twelfth floor and all and the taxi and I guess we'll try again. Maybe St. louis. Maybe a visit to your Aunt Harriet in St. Louis."

"So, you didn't see whoever you needed to see?"

"No, son. We'll try St. Louis."

We sat for another few minutes and when I got tired of the silence I stood up, brushed my trousers and made a show of it being time to head back and finally I said, "I'm head'n back, Dad." I tapped his shoulder and added, "Mom'll like seeing Aunt Harriet."

I waited, and added, "She'll like St. Louis better. Everything'll go right as planned in St. Louis, Dad."

I made my way back along the high wold of blooming chicories and honeybees. The languorous monotony of two Bobwhites hung in the air like a sediment, perched on the weathervane atop the barn overlooking Max and Givens firing test rounds. And on up the rise I could hear the voices and laughter from the lawn and pausing on Slave Hill with the hint of a breeze dangling the colored bottles to see Father still sitting in the distance, no bigger than a honeybee, and I wondered if he was thinking of the visit from the University or how just a half-inch would make all the difference with the barley and alfalfa or how people were going to react to the garden sale. Or Chicago, and whatever it was that went wrong in Chicago.

ELEVEN

Every year on the first Saturday of the new school year, we had held a roadside sale of fruits and vegetables harvested from the house garden. Like everyone else. A predictable annual event and to my memory, the only opportunity for those outside the valley to meander our roads as welcomed guests. Buying our perishables, taking photographs, striking up conversations, or simply stopping in the middle of the road to stand leaning against their vehicles gawking at the likes of the old-world equipment sighted in the fields of the half-dozen Amish spreads. Their chance to make an exchange of organic carrots for coins and a word or two with the inbred descendants drawn down from the James Madison administration.

An open house, similar to the prearranged field trips from the outer-lying school districts when the school buses navigated the maze of unmarked roads en route specifically to the Roe farmhouse. A busload of children tolerated by the others because they were rare and because they were children and because it was Mother they came to see. That small part of Mother belonging to an unknown and rarely acknowledged public of young readers captivated by the make-believe garden of three illustrated children's books. *The Adventures and Misadventures of Little Miss Meadowsage.*

56

But unlike past garden sales, it was only late July. Five weeks early, and due to the continued drought, the only garden sale to take place that year in the entire valley.

We went out to the west field on Friday, pulling the little wagon, giddy with the anticipation of making a killing. As our one source of income, beyond a meager allowance, and often lasting, in Verity's case, for the course of the entire year, my sisters and I imagined a reaction and resulting sales that would make us stinking rich. And why not? We were stacking the wagon with cantaloupes the size of basketballs.

We set up the long table at the foot of the drive and carefully placed the bounty from the west field throughout the house garden like props in a stage show and took our places. And waited. Waited as the sun rose higher and the heat matured to a thick stifling afternoon and it was only the Fallers and the Marshes and a few passersby from town out on Pond Road by sheer coincidence. We divided $1.29 among us and imagined how we might otherwise have passed a perfectly good Saturday.

The following Saturday we arranged the table with samples and Mariah wrote out labels with the flourishing script she was known for. Swooping letters that appealed surely to Mother's fans, the kids who wrote their cards stuffed in envelopes addressed with colored crayons and answered by Mariah because that was Mariah's job, but also because Mariah loved to make a show of handwriting as if it were something more than handwriting.

Mr. Arthur himself was our first customer. Walking up Pond Road alone to stand at the table with his thin smile, fondling the samples one at a time. Rolling them across his bony fingers and stepping back to consider the garden, running his fingers through his beard, and returning to the table to select a single tomato and set his money down and say, "Didst thou grow this?"

"Yes, Mr. Arthur," Mariah answered. "Of course we grew it."

He looked at her and smiled and added, "In the dirt?"

"Yes, Mr. Arthur. In the dirt."

"Reg'ler God-fearin dirt?"

"Yes, Mr. Arthur."
"Anna Mirah."
"Yes, Mr. Arthur?"
"It wonders me, arst you the girl who butted the bull off the bridge?"
"No, Mr. Arthur."

That evening we split up $13.25 among us and set our sights on the last and final sale a week away.

At the *Gazette* mid-week, I sat at the back composition table swimming in words. So many words. So many choices. All toward my bi-monthly sidebar column *A Word More* under the new pseudonym Linkum Regards.

> *Here ye. Here ye.*
> *Believe it or not.*
> *Something's afoot out on Pond Road. Reports of an early garden sale.*
> *Scheduled tomorrow, Saturday, July 26, without fail.*
> *Feast all week on a single otherworldly cantaloupe.*
> *Fall in love with the super scientific avocado elixir.*
> > *Builds muscles. Cures aches. All natural.*
> *What they are saying:*
> *'I've never felt younger.'*
> *'I feel like a kid again.'*
> *'I feel all tingly. Love is everywhere.'*
> *Scooter Morrow, our local track star, runs a mile in two minutes flat.*
> *Brother Reeves delivers invigorated sermon of pious proportions.*
> *Dr Steadfast Stewart endorsement of amazing breakthrough.*

And that same week in Letters-to-the-Editor—

> *-What's going on out there is pure blasphemy.*
> *-The devil lives out on Pond Road.*

-The Beast is returned, possessing you know who on Pond Road.
-The Devil/Beast lures us with lies and potions.
-The devil marries his way in and for 17 years waits like a snake in the grass and strikes!

"Oh, Bim, really?"

Aunt Bim Bim sat over coffee at the kitchen counter early Saturday, not wanting to miss a moment of the big day, watching me at the far end of the counter spooning oatmeal. Clare stood at the stove and Mother against the sink reading aloud.

"Marries his way in? Was that necessary?"

"It's satire, Grace."

"Satire? Satire? *Really?*"

Verity arrived and Clare set her bowl out and a moment later Mariah skipped in with a pirouette and a twirl and Clare stood at the stove, thinking aloud, "I spek they gon to come. A circus a comin today."

They came that Saturday. Like a circus. Locals and sightseers and Father's scientists from Champaign clogging Pond Road to see for themselves this early harvest in a drought year with tomatoes so bright they gleamed and string beans as green as candy and cauliflower big as beach balls and zucchini the size of submarines and we played to them, my sisters and I, like giddy fools. We performed, as if it were a vaudeville act. Cartwheels and somersaults, prancing and dancing about like idiots. And they applauded, leaning against their cars or standing in the bed of their trucks or wandering up and down the driveway, filling our shoebox with sumptuous leafy cash, buying as if they were buying collectibles, an investment in something odd, something original, something to show the others back home from that county where farming was an art, that county tucked like a lush watershed between Kickapoo Ridge and Moingwena Rise and fed by a river as thick as soup in turn fed by the mighty Ohio and Mississippi and Wabash and Cumberland and they believed the bedtime stories they had heard since they were children, the superlatives of a topsoil so rich it had the stench of fresh dough and so fertile that Puritan virgins could wallow naked in the dirt for an immaculate conception that practically insured the propagation of a heavenly species. Etc. etc.

They believed because they wanted to believe. In spite of the Marsh corn and the Faller beans flanking the road on both sides with the sad truth. They wanted to believe the entire Missouri Valley had been baked crisp but for Salt Fork, but for an oasis of prayered mystery and pious fertility and there was no doubting the proof of a rhubarb in late July as purple as a coloring crayon.

And among them were the speculators from the north, lured into the forbidden fantasy where rumors spoke the reality of farmers on the brink, clinging by their fingertips. Bottom feeders drawn by reports of the Sapp place transferring title weeks before to a Kentucky horse farm and goat breeder. The Javitts. The Javitts-from-Kentucky who had made inquiries into Clare's beau Max with offers to manage their thoroughbreds and learn the goat-breeding trade. Oversee an enterprise of replacing crops with goat sperm in a slow irreversible revolution against milk, against lovely pet milk cows who had never done anyone any harm with their thick sweet creamy glasses of milk washing down our suppers in lieu of… of…in lieu of sweet creamy glasses of goat sperm?

Later, we joined the others gathered off the back porch beneath the shade of the twin elms. With iced drinks and Clare's pastries and their hand-fans generating some relief from a heat so oppressive and heavy the conversations were muted to whispers. I laid back on the grass and instantly Bo straddled my face while Mariah counted the money. I moved and Bo moved and the girth of his belly swayed back and forth, brushing my nose as a puddle of goo dripped onto the grass beside my ear. Verity had gone straight from the garden to the barn to come out with Horse following off the corner of the Quarters where Max sat his steed, waiting. He was talking to a few of the hands, like one of them but not like any of them because Max owned a steed and an English riding saddle and wore jodhpurs and rode with the postcard bearing of an equestrian; Max's people from New Orleans had French noble blood. So, Max was noble, and the hands were not. He and Verity disappeared off Slave Hill toward the river and Clare stood watching with a plate of cakes in one hand and Aunt Dee said, "I spect Max is about the handsomest horseman on this planet earth."

Clare smiled and straightened her shoulders and from where I lay lounging on the grass, peering through Bo's flopping jowls, her eyes seemed to go soft and watery.

"He's a nobleman," Aunt Elizabeth said. She sat next to Aunt Madeline, both of them bone-thin and sitting stiff and rigid and it was as if they had strapped planks to their spines.

"Noble blood from Australia," Elizabeth added.

"Austria, you boob," Aunt Bim Bim said, rolling her eyes. *"Austria."*

"France," Aunt Dee said. "It's paris france, not Austria his people are from."

At the mention of paris france, Mariah looked up from stacking cash in the grass and Bim said to her, "You can lookem up when someday you go there, Anna Mirah. Look up Max's people."

"They don't speak english," Madeline said. "You can't just go knocking on doors like that. They speak…they speak…"

"French," Mother said. "They speak french in france."

"French," Elizabeth repeated. *"Fre-ench."*

Dee turned to Mariah and said, "Honey, do you speak french? Do they teach that at school?"

Mariah shook her head without looking up from thumbing the bills into three stacks on the verge of teetering. I reached to separate them from collapsing onto one another and mixing my profits with theirs and

61

Mariah slapped my hand and looked me in the eye and said, "Stop it! Just let me do this, Jussie."

It was the side of her I often required. By default, Mariah was the only one who agreed, reluctantly, time and again to take her place at the manure pile in the barnyard where I would have spent days arranging my lead soldiers to the exact historical placement of a given battle at Antietam, or Gettysburg, or Bull Run. She would arrive to carefully take her place in her immaculate wardrobe and suddenly become a savage. Dead soldiers flung everywhere. Sound effects. Explosions. Agonizing screams. And then she would stand up and brush her black stretch pants and pat her hands and head back off toward the house without a word.

Whereas Verity would make horse sounds, prancing her general as if he were out for a Sunday ride to cross enemy lines and suddenly opposing generals were talking and laughing, their horses nose to nose. Kissing horses.

Bim worked her fan and wiped her neck with her kerchief and said, "French is just stretching the end of the words and adding a W. Word-*wha*. France-*wha*. The words are the same as us, only they sing them with w's."

"Phew!" Dee fingered her pastry and fiddled with her stockings rolled just below her knees and exhaled with an exaggerated sigh and added, "You learn *anything* at that paper up to Champaign but satire? They teach you *anything* else? Grace got an education now."

"In art. Has nothing to do with…"

"A college education…almost[4]."

"In art."

4.　*Mother never actually graduated, falling prey to the spoils of love, to the meticulously arranged midnight break on Hamilton's Illinois Central to Centralia where they switched to Carl's Wabash run, hidden in the cupola of Brakeman Robert's caboose like squirrels, Bim and Mother and Father, one imagines, laughing hysterically as Carl steams his marvelous mechanical beast without stopping at Du Bois or Du Quoin or De Soto, not so much as a signaling whistle until the very scent of the milk 'n' honey valley permeated the cupola and when they finally climbed down to stand with Brakeman Roberts off the bay window brakewheel and introduced Father to the rest of his life.*

"College, Bim. Col-leege. You go on to france with your *france-wha* talk and see if they know what in heavens yer sayin. Lord."

"One hundred and eighty-six dollars and thirty-three cents."

The others went silent, their eyes on Mariah, then lowering to the bills and coins in three neatly arranged shares.

"Sixty-two dollars and eleven cents each," Mariah declared, as she put each share into separate paper bags and stood up to brush the grass from her pants and turn toward the back porch as the sound of Verity's voice carried up off the rise of the lower pasture. Her singing voice, similar to an oboe or a violin, but never in the sense of actual songs or melodies. An oboe that held a note, and then anothern, and anothern.

Clare appeared out the back porch and went to stand in the center of the lawn fully exposed to the sunlight, facing the river. Off the back corner of the Quarters half a dozen hands appeared, hurriedly gathering at the Bottle Tree to face the river and to them, to Clare and the hands and any of those migrants still camped under the bridge hoping for a day's work, Verity's singing notes were something more than just Verity singing.

She stopped and yet the notes lingered, occupying the airspace as if held and harbored in the upper reaches of the twin elms.

"Nothing prettier," Bim said, finally.

The others nodded and yet said nothing because Verity's singing was something known but not acknowledged. The singing language. Her language with Horse and Cow and the Sows and who knows what else. The birds and muskrats and Herefords maybe.

Father and his three visitors left the Annex and crossed the barnyard, creating little explosions of dust with each step as they arrived at the rail fence separating the lawn from the barnyard. Mother turned in her chair and smiled and said, "Hello, Wesley."

"Hi, Grace."

From the shade of the elm the others all looked at Mother and to the fence and back to Mother and Mother said, "This is Wesley. He was in school with Hank and I."

"Another lifetime," Wesley said.

Mother smiled. Too much smiling, it seemed.

The others continued staring at Wesley as if he were from another country and Wesley said, glancing at Father, "It looks as if I'll be getting down from time to time." He motioned to the Annex and toward the fields and Father stood beaming.

When they were gone, making their way down the fenceline toward the peach grove and the driveway, Bim said, "From time to time? What does he mean?"

"Hank and the school are collaborating. It was worked out in Champaign last month. Wesley works for the school. Assistant Dean of Natural Sciences, actually."

Bim turned to the twins and said, "Maybe you two should go up to Champaign. This Wesley fella could get you the proper permits."

The previous week Madeline and Elizabeth had been cited and fined for the umpteenth time by the University Police in Carbondale for peddling bibles on the street corners without a permit.

"Maybe you could just *move* to Champaign," Dee added. "Make lots of money and live there and come down for a visit once a year. Or every other year."

The twins were silent.

That night, dinner included Max and Clare and Aunt Dee and Sheriff and after dinner they danced to music. My sisters and I sat watching, eating popcorn, and eventually Aunt Dee and the Sheriff left, and Clare and Max went to her room off the laundry, and Mariah and Verity and I went to bed and for a long time I listened to the music. The sound of the music and Mother's laughter carrying up the stairs.

TWELVE

By late August everyone had plowed under the wilted excuse of a harvest and turned to Allerton's for store-bought feed on a run for credit that staggered Listen Allerton, who in turn borrowed from the bank that was suddenly as staggered as Allerton Feed. Listen could have refused their credit and closed his doors and harbored his relative wealth, but what good is wealth if everyone you knew was poor? He and everyone else banked on the beef and pork markets in a leveraging strategy for the coming winter and the assumed spring rains for a return to good harvests the following year. A gamble not only on the fluctuating beef markets in Greenville and Cape Girardeau, who fixed their prices based on a volume that included the entire drought-stricken Missouri Valley, but a gamble on no drought in recorded memory having ever extended for four consecutive seasons.

By early September we had opened the barley and alfalfa to a herd who had for weeks been nibbling on the thorny bramble along the river and the Herefords gorged themselves until they were like ripe peaches. A crop, like the west field, hand-watered from Dad Pond's meager well, but unlike the west field, with just enough irrigation to break ground for the benefit of the subsidy review, while also avoiding store-bought grain toward a fattened beef market. The following week Mr. Arthur's smaller herd finished off our east field while the Marsh and Faller herd were set

65

loose on our north field until it was drawn down to stems and stalks.

I explained all this and more to Mrs. Hall and the entire class when caught daydreaming at my desk along the bank of windows, gazing out onto Sycamore Street and Carl's tracks while imagining a train wreck. A train wreck scattering Herefords across the schoolyard. Starved skeletal Herefords no one could sell and rejected by the slaughterhouses and the consequences of all that.

"Mr. Roe? Are you with us?"

I glanced at the times tables on the blackboard and thought how a much younger Mrs. Hall would have opened the door of this same classroom long ago when my mother's sisters stood released from their own classes to fetch their baby sister on the day their mother died. Less than one year after their father died. Twenty-eight and twenty-nine years old, ravaged by the unmentionable TB, and *when* mentioned, never with more than a whisper.

I explained the math of multiplying store-bought feed on credit by a mass run on the beef markets divided by the only thing between now and next year's harvest and how with all that multiplying and dividing you could end up with a negative in a world where multiplying two negatives never came up positive.

Mrs. Hall said nothing and, in the silence, I glanced at Acceptance who sat watching me with that look I would see for the last time sixty-six years later in the same bedroom where Father saw Mother's look and where my grandmother Vanity saw my grandfather Silence's look and where my great grandparents both saw my grandmother Vanity's look, with no time to blink.

At recess, Bump and Scooter and I made our way across Sycamore to the tracks where we tossed stones waiting for Carl's *Wabash*, and Bump said, "What was that all about?"

I shrugged and turned to find Acceptance waiting for her turn at the tetherball pole and Verity behind her and Scooter said, "It was like you lost yer mind or something."

The whistle sounded from beyond Birch Street and a moment later the engine appeared with its bursts of smoke and steam and Scooter hoisted himself onto the rail, gripping the rail with both hands and the rest of his body as straight and rigid as a pole as Carl drew closer, sounding his whistle again and shaking his fist out the cab and when he was close enough that the ground shook, I reached to grip Scooter's belt and yanked him back to go sprawling across the trackbed as Carl passed us, yelling and hollering, followed a moment later by Brakeman Roberts in the caboose wielding his mailpole to clip the duffel bag slung off the hook. In his wake, he tossed out a batch of bananas, smiling and waving until he disappeared around the bend en route to Centralia.

Scooter stood up, smiling like an idiot and I thought how in any other school he would still be in first grade. Teachers kept passing him because Scooter belonged to the whole town and the whole town pretended everything was just fine.

I had no cause to consider doom everywhere. Father's gamble had paid off big; the third garden sale had attracted enough attention that the *News Gazette* in Champaign announced that Wonder Boy had resurfaced, cooking his magic all along, and Chicago's *Tribune* dispelling rumors he had been kidnapped back in '41 by the Dominican Republic to play ball alongside the young Roberto Clemente[5]. With its original stolen patent by now expired, the University was suddenly in competition with the World Food Organization and Wes, as the chosen emissary, arrived with his back to the wall. Ready and eager to make a deal: a year's steady income for the second rights to certain logbooks in the Annex and next year's barley and alfalfa in the field. Trucking was already arranged for the combined Roe, Arthur, Faller and Marsh livestock—fattened on the last barley and alfalfa leafage—to a Greenville slaughterhouse for four

---

5. *To the consternation of bodyguards posing as students, Father played baseball. A poetic relief from the lab and those hours glued to the microscopes. His record-setting errorless defense on second base contributing to a Big Ten title that same year Joe DiMaggio and Ted Williams left the game at the peak of their careers in a much-publicized induction ceremony. There were others who read the* Tribune *article. Others who had never heard of Roberto Clemente but possibly Dominican Republic, that and a host of random third-world countries purportedly welcoming with open arms the oppressive oversight of someone else's Manifest Destiny.*

times the rate what all those in the larger Missouri Valley would get three weeks later in Cape Girardeau.

Nevertheless, with doom on my mind, with the nightmare of Scooter one day losing his balance and toppling across the tracks and sliced in half by the weight of a twenty-ton engine, I slapped him hard across the cheek.

He stumbled back and raised his fists and I slapped him again. Like slapping the flank of a hog.

"You shit!"

He lowered his arms and stood for a moment as the sound of my words lingered, drifting to the schoolyard and everyone's eyes on Scooter who had been slapped as if by someone's mother, which was nothing at all like being hit with a fist.

After school, Verity and Acceptance and I walked the three blocks between school and downtown under the shading umbrellas of the old elms lining that street like antiquities, like ruins from Linkum's day, which they were. But the seasons were changing and the upper reaches were thinning to expose a maze of lonely stout limbs slung out over the street without the living quality of a full canopy and without the deafening birdsong that had in recent weeks gone south. Hundreds of thousands of whip-poor-wills and Chuck-will's-widows and Pine Warblers and Herons and Robins and Swallowtails and Bobwhites all somewhere over Nebraska by now and I imagined how they must stay together, a migrating cluster like that. A huge extended family leaving me always with that sensation of being abandoned, of being left behind with the silence of the long dull winters without the hibernating crickets or the Copperheads or the bull frogs. Without the flowering dogwoods and chicory and coneflowers and mimosa, and the sycamores and cottonwoods along the river stripped naked, stripped of their fullness and exposed to the ravages of the endless bitter winters simply because they couldn't fly. Trees can't fly. Because God had refused them, and me, an ability to soar over Nebraska en route to Costa Rica and avoid all together the blunt hammering ugliness of the most unapologetic season. A stretch of so many months so ruthless and dull and unrelenting that the oldest of us, the aging trees and animals and people, die off in the throes of winter, denied something called spring. Something waiting at the end of that ugliness that spoke of beauty better than any God or any Heavenly Ever-After...

"Hello?"

The sound of her voice, Acceptance, floating somewhere.

"Jussie?"

"Where does he go when he does that?" she said, turning to Verity. "Sometimes I'll be talking and then I realize he's not here. He's somewhere far away and it makes me sad because I don't know how to go there. I don't even know where there *is.*"

We drew abreast of Mercy May Jenkin's little house and I paused and the sounds of town return, the warbled voices of Verity and Acceptance and the rhythm of the arpeggios up and down the scales of Mercy May's piano and I said, "It won't be long before winter."

"Winter?" Acceptance touched my arm and looked at me close and added, "Is that it? You're thinking winter? It's still fall, Jussie. It's still September. Septembers are perfect. September is everyone's favorite."

We crossed Main Street and below the Café windows and up the slight incline of Sycamore Street and everything seemed fine. Three abreast, likely unaware that Acceptance had hold of my hand and Verity had hold of Acceptance's hand as we turned up the steps to the Davis porch. Acceptance's mother was waiting, setting out the iced tea and cookies and I took my place on the swing beside Granny Davis. Quickly, instantly, they were talking, Verity and Acceptance and her mother sitting and talking like music, their hands moving and their three voices going at once and for a moment my eyes fell on her brother's belt, dangling casually off her waist with that indifference to what mattered and what didn't matter. Her walk, replayed like a reel of film the last decade of my life, the stride and rhythm of her step with her feet slightly splayed and my joking associations to a platypus. The easiness of that walk and that dangling belt.

"Is that the Pond boy?"

Granny's hand patted my knee and leg and found my arm and when she pressed it between her fingers, I felt the warmth of the oldest living person in Salt Fork Valley.

"Hi, Granny. I be a reckon'n it's mighty good to see you."

She smiled and her face was all folds and wrinkles like the bark of an elm and she said, "So that's it again?"

"What again? I cain't says I be a follow'n, ma'am."

"You're silly talk."

"Ain't silly, ma'am. Twenty-thousand casualties. Linkum grieved and grieved."

"That many?"

"No one knows fer sure. Unless you counted and most of those solderin' ain't learned their numbers."

"They were just boys, Mr. Pond. Nice farm boys. Plain boys on both sides."

"Did you talk to them?[6]"

"They all wanted to talk to Reliance," Granny began. "She was so

---

6.   *Granny Davis' father left Salt Fork for a job with the C&O canal close to Lincoln's Washington. He moved Granny's mother and sister and eleven-year-old Granny—the original Acceptance—to a little hamlet called Sharpsburg, Maryland along the Potomac River, where Granny and her sister and mother watched through the attic dormer of Dunker church on a morning when Robert E. Lee appeared through the corn fields along the west woods with 40,000 troops and the dandy General McClellan with 90,000 troops along the sunken road to the east and by the end of the day, there was more bloodshed than any one-day battle in the history of the United States. And on the following day, when the armies moved on, some from both sides were left behind to bury the bodies and they worked side by side, talking and chatting and calling one another names while digging 4,000 holes in the ground and Lincoln shoulda considered Granny's sister Reliance for a Vice President because when she and Granny came down from hiding in the attic of the Church and walked outside and then onto the battlefield, the boys stopped digging and leaned on their shovels and made nice talk to a pretty fifteen-year-old girl who talked back and suddenly the young rebs and yanks are going on like it was a Saturday dance and for a while, they forgot all about the war. But of course, the story was never exactly the same; Reliance danced with them, tip toeing and high-stepping on the blood-stained Antietam meadow; Reliance kissed them and made them promise to be nice to each other and not hurt one another in the next fight; Reliance and Granny walked among the dead while reciting prayers and singing hymnals they learned at Fall Ridge Baptist Church; Reliance with her genetic Anabaptist beauty stole their hearts and gave them something they didn't otherwise know existed and how the Reb boys thought if such a thing exists in the north, then the north might not be so bad and the Yank boys thought if such a thing exists, then the quicker the war was over, the quicker they come back to Antietam and get more kisses.*

pretty, you know, and fearless. We walked among them, I recall. Through the cornfield and across the bridge and they followed us, followed Reliance, who was singing hymns and dancing and tellin all those boys she loved them and them whispering they loved her back and I do believe they thought she was sent down from heaven, this beautiful spiritual creature appearing out of nowhere arriving surely from God's heaven[7]."

The porch went silent. Verity and Acceptance and Acceptance's mother Laura had stopped talking and were watching Granny who sat beside me on the swing with her thin little hand on my arm and in her blindness looking off beyond the porch lost in memories real or imagined and I said, "Any a them you meet injured? Missing arms and legs and…"

"Jussie!" The sound of their voices, both Verity and Acceptance, like a single voice. Acceptance's mother looked at me and smiled and shook her head and Granny said, "It's likely, Mr. Pond. But you are right about Mr. Lincoln. I believe he grieved and grieved."

"Linkum walked with Jesus."

"Oh, Mr. Pond. You are the most interesting young fellow. Are you going to write about this in your little paper?"

"Yesum. I reckon so." I thought for a moment about those digging the graves side by side, insulting one another and then bantering like chums, when suddenly Mother appeared along the walk, turning up toward us on the porch and both Acceptance and her mother Laura were on their feet as Mother paused on the top step, catching her breath. Catching her breath from what? Climbing six steps?

---

7. *When the Davises returned to Salt Fork at the end of the 1864 drought, Reliance, at seventeen, remained behind. She kindled a friendship with President Lincoln's personal secretary John Hay, who she had first met days before the battle of Antietam when Lincoln had visited his lackluster General McClellan in an effort to incite in him the cry of battle. Reliance lived out her long life in a splendid home on Lafayette Square in Washington, at the center of a social registry spanning five administrations and the subject of lasting romantic gossip linked to the notables of the era. She never returned to Salt Fork, and in her wildly popular tell-all autobiography penned during the Roosevelt administration, she claims to have been born in paris france and raised in Sharpsburg, Virginia, where her father had been hired by L'Enfant to engineer the complexities of the canal's many tunnels. Reliable was a liar, never far from her Salt Fork heritage.*

POSSESSING THE SEASONS

"Who's there?" Granny raised her head, looking blindly about and Acceptance pulled a chair beside Granny and Mother sat down and laid a hand on Granny's wrist.

"It's Gracious, Granny. Gracious Roe."

"Who? Gracious who?"

"Gracious Roe, Vanity's girl."

"Vanity? Vanity who?"

"Vanity Pond. Ma's girl."

"Ma?"

"Mariah…Mariah Pond?"

"Mariah? Why I was just thinkin of Mariah. She here? She here, too?" Granny raised her head toward the porch ceiling, searching.

"Mariah is gone, Granny…at least *that* Mariah. Her granddaughter, though…she lives nearby. Mariah Ann? Bim? Bim Bim? Owns the *Gazette?*"

"Bim Bim what?"

"Bim Pond."

"Well, where'd Mariah go? Does Silence know?"

"Dad Silence is gone, too, Granny."

"Gone? To where? There's only Fall Ridge?"

"They're passed."

"Passed? I thought you said she owned the *Gazette,* where the boy works. The Pond boy."

"No, that's Bim, or Bim Bim, my sister, who was named after Ma Mariah. There are six of us, all girls, born from Vanity, Obedience's girl."

"Well then, who are you?"

"I'm Gracious, or Grace, the youngest."

"You the runt?"

"Yes, Granny, and Fortune's the oldest. Although she changed her name to Harriet when she moved to St. Louis. She's in St. Louis, you know. She lives in St. Louis. And she's followed by the second oldest, Redeemed Pond. Dee, who runs the fabric shop?"

72

"Tea? No, not fer me, thanks. Laura?"

"Yes, Granny?"

"The Pond runt here's offered us tea."

"No thank you, Granny."

"No, me neither. Very nice of you to offer, Mariah."

"I'm Gracious, Granny."

"Oh, Mariah, it's just a cup of tea."

Mother had turned away, confused, gazing across a Sycamore Street that had gone to shadows. The graying light of a late afternoon sat off the neighbor Avery's gable with that golden antique light restricted to those few precious weeks between the vulgarity of summer and brutality of winter. The smell of approaching fall was in the air.

Mother stood, smoothing her dress as a signal to Verity and I as Laura Davis came over to take her hand and for a moment they exchanged looks and Laura Davis' eyes were wet.

We drove home silent, the three of us in the front seat passing the lifeless fields of one lost crop after another and there was only the sound of the gravel shifting and crunching and relocating beneath the wheels like corn popping on Clare's stove. I thought how Mother lately wasn't so different from Granny, or Bump's granddad with his meandering pointless stories and how it wasn't like a sputtering engine, something that could be fixed, like a broken sputtering engine.

THIRTEEN

In that week before opening the fields to grazing, the crops by appearance were a flourishing testament to something. To a farm who prayed harder and was rewarded with the blessings of Eden; to the hocus pocus of the farmer himself up to something ungodly and possibly blasphemous; to a pact with the devil inhabiting that farm as an historic beast turning against everyone but the Pond/Roe spread; to a pact with Washington to feed only favorable portions of a starving post-war Europe; to a syndicate of Stalinist thugs with shoulder holsters posing as students under the guise of protecting the prodigy until the prodigy pulled off the Great Escape and disappeared and it was seventeen years before they returned?

That week seventy-some summers ago, the east, west, and north fields were the culminating result of our father's notebooks kept for decades in the Annex and then the cellar and then stolen away and eventually recovered and donated in their entirety to the archives at the University of Illinois. His earliest references to a hybrid seed are found in Notebook #1 with his last year in high school and as long as we're keeping records—and records are obviously something my father cared a great deal about—the *suddenness* of that revelatory debut hybrid can be traced to Notebook #1. Scattered mention of stem cells and grafted genetics and of hormone additives mingled amongst notes for algebra and biology and to confuse, even amuse, the historians who continue to hover, there are within those earliest notebooks the entreating pleas of any number of young women—girls, really—understanding even then how the only way to Henry Roe's heart was through his head, to use what weapons they possessed as sixteen-year-olds to discover the combination to that locker in the hall of Champaign High School and in pink- or red- or violet-colored pens scrawl their intentions and hopes and desires over the formulas and equations and meticulous notes like an exploding sunrise.

Thoughtful, poetic epithets like, *I want to fertilize yer seeds, HankyPoo.*

So breeding, and the thoughts of breeding, of manipulating, arranging, mutating, wangling a given entity into an unknown entity had begun perhaps at that hormonal stage when boys, normal boys, dwell naturally on images of seeds and fertilized eggs.

75

FOURTEEN

There were forty-seven land rights awarded to the original founding settlers of the valley as per an arrangement made by the short-lived Continental Congress in a 1789 doctrine that opened, with the stroke of a pen, many pens, a portion of the continent so vast and so unknown that it was named nothing more specific or succinct than simply the Northwest Territory.

Within weeks of the signed ordinance and given the boneless assurances of scattered forts and relative safety, the population formerly congested along the eastern corridor began to leave with an exodus of such proportions it redefined the continent. People and their relative density shifting, repositioning their mass until the balance teetered westward like a listing ship, abandoning their known world for an unknown world on the strength of rumors and the rare firsthand accounts of former trappers or scouts or Indian fighters with their lonely dispositions and cauterized hearts who had faced death, apparently, at the bend of every river and behind the trunk of every tree. And there were, we assume, no shortages of rivers and trees.

If you were young and in love, like Experience and Chastity Pond, the restrictive existence of southern New Hampshire's old-world Puritanism was itself reason enough to join the exodus. To break from the elders and embark on a traveling adventure in the timely spirit of revolution and a yearning for liberty and along the way, found a new more lenient faith that came to be known as Anabaptist.

Although present-day planting logs are still being written and recorded with the seasonal conundrums of weather patterns and crop rotations and harvest schedules, those earliest logs dating from the original founders, arranged in sequence to their ancestral authorship, survived in everyone's attics like dissertations in a foreign language. And although translating their pompous overly pious script could make for tedious reading, the rewards were the scattered truths and wildly imaginative suppositions considered by the descendants as only mildly fanciful facts, while by later historians as pure gobble-de-gook.

Virtually all of the logs made mention of the Great Kickapoo Raid of 1793. Laying siege to thirteen cabins elevated off the banks of the Salt Fork River in a three-day stand-off between musketballs and arrowheads that by all accounts appears to have circumvented a theme common to most historical skirmishes and battles. Death itself. A conspicuous absence if you were a present-day youngster fascinated by death, and battle, wading through the early family logs as tales of adventure. Preposterous encounters and blood-curdling bravery and yet the cowardice slight of my own ancestor's inability to take aim with the family musket, to fire upon and kill an enemy. To adopt the savagery of warfare as a noble manly endeavor. With the exception of religious exemptions as Quartermasters and Agony Pond's ceremonial ribbons from his 1862 Honor Guard post along the Wabash, and Dust Pond's brief and peaceful foray into the Black Hawk campaign years earlier, the Great Kickapoo Raid is the only act of open warfare in the long recorded history of the new order settlers, successfully defending their high ground cabins without a single casualty at the hands of a physically prodigious enemy who not only reached the high ground but pierced the defense of a single, seemingly specific cabin, the Pond cabin, and made off with the spoils of the comely Chastity.

Not one of the logs drawn from those early entries summarize that loss with any comparative analysis. Experience himself devotes only a single sentence: *The savages held off with the requireth of 33 preshus musketballs at a loss of one personage.*

And it was Experience's son True, remembering the event decades later, who elaborates on how his mother went missing, *whence our lovely mother layeth herself before the savages and abideth their demands for the safety of her childrens. Returning to us therewith fully one year later. Pregnant with evil.*

It's the *pregnant* that sticks. Who in our heritage had the high cheekbones? And where are they now, those cheekbones? A bastard offspring banished to the woods? To the river thicket?

And why couldn't they write with clear and common usage? Noah Webster, by then decades into his definitive study and resigned to the impoverished life in western Massachusetts, would have cringed at the lack of clarity. The superfluous use of archaic pronouns and meaningless suffixes and the persistence of an appalling leniency toward a standardized spelling. But then again, as the Kickapoos were making off with their comely prize, George Washington was taking his oath of office on the balcony of the Federal Hall in New York with a third-grade education and only a rudimentary grasp of the written language.

Lamentation Goodwin of the Goodwin logs mentions, *He may do with us what he pleaseth, for his own honour and prase; but it is His will that the poor Chastity serveth the savages willfully.*

Willfully?

True Pond, who built our present-day barn in a timber-framing schematic of tenons and fanciful wedges, opened his log on the same day Alexander Hamilton honorably, and fatefully, fired his dueling pistol straight into the skies over the Hudson River. True returned once again to the subject of his missing mother in an entry dated 1821, rejoining her family from a year's absence, *returning tongueless and a lost vacancy in her eyes* to sleep on the cabin porch, expunged by the bewildered Experience as tainted, too soiled to share his bed once again. And less than ten days later she disappeared, again, kidnapped by the original Listen Allerton for ten interminable days and held in Listen's cabin at the foot of Moingwena Rise. An episode that appears in various other logs within the valley as an *exundation of a bedeviled debauchery.*

The Allerton family logs of course depict the incident as a willing elopement, as a womanly fever caught fire by the animal magnetism of Listen's favorable attributes.

Seems everyone wanted a part of the fair Chastity Pond. A reputation that likely began on the heels of their original arrival in the valley, having successfully traversed the pass over New Hampshire's White Mountains and forded the Connecticut River to scale the Green Mountains and then the Adirondacks and across the endless stretch of the Ohio Valley on the strength of heresy, a flimsy rumor about a valley situated at the southernmost outreaches of this new Northwest Territory between the confluence of the Mississippi and Ohio and Wabash and Cumberland rivers and traversed by the muddied nutrients of the Salt Fork River with banks of blossoming meadows, with topsoil as dark and moist as a chocolate cake and Indian corn so stout you could shimmy up its stalks. And where propagation was, well, immaculate.

Where our impressionable, God-fearing Anabaptist beauties would tiptoe from the crude porches of their newly staked cabins and in the last weeks of April, when the corn had been seeded and the furrows were rainsoaked, leave their frocks to ford the river naked and lie face down in the earth, wallowing and gesticulating in a communion with the rumored fertility of the Salt Fork Valley until they conceived in a shivering trembling consumption of moonlit fertility. An immaculate something, if not conception, leading to the first and original entries of the pale colorless giant who lurked within the cool shade of the thicket, waiting for the naked beauties to make their break back across the river, to wade the waterline that buoyed their engorged nursing breasts glancing nervously left and right, exposed by the strength of the moonlight and the skittish pulse of their breath to a creature that fed on newborns. *The*

POSSESSING THE SEASONS

whitish giant beast pearing from the thiket and beholding their fruit...the tender lathered flesh of newborns and although nearly all of the new mothers returned to the beds of their waiting husbands with the continuum of heirs and heiresses to what was then known as the *Valley of Heaven on Earth*, many did not.

Many drowned themselves, simply losing any will to go on empty-handed and allowing the sluggish current to enfold them and gently, kindly, soften their grief in an act that is described repeatedly and with great embellishments.

FIFTEEN

In the attic on a Saturday morning before dawn, I stood in my slippers and pajamas, adjusting my eyes to the thin light over her easel at the dormer window, the easel and brushes and the pallet of colors for Saturdays, and sometimes Sundays. A portion of her right hand wielded a brush with even steady strokes to move across the canvas with the fluid rhythmic motions of an instinct. A certainty, a knowingness of what existed in her mind in its wholeness and how the act of transferring that to paint being simply a mechanical discipline, as with language and learning to speak and write what one thinks with a learned diction. A mechanical discipline like the foundation of a beautiful building or the upbringing of a child, rising thereafter on this reliance of a musical imagination that comes to define the building as a whole, the child as an adult. I envied that gift of a mechanical application and the embodiment of how she occupied the attic alone while the world slept but was not, strictly speaking, consciously there.

She was somewhere else. Contained within the narrow sphere of light in some state of transcendence that allowed me to move quietly across the expanse of that sprawling attic, beneath the exposed timbers and girders laced together by generations of spiderwebs doing whatever

81

spiderwebs do in the airspace of cavernous rooms, beyond the bureaus and tables and chairs and the assorted miscellany arranged like items in a museum. The Pond Museum.

In the center of the attic was that featherbed that had conceived a continuum of Ponds for generations and moved to the attic upon the deaths of Ma and Dad Pond. In the darkness, I would creep stealthily across the floorboards, led by my navigational heart to approach the mass of that bed and climb up onto the heights of that mattress and then slowly, silently, sink within its folds like giving in to a cloud. Ingesting, with several deep silent breaths the scent of the paints, the oils and solvents permeating the attic air.

And there I would remain, wide awake. More long deep breaths to encourage the light headedness of her kerosene solvents and eventually when the morning light appeared through the dormer, I would reach for a random planting log from the shelf housing the entirety of *Pond Planting Logs* and begin reading from a bound volume the width of my chest and as tall as my arm such sentences as:

April 17, 1861

Cool cleer skies

Apple, peach, and cherry trees all leafing

Two selection of tomato seeded to the house gardin

32 lbs. of test corn seed to the 13 east furrows of the west field.

Twelv black'ns arriving at dawn. Some near starved. Remember nurshished them and doctored their scars and in the morning the able-bodied will set to the west field seeding. Among them, a gient speciman all white who sings heavenly like the messiah.

From the drawing board came the sound of her sighing, followed by a shifting and the chair legs scraping as I looked up to watch her toss a brush over her shoulder that caromed off the wall behind her to land on the floor before the scores of drawings and paintings stacked against that wall. My cue. I scuttled from the folds of the featherbed and made my way to stand beside her, reeled in by her arm and nuzzling like melting wax to the scent of her breath against the back of my neck and for five full minutes there was nothing more. Nothing more to my existence. No farm or river or barn or bridge or aunts or sisters or anything beyond the contained silence and the physically addictive scent and texture of my mother's skin.

And then I would snap out of it. The distant hum of our tractor down along the river, the headlights bobbing as thin narrow ribbons of light along the riverbank thicket, well ahead of the herd lumbering away from the barnyard to feast on the barley in the east field. And Givens, Givens Marsh. His tractor paused off the bridge at the mouth of the old cow trail leading ultimately to the forbidden west field. I leaned forward, my nose grazing the glass of the dormer window and Mother's fingers slipped from my scalp to crease my spine at the nape of my neck, as if scruffing a possum.

"That Givens?"

She joined me at the dormer. "Maybe."

"No maybes, Mom. That's Givens."

Quickly, as if given to the guilt of being caught by someone, by Scooter or Bump or even my father, I broke from her embrace and almost ran to the landing, pausing at the top of the attic stairs long enough for a glance of solidarity, the reassurance of her at the drawing board watching me watch her for a few frozen seconds and then I was gone, skipping down the winding steps to dress quickly and see Verity's empty bed off the adjacent wall, the shelf of plastic horses branding her side of our shared bedroom. I skipped down the main stairs to pass through the library and living room and into the kitchen, where Clare was already awake and preparing breakfast. Clare, who was once among those who migrated up every spring from Cairo, from Mississippi, camping out under the bridge and lining up along Pond Road every morning hoping to be hired for the season and housed in the women's wing of the old Slave's Quarters up on Slave Hill overlooking the lower pasture and river.

83

For some reason, before I was born, Clare stayed on. Perhaps she was a good cook, or had a favorable disposition with children, or possibly because she and Mother simply got along and their relationship, their friendship, was unlike that of Mother and her sisters or even Dolores Faller, Mother's closest friend since they were toddlers—Dolores, who would come straight to the house after school during Mother's early sickly years, summarizing the school day highlights with notebooks sent along by Mrs. Hall.

At this hour, Clare was all mine. Before I had settled onto a stool at the end of the long counter, she set out a bowl of cereal and stood for a moment, leaning into the counter, watching me add spoonfuls of peaches to a mouthful of cereal until my cheeks were the cheeks of a hoarding squirrel and she said, "Well you, Mister Whister," and I'd look at her, searching for something to say.

"You know old Mr. Arthur don't speak cause he had his tongue cut out by the Kickapoos. That's a fact."

"The Kickapoos?"

"That's right, Clare. The Kickapoos. Or the Moingwenas. I ain't sure."

"He just an Amish," she said, wiping her hands on her apron and returning to the stove. "They mostly don't talk much," she added.

"*Tongue*, Clare. *Nooo tongue.*"

Mr. Arthur, as mentioned, farmed the adjacent east field of their 125 acres with a draft horse and plow and lived by oil lamps and no plumbing and had a gray beard. The Amish, they all had long beards as thick as cotton candy. Mr. Arthur, like everyone else in the valley, fertilized his fields with manure. Mounds of nutritious redolent manure stockpiled as just one of the many byproducts of maintaining a herd. He and Father were friends. Not friends, precisely, but likeminded on their close relationship with soil.

Clare made a face and said, "So, the War of the Kickapoo, you say'n?"

"Maybe. Or some other war. I might be talking bout a war you ain't heard of."

"Hmmm. Amish don't fight."

"It was more a raid. The Tongue Stealing Raid of 1820."

"How old he be, ole Arthur?"

"First thing...Amish live longer'n us. A fact. And they fight only when they's protect'n something...like their *tongues*, Clare."

Mother, as the embodiment of Chastity Pond, entered the kitchen to stand at the small window overlooking the peach grove and the silo and the prancing barnyard banshees. The full light of day was upon us. Clare and I watched as she steadied the carving knife over the apex of a mammoth cantaloupe the size of a basted turkey. Intent on slicing this aberration to the precision of perfectly equal halves with Clare standing by, watching, humming, dallying through the chorus of *The Sweet By and By* as Mother steadied her knife still poised in indecision.

"You want help, honey?"

Without waiting for an answer Clare took the knife and sliced the cantaloupe and sliced it again and set the servings on the long adjacent counter while Mother settled into the alcove at the far end of the kitchen. A small desk situated against a small window overlooking the farmhouse gardens and the not so small expanse of the north field. In the distance, at a height of land along the road, the Fall Ridge Church and the adjoining cemetery littered with the granite markers of our founding settlers.

"Where's Verdi?" She asked.

"She up to the barn," Clare answered. "Early. Brushin down Horse, I sume."

Mother slowly situated herself into the desk chair sidled against that small window with its lifting panorama, and with the lethargy of a confounding drizzle she considered the stack of mail. Accumulating like dust, the stack grew with a maddening accountability and if ignored, if dismissed, the arriving letters would overwhelm the quaint little desk and scatter themselves across the laundry room floor. Whiffed by the repeated draft of a back door opening and closing until the laundry room floor was a drifting dune of envelopes addressed in red or blue or purple crayon.

Humming another melody now, lingering from last Sunday's service, Clare retrieved little envelopes from beneath the washing wringer.

"You want help, honey?"

But Mother had yet to get started. On the wall, pinned to the bulletin board was a list of to-dos, written in her new scratchy script of abbreviations and codes and acronyms. Yesterday, or the day before, or whenever the current list was composed, the codes and abbreviations would have made perfect sense but now, now the list on the wall was a puzzle unraveled.

She pulled a single envelope from the pile to her right and opened the letter and read the careful deliberate handwriting of an eight-year-old. At the bottom of the letter, she penned a short reply and it was impossible to ignore the disparity between the clean and ever so careful cursive of an eight-year-old to the nearly illegible reply scrawled across the bottom of the page. She returned the letter to the same envelope and set it to her left as the start of a new pile that Clare would eventually address and stamp and post when Mariah's footsteps vibrated lightly through a system of aged floor joists linking the old house from one end to another.

A fashionable tardiness. The last to rise.

And as the last to rise, she descended the stairs and passed off the den and through the dining room and into the kitchen with the delicate step of an aspiring dancer. She sat at the far end of the breakfast counter and her eyes traveled the length of the counter to the small desk in the alcove and remembered, surely, that she had agreed to help, to offer a penmanship so affected and conscientious it bordered on calligraphy. To work her way through the stack of imbecilic fan mail in a trade to have her hair set and curled for Saturday's dance at the Town Hall in Fall

Ridge. Where she would meet Buddy…Buddy Faller.

Clare had finished slicing the cantaloupe—like milling a tree trunk—stacked and assorted on a small dish on the corner of the counter claimed as Mariah's corner and Clare asked, "You wants some toast, Miss Sheba?" Which would be the Queen of Sheba, and a subtle reminder that the rest of the house had been awake for some time.

Mariah shook her head and spooned into her fruit, likely considering Mother quietly occupied at the small desk.

"I'll be right there, Mother."

But Mother didn't respond, and Mariah would've understood that Mother understood that the understanding of the trade to set her hair was no guarantee of anything.

Clare turned from the linens and glanced at the back of Mother's head and then to Mariah at the far end of the kitchen with a wordless exchange of raised eyebrows that was linked somehow to an unlikely alliance, a sisterhood between Clare with her slave's ancestry and the Queen of Sheba.

But Mariah took her time, one bite followed slowly by another because she had every right to see Buddy. He was not a criminal. He was not, as Father once quipped, '…*as dumb as a milk pail.*' Buddy was simply the frontrunner of a selection based on a rudimentary curve, a relative scale drawn up by Mariah and her friends listing who was available and Buddy, well…Buddy was available and convenient and who could deny the adrenalin of rollercoasting the gravel roads in that guttural toy, the ultimate rebellion against…against, something. Anything.

Mariah set her dish in the sink and turned to consider me as she leaned against the sink in her svelte stretch pants and her linen blouse and it was as if she didn't see me at all. As if I were a still-life framed and hung on the wall. She made her way to the desk chair with a vainglorious sigh loud enough to punctuate just about anything. She took an envelope from the pile and opened it and signed Mother's name and replaced it within the envelope and set it to the left and Mother exclaimed, "Mar-i-ah."

Mother, leaning against the counter, looked to me and for some reason I said, "Hey, Mom, you know old man Arthur ain't washed his beard in ten years?"

"He *hasn't* washed his beard."

"I know."

"Well Whisty, how do you know this?"

"Cause he told me is how."

Mariah glanced over her shoulder at Mother and then returned to the stack of mail.

"So you spoke to Mr. Arthur, did you?" Mother asked.

"He's lying, Mom."

Mother looked at Mariah sitting with her back to us and said, "Be sure to read them, Mariah. Answer them nicely. Don't just sign them. *Answer* them."

"He's lying," Mariah said, her back still turned to me. "He always lies. He lies about everything."

"Just answer the mail, honey. And Saturday we'll set your hair. And by the way, Buddy is not picking you up. Your father will give you a ride."

Mariah turned and stood so quickly the chair toppled, clapping the floorboards like rifle fire. She stood with both hands on her waist and one hip slung out like an elevated teebox and Mother sighed.

"Your father will drive you, period."

And turning to me, Mother added, "I believe I saw the boys waiting for you at the barn already."

That fall, and it's that fall I'm concerned with. Chronologically speaking. That last fall of the long drought and the coming winter of record freezes and the following spring of record floods, that period of eighteen months as opposed to some other eighteen months...when practically every Saturday morning I would head out early to cross the lawn and up beyond the Bottle Tree beside the Quarters to find Bump waiting on the rise beside the old Farmall. And Scooter who would have arrived by traversing on foot the handful of north-south streets comprising all of Fall Ridge to arrive at the edge of the Sneads' place to light out across their corn field and cross the river at the Point where the logs jammed up for a natural, slightly dangerous bridge and on up through our forbidden west field to arrive at the back side of the barnyard.

We occupied ourselves with the relic Farmall, stripping away the vines and thicket with the pointless pastime of painting it orange. The casing, the wheel-wells, the tires, even the engine block itself. Or in the loft of the barn, where we searched the girders for pigeon nests with hatched eggs, binding their spindly legs with string to hang upside down, lowered into a bucket of tractor lubricant headfirst. Or milling about the Quarters thick with the scent of sausage and grits and where the hands were readying themselves for the fields, sitting on the long porch or against the same railing their ancestors once embraced, drawn back then by the billowing yellow flags strapped to the weathervanes as signposts to a freedom from bounty hunters.

But this morning, grasping the last vestiges of the summer pastime, we headed to the river. We stripped naked and wallowed in the shallowing current with the last swim or two before the weather turned from fall to winter. With Father downriver, turning the herd loose on the leafy smorgasbord of barley, Verity arrived bareback on Horse to find Bump and I smoking dried hickory twigs as Scooter dragged on the rolled cigarette stolen from his mother's bureau. Lounging amidst the wildflowers and head-high weeds, safely distanced from a riverbank pitted with snakeholes.

Verity was changing. At thirteen, she no longer swam in just her underwear, and both Bump and Scooter were reacting to the change, pulling on their shorts as she rode up and adopting an awkwardness that had them noticing Verity as if she were the only female they'd ever seen.

Bump fingered the hickory stick as if it were a cigar, lolling in our private haven, harnessed by walls of milkweed and gazing up into the blue, the coppery blueness of mid-September, and he suddenly said, "Some folks saying what yer dad's doing ain't right."

"Shit them," I answered, for a lack of anything else to say.

"Jussie."

Anymore all it took was just the sound of Verity's voice. It didn't matter what she said, just her voice alone and Bump and Scooter turned to her like drooling disciples.

"They's shits. Stuck in the past like stupid shits."

"Jussie!"

"They just don't understand." Bump said. "They don't understand what yer dad's doing is all."

On his back, Bump borrowed a drag from Ruby Morrow's tobacco stash and exhaled slowly, watching a smoke ring float and drift in the protected airspace, rising up beyond the wall of weeds, gently whipped and eddied but still rising. A moment later, he passed the cigarette back to Scooter and rose to leap onto Horse behind Verity and they rode off toward Father and Givens down near the Point as I watched Scooter trapping a carp in a shallow pool of mud, splattered in mud, wrestling this half-dead carp with his hands and arms and the cigarette slung from his lips and laughing crazy when we heard the familiar sound of his mother Ruby's little MG sputtering from up Pond Road.

We stood and from that vantage watched her approach on the higher elevation of the graveled road as she neared the bridge. A tin cup, as Buddy Faller called it, her MG, sputtering and coughing like a sick toad. The top down and Ruby's signature yellow scarf trailing off the trunk, flapping in the wind while from the other direction appeared the twins, Aunt Elizabeth and Madeline's old Plymouth inching along past the Arthur place. As they drew closer to the bridge with its elevated rise, we watched Elizabeth leaning in with both hands gripping the wheel and no visibility of what was approaching and Ruby braking hard on the wood planks of the bridge. The twins rolled to a stop and for a moment they sat watching Ruby watching them. Ruby tapped her fingers on the side of the door waiting impatiently for the two badillacs to back up and clear the way and the twins sat, confused, when Ruby raised her hands in frustration and stepped out and started walking briskly toward the Plymouth when she dropped flat on her back and out of view.

Scooter and I clambered up the aggregate of the roadbed to stand at the edge of the bridge. Covered in mud and a cigarette still wedged between his lips, Scooter trotted to where his mom was spread out on the bridgeplanks. He yanked the scarf free from under one of the rear wheels, freed the other end noosed around her neck, and helped her up to the sound of Father's raised voice carrying from the distance. Givens and he were arguing, Father leaning over the tractor wheel-well and Givens standing with flailing arms and suddenly Verity's voice. Her singing voice.

I abandoned Scooter as he brokered some kind of peace between his mom and the unlikeable twins as I ran off in the opposite direction, dissecting the river bramble and through the long linear geometry of browsy barley to reach the Point where Father sat the idling tractor with the intoxicating scent of oil and gaseous exhaust coughed through a thin vertical pipe vibrating off the block. I climbed up to take my position against the wheel-well and called out, "Hi, Dad!"

Something was wrong. The Herefords had moved away from grazing the brushwood, driven in a wide swath between the edge of the barley and the river thicket and I leaned in close and yelled over the rattle of the diesel, "They look jittery, Dad!"

Father nodded. He motioned to the west field, to the hired hands clustered against the split rail separating the alfalfa of the west field from the barley of the east pasture. He raised a few fingers toward the nearby Givens as if to end their conversation and we rolled slowly along the brushwood before clutching and again, over the idling engine I said, loudly, "It ain't right, Dad. Somethin ain't right."

The herd was agitated, shuffling in place, bunched close and bellowing their refrains. Those hands on this side of the river, another forty paces beyond the herd, stood against the fence with their hoes like walking sticks to face the river where along the opposite treeless bank another group of hopeful hands stood, seemingly flushed up from their encampments along the riverbed.

The engine died out and we sat in an abrupt and sudden silence punctuated only by the whining herd. The light slanted off a stand of sinewy dogwoods with long thin shadows extending beyond the herd and well into the crop where Verity sat Horse. Our eyes were on Verity now, as Bump had dismounted and made his way on foot away from Horse and the herd toward Father and myself. Verity was holding a single note, reining Horse toward the herd, cautiously, to just beyond the shaded margins of the dogwoods where the light of the clearing was unimpeded and where she paused, surrounded by one-thousand-pound Herefords who had gone silent. Verity skipped along a quick succession of familiar hymns and then she waited. From the clearing down in the river thicket a series of quarter notes, rising and lingering with the impasse of a lifeless painting. A single crow cawed from a lone cottonwood across the river and the sound floated, drifting like a falling leaf.

He stood positioned in a hollow along the river's deeper trough, a chambered clearing without groundcover or the shade of the canopied tupelo wood and with the open exposure of an amphitheater He issued a guttural incantation and Verity responded. Fluctuating single notes colliding somewhere over the herd and the conversation advanced, quickly, to multiple flexible octaves more like a coloratura than a song, trading back and forth between them a musicality beyond Verity's animalspeak. Beyond her language with Horse and the barnyard critters.

And then it stopped, replaced with an unsettling silence.

I rested a hand on Father's shoulder and leaned so close our cheeks touched, so close I could drink in the scent of his skin as the herd resumed their braying and muttering and the hands up along the west field fence and the latecomer migrants positioned along the opposite bank dropped to their knees. As if praying.

He began again. Not a song, not a recognizable melody with meters and measures and the complimenting progressions of an expected rhythm. Not that. The sound of His voice carried off the river and settled over the sunlit fields like a thick lingering cream, resonating with a persistence that allowed another measure of a new octave to occupy the same airspace as if it were two voices rising at once off the river. A third measure, and a fourth, and fifth, and each octave sustaining itself with its original throttle that became essentially, a chorus. A half dozen layers occupied the various registers of an extended scale hovering and dawdling in the airspace with the harmony of a metaphysical chorus.

And again, in the ensuing silence the notes lingered and drifted and gradually died away.

I turned to Father as a corroborating witness but Father's eyes were on Verity. He and the hands on both sides of the river were watching Horse and a thirteen-year-old weighing all of seventy-five pounds followed by a herd of hypnotized Herefords moving obediently away from the indigestion of the bramblebush to the newer intended diet of tampered barley. A genetically tasteless barley?

We sat the tractor a while longer. Eventually Verity and Horse left the herd for the open plain where Bump rejoined them as Father scanned the riverfront and then back to Givens, as if to identify the witnesses. Along Pond Road, Widow Drew and her grandson were parked, likely on their way to Lorraine Snead's little daycare school. And Dr. Steadfast Stewart behind them, making his morning rounds.

I broke the silence with, "I guess by now pretty much everyone knows anyway, Dad."

He nodded, and I wondered if we were talking about two different things.

By my own *accurately* reported account, he sang for ten minutes, although later recounted and embellished by some, by me, to as long as an hour because the gift of storytelling and the sovereignty of the narrator's version, of the great writer Linkum Regard's version, with all its embellishments and privileges, rested on nothing more grounded than the ephemeral rule of believability. How the storyteller can set his type one letter at a time and sell his story to a wanting audience that rises or falls to the timing of his delivery, to the steady pace that reads with the timbre of a spoken voice explaining how...*the sky went black with all the birds in the valley flocking to the voice of a timeless Beast. This Messiah, frozen in time, trapped between history and eternity as the river's current paused and the water level rose to brim the banks with the floodplain marked and compared to the epic Spring of Ought 8. A metaphysical incarnation witnessed firsthand by credible sources out along the Pond place.*

Givens Marsh stood a few feet off, his thick hands shoved into the back pockets of his overalls as Father killed the engine and leaned out over the wheel-well as Givens raised his chin with a faint gesture and for a moment no one said anything. Up on the road the twins had resumed their Saturday drive as Scooter and his mom headed the opposite direction in the sputtering MG. Across the road Guy Faller stood on his tractor with his hands on his hips and in the opposing field across the looping current of the river old Mr. Arthur stroked his beard. Inescapable reminders of unharvested dehydrated soybeans.

"I got the Ag people over to Fall Fork testing samples," Givens said, out of the blue. He stood with his thumbs behind his suspenders and a twist of tobacco working against one cheek. He leaned and spat and wiped his mouth and a moment later added, "Thought you should know that."

From her vantage in the attic where she had returned in search of predictable results... Mother watched, with brush in hand, the proceedings down along the river. With the dormer window open to the September air, she had sat listening to the birdsongs, as she later recalled, sharing the shade of the side-yard elm with Dee and Bim, how she thought of Verity's voice, like birdsongs, how Verity's little secret was no longer a secret; how there would be repercussions and more Devil-talk. And then her husband and son who appeared to be engaged with Givens in what was surely the growing debate over the crops, the chemical drift at the heart of her neighbor's unspoken complaints and how there would be repercussions and more Devil-talk. And then to the wild but goodhearted Scooter ensuring his mother got home safely, and then to the sound of the half-crazy twin's Plymouth pulling into the driveway. She had never felt so alone.

SIXTEEN

The afternoon developed...building steam with a call on the party line from Dolores Faller. And from Clare's Max so proud of his new personal phone in the stables over to the Javitts-from-Kentucky place looking for Verity and wanting likely to know if she would be helping in the stables and then a call from the twins looking for my help with that coming Sunday's sermon they were commandeering from Brother Reeves because, with my celebrated *Gazette* fame, it was now believed I had a way with words. A call from Aunt Dee looking for Mariah's help in the shop and how there had been a mix-up with the Shriner's job in Mount Vernon receiving the uniforms that should have gone to a pom pom squad in Vernon Heights and how the pom pom squad received four boxes of tasseled hats. But Mariah wasn't interested lately in anything but the art of insolence and aloofness, and Buddy Faller.

I considered calling Acceptance, expecting to hear from her regarding our apparent celebrity status but the party line was a beehive and I dialed up Bump just across the road, unconcerned with the lack of privacy as we listened to Givens talking to Listen Allerton over to the Feed Store, and Diligence Wiseman, Ruby's secret lover, who pretended as a concerned neighbor to inquire about her mishap at the bridge and

CHARLES PROWELL

then Aunt Elizabeth who chatted with Mercy May Jenkins about the musical score for Sunday's hymn selection and finally I got through to Bump who kept asking what Verdi was doing and I interrupted the Wiseman-Ruby conversation to ask the short-circuited Ruby if Scooter was home and for some reason I was suddenly thinking how both Bump and Scooter were replacements for Meek, Bump and Buddy's youngest brother, or once their youngest brother before being dead. The thought of Meek's death was strictly off limits. There had been enough sleepless nights, sweatdrenched dreams of his pantleg shooting up through the ice, wriggling and kicking and then gone and suddenly I was thinking of it again, when I swore never to think of it again, not for the rest of my life.

Sheriff Sam Ditmar also called, wanting Mother's help with Aunt Dee's habit of shooting the crows from her sycamore and her neighbor the Widow Drew's objections to the calamity of buckshot at eight in the morning and how their back-and-forth exchanges from window to window were immature and unhealthy, and eventually Sheriff brought up the idea of an investigation. Investigating the *occurrence*. Coming on out to *investigate*.

"What occurrence is that?"

"You know. His little piece in the Gazette this morning. The Beast, and all."

"Don't bother, Sheriff."

"Is it still there?"

"We don't need an *investigation*, Sam."

At mid-day, I approached the Annex with a platter of lunch fruits and vegetables and sat in the corner struggling to breath, swallowing artificial air thick as pudding in a room lined along one side with hundreds of potted plants flourishing in the indirect light of a frosted glass wall. On the other side was Father's long work bench and the logbooks stacked along a shelf, consisting of secrets and mysteries and cryptic computations and it was clear to me that no Roe descendant would ever read the Henry Roe Planting Logs; they lacked the heart and the soul of what makes something readable. They lacked the peculiar dialect so pervasive to the valley history. They lacked the sort of imagination my sisters would find fault with decades later, the embellishing and fabricating and stretching of the truth all for the sake of a good story at the expense of credible history. But then they had always accused me of lying. And rightly so… they don't understand how a well-told lie is worth a thousand truths.

Justus Roe's Planting Logs began five and half decades ago, concerned with births, deaths, crop rotations, and general sundry. Linkum Regard's Planting Logs are of a recollective nature undertaken during my seventh decade. What you are reading now, concerned with only a portion of time near the end of my first decade and as a clear departure from the very purpose of all our ancestral logs and while Mariah once objected from her removed distance of having once spent two years living with Aunt Harriet in St. Louis, or Verity from her professional scrutiny as one of the foremost large animal veterinarians in all of Illinois, what is the point of a log no one reads, as in Father's logs—studied, admittedly, three-quarters of a century later not by the Roe family, my sons and their own sons and daughters, and their sons and daughters, but by tropes of questionable scholars and research assistants and graduate students and shoulder-holster thugs and global economists writing papers on where and how it all began. How farming changed. When it changed. Who changed it? Who was responsible? What horrific megalomaniac was accountable for poisoning half the world? And to others, for feeding them.

Father stood to leave the Annex and I followed, carefully mimicking his footsteps, stretching to fill the bootprints that with each step incited powderpuffs of dust off the barnyard floor as we entered the barn. Verity was dressing Horse, with the Sows One and Two and Cow watching on with an idle interest. We climbed the ladder to the loft and moved among the meager stockpiles of last year's hay as Father paused and stepped around an open bucket of lubricant and gestured as if to say, "What's this?"

He glanced at me and I shrugged as if the bucket might speak up and offer some explanations. I turned to the bales of hay, wisely, and asked, "So, how's it look, Dad? We add the barley and alfalfa and it'll be enough to get through, right? That's the plan, right?"

Father shook his head and raised his pencil and poked the air, transferring tallies to the little notebook pulled from his shirt pocket and he said, "Probably not."

I considered this. "So then there's the money from the Ag people, from the school. We can *buy* feed from Listen Allerton and in April it'll rain and everything's good, right? Everything'll be just good."

"The school money is for what really matters. The herd, and the alfalfa and barley, don't matter as much. The Annex and the west field are what matters."

"Then they'll know. Everyone else will know."

"Know what, Sport? I don't care what they know."

I didn't understand. Father wasn't seeing the big picture. If come spring we were doing fine and everyone else wasn't doing so fine, they would know.

"They'll know we belong to the school, Dad. That we're not farmers at all, but somethin else."

Father turned and studied me for a moment. He might've been thinking how I wasn't an academic or that I lacked the patience for delayed rewards but that I had the intuition, the congenital understanding of the do's and dont's of solvent farming drawn from a heritage above reproach. It wouldn't be accurate to say now, in hindsight, that my father, as an outsider, was jealous of that heritage. Not quite accurate, but something close. Something close to jealousy.

"I thought you were going to the paper today," he said, changing the subject.

"Bim's off to Granny Davis'…you figure she's the oldest person around?"

"She pretty old."

He sat close, sharing the same bale of hay and gazing through the trap to the ground floor where Verity's voice had begun drifting up. Her soft singing voice.

"Hey Dad, you think Acceptance is pretty?"

"What?"

"Acceptance. Acceptance Davis. You think she's pretty?"

"Sure, Sport."

We sat in a silence flushed with the scent of feed grain, hay, hides, and dung, listening to Verity, to the chorus of conversations developing down below in a language neither of us understood. People should know that Verity's language is nothing more than what she taught the Sows and Cow and Horse as a dialect of octaves and syllables begun at birth with a Pavlovian simplicity.

Suddenly the sound of Mother's voice, whispering from the barn doors and rising up into the loft, "Just stay in the barn, honey. That's all I ask."

The chorus went silent, the animals and pigeons and wrens along the girders suddenly quiet, and as Mother was seen returning through the barnyard toward the house, the chorus slowly returned.

There are stories of magic, and stories drawn from a premise of fantasy and disbelief, and stories rooted in a fiction drawn from science. The credibility of the planting logs comes from a trust in the simplicity of the prose and the irrefutable evidence of stated fact and when the dry rough-hewned usage is broken with the colloquialism of something fantastic, such as singing critters, the entry is read with impact. A measurable credibility. Do you understand?

Born with the mental orientations of science and the empathic reservoirs of an angel, Verity had simply adopted a language of recognizable sounds translated into equally simple associations. Beginning as an eight-year-old in the barn and the birthing of a new foal, Verity passed entire nights in the stall cradling the newborn and repeating a series of sounds the way a mother might sing to a child. Each sound had a translation, such as a simple Hello. A hierarchy of sounds matching the intelligence of Horse over the course of that first year and like the Sows, One and Two, they grew into a language of varying octaves and sustained notes that must be described as incantations. Each octave was associated with an emotion, such as happy, sad, danger. The notes within, say, the sad octave, were equally associated with the translated derivatives of the basic nouns of a building vocabulary.

The language of the lesser-developed brains such as the Herefords and the muskrats were more elementary and relegated to fewer octaves and with the pigeons it consisted of only two notes drawn from two distinct octaves. Hello, and Goodbye, and whether they were in the upper reaches of the blossoming dogwoods or perched on the beams of the barn, they responded to their simple language by acknowledging Verity's presence with the social graces of a tutelage that began in the nest.

As the population aged, the proportion of those raised under her directives increased until by the time she was thirteen the majority of the critters associated with the farmstead were linked not only to the Verity Language, but understood on a sliding scale the language specific to any given species—as the octave language was common to translation. So, a single note on the middle octave issued in the mornings as she entered the barn was heard and understood and responded to by virtually every species within earshot. Whereas the complexity of a conversation reserved for Horse, or Sows One and Two, was a dallying range of arpeggios and sustained notes that was closer to a musical dance than a spoken language.

A simple insight drawn from a Pavlovian approach that had nothing to do with magic or the peculiarity of the supernatural. A gift, nonetheless, known to us and our aunts and the Fallers that would be cited in the decades to come and forevermore, as a significant, innovative reach in the science of animal behavior.

And so we listened, Father and myself, as she brushed Horse down below in a barn that was something of a symphony. A cacophony of syllabic banterings in a crossfire of bilingual conversations that had drawn, by its very proportions, a gathering of critters rivaling a social jubilee that began to carry up the road to Dolores and Guy Faller sitting on their front porch and to the older Givens and Vivian Marsh on their own front porch and to old Mr. Arthur and his aging wife listening through their open window and of course Mother and the others gathered under the elm off the side of the house. And then silence. Absolute silence.

Father and I glanced at one another with measured breaths, careful not to give up our presence. A moment passed and a single soft note. The first note in the lesson plan presented at some juncture to all those critters present and perhaps it was considered insulting, the baby-talk of this single note. Perhaps all those present had long been aware of a creature who is far beyond the limits of Horse or the Sows and perhaps beyond that of their own tutor.

A series of quarter-notes scattering the scales beyond the known simplicities, followed by another silence and as we listened to the sound of Verity's brush smoothing Horse's silky flanks He sang from beyond the back open doors. Stationed just outside the barn, He lifted a series of almost inaudible notes to rise and fall from a sliding scale, and the sound that carried through the barn was both new and agreeable.

Verity responded, settling the same range and tapering the staff to a series of sharps and flats and they began, stretching a known language through a pianissimo of soft flexible exchanges that soon floated across the staves with the subtle shadings that had their voices lingering to the acoustics of the cavernous barn. The fragile registers of the soprano rose and suspended, hovering along the vaulted beams and layered with His metallic tenor as entire octaves came to occupy the airspace simultaneously.

Eventually the others participated, each within their own range of relative offerings and the result is unlike the babble of conversations earlier that afternoon, but something closer to an orchestra. An orchestra with the grounding acumen of a masterful conductor and yet in the end it was only the two voices in their unceasing exploration.

Verity's singing counterpart, I decided, needed a name. Harlan, because it rolls easily off the tongue. But to the hands, however, He was *Massiyah.*

Father and I waited until Verity left the barn and we made our way down from the loft and back to the Annex where the logs aligned on the shelf were brought out and splayed along the potting bench, poised for the scrutiny of the first real subsidy review. To be conducted by three administrators who on that very morning would have embarked at first light on the second leg of their journey, leaving an overnight stay at the county seat of Fall Fork and dropping down off the grade to pull off the side of the road to stretch their legs and summon their readiness for a descent into the Valley of the Unknown.

Of course, it was an inconvenience and in their own minds only Father, Henry Roe, could have warranted such effort. More than inconvenient, it was. Leaving the civilized social graces of their clean brick homes in the manicured neighborhoods of the northern campus for the heathenism of third-world folklore and hand plows. In their middling minds only Roe, with his history, could have lured their descent off the ridge to the junction of Route 10 and on through the glade of blossoming dogwoods to mark the valley-proper with the farmsteads unfolding like portraits. A confusion of unmarked winding graveled roads graded once long ago to the width of a horse-drawn wagon and the three administrators would have debated and disagreed on which road as the dust eddied through the open windows and the September sunlight bore down on their black sedan and they drove on like dusted cupcakes.

Meandering along a current of seemingly endless options, the schoolboys frequently paused and left their idling car to again stretch their legs and on foot they would have infiltrated the fields flanking the roads to pinch the leafage of a crop similar to the drought-stricken fields up north.

At Snead's Corner we know they progressed alongside the Arthurs' field, smiling certainly at the sight of the gravity wagon and the piano-box buggy as visible reminders they were in the heart of the valley and as they approached the bridge, they would've paused and cut the engine and left the car to walk among the Faller soybeans. Scrape the silk from the prop roots and tap it into their vials and maybe compare the pale colorations of the Faller crop to the flourish of the barley across the river. A yellowing patina demarcating the leafage as something beyond dehydration.

Givens Marsh would at that moment have maneuvered his tractor across the river at the surviving stone reach so soundly engineered during the Black Hawk campaign by Captain Abraham Lincoln and his volunteer charges in search of an enemy they never found. But instead of turning up the back access toward the church and his own barn, Givens followed the western access to surpass The Point and en route to Guy Faller's farm where he idled the engine and climbed from the tractor and approached on foot toward those three trespassing strangers. And as

Givens afterward always said, again and again, they had a conversation is all, nothing more, occupying the western reach of the Faller field until Givens returned to his tractor and set it to gear and disappeared into the dale of a former Shawnee encampment.

The schoolboys returned to the car to cross the bridge to pull up the Roe driveway and made their way on foot directly to the Annex as Bo the hound appeared off the corner of the barn. He loped to a position that checked their advance with a low gargling sound, drool streaming from his loose jowls, and from the barn's sliding doors, Father appeared. Bo pivoted and wagged his tail and disappeared around the silo to play with his friends, our resident barnyard muskrat or skunk or the three of them teaming up to taunt and tease the bullish copperhead.

As a rehearsed appearance, as I believe Clare remembered it, Mother, on cue, had crossed the lawn and the barnyard to enter the Annex with the platter of oatmeal. One of the schoolboys sat with his back to the door bent over the logs while another examined the rows of potted graftings and their index of hormone dosage and when neither acknowledged her, as expected, she eventually said, "Good morning."

They looked at her and because she was pretty they quickly looked away and nodded and mumbled a disarming good morning and Mother left the Annex, on cue. She walked to the edge of the barnyard as Clare appeared from the barn to join her, overlooking the river where in the distance Father stood in conversation with the third schoolboy. They occupied the grassy swath off the west field where Father spoke with his hands, moving his hands and arms with the gesticulating mannerisms of a snakeoil salesman. She caught his glance, his cue, and the two pretty women watched a moment more before turning to make their way barefoot back across the barnyard as Clare released the waistcord of her thin cotton wrap and Mother re-pinned her hair up off her shoulders.

Clare took the platter and together, as they returned to the house, Mother smiled and said, "We have visitors this morning."

"It would 'pear so."

"They're from upstate...the University."

"Look to me theys from somewhere. Somewheres but here."

"Upstate."

Clare nodded silently and a little further on she added, "Upstate."

Mother, as if dismissing the flies, drew a hand lazily toward the north field and Clare nodded and began to hum a melody lifted from an ancient bible hymn. They took the long way around the silo and past the manure pile where I was on my knees, in full regalia, utterly unaware of everything but the historically correct placement of my little lead soldiers and as they entered the peach grove Dee and the Sheriff and Bim had pulled into the drive to make their way on foot up the house garden toward the grove where Clare and Mother had appeared arm in arm, eating peaches and singing bible hymns. Clare broke for the back door and the others idled round the side of the house humming the same infectious hymn and by the time they approached those chairs under the shade of the front elm, Clare had by then set the small table and returned through the porch door as Bo left the manure pile toward the elm on the scent of fresh pastries.

They sat, appreciating the cooler September air, twirling their glasses to rotate the ice to cool their tea and as they fanned themselves, a lingering summer habit, a thin breeze arrived from down off the gorge. Drawn from the high-country waterfalls as a mist, swirling between walls of mossy limestone to carry down onto the open fields and along the depressions of the riverbank and lifting ultimately off the lower pasture to reach the elm as a subtle caress.

With a percussion of sound effects drawn from the manure pile, a flurry of young sparrows was flushed from high in the elm to take flight out over the front lawn, sweeping left and swooping right in a formation so tight and so perfect it appeared like a shadow that quickly disappeared back into the upper elmleaves. Tufts of dried dung hurled upward into the sky to my animated cries of wounded soldiers. Colorfully painted lead soldiers destined for the debacle of Picket's Charge turning somersaults in the air and falling to the ground with more sound effects and moments later, I looked to the elm where Sheriff raised a thumbs-up as I negotiated with some awkwardness the gaps in the fencerails to approach the small table with the kepie drawn down to my eyebrows and the oversized greatcoat dragging the lawn and the long scabbard strapped to my chest to clap the back of my knees to the rhythm of each clumsy step.

"…and how long will you keep it?" Dee was asking.

"Keep what?" Mother replied.

"It's like a pet, right? More a pet than another hand."

"Who sings," Bim said, chuckling.

"A white pet. Very white pet," Dee said.

"A giant singing white albino pet," and at this Bim smiled and a moment later Mother said, "Stop it. Both of you," and turning to Bim, "Do you *edit* what he writes?"

"He sells papers, honey. Oh, does he sell papers," Bim quipped, as if I weren't present.

"Well, one thing," Dee added, after a short pause, "Verity sings like an angel. Always has."

"Of course," Bim added. "And people will talk. Oh, they'll talk, the same devil nonsense."

"They *believe* it, Bim," Mother said. "What you're printing is just fueling the fire."

Sitting at the same table, the Sheriff was no more a part of their conversation than the sparrows in the elm. And when, following a lapse, the conversation changed to that morning's confrontation between Dee and Widow Drew, he looked away, likely regretting he had ever mentioned it to Mother over the phone.

"Sam is simply concerned for your safety, Dee," Mother reiterated, looking to the Sheriff who turned his eyes from the manure pile to Mother and Bim and he nodded and turned back to me.

"Total and absolute annihilation, Jussieboy."

"Colonel Picket was a fool."

"A brave and courageous fool. He believed they could do it. The Yanks held the high ground. It was Lee's last chance, or retreat to Virginia."

"It was a massacre, Sheriff. Like shootin pigeons on a fence."

"It was a horrible day. The bloodiest three days in American history."

And as the Sheriff fell silent, his eyes lost their focus and as was so often the case, he returned to his own memories, to the battle of Arles with all the fear and adrenalin and decades later enough shrapnel still scattered in him to send occasional radio frequencies into a static of confusion[8].

But I was more absorbed with the back of his hand, with the silver dollar rolling end for end and disappearing somehow into the palm of his closed fist and reappearing, rolling again end for end and when I reached, it quickly disappeared.

"Teach me that," I said.

"Cain't teach magic."

"It ain't magic. It's a trick."

The coin reappeared, cartwheeling along the back of his knuckles and I reached with a quick stabbing motion and again the coin disappeared and I gripped hold of Sheriff's fist with both hands and Bo barked and in a brief tug-a-war a half-smoked hickory stick fell from the breast pocket of the greatcoat onto the grass to sidle against the sole of Sheriff's right boot.

---

8. *If, on those summer evenings with everyone gathered on the back porch and the twins stationed on the living room couch glued to radio broadcasts, if on those evenings Sheriff was present, the radio console sputtered with static to interrupt the fights, the full nelson violations, until the twins moved from the couch to stand before the console with their backs to the porch as waifish barriers against the source of interference. Or if when dropping into the* Gazette *on a morning when I happened to be setting type, gainfully employed with the minutia of setting the trays and magnets when the trays were suddenly like Ouija Boards and the magnets were like mavericks with a mind of their own, sliding toward the shrapnel embedded in Sheriff's skull. He had survived, when many of his comrades had not. The blood and guts and death and desolation of Arles, France.*

He looked at me and raised one eyebrow and I shrugged and he shuffled the toe of his boot over the hickory stick while glancing at the three women lost in a conversation that had returned to their twin sisters.

"Why don't they just apply for a permit[9]?" Bim asked.

"They believe they have a right to Spread the Word," Dee said.

"On the street corner, like a couple of carnival barkers."

"And the fines...how much are they?" Mother asked.

"Ten dollars. Paid for by peddling more bibles, with more fines, with more peddling."

They allowed this to settle, the three sisters, sitting quietly for a moment, vacantly studying the plate of remaining pastries as Bim raised a single eyebrow over the frame of her glasses and whispered, "Nutty as hoot owls."

Sheriff looked up, drawn by the tenor of Bim's whispering voice as I made my move, lunging to grasp the coin in one hand as I fell onto the Sheriff's lap and the scabbard clapped the edge of the table and the pastries went airborne, sailing through the air like frosted tennis balls.

It was late that afternoon when the visiting sedan backed out the driveway and made its way up toward Bonnel Road and on toward Fall Fork and the following morning they would have traveled north without delay. It's how they operated, quickly furthering themselves from the Valley of Voodoo with an agreed consensus against any future excursions and with each mile their mood lightened and by the time they arrived

---

9. *If you happen through Carbondale for business at the University or on your way to somewhere, nowhere, you may have seen the twins stationed on Mill Street or Grand Street with a stack of cheap bibles placed on a cardboard box along the curb amidst the throng of passing intellectuals, students with their minds on engineering and architecture and eighteenth-century french comparative literature smiling at one another, bemused by the two spindly figures in matching pleated florals from that world, another world, and how to the twins, it was a badge of sophistication. Carbondale. To speak of it with an intimacy, a familiarity with the high-mindedness of somewhere beyond the valley. "You know Mill Street of course...at Grand Avenue...etc. etc."*

home to the cultivated lawns of their own culture, they'd have practiced their valley dialects to an invented vocabulary of hayseed quips and references of essentially no value beyond their own amusement. Or maybe not. Maybe they spent two days traveling in the silence of those who have no capacity to amuse themselves.

While still making their way up Pond Road, however, Father closed the open logs and returned them to their rightful sequence along the shelf on the same wall shared by Cow and the two Sows. He turned to shuffle the potted cuttings back to their previous labeled order and then lowered himself onto the stool and listened for a moment to the sounds beyond the wall, to Horse and Cow and the Sows that told him Verity was in the barn and, as I believe he once mentioned, he had pictured her life. Verity's life. The years ahead and the decades waiting to be lived and how a life like that was all about options and how time passes and the options are narrowed and how you live with the decisions that have narrowed those options, as Sheriff and I entered into the thicker air of the Annex with the door closing on its squeaky spring hinges to trap the tail of the greatcoat. I tugged and tugged again and then slipped free of the coat all together and it fell to gather on the floor of the Annex. The thickest purest wool drawn from the thickest purest cotton cultivated in the long-ago south to clothe an enemy in the long-ago north.

The Sheriff's eyes wandered, his first exposure, actually, to the inner sanctuary, browsing the mutant plants along the two walls and the vials of hormones along a shelf to the left of the logs and then to the stool and to Father who was either daydreaming or hypnotized. The Sheriff was aware of the subsidy's importance, and with the visitors now gone he would easily, as a trained professional, have known how no one seemed right anymore. Little wrongs appearing all over the place. Subtle malfunctions, scattering here and there all over the valley and yet nothing specific. Nothing he could put his finger on, specifically. Nothing to actually investigate.

POSSESSING THE SEASONS

Father returned from somewhere distant and looked at Sheriff and then to me, the kepie and the scabbard, and for a moment he seemed to consider my own legacy and my rightful turn in the years to come. A subject he returned to now and again, the continuum of a lineage and the efforts of Experience and Wrestling and Dust and Dad Pond, all of whom maintained a safe and cautionary planting schedule that had preserved and flourished acreage founded and cleared at about the time Washington was crossing the Delaware.

But his mind could wander, wallowing with a sluggish edge through a medley of potentialities and possibilities. Sheriff, seeing this, gripped him by the back of his shirtcollar and pulled him from the stool and moments later we were crossing the barnyard, the dragging scabbard marking the dust with a course coming adjacent to the little table since righted beneath the elm and the women since repaired from the elm and we made our way round the manure pile and behind the peach grove to arrive at the towering silo for that mindless pastime of feeding cartridges into a chamber, of triggering firing pins, of drinking in the scent of gunsmoke and the resulting thrill of empty cans shot to smithereens.

SEVENTEEN

Lately, as in the past decade, there are visitors. Officials, from some officiating department or another. Officials unofficially linked to various officious anacronyms, asking questions.

"How is it you never spoke of his ultimate goal?" they ask.

"I was eleven or twelve. I was a kid," I answer.

"Reading you and it seems you were a bright kid. Bright enough to understand."

"What I understood, decades later, was the culmination of research. The slow process of that. Seventeen years. He was caught up in the collection of data, the analysis of what was in the logs and later, the living results of what was in the fields. Z-scores, analysis of variance, statistical permutations, algorithms. Escalating until nothing mattered more. Not the solvency of the farm, nor the University's self-interest on a regional scale, nor even Harriman's Lend-Lease relief program or later, the Marshal Plan. My father's life had been reduced to how a species of the original hybrid dramatically shortened harvest timetables; how another strain was resistant to the most common crop-killing diseases, thus eliminating pesticides and the ensuing issues with watertable erosions; and then the succulents, the studies toward thickening the cell walls to insulate the capillaries from normal evaporation and how that two-thousand-mile stretch of coastal desert along Peru and Chile could be irrigated, in a way they were once irrigated by the Incan viaducts, but with only a fraction of needed water. The

POSSESSING THE SEASONS

arid deserts of North Africa; the entire Mideast basin; and any of the global fertile valleys historically subjected to recurring prolonged droughts. And of course, Europe. Post-war Europe.

"This was the premise...until one day it wasn't. That spring when both Mother's health was no longer imagined and he lost possession of the logs. That spring."

EIGHTEEN

That last summer of the drought Father had hired a geologist from the county seat and a drilling rig from Paducah, Kentucky to search for well water in the event of another winter without precipitation. Without snow or sleet that could be melted to provide potable drinking water (Dad Pond's silty little well behind the silo was giving up a whopping half-gallon a minute).

The lumbering rig moved from one spot to another and then another, dictated by the geologist with his gauges and instruments, paid by the hour. And each time it bore down thirty feet to a watertable that smelled and tasted like cow dung and at one-hundred-twenty feet to a loamy substrate and eventually Father hired Diligence Wiseman, who arrived with a widget he cradled in both palms as he walked the barren west field and the east field and the north field. He returned the following day towing his rattling rig and started drilling two-hundred yards behind the barn to ninety feet, tapping a vein of clear potable water pumping at two gallons an hour. Father paid Diligence in cash. Diligence Wiseman was now officially a well driller who farmed on the side.

With credit by now an improbable option to most of the farms, and cash, following three seasons of withering harvests, an even more

113

improbable option, the talk at Davis' Café on Saturday mornings widened the gap; it seemed clear that our farm was insulated from the clear and present danger facing most everyone else. By either the income of Mother's little books or that the unconventional alfalfa and barley was being subsidized by the University up north. To the others, it appeared Henry Roe was being paid to fiddle with Mother Nature.

Later that same week, well into October, Mother had tried to take it easy and get some rest, as old Doctor Stewart had prescribed. She entered the bedroom in the middle of the day and closed the door and lay down on the bed and stared at the ceiling, and it was the songbirds, she would recall, chattering in the elm with a splendid racket but a racket nonetheless. And then the banshees, muttering like an incessant white noise. And Hound, maybe, chasing something in the distance, and from somewhere in the house, beyond the bedroom door, she dwelt on the sound of Clare singing and how having Clare around was like having her own personal portable choir, which inexplicably led to the twins who had been arrested and fined, yet again, for peddling their bibles on the street corner over in Carbondale which flowed to thoughts of their failed insurrection to upend the aging Pastor Reeve and then the insanity of entrusting an eleven-year-old to compose a sermon that was a curiously skewed version of creation culled, curiously, from Henry's curiously skewed version of creation, and if you included all the uneasy reactions to Verity's own curiously inexplicable gift, everything was just plain skewed up.

How do you shut off your brain in the middle of the afternoon?

She closed her eyes and blanked out everything but the sound of Clare's voice.

She had never understood naps. Her great grandfather Dad Pond had taken a nap every day, right in this very room, and she often waited just outside the bedroom, sitting with her knees pressed to her chest and her back leaning against the door and counting the books on the shelves of the family library until he *finally* woke up.

She opened her eyes and studied the ceiling and left the bed for the long bath off the bedroom and in her continuing explanation to the girls and myself of that lost afternoon as if it was worthy of an explanation, she opened the medicine cabinet and stared at the little bottle of pills. She returned to the bed and studied the ceiling and folded her hands across her chest and waited. Guy Faller's tractor coughed in the distance and another songbird symphony, somewhere close, possibly from the elm off the sideyard window, when Henry opened the bedroom door.

"Is it working?"

She slowly shook her head.

He pulled off his boots and lay down beside her and studied the ceiling in his own futile attempt to understand this concept of naps when he always later claimed how naps were for the very young and very old. He held her open palm and listened to the blending sounds of a mid-day beyond the bedroom monastery. The sound of Guy's tractor reminded him that Guy had begun to plow up his futile crop and the news from earlier in the week that Guy had been approached by a consortium of St. Louis businessmen interested in paying cash for the place with the intent of creating a commercial hunting retreat. The news had been greeted with hearty laughs by everyone in the valley. Except Guy and Dolores Faller. They weren't laughing.

He looked at her open eyes and whispered, "Maybe if you closed your eyes."

She frowned and said something like, "I don't feel anything. I feel wide awake."

"Does your head hurt?"

"Some. Better."

"Well, then maybe they're working. Maybe they just make the headache go away."

"I was thinking about that, about how making the headaches better isn't like knowing why I have headaches in the first place."

He raised her hand to stroke her open palm against his cheek like a salve, and forgive me while I retreat, shamelessly, to my imaginative license...her palm against his cheek, drinking in the scent of her. Getting drunk on the scent of her and not fully comprehending this idea of her at less than full throttle while exploring the length of her neck and along the stretch of one arm and down her breastbone and along her legs. A slalom run up and down the groomed slope of her legs ingesting the smell of her and the feel of her born from flagship chromosomes.

"I'm worried about Dolores. About the offer from..."

"They need to hold on," he interrupted. "Get through the winter... and with weather in the spring, just a little, then the barley and alfalfa will win them over. Everyone will come around. There's time. It'll work out. Go with what makes sense. What makes money."

"They're not like the farmers upstate, Hank. You should know that by now."

"Religious limitations."

"Henry."

"How do you talk reason with religion? Not in seventeen years have I had a normal conversation with your sisters, the twins. What middle-aged women peddle bibles on the streets? It's pure charlatanism."

"Too many syllables. You use words with that many syllables and you'll have no one left but Verity to talk to."

"Who believes a girl who can talk to animals is sacrilegious?"

"Too many syllables."

"...a fabled creature who sings is the Messiah? A boy who writes a sermon, a Jeffersonian sermon..."

"Is it so different from my own little books, his sermon? He's a storyteller is all."

"That he is."

"They're all brilliant, Hank. They have your brains."

"And your heart."

He allowed himself a thin smile and she said, "Can't we help Guy and Dolores through the winter? He believes in you, and, well...they have an offer, Henry. I'm worried they'll have to take it. To move into town."

She rested her chin on top of his chest and combed her fingers through his scalp, gathering tufts of hair like shocks of straw and said, "People are talking about us."

He said nothing.

"About Verity. They don't understand her. They don't understand how smart she is. She learned it from you, Hank."

He sat up, looking intently at her.

"She got it from you. The way you've always talked to the Herefords."

"I can't imagine, Grace. What Verity's doing. I don't understand what she's doing. I don't understand it at all."

"She grew up listening to you and apparently decided, long ago, that she could do it better. Much better."

He returned to their shared pillow and the view of the plastered ceiling and said, "It's not necessarily a bad thing."

"Not necessarily."

A moment more of silence and she said, "Bim said Vivian said Givens was having samples of the barley tested up at the county seat."

"Hmm."

"Seems like everyone is against us."

"..."

"Hank?"

"I heard you."

"So, it's not like the garden?" she added. "The barley and the alfalfa need less rain is all? That's all there is to it?"

"Pretty much."

"Is that a yes or a no?"

"It's a pretty much."

She frowned and lowered her eyes and he said, "It's about progressive farming, Gracie. Mostly it's about that. It's about increased production for a world whose population is growing exponentially."

With the head of their bed to the window and the sash opened to a sliver of the looming winter, she considered the idea of St. Louis.

"I'd like to see Harriet."

"Perfect. So then it's set."

"But I don't want to go to St. Louis."

"Oh."

"They'll laugh at me again."

"No one laughed at you in Chicago."

He studied the ceiling with the déjà vu from months earlier. The same conversation. Her fear of some imagined hostility beyond Salt Fork Valley. Her grip on his hand loosened and when he turned to her, her eyes were closed and her breathing was steady and he stared up into a plastered nothingness and writing this even now, well into my eighties and the page is suddenly spotted with the wetted dollops of regret. Regretting this voyeur's entitlement of mine.

NINETEEN

There was a dull temper to the rest of September and all of October. The dust from the fallow fields lingered and drifted beneath skies that were as blue as sapphire until it gathered like cotton, clinging to the back of your throat. It was everywhere, permeating the walls of the house so that every room, even the books in the library, were coated and sheathed beneath a thin blanket of dust that nearly drove Clare to exhaustion. It became routine to blow off the plates and silverware before every meal.

We put up the storm windows with the anticipation of winter and eager for a change in the weather, any change, but also as an act of perpetual motion and the avoidance of inertia; the field work was over and most of the hands had returned to Cairo or farther south; the livestock was being flanked in the stockyard plants in Greenville and Cape Girardeau.

On an evening in late November, Givens and Vivian Marsh and Guy and Dolores Faller sat with Mother and Father at the dining room table for cards and coffee and during a lull in the chatter, Dolores announced their decision to sell. Buddy and Mariah were picking up WLS-Chicago on the radio in the library and Verity and Bump and myself were playing word games in the adjoining living room.

119

There was an abrupt yet almost apologetic tone to her voice, as if she had rehearsed the words a thousand times. The rustle of shuffling cards stopped. A long, awkward silence, a cloak of silence freezing this moment as if a death had been announced.

Guy occupied one end of the table like a sad giant, his glossy eyes studying the fan of cards in his huge hands but the cards meant nothing and he eventually turned to look at Dolores, and then to the others and with a shrug and a faint smile he added, "Hey, on to bigger and better things, eh?"

Suddenly everyone was talking at once.

TWENTY

Mother and Father left for an overnight stay in Fall Fork, without the hoopla of Chicago. A single satchel between them, and winter coats for the higher elevation weather. In the school cafeteria that afternoon, I sat with the brooding Bump, our eyes on Verdi and Acceptance sitting across the room. Mariah sat at the far corner of the cafeteria surrounded by upper classmen so far removed in the social order they might as well have been adults; to approach Mariah during school hours was unimaginable. Yet she found my look and returned it, distant and lofty and as blank as a wall. A moment later, however, she looked again and now there was a hint of confusion in her eyes, a passing glimpse that cut briefly through the veneer to acknowledge the same unsettling vacancy.

After school, I set the type at the *Gazette* while Aunt Bim put notices of the auction in both the *Southern Illinoisan* and the *Fall Fork News*. I caught a ride home on Max's steed along the old horse trail through the Sneads' back field to come onto Slave Hill as Dee and the Sheriff were pulling into the driveway with Verdi and Mariah. Clare was standing at the bare bottle tree, waiting, watching our approach as we carried the hollow of the west field and because Max would be staying over, he wore his jodhpurs with the black wool vest and the sharp riding derby.

121

That evening, Clare fussed with his buttons and smoothed his thin pockets with her open hand and fiddled with the brim of his derby as Max studied his cards fanned out in one hand and the fingers of the other glazing her arm, while across the table Dee fiddled with the Sheriff's new vest as a work in progress, as if the Sheriff was still in the shop on the fitting pedestal and as he shuffled the cards, she tugged lightly on the neckline and smoothed his shirt collar to lap the stitching at the back of his neck while we lounged near the first fire of the season.

A traveling sky with a light breeze drawn from the north that was well within the promising expectations of November. An initiation that may or may not settle as an overnight frost but was enough to light a fire. I settled a new log onto the hearth and rearranged the embers and returned to a book with photographs of Antietam Bridge—dead soldiers shot and bayonetted and strewn along the trench like table scraps and I studied the photograph with an eye toward reenactment, toward creating the trench on the manure pile and partially melting a few lead soldiers so they were bent and contorted to fold over other bent bodies when I looked toward the card table and said, "Sheriff, you ever been shot?"

Mariah looked up from one of Aunt Dee's fashion magazines with a face often reserved for me and said, *"Jussie.* That's none of your business."

The Sheriff looked up from his cards and hesitated for a moment, as if the question was being considered for the first time and when he said, quietly, "I reckon," his words lingered and we all imagined the war we couldn't imagine, the shrapnel still lodged in his right shoulder and left thigh and the crooked scars on the back of his neck and dissecting his stomach as if the surgery had been performed in a tent with the scalpel zigging and zagging every time the ground around arles france rattled and shook.

Sheriff had battle scars, as I've mentioned. He also had a solid steel badge and a rotating blue and white light kept behind the seat of the truck and a war pension and he had Aunt Dee. Sheriff had Dee.

Beyond the windows running the length of the living room, the breeze had gone from a breeze to a blow that carried down the chimney to flutter the flames. Max listened, distracted from the played hand to acknowledge the wind and Verity looked up from the work on a school essay to follow his gaze.

"We should blanket the horses."

She said this in part to remind the rest of us that she had a job, and in part to remind the rest of us that she and Max were actually co-workers whose concern was the health and welfare of the Javitts' prize thoroughbreds, which for Verity included and was in fact relegated solely to cleaning the stalls. To shoveling horse droppings.

Max, relishing the role of wisdom to an understudy and maybe to remind Clare that he possessed family-man qual'tys, turned to Verity and in the precocious language of job talk, of co-workers conversing in the distinct vernacular of their distinct trade, he said, "You 'pear it's fixin a big'n?"

Verity shrugged and adopted a solemn consideration as she looked to the windows and back to Max and Max added, "The warmbloods and broodmares are the mostest concern. The geldings be fine with some exsta shavings in they stalls and some turnout blankets and maybe anklers for the fetlock feathering. Importantly, we'll be cognant of the sit'ation."

Cognant? I glanced at Bim, my wordsmith cohort while Clare leaned her head back and started laughing. She laughed until her eyes watered and her face suddenly had the color of a girl Mariah's age, although Clare herself was only twenty-five. Twenty-eight at most. No one knew, really. Including Clare, who, as the story goes, arrived one day from nowhere to help Mother around the house but mostly to help with the boy, me, who, as Clare repeatedly reminded me, if compared to the girls at that age, was like Rachmaninoff hammering out Brahms' Lullaby. A boy who at eight weeks, she claimed, could throttle the old house with a voice that found comfort in Clare's arrangement of the humming

Lullaby as she walked him in her arms around and around and around the dining room table in the middle of the night until eventually, he was conditioned to either the drugged measures of Brahms or the nurturing scent of Clare's swaddling arms, and the midnight interruptions were reduced to something brief and tolerable.

Clare's laugh was close to music. Unimpeded by anything but the clear passage from somewhere down deep in her diaphragm and up her throat as if her throat was coated in butter. But Max failed to see the humor and stared at Clare until Clare sandwiched his cheeks between her hands and kissed him on the nose and stood from the card table and Max's eyes followed her until she disappeared into the kitchen.

"The Javitts are lucky to have you, Max," Dee said, looking up from the cards fanned across her fingers.

Max nodded, with appropriate modesty as the Sheriff looked up at the sound of the wind against the plate glass windows and said, "They left early. They'll be settled and safe by now."

Verity stood up and said she would break down Traveler, Max's horse, and a moment later she had put on her coat and left out through the front porch as Clare returned with a platter of snacks and I said, "The train won't care about any weather, right, Sheriff? Trains don't care anything about weather. Ole Carl can come through anything as good as any engineer anywhere."

The Sheriff nodded and Dee looked out the windows and then up into the Sheriff's eyes as she ran her hand up the side of his arm and Mariah said, "Train tracks can…"

But she stopped, caught in Dee's look thrown across the room like a reprimand and for a long time we sat in silence, the cards on the table forgotten and the snacks untouched as everyone imagined in their own minds the train and the weather and the high country of Fall Fork.

That night I woke to the sound of the wind pressing the glass beside my pillow. While we slept, Verity and I, Aunt Dee had been in our room. I could smell her. She had been on the edge of my bed.

TWENTY-ONE

A few days later I stood at the top of the attic stairs, rethinking the featherbed and the comfort of those early morning routines as I watched Mother and Dolores staring into the total darkness beyond the dormer window. Dolores with her embroidery, and Mother poised over the drawing board with a pencil in one hand and a feathering tool in the other. I slipped back down the stairs and out to the Annex where Father had his logs splayed out on one of the workbenches alongside a folder of medical data sheets from their time in Fall Fork. He looked up, held his gaze for a moment, and quietly returned to the logbooks. I wandered over to the Quarters, led by the scent of sausage on the woodstove. Laney and Septimus, the two winter hands, sat warming themselves with their backs to the door. Just the two of them, and no Harlan. I made my way around the back of the barn to the hen roost I had repurposed a week ago, swept clean and furnished with fresh fluffs of comfy hay as an invitation. But Harlan had not been seen since Verity's encounter in the barn weeks ago.

An hour later, the first light carried off the ridge as the tractor coughed and sputtered, throwing plumes of thick white exhaust into the brittle air. I climbed up to stand leaning against the wheel-well and said, "So, where we off to, Dad?"

125

He pulled a jacket from the carrier under the seat and handed it to me as we made our way behind the silo and along the back of the peach grove to head out to the edge of the north field where he clutched and waited. Givens approached alongside us, separated by the common fenceline and several minutes passed before Givens muttered, "Hunting retreat."

Father shrugged and pulled his collar against the back of his neck.

"They'll need a guide," I said. "They won't know the land. They'll need someone like me to teach them how to shoot and where the game is and Bo...we can rent them our hound."

Eventually Father asked, "What'd they get you from the labs?"

Givens shrugged his shoulders and his eyes went sheepish as he cut the engine and Father repeated, "What'd they find, Givens?"

Givens sat for close to a full minute, perched in his tractor seat with his frustrated eyes leveled on Father. Eventually he leaned over his wheel-well and spit tobacco juice and wiped his mouth and said, "They come up with a whole lot of things. A list a things no one ain't ever heard of. They spek it would take time to identify them and years, maybe decades to know if they's good or bad. I'm no scientist, Henry, but yer fiddling with somethin you should leave well alone. I've said it all along."

Heading back toward the house I asked, "We in trouble, Dad?"

"We could use a little help."

"That's what they said at the Alamo."

"What's that?"

"We could use some help."

"You think so? You think they knew?"

"Oh, they knew, Dad. Santa Anna had seven-thousand troops they could see, positioned just beyond cannon range. Just waiting for the white flag."

"Maybe they should've surrendered...once they saw the size of Santa Anna's army. They could've regrouped and waited for reinforcements and fought the battle on better terms...maybe won."

We rounded the peach groves and I added, "They'd have been cowards."

"They'd of been alive...something their wives and children would've appreciated."

"It was a battle of honor, Dad. Wives and children got nothin to do with it. You fight with honor and courage...like the Civil War."

"It was greed. They wanted Texas is all. Now Santa Anna controlled Texas. Am I right?"

"Mexico, Dad. It was Mexico's."

"He didn't like the terms we offered—if in fact we even offered terms—so we eventually took it by force. If I wanted the Arthurs' field," he said, motioning toward the river, "and Mr. Arthur doesn't like what I'm offering, then is it right to just take it? Mr. Arthur's an old man, I could take it easy enough."

"That's different."

"It's the same."

"Not with the Revolutionary War. We took America from England and that was right."

"That was oppression. It gets confusing. You can fight against oppression, but to fight for greed is wrong. Custer, Pissarro, Alexander the Great, Napoleon, the Romans...they were all driven by greed and they were all wrong. I don't care what the history books say. To fight against oppression is right. To fight *for* oppression is wrong. Clear?"

"How bout the Civil War, Dad?"

We had passed behind the barn and out along the lower pasture, feeling the sunlight, climbing the gully onto Pond Road to cross the bridge and past the Arthurs' field, going nowhere in particular. In the distance was the sound of an approaching engine.

"You think Verdi will go to college?"

"Yes."

"You think we should rent Bo to the new hunters? We could make some money there."

"Bo."

"Bo the hound, Dad."

"We don't have a hound, Sport."

"Sure we do. Bo the hound."

The approaching engine heading up from Snead's Corner was loud enough to recognize the throaty roar of Buddy's Ford.

"You think the twins should be arrested and go to jail?"

"What?"

"The twins, Aunt Elizabeth and Aunt Madeline."

"Why should they?"

"Cause they keep breaking the law, Dad. It's simple, you break the law, you go to jail."

Buddy approached up from the south to clear the rise at Snead's Corner in a cloud of dust. He accelerated and the roar of glass-packed headers carried down the road like the sound of a freight train at full throttle. Forty yards off he decelerated with an exploding clap and a succession of sharp backfiring reports as he worked down the gears with the whine of a tightening coil, gravel scattering like hail against the side of our tractor as he fishtailed through the intersection and came to a stop. The dust cleared and Buddy waved an arm through the open window, and over the raw sound of an idling engine he called out, "Mornin."

I waved and he added, "New carb…needs a little tuning."

He carried on up Pond Road with a sequence of rising gears and guttural blows.

"That baby really moves, eh, Dad?"

"I think it's Buddy needs a tune-up."

"Sheriff won't let him do that when they move to town." But the moment I spoke I knew it was wrong. Mentioning the Fallers' move.

We paused on the bridgeplanks and the bridgeplanks rattled to the vibrations of the diesel as we sat with a view of the house and the yard as if it were a painting.

"So, what about it?"

"What about what?"

"The Civil War."

"Civil wars are a little different. I guess you could say the South felt oppressed by the North, the way the slaves were oppressed by the South. But I don't think it's that simple. To Lincoln, slavery was the dividing issue within the larger issue of preserving the Union. They went hand in hand; if the South won the war and slavery was allowed to continue, the South would succeed as its own sovereign nation. The northern union would survive, but with eleven fewer states. Non-slave states."

"It's like families," I added. "I might be treated okay, but if I wanted to leave, well there'd be trouble."

"Why would you want to leave?"

"Mariah's leavin. She's goin to paris france, or St. Louis, like Aunt Harriet. And Verdi's leavin someday to college."

"So, you're leaving, too?"

"I just said if, Dad...if I was leavin."

"Okay, if...then where would you go?"

"I'd go to a war somewhere."

"Wars are dangerous."

"They're about honor and courage, Dad...and weapons."

"They're dangerous. Your mother would never allow it."

"So, there you have it...Mom is Abe Lincoln and I'm the Rebs and she'll try to keep me from leaving the family union."

"I read where the Confederates were so hungry, they ate rats and leather."

"Not rats, Dad."

"Too many bones?"

"Teeth."

"Teeth?"

"Teeth, Dad. They got teeth can chew through your stomach."

TWENTY-TWO

Later that afternoon I followed Father into the Annex where he quietly gathered an armload of selected logs off the shelf and moved them to the back reaches of the cellar, behind Clare's stores of canned goods and preserved fruits, behind even those dating back to the hand-scripted legends of Donation Pond.

TWENTY-THREE

Wesley and his schoolboy colleagues had been fed what Father provided. A summary. A guarded penetration into how seventeen years of unimpeded research had elevated the original patent along multiple fronts.

The barley had been bred to drought conditions. The official story. But what Father had failed to disclose, to Givens and to Guy and to everyone else, including the subsidy board, is that the crop also produced its own introgressed genes, or toxins, back-crossed to resist the blight of earlier trials. Thus, the new derivative was prone to drift, hybrid pollens carried by the wind to cross the road and the river as an infection to the neighboring crops. The vulnerability of virgin fields harvested without chemicals or pesticides, as if the common cold was exposed to an indigenous culture. The milkweeds provided the first clue. Flanking our crop, rubbing shoulders with the barley's alleles, they broke ground with a flourish before giving way to yellowing blight. The leafage coated with a residue not immediately evident to the naked eye. Givens' crop itself, soybeans, suffered from this drift.

POSSESSING THE SEASONS

But there was more. The gene, or allele, was an organic poison, but unlike Givens' rotation sequence, coupled with organic fungicides, which were only partially effective and required additional application cycles over the season, Father's inbred poison was perpetually regenerative. The pest ecology is minimized, but not eradicated, during cycles, returning in force between cycles. Not a single caterpillar or butterfly was seen in our fields since the crop broke ground. In turn, the bird population who fed on the crop's ecosystem, had largely diminished—far beyond the normal migratory species, the songbirds. One wonders, had anyone else noticed? Do we notice the absence of something? Go searching the furrows for an absence of caterpillars? It was still too early that year to know just how far the prevailing winds would carry our pollen, our toxins. Unlike corn, with its exposed tassel, Father understood the barley floret to be relatively protected, still wrapped in its leaf sheath at the time of pollination, reducing the amount of drift. And yet, there was drift. And to what effect?

To the farmers and agriculturists from up north and beyond, the valley was considered a poor man's Eden. Good soil—perhaps the best soil. Talented farmers—perhaps the best farmers. But an area mired forever and without explanation with the hapless yield of a third-world economy. An assessment, one should note, based more on the standardized forty bushels per acre of corn yield—a comparison of volume over the quality of what was yielded. The disparity was discriminatory, biased by what was considered backwater renegades and Anabaptists and the non-negotiable Amish with their amusing horse-drawn plows, drenched in folklore and superstition and pulsing with a stubborn contempt.

132

TWENTY-FOUR

We left the house that Saturday morning in late November to walk the quarter mile up a Pond Road narrowed into a logjam of parked cars and trucks. The air was cool, crisp with the scent of a new season.

"What if no one buys anything?" I asked, to no one in particular.

"It's an auction, stupid," Mariah snapped.

Mother threw a look at Mariah and Mariah rolled her eyes and I smiled.

"It ain't a law…no law that you have to buy something…Miss Priss."

Mariah stepped toward me and I shuffled back, dancing like a boxer, fists raised with a mock pose until Mother turned to me and I glanced at Father, probing for support, but Father's thoughts were elsewhere.

"You're mad cause Buddy's leaving."

The sort of remark you made from a distance and with a clear means of escape worked out well beforehand. The sort of remark we had been flinging at one another all week, a week that, since the Fallers' bombshell, had seen our normal gaiety give way to somberness and then to the squabbles and bickering that ended only with the intervention of an adult.

POSSESSING THE SEASONS

Poised for the worst, I backed into Verity who cried out and shoved me forward where the full impact of Mariah's swing sent me sprawling to the gravel. She stood over me with her feet spread and her fist still clenched when the auctioneer's truck turned off Pond Road and onto the Fallers' drive. It was an older truck, with dented fenders and a cracked windshield and the faded lettering *Robinson Auctioneers—Jackson County.* The driver hurled a stream of tobacco juice toward the gravel and to Father he asked, "There the Faller Place?"

Father nodded and the driver, the executioner, looked to Verity and Mariah and me. He winked and smiled to expose a row of yellow crooked teeth.

Up the driveway we'd walked ten-thousand times toward a barnyard filled with a crowd that rivaled the county fair. Mother and the girls disappeared toward the house.

To Father, I said, "We buyin anything?"

"There's nothing we need...is there?"

"What if no one buys anything?"

With his fingers running along the back of my neck, he said, "Why are you so worried about no one buying anything?"

"Cause no one but us has any money and if we don't buy anything, well...then no one else will."

"Who told you that?"

"No one...but I have sixty dollars from the garden sale and I'm buying, Dad. I'm buyin *somethin.*"

We joined Guy and Givens along a fenceline shared by Listen Allerton and Dilligence Wiseman and Pat Davis and the Sheriff, Sam Ditmar, all of them forming a sort of bereaved shield around Guy, insulating him from the proceedings with some awkward small talk and a few stiff chuckles as Bump and Scooter and I sat perched atop the fence, surveying the crowd.

Mariah left the house to sit with Buddy on the back steps and Bim appeared to take a seat on the bench beside Dee. Brother Reeves stood

134

with the twins and judging from the atmosphere and the awkward silence of the crowd, it seemed reasonable he would stand to the platform and deliver a eulogy. Off the corner of the barn lingered the winter hands from several of the surrounding farms.

The auctioneer stepped to the bed of his truck and clattered the bell and motioned to the old Farmall stationed off the barn and he began singing, words strung together as a single breathless syllable and a brief pause. "...do I have an opening bid?"

No response. He returned to his song, and "...do I have an opening bid?"

Silence. Someone cleared their throat and from near the house someone coughed and in the distance a dog barked. Father turned to study the machine behind him as the voice returned to its melody and Guy leaned into the fence with his forearms on the top rail and his face buried, staring at the ground as the auctioneer paused and again entered his plea for an offer, any offer when, with the silence so pervading you could hear the weathercock squeaking over the barn gable, I raised an arm and called out at the top of my voice, "Sixty bucks!"

All eyes turned to the fenceline, and the silence was replaced with a calamity of voices and muffled laughter as Bump jabbed an elbow and whispered, "You nuts? You cain't bid."

"Sixty bucks...it's all I got!"

The chuckles faded to an awkward stillness as the auctioneer looked away, shaking his head. I felt Father's eyes, but refused to meet his look.

The auctioneer raised his cap and ran his hand over his thin scalp and replaced the cap on his head and tugged at the beak and scratched the stubble on his cheek and raised a limp arm toward the fence, shrugging as he smiled.

"Kay, why not...I got me sixty from the young'n on the fence...all the money he has...do I hear more, do I hear seventy, seventy dollars, do I hear seventy?"

Leaning over the kitchen counter, Vivian, Dolores and Mother peered out through the open window.

"The bid stands at...at sixty dollars, do I hear seventy, seventy dollars?"

From the porch stoop, with one hand on the screen door and the other raised, wielding a soup ladle, Mother called out, "Seventy-five!"

Her voice carried with resolution and lingered with the dictum to everyone that this was an auction and not a side show.

"I hear seventy-five, seventy-five dollars, do I hear one-hundred, one-hundred dollars?"

Father raised a hand and the auctioneer sang, "I have one-hundred, one-hundred dollars, do I hear one-fifty, the bid stands at one-hundred..."

Mother wagged her ladle and glanced at Father with a slim curling smile.

"One-hundred-fifty dollars, I have one-hundred-fifty dollars, do I hear..."

Back and forth between Mother's ladle and Father's calloused hand until both her hands came to rest on her hips with her lips pursed tight and her eyes gleaming with excitement and she pivoted and pirouetted and waggled her backside while disappearing back into the kitchen and the barnyard erupted.

"Gone...one two three, three-hundred smackers to the strapper along the fence."

A hullabaloo of exhilarated voices and laughter and hours later, with the barnyard emptied and the sale tags collected and the auctioneer paid, we sat for dinner at the Faller table, Dolores' fingers drifting lightly along Guy's arm as she attempted to set the day's events into some perspective. "There's real value, and relative value. Relative value is like a rumor. Ignore it. It's the real value that counts...what the market will bear... what people will pay."

Fine words. But to Buddy, sitting beside Mariah, it was nonsense. He sat grinning, openly fingering a wad of bills in the unexpected sale of the Ford to a man from Pinckneyville. A man who was caressing the flecked candy-apple paint when Buddy approached and said everything has a price. He turned over the engine and the glass-packed headers rocked and vibrated the entire chassis and a deal was made and the buyer inquired if there would be more. If Buddy would be building another. The others at the table made a point to congratulate him, stroking the young confidence while Mariah allowed herself the premonition of a shop with Buddy-built hotrods selling like hotcakes and she moved a little closer.

Vivian and Dolores and Mother set out the food and Givens said a short prayer and we looked to Verity, all of us, for a whispering salve of *Saving Grace.*

Vivian stroked Verity's curls and fingered the collar of the new blouse where Dee had embroidered a horse and Vivian looked to Bump and said, "Isn't it nice, Bump?"

Bump swallowed hard and nodded with a reddened face. Verity smiled quietly with her eyes cast to the tablecloth and her heart where it belonged…where it would remain for sixty-two years, when the sound of Mother's fork bounced off the table.

She made a clumsy attempt to catch it, grasping at thin air with her eyes closed, and we watched, all of us, as she tried again, in slow motion, but the fork was long gone, bouncing off the floor once, then twice to settle somewhere under the table as Mother's hands returned to the table, gathering the edges of the tablecloth in her fingers as she leaned back and took a deep breath.

Dolores leaned close with a hand over Mother's arm. "You all right, dear?"

Father shoved his chair from the table but it was too late. Mother was on her feet, one hand clutching the tablecloth and the other reaching for the toppled chair when she dropped to her knees and then to the floor, pulling on the cloth to send dishes smashing to the floor.

POSSESSING THE SEASONS

A moment later, Father beside her, she looked up with a frightened apologetic look to study the scattered dishes and said with a surprising lightheartedness, "Good heavens."

And for reasons I've never understood, to this day, we all started laughing. The sort of laughter that begins slowly and builds into a chorus of lunatics who can't stop laughing.

Ultimately the women, all the women, including Verity and Mariah, retreated to the one upholstered chair in the front room and the men, all the men including Buddy, Bump, and myself, set about picking up the pieces and if Father swept the fragmented shards into a dustpan wielded by Buddy it was because we were all reminded of the uncertainties of a lost home or a lost crop or a loss of assumed good health while in the darkness beyond the kitchen windows a cold fierce wind eddied through the barnyard. Bullying its way through the gorge and down off Moingwena Ridge and settling over Salt Fork Valley with the first intolerant freeze of the new season.

TWENTY-FIVE

On these mornings, early, when the frost patterns the glass and the view out my little window is a confusing distortion of naked trees, I imagine on the brink of winter the season's first snowfall. Fat bulbous tufts of snow gathering on the sill, or as drifts accumulating in my sleep to rise and pile against the fence, or weighted on the outer reaches of the most fragile branches of the old elm with that anticipated snap. That report like a muted firecracker when the most vulnerable limbs succumb to the inevitable.

My legs seem pinned in place. I glance down the darkness of this bed I returned to the day after Acceptance left us to see them curled up on the bedsheets, little snowdrifts, Whisty and his sister Mademoiselle, wrapped together. With an effort and to their murmuring objections, I pull them up one at a time and stuff them under the heavy blankets to each side of me and turn my head back to the window, back to that winter long ago. That mosaic tapestry, when the front porch thermometer registered eighteen degrees. When the lawn outside the kitchen window was blanketed beneath a thin layer of frost. Mother cooking oatmeal—thick as clay—and for the first time that school year she drove us to the bus stop at the end of Pond Road.

"It's late, Mom. We're gonna be late," I said.

"We're fine."

"Eart don't wait for nothin."

139

Down the rise and approaching the crossroads we watched Eart's bus pause and then continue beyond Pond Road.

"Dangit, Mom."

"Jussie, stop it. We're fine."

She turned onto Deere Road, hoping to close the gap but when we arrived at the Chestnuts' drive, Eart was pulling away.

"Bless it, Eart," she muttered. She honked but the sound of the horn was lost in the wind.

On Fall Ridge Bridge we slowed for a slick of ice and Eart padded his lead and Mother accelerated, watching for ice, to arrive at the Cushman stop and once again the bus pulling away.

She angrily pressed the heel of her hand against the horn with Bump on his knees waving like a lunatic through the back window of the bus.

"Mom, I'm tellin ya…"

"*Jussie.*"

"Just take us all the way, Mom," Mariah said. "We're practically there."

Along the straight open way of the paved Bonnel Road, she broke the law—although, technically, we had no laws beyond the common sense of right from wrong—and passed the stopped school bus, and Eart thrust his arm out the driver's window, yelling something no one could hear. At McPhee's Corner, she pulled to one side of the road and we hurried from the car and a moment later boarded the bus for the remaining half-mile to school.

It warmed to only twenty-three degrees that afternoon and because Eart refused to detour from his route, we ran home along Pond Road headlong into a biting gray wind that put the wind-chill factor near zero. Nearing the house, we watched a car pulling from the drive, approaching through the blowing snow. It came to a rolling stop in the middle of the road and Dr. Steadfast Stewart called out through the opened window that it was no weather to be out walking. We nodded silently, our backs buttressed to the wind, waiting for him to drive on but he just sat there, staring at the three of us as if expecting a conversation until he finally added, off-handedly, that he had simply stopped by for a social call.

We found her in the warmth of the attic, leaning over her drawingboard with a shawl draped comfortably over her shoulders, humming, oblivious of the weather or the time or her morning's promise of a ride back from the bus stop. We stood at the top of the stairs, the three of us, with the ice melting off our eyebrows like tears and our cheeks still red as an August sunset until she eventually turned and looked over, surprised, "Ah, you're back."

That night it dropped to four degrees. In the morning, Saturday morning, Father and I left the house to find Harlan waiting beside the truck with his back to the wind. We paused, surprised by his reappearance, anticipating an explanation. But he simply stood there, in the freezing wind. We worked the truck doors open and crowded ourselves into the cab but the truck, caked in ice, refused to start. The firing pins were frozen and the click of a stubborn ignition led us to the car but with similar results and eventually I convinced Harlan to come inside the house. He sat at the kitchen counter with a long face, dwarfing everything. His exposed skin, his arms and neck and face, had the coloring of a ripening tomato.

It warmed to eight degrees that afternoon and by nightfall I finally convinced Harlan to stay in the house (Septimus and Laney had recently returned to Cairo; the walls and roof of the Quarters were not insulated and the tiny wood stove couldn't overcome thirty-mile-per-hour winds). Harlan slept in the attic featherbed and that night, as the wind rattled the windows and twisted the timbers, I lay awake listening to the sound of his frightened moans carrying down the attic stairs.

"Harlan's spooked," I whispered.

"Who?"

"Harlan. He's spooked?"

"Who's Harlan?"

"Your singing friend. You know…"

141

"Singing friend?"

"Yeah."

After a long silence, Verity whispered, "He must be scared."

"Yeah, me too…but I ain't moanin like an ole dog."

By morning the weather turned. Through the window beside my bed, I woke to see the world sheathed in ice; the fields—ours and the Arthurs' and the eastern corner of the Fallers'—glittered like plains of ground glass and the trees, the big elm in the yard and all the cottonwoods and hickories and tupelos scattered along the river, gleaming like prisms. Lying perfectly still, I listened; I could hear the creaking and pinging and the snap of a limb giving in to the weight of the ice. The sun was clearing Kickapoo Ridge, not like the blood-red sunrises of August where the colors changed and feathered gradually into an endless blue, but a cold and brittle sky, a sky so colorless it blinded the eyes.

I watched Father standing off the barnyard doors, turning his face from the wind as he moved stiffly toward the house. With the girls still asleep and Mother in the attic—with the sleeping Harlan?—I slipped from bed and hurried down the stairs as Father appeared through the back door, stamping his feet, bundled so heavily only his eyes were left exposed. He held a canvas of logs in one hand and the coal bucket in the other. The hall was dark and cold.

"The power out?" I asked.

I followed him down the hall and into the living room where the morning light splintered through the iced glass of the picture windows.

"The power out?" I asked again.

He set the logs and the bucket onto the hearth and nodded, mumbling that the barn thermometer was cracked clean open. He turned, his eyes resting on me as he cupped the back of my neck with a gloved hand cold as ice.

"I don't want you outside today, Sport. Not without me."

"Sure, Dad. It's cold."

"It's not just cold, Whisty. It's more than just cold."

"Sure, Dad. It's *really* cold."

And yet a moment later, driven by curiosity and still in my long-johns, I opened the storm door to stand at the thermometer tacked to the corner of the screen porch when I sensed a cold like I had never known. A cold that burned and stung and drew the flesh numb.

"Twenty below, Dad!" I declared, almost yelling as I slammed the door closed.

"What did I just tell you?"

"Sorry, I forgot."

"Well, are we clear on this? I don't want you outside today…not unless you're with me and in full gear."

I turned and kneeled before the fireplace, structuring the kindling over the grate and then the smaller chunks of coal laid out to create a cradle of sorts for the hickory round. I moved over beside him, not sure if he had heard, "Twenty below, Dad."

He looked at me and then back to the hearth as he struck a match and set fire to the kindling.

"Twenty below?" he said, watching as the kindling took hold and the flames grew to engulf the coal and he added, "Well, how low does that porch thermometer go?"

"Twenty below…it only goes to twenty below, Dad."

The fire gained strength, throwing its warmth against the brittle air of the living room as he drew a chunk of coal from the tin and set it on the fire. He pulled off his gloves and then the hat with the sheep's-wool havelock that's snapped to the collar of his jacket and he looked at me, gathering his thoughts.

"The power's been out a couple hours," he said, as if thinking aloud. "The furnace has an electric ignition, so we'll want to drape off the stairs this morning…keep the heat downstairs. There's no water, the pipes are frozen, so later, after breakfast, we'll clean out some buckets and get geared up and we'll collect some icicles. We'll need to rig up a cooking grill over the fire…your mother will need it…and check the deep freeze and ice box and set some things out on the screen porch, just in case. Don't want to run out of food, do we?"

I imagined Mother cooking. On a fire grill. Clare was at the Javitts' all weekend and I said, "Think Clare's all right?"

"She's with Max. She's fine."

I nodded, excited and ready to begin doing whatever it was we needed to be doing. Where was the camping stove and which blankets would be used to close off the stairs and would they be nailed or held with thumbtacks and where were the buckets for the icicles?

"We'll want to bring down the bedding from upstairs," he continued, more thinking aloud. "Everyone sleeps down here, by the fire. And the transistor radio, Mariah's…find that, and the flashlights and lanterns."

"What about Harlan?"

He studied me for a moment with his crooked smile as he ran his fingers through my hair and continued, "And your mother…she's been a little under the weather lately."

What did he mean, *under the weather?*

"…Now there's the livestock…there's a fire out behind the barn and that needs to be checked every couple of hours round the clock, keep it burning. Check in with the Marshes and Fallers and your mother's sisters. Phone still works but I doubt for long…oh, and the Arthurs, may have to walk down there. Definitely…better do it this afternoon."

He paused, resting his eyes on me but his thoughts were elsewhere. My head reeled. Was he expecting an answer, an acknowledgement of some kind? My mind wandered and I imagined him injured and incapacitated, possibly dead, and what if I didn't remember and understand all he had just told me?

"What about the barn fire?" I asked. I made an effort to speak clearly, competently. "There enough wood?"

"The barn *is* the fire…plank by plank if we have to."

He turned to stoke the fire and stood to his feet and started for the stairs. At the dining room he paused and turned back, adding, "Don't worry, Sport…we'll be fine."

Mother was on the phone to Vivian and Dolores and the Allertons and the Wisemans and by late morning she finally got through to Aunt Dee, who had been trying all morning to phone the farm. Dee and Bim and the twins were all together, kept warm by Dee's propane furnace and worried to death about us and already, after only a few hours, they were bickering like hens. Dee asked Mother, who later recounted the conversation, if it wasn't so improbable that ole Steadfast had made a mistake, a mix-up, and that the twins weren't really Ponds after all. And then the connection was lost and suddenly the Roes of Pond Road were isolated and unable to communicate with even our closest neighbors.

We spent the morning carrying bedding down from the upstairs bedrooms, locating the camping stove and the fuel and the oil lamps and nailing old blankets to the dining room pass-through, closing off the rest of the house to leave only the living room exposed to the heat of the fireplace. Throughout the night, with the temperature dropping and the winds persisting, Father rose every few hours to feed the hearth and tend the fire behind the barn.

In the morning, Mariah's transistor reported the temperature in Fall Fork at twenty-eight below with a wind chill of minus fifty. The radio was put on rationed time.

As Mother cooked oatmeal and warmed a pan of fresh milk, Father readied himself to leave for the Arthurs'.

"The tractor's still not turning over," he said.

Mother studied the cooking pot, refusing to meet his look.

"Why don't you take Horse?" she asked, finally.

"No one can ride that animal but Verity and I'm not having her out there."

Verity stepped forward, ready to object, but Father moved to the fire, buttoning his coat to pause beside Mother and for a moment they studied the oatmeal on the grill. A minute passed, another, Mother finally breaking the silence with, "At least go to Guy's first…and the two of you can go down together."

"That's a half-mile the wrong way. By the time I get to Guy's I could be at the Arthurs'."

"Yes, but Guy would be with you. You wouldn't be alone."

He rested his gloved hands on her shoulders, turning her from the fire and raising her chin with a clumsy thumb until their eyes met and he kissed her, running his cheek along hers, inhaling the scent of her skin.

The small Christmas telescope was located in a buried corner of my closet and stationed at the living room windows. We were to monitor his progress down Pond Road. Once he had reached the Arthur house, he would step out and fire a round from the .22-caliber single-shot slung over his back, signaling that all was okay.

Resigned to the inevitable, Mother followed him to the back door and from the hall we watched as she checked his straps and buttons and zippers and then clung to him for a moment before he opened the door to a blast of freezing air and he was gone.

I positioned myself at the telescope. My telescope, my job, setting the sights on a landscape sheathed in ice and flanked by miles of whitened countryside as Mother and the girls feigned an interest in *Crazy Eights*.

I sighted him clearing the elm with only his head and shoulders exposed above the yard fence, a heavily padded bundle moving briskly down the road toward the bridge. As he cleared the fence and came into full view, he raised an arm toward the house and I signaled back with the twelve-volt flashlight. Fifteen minutes later, he reached the bridge and again we exchanged signals. He paused for a moment to adjust the rifle and the small pack that was strapped to his back before crossing the bridge and disappearing down the opposite slope and out of view.

I know my father. No less so now, eighteen years after his passing, than when I was twelve. It's no stretch to become him, to embody him. My memory of what he remembered, his version, but it's no stretch to be there as if I was there.

'...It's cold...colder than the barnyard. The wind down here... carrying off the fields. Grace was right...he should've gone to Guy's first but that would've been an hour more and the Arthurs...the Arthurs. He should've gone down earlier...but when? In the middle of the night? No tractor, no truck...making this in the middle of the night on foot and then what? A sudden gust off the fields and everything blinding whiteness. He stood braced into the resistance of the wind realizing he had no plan for transporting the Arthurs back to the house. In their seventies and not capable on foot...not in this.

It was difficult to get his bearings. Had he reached the Arthurs' field yet? Sure as hell don't want to pass it. Cold. Hard to breathe. Trotting, maintain the circulation, prevent the toes from going numb but the road is slippery. Too dangerous. He returned to a walking pace, raising his knees and moving his arms. Damn...it hurt to breathe. The wind died down and he paused, turning for a look at the house but the house was obscured by the road. So he was still in the hollow and the boy wouldn't be able to see him until nearly at the Arthurs' drive.

Nothing to worry about him. He'd do as told, as told. If brain waves went everything went, went. Keep moving. Farther to go back now, can't go back now.'

Back in the house it was not a question of competency. We were capable of surviving without Father; there was more than enough fuel for the fire and a surplus of canned goods in the cellar that would take weeks to exhaust. It was something else, something that lingered in the warmish stagnant air of the living room. Something I couldn't identify.

Mother set her cards on the hearth and stood up. She looked to the windows. "You see him yet?"

I shook my head and said, "He's still in the hollow, Mom."

"Shouldn't he be coming up by now?"

"Pretty soon, Mom. Should be pretty soon."

She looked down at the girls and reached for one of the blankets piled near the doorway and draped it over Verity's shoulders and said, "I think I'll go check the stores."

I turned from the telescope, "Shouldn't you wait, Mom? Dad said for everyone to stay here."

She moved to gather her coat off the corner chair.

I looked to the girls for their support and Mariah said, "Check'm later, Mom. When Dad gets back."

"It's okay." There was a sharp abrupt tone to her voice. "I'll be right back."

I nodded, frowning, watching as she bundled herself for an expedition that would take her out the back door and along the side of the house to the storm cellar. Twenty steps at most. Stepping away from the telescope, I glanced from Mother to the windows and back and reached for my coat.

"I'll go, too. Verdi and Mariah can watch for Dad."

"Sure, honey. We'll bring up some rations."

Mariah approached the windows, absorbing my explanation of the signaling system and a moment later Mother and I were making our way down the cold hall and out the back door.

'...At the fenceline he turned toward the Arthur house and raised his arm in a wide sweeping pattern. Instantly, the signal, two successive beams. Back to the road, he continued in the utter silence of a world without movement, quickening his pace, still a hundred yards from the gate thinking, strange, how quiet it was...and if he stopped thinking, his brain would freeze and his toes were probably already frozen and weird stuff like how death creeps up and then his Nana and if she had any pull up there at all to lock up the Gates of Heaven cause he tweren't ready quite yet. Not quite yet, Nana.

He reached the edge of the Arthurs' dormant garden and a moment later kicked the gate open and started across the barnyard. No smoke from the chimney.

✳ ✳ ✳

Without the telescope, with just the naked eye, Mariah's father was no bigger than a fingernail, as she would tell her own children until they knew the story by heart, her father moving slowly over a lifeless landscape where even the trees, so heavily weighted with ice, were as still as a painting.

"He's there," Mariah announced.

"Did you signal?"

"He didn't wave. He's crossing the garden, though."

A moment later and she watched him disappear around the side of the unpainted house and she waited. She moved the eyepiece to canvass the barnyard and then the barn, wondering how Mr. Arthur's team was faring; there was no smoke nor any sign of a bonfire and she thought how the horses might survive in the wind-blocked stalls, insulated by the hay and warming each other with their own body heat.

Verity poked the fire and paced the room and turned to Mariah and said, "Mom and Jussie've been gone too long. It's been too long."

Mariah turned the telescope back to the Arthur house, a plain and unadorned structure that had gone unchanged since it was built in the 1840s. There were no curtains, just shades that had long ago been yellowed by the sun. They were pulled now as they were in the spring and summer. The area surrounding the house was without the usual clutter of the other farms; there was no machinery, no cars or trucks or tractors with their endless implements scattered about, rusting and overgrown with weeds. The house and barnyard had the unmistakable austerity of the Amish.

There was the large vegetable garden where Mrs. Arthur toiled in season and where she might acknowledge a wave if you happened by, if you caught her eye, but never a spoken word, not once. Mr. Arthur was different, slightly. When she was younger and would occasionally accompany her father in the fields, straddled atop the tractor, they sometimes came abreast of Mr. Arthur, separated by only the fenceline. Her father would talk about the soil or the weather or crops while they shared a cup of ice water from the thermos strapped to the tractor and at some point, Mr. Arthur would turn to her and ruffle her hair with his long coarse fingers and say what he always said, "You the girl who butted the bull off the bridge? Who let the canary out of the cage?" She would laugh, mostly because he laughed, turning back to his team, chuckling to himself.

It was only her father who had any sort of friendship with him. A few years before when Mr. Arthur had double pneumonia and was laid up only half conscious while everyone in the valley was hurrying to beat an early frost, he had harvested Mr. Arthur's crop without permission because Mr. Arthur would have objected to the machinery. Mrs. Arthur crocheted Mother a shawl as a token of thanks and it was about then that Mr. Arthur began with his jokes, the stuff about bulls and canaries.

✳ ✳ ✳

Mother and I opened the cellar doors and descended the concrete steps into the darkness. She would have known we had enough supplies in the house but it was the waiting; to her, the waiting was intolerable. Better to stay busy. With her, in Father's absence, and I was suddenly apprenticing the man-of-the-house role. Good. Fine. I took it seriously. She wouldn't undermine me—allowing me to pull open the doors and hold her arm down the steps, standing ready at her side with the basket in one hand and the flashlight in the other. Standing so tall, so erect. Little Wonder Boy.

"Whatya we need, Mom?" my voice lowered a full octave.

"Oh, just a few things. Of course, we'll have to thaw it out...set it by the fire."

"No problem, Mom. There's plenty wood and coal."

She moved over toward the back wall of shelves, rubbing her gloves together and tightening the muffler, pulling jars from the shelf as I held the basket close and when she encountered a stack of log books, Father's hidden logs, she paused, fingering their bindings. With a quizzical look she turned to me and I shrugged and said, "It's cold, Mom. We shouldn't stay very long."

"I know. We'll..."

A gust of wind carried down the steps, swirling in a box canyon to steal our breath. Moments later one cellar door clapped shut, then the other, echoing off the cellar walls.

'He rounded the corner of the Arthur house half delirious, glancing to the barn where there was no smoke nor sign of a fire—which he later always described as the moment he knew something was very wrong. He advanced through the back door, trotting, and through the kitchen with its cold box and wood stove from another age and into the dining room as lifeless as a mausoleum and then the sitting room where they occupied the floor wrapped in blankets before the hearth of a fire long extinguished. The embers cold. On one knee, he removed a glove to feel her body wrapped in Mr. Arthur's arms when old Arthur opened his eyes. Quickly to the fire, he built the kindling and struck a match and returned to the bedroll knowing they had fallen asleep and in her sleep she had frozen…no pulse.'

Mariah stood fixed to the telescope, her view narrowed to the Arthur house. Surely, he was inside by now. Had he forgotten the signal? Had he been visiting for the past ten minutes, warming himself beside their fire, unaware that she was waiting? She shifted her weight, worried she had misunderstood Justus' explanation of the signals when a thin, lariat-like plume of white smoke issued from the chimney that she always said she mistook for blowing snowfall, but drifting up, lazily, before being whipped away by the wind.

Had there been no fire before? Surely, she would have noticed but without a fire how could they possibly have survived? She understood why her mother had insisted on going to the cellar. She stepped away from the eyepiece to find Verity on her knees, stoking the hot coals.

"Shouldn't they be back by now?"

Verity stood and said, "I'll go check."

"No! We have to stay together."

But Verity was gone, out the back door, and Mariah returned to the telescope. Nothing. Ten minutes later, she glanced toward the empty living room, staring into the hearth of a fire she suddenly realized had burned itself out. An unnerving silence, so quiet with only the wind in this room so abruptly cold and cavernous and empty. She was torn between abandoning her post and leaving the telescope to renew the fire and go searching for everyone when she heard the sound of her father's rifle, the distant pop of a single round fighting the wind. Before she could adjust her eyes back to the lens, there came a second shot.

I tried the storm cellar's heavy doors, again. Mother wielded the flashlight and then the two of us together with the flashlight on the cellar floor growing dim. But the doors had been wedged against the concrete opening by the force of the wind. I moved to the center of the cellar floor and called out but the walls were concrete and the ceiling joists heavily insulated and the sound of my voice died off instantly when the light gave out and in the absolute darkness of a cave, the cold threatened. Mother feebly tapped a jar of peaches against the underside of the doors as I moved in tiny circles, petrified of the dark and the cold and the sudden claustrophobia of cellar hell.

"Mom?"

"Here, Honey."

"Mom?"

'He stood off the corner of the Arthur house, braced against the wind with the old man warmed and revived and strapped like a bundled mummy on a draft horse weighing half a ton. He stepped away, distancing himself from the animal to extend the rifle and fire off three shots, studying the window across the river for the expected signal.'

Mariah heard a shot, confused. Justus had said nothing about three shots. The plan, as she understood it, hadn't gone beyond a single shot, a single shot to indicate all was fine, but she knew as well as anyone what three successive shots meant. She flashed back the Morse signal for a question mark: two shorts, two longs, two shorts, and waited…knowing it was impossible for her father to answer.

'He returned to take the reins of a horse twenty hands high, leading it to where he could mount from the elevated well-pump, securing the old man between his arms and the bridle reins and together they started off across the gardens and through the broken gate and into the headwind of the road.'

※ ※ ※

Verity discovered the closed cellar doors but later had no explanation for why she turned and crossed the barnyard to search the barn and the Annex, calling out with a voice that went nowhere. She hurriedly fed the smoldering fire from a stack of barnplanks along the opened back wall and warmed herself while comforting Horse and Cow and the two Sows, angry she hadn't thought to grab a scarf, gloves, nor even a hat. She returned to the living room where Mariah was on her knees rebuilding a cold fire.

"Where've you been?" Mariah snapped, her voice angry and sharp.

"I don't know where they are."

"Who cares? Who cares at all, Verdi? You left me to watch Daddy and the fire went out and I really don't...they're not in the cellar?"

Mariah shoved new paper beneath the grate and angrily slapped out kindling sticks and some fragments of broken coal and a split log and when she struck the match, the flame trembled in her hand.

"Where's Daddy?" Verity asked. "Did he signal? I don't know where Mom and Jussie are."

"Of course he signaled. It's only been about ten hours since you left."

"I don't know where Mom and Jussie went."

"They went to the cellar. The *cellar*, Verdi!"

"The cellar doors are closed...locked. They weren't in the barn either. The barn fire was almost out. Where's daddy?"

"They're on one of the Arthurs' horses."

"They?"

"Daddy and one of the Arthurs."

Mariah turned from the fire as Verity turned from the telescope and in a moment of clairvoyance Mariah moved to strap on her coat and pull on her boots and her gloves and then the wool muffler wrapped tight to her face. She tied off the muffler and as Verity returned to the telescope, Mariah made for the kitchen and down the hall and out the back door and into a raw icy wind that stung the exposed skin of her cheeks like a hard fucking slap, which I believe, when among adults and after a glass or two of wine, was how she always described it.

Reaching the cellar, she kicked the doors with the heel of her boot and hollered.

A faint knocking from below. The sound of Mother's voice, "It's stuck. The doors are stuck."

On her knees, crouching close, Mariah answered, "Where's Jussie?"

My voice, a whimpering, barely audible whine, "There's a crowbar, behind the seat of the truck."

Mariah scuttled to cross the drive where the truck sat parked like an iced ornament. The door was frozen shut. She moved to the garbage pit near the gate, braced into the wind, grabbing a rock the size of her head, thrusting it against the truck window. Glass shattered, scattering invisibly over the iced drive. From behind the seat, she grabbed the crowbar and moved quickly back to the cellar, slapping the doors with the iron before working the blade against the frozen hasp.

"Anna Mirah?" Mother called. There was an odd sound to her voice, a soft almost pleading sound. "Open the door, Anna Mirah."

"I am...I am, Mom."

POSSESSING THE SEASONS

Mariah heard Father's rifle, a faint, reverberating report dying off instantly. She chipped the ice from under the latch, wielding the bar awkwardly with both gloves before wedging the blade in place and pulling back with both hands when the blade slipped and from within the cellar I could hear the bar spring free to fling itself against the clapboards of the cellar doors. She hurried over to pick it off the ground and felt the cold curling through the ends of her fingers, or had she always said her toes? I can't be sure. A moment later, there came another rifle shot that was quickly muffled.

She started toward the side yard where she could signal but realized she had left the flashlight inside. She returned to the doors, in tears, aware that Father was waiting for a signal and she had neglected to brief Verdi and she considered running back to the living room to flash an S.O.S.

"Hey, Mariah," I called out. "Hey, where are you?"

She returned to position the blade a second time, scraping the cellar door for leverage when the hasp broke free. She yanked and yanked again but both bottom rails had been blown to wedge against the riser of the top step. Was she sweating? She could feel moisture beading against the back of her neck and chest and yet her face and fingers and toes were almost numb with cold. She wondered how heavily Mother and I had dressed before leaving the house. Had we put on only our coats for the short jaunt to the cellar? Had we thought to wear gloves and mufflers?

I moved to the center of this cellar I had always disliked, the claustrophobia of this cave, and then back to stand beside Mother at the foot of the steps and then back to the center of the room, moving in tiny concentric circles.

"For heaven's sake, Honey…hurry."

"I am…I am, Mother. I'm hurrying."

"Where's Dad?" She could hear my voice but it wasn't my voice. It was the voice of panic and fear and she was beside herself now, oblivious of everything but the blade of the crowbar, driving it between the rail and the concrete rise with a rock that sent shocks up her arm with every impact.

But the blade found its place and she stood to her feet with pant legs that were hard with ice. She pulled on the shank of the bar. Nothing. She crouched down and wedged her boots against the top step like saddle stirrups and pulled again as if she were hauling in the reins of a spooked horse. Still nothing. She stood to her feet and took a step back and hurled her shoulder against the shank and the hasp snapped with a clean break that ripped away a corner of the planking and sent the broken hasp flinging into the air above her head. She crawled back, panting, sobbing, bracing her feet to yank on the door with a dead pull but the door didn't budge. She returned to her knees and peered through the hole to see Mother staring toward the light with empty eyes.

"Daddy's not back yet," she said. There was an exhausted, resigned sound to the words as she caught her breath, watching her mother's eyes.

"Try again, honey...keep trying."

She found the crowbar lying on the ice several feet from the drive and started back for the cellar confused and frightened and feeling the first pangs of terror rising in the back of her throat when she heard a voice and turned to the road. A horse moving against the wind, obscured by the flurries and the driving sleet and as it drew closer to the driveway, she recognized the color of Mr. Faller's overcoat. He raised his arm, pointing to something beyond her line of vision, something toward the bridge. He carried on past the drive, trotting. She moved away from the windblocked house and into the force of the storm to see the draft horse bearing Father and Mr. Arthur reaching the edge of the lawn. The Fallers' quarter horse drew abreast of the Arthurs' massive animal and she watched Mr. Faller reaching up, clutching her father's shoulders.

'He felt someone shaking him, yelling, but it was all a dream. His head, as he told it, was filled with nonsense, riddles to keep the brain alive but the brain wasn't reasoning and the riddles were little more than repeated stutterings. He heard the voice again, louder, and he raised his hand to dismiss it as a teasing insanity and the voice was gone.'

Mariah watched, helpless, as Guy Faller gripped the bridle of the draft horse and stroked the muzzle before turning away, starting up the road riding low to the neck, cantering along the frontage when the quarter horse turned and cleared the side-yard fence. He crossed the width of the yard at a full gait to pull up at the house with a fist of rein so violent the horse nearly slipped to the ice.

Mariah merely pointed to the cellar. There were no words. He was at the cellar, lowering himself to call out through the hole in the door. He placed the reins into Mariah's hands and ran over toward the truck parked like a block of ice near the barnyard gate as the draft horse appeared. It sat uncertain off the head of the driveway and Mariah tried calling out but there was no hearing anything over the wind.

Guy returned with a coil of rope stiff as a cable, slamming it against the house with an impact that loosened the corner boards. He lashed one end of the limp rope through the hole in the cellar doors and around the stile and threw the other end to land on the ground at Mariah's feet and without a word he motioned to the quarter horse, explaining the sequence with nothing more than a sweeping arm as he left the house, running toward the road where the draft horse had passed the driveway, continuing up Pond Road.

Mariah reached for the rope at her feet and unraveled it the few feet to where she stroked the quarter horse Dixie, looping the rope to the saddle pommel and stepping away to sight the road. Guy had caught up with her father, leading the draft horse back toward the drive and she turned to rest her glove over the hindquarters like sighting a target and took two steps back and charged in with a leaping kick square to the flank. The horse jolted, spooked, slipping over the ice and onto the gravel of the drive as the slack in the rope tightened and the cellar doors ripped away, splintering like kindling.

Much later, with only his eyes exposed, Guy ventured back into the storm and when he was lost from view, Mariah returned to the rest of us huddled near the fire in the last failing light of the day. Darkness overcame the room but no one stood to light a lamp. Half asleep, I watched Father bundled on the floor between the Amish eccentric and Mother. I watched him watching Mariah's face silhouetted against the light of the blazing fire.

"Hey," he whispered.

Mariah, beleaguered by her own thoughts, turned to where he lay motionless, wedged amongst the others. The hint of a smile creased her mouth.

There had been no discussion regarding the livestock but it seemed obvious; as Verity stirred a pot of warming soup, Mariah pulled on her coat as I watched, following her movement. She wrapped her muffler and buttoned on Father's havelock and glanced in my direction, seeing certainly the vacancy in my eyes, the frightened hollowness and she stepped over and lowered herself to one knee and tucked the blankets tight to my chin the way Mother might have done.

"You okay?"

My eyes were wet. Silent tears welling up like pools.

She wiped my face with her glove, "So, you okay, or what?"

Hesitating, not sure how to fulfill her role, she eventually leaned in and grazed her cheek with mine and I filled myself with the smell of the Arthurs' draft horse still strong in Father's havelock.

POSSESSING THE SEASONS

* * *

Givens and Vivian, in their 60s, settled in at the Fallers on the first day of the ice storm. Strength in numbers, and body heat. Moving the Roes, all of them, and the weak Mr. Arthur, was improbable. There would be three signals a day, they had decided, fired off between the two farms in the morning, afternoon, and evening. If a signal went unanswered it meant, well…three signals a day.

The radio batteries died away and over the next several days it was only from the gauge on the screen porch that we knew the temperature remained at least twenty below with strong winds. Within a day Father had recovered to relieve Mariah, replenishing the stores from the cellar and maintaining the fire in the barn. Mr. Arthur hadn't spoken, occupying the couch, grieving his lost wife.

Father fueled the barnyard fire with the dismantled stalls and feeding cribs that had once partitioned off the west and east wings of the barn. The coal and split logs, generating a longer and hotter ember, were reserved for the house. From the cellar, stores of canned goods and preserved fruits. From the deep freeze, separating the shelves of canned goods from the bins of coal and wood, we renewed ourselves each evening with the slaughtered surpluses of poultry, pork, and beef. The water supply, drawn for cooking, drinking, and sponge-baths, was refreshed every afternoon with dagger-length icicles snapped from the eaves of the porch and plucked from the naked boughs of the peach and apple and cherry trees in the garden's northernmost precinct, transferred to melt in a larger can situated near the fire. The rainwater tank, constructed and enclosed off the kitchen by Dad Pond seventy-five years before, was a solid two-foot-deep block of ice. The well behind the barn, bored by Diligence Wiseman, was no longer operable; the pump was frozen and locked up stiff as rusted steel.

We woke each morning not anticipating an end of the siege nor considering even the full range of the given day. We looked instead to the

160

immediacy of breakfast and then to the morning signal fired off from the front porch and the anticipated reply. We warmed water to clean the breakfast dishes and then washed ourselves from the same water. We thawed the provisions rationed out for the afternoon and evening meals and on Father's return from the barn and the cellar, we laid out his boots and coat and gloves to warm by the fire while listening to his account of the livestock and a metered inventory of the staples in the cellar.

We ate lunch and following the mid-day signal, Mother read aloud from a variety of our favorite novels drawn from the cold library and then we warmed the water to wash the dishes and spent an hour or so reading and reviewing assignments from school texts. The new normal.

No one came to the house nor did anyone leave but for Father's excursions to the barn and the cellar and to collect ice. One day mimicked another, the relentless cold and wind and sleet driving against the clapboards of the house. The only contact with the outer world were the muted, crackling reports of riflefire between the two farms, assuring us we weren't alone but leaving us hungry for more than could be conveyed by the sound of gunshots. There was only the Roe farm and the Faller farm, while the rest of the valley remained a mystery. Did Dee and Bim and the twins have enough resources to sustain four women for nine days? Did anyone? Were the cellars and basements and pantries throughout southern Illinois all as bountiful as our own? And if Mrs. Arthur was gone, were there others?

Mother's afternoon naps grew in length and in the mornings she was slower to rise. The unknown fate of her sisters and the unrelenting pace of the storm was affecting her with a listlessness that threatened us all. And on an afternoon when Father was late in returning from the barn, delayed by more than half an hour with the death of Sow One, she prayed beside the hearth alongside Mr. Arthur before bursting into a fit of inexplicable tears. Her frail hand cupped between his was the first hint of Mr. Arthur's revival.

In the morning, following breakfast, she left the house for the first time in eight days to stand on the screen porch and scold the wind with a long, cleansing scream. She then walked to the far end of the porch and began hollering again, shaking her fists at nothing, at the eternal whiteness whirling and eddying with its incessant noise, yelling out in a long continuously pitched cry that ended so abruptly it was as if the door had been closed. She turned back to the living room where we stood dumbfounded, galvanized by the interruption. With an iniquitous look in her eyes, she smiled and curled her finger and motioned everyone to the porch.

"Try it," she said.

"What," Mariah asked. "Try what?"

"Yelling. Try yelling."

Mariah looked to Father who simply shrugged his shoulders and I said, "It's cold out there, Mom."

"It feels good," she proclaimed, opening her hands toward the lawn and the dull unfurling fields.

"Well, what do we say?" Verity asked.

"You don't say anything, honey. You just yell is all."

Mother stood with eyes shimmering, smiling for the first time in days. Verity stepped to the opened storm door and embarked on a modest note and she sustained this note from octave to octave with that mellifluous tone recognized and responded to by Horse and Sow Two and Cow, and ultimately an ecosystem of hibernating critters in a ridiculous hootenanny joined by Father and the girls and cut short when I hollered, "Got-dangit hound, where are you?"

"Justus Charles…"

The porch turned quiet and I turned to the others wide-eyed, as if confused by their silence.

"That's enough, young man…not what I meant."

It was a discovery, of sorts, a missing link to our psychological survival. Four times that day we returned to stand at the porch threshold, screaming with a glorious delirium, and each time the wind and the cold was less threatening.

❋ ❋ ❋

The following morning, we woke to silence. There was no wind howling against the house or sleet slapping the long windows and we opened the drapes to the first visible sunrise in eleven days.

Over the next several days, the temperature rose to a windless seven or eight degrees Fahrenheit but to us and to everyone in the valley, it was like summer. The sky, by day, was as clear and as blue as a lake and by night so congested with stars, we opened the drapes and lay on the blanketed pallets, identifying constellations. We met with the Fallers and the Marshes and stood chatting in the middle of Pond Road as if it were July or August. The truck was coaxed alive and Father and Guy retrieved Mrs. Arthur's body and with the rest of us following in the revived station wagon and the Faller sedan, we traveled to town like inmates released from an asylum, honking to exchange waves and inquiries with every farmhouse we passed.

At Dr. Steadfast Stewart's, we learned of those who hadn't survived—older residents, caught alone and without provisions or sufficient heating fuel—and at Grant's Funeral Home, Father and Guy and Mr. Arthur stood by for nearly an hour before Josh Grant found time to accept the body and schedule a burial. Brother Reeves, in an everlasting reward, was among the seven bodies at rest in the receiving chambers.

By the time we arrived at Aunt Dee's, the power had been restored and Bim and the twins had already left. We walked down to Bim's and then the twins' but the sisters were all so fed up with one another no one would leave their own house so we had cocoa and cookies at Dee's and muffins at Bim's and finally with Madeline and Elizabeth who swore if they never laid eyes on either Bim or Dee again that it would be too soon.

"Well, it couldn't have been *that* bad, Elizabeth," Mother responded, accepting her third cup of tea in less than an hour.

Elizabeth turned from the stove with that thin whippet face to stress her words as if scolding a child, *"Ne-ver."*

It was dusk before we left town beneath an unfettered crescent moon so clear we could see the static windmill from as far away as Deere Road. We pulled down the partitioning blankets and over the next hour cleared out the living room to eliminate any trace of the past eleven days.

Later, Father found Mother in the bedroom, beneath the blankets and with her eyes closed and her fingers interlaced over her chest. In his long johns and his sleeping cap, he settled in beside her, studying the ceiling, the geometry of the moonlight through the east window, listening, and I can easily become confused, as I write, with that of myself and Acceptance, in the same room, same bed, same plastered ceiling, hearing the same barn owl, his callings slow, metered out like a meditative chant to linger, suspended in the airspace beyond the window like the soft repeating notes of a somber sonnet. He quietly shifted an arm along the pillow and allowed his fingers to graze her hair, gently brushing her hair until the day and the day before and the day before that and every one of the past eleven days were gone. Gone away.

TWENTY-SIX

From a three-legged stool in the Quarters, I watched Mr. Arthur pacing, sizing up the offerings of a bank of bunk beds along one wall before settling gingerly on the edge of a thin mattress near the stove. I moved over to the opposite cot, close enough to taste his breath.

"How's it feel?"

"…"

"Feel pretty good?"

"…"

He removed his boots and stroked his beard and I said, "Wanna play some checkers?"

"…"

From the table, he lifted a bible as old as time and laid himself out and I leaned in closer, hoping he would read aloud so I could get a glimpse of his cut tongue.

"Mr. Arthur is depressed," Mother said.

I considered the idea. "He's tired. He's old, so he's tired."

"It's different. Being depressed is different."
I considered this. "So, he's really tired. Too tired to go home?"
"His home is empty."

On the evening of Mother's thirty-eighth birthday, Father and I were in the barn pitching alfalfa against the remaining feeding stalls. Mr. Arthur was busy relieving Cow's udder with the two-handed rhythm of a subtle percussionist. Although the storm and the funerals had passed, the weather remained cold and severe. The days were clear and windless with highs in the teens and the nights dropping to near zero. The back wall of the barn was like the carcass of a ravaged animal; there were huge, gaping cavities where the planks were still being pulled to fuel a fire that was kindled through the nights but allowed to die out in the sunlit warmth of the afternoons. Beyond the glow of the fire, the barnyard shimmered under the light of a full moon, the trees and fenceline and even the tractor glistened beneath a blanket of icy dew. The air smelled of oats and hay.

"Hey, Dad," I hesitated, searching for the right words. I raised the tails of the greatcoat and fussed with the kepie slipping low on my forehead. "You notice anything different about Mom lately?"

He stepped over to spread the alfalfa evenly along the stalls before returning to slap the flanks of Sow *Two* with the back of his pitchfork. Sow *Two* snorted and a cloud of white breath dissipated into the cold thin air. He slapped her again with an open hand and a stiff-armed shove and the animal lumbered closer to the fire.

"Different? Different how?"
"You know...jes different."

He turned, pausing just long enough to consider the question before shrugging his shoulders and pitching more feed toward the stalls.

"She's just under a little stress…everyone is."

"Ain't that. I ain't a mean'n that. It's different."

"*Ain't a mean'n?* I don't think they said that."

"Oh, they said it, all right. The Rebs weren't school taught, Dad… and if you actually *read* their letters home, you'd see they couldn't spell neither."

"Aren't you taking this too far? You've got Scooter doing it and maybe even Bump and one of these days, you boys will wake up and realize how silly you sound."

"I wouldnt be a worryin bout that, Dad."

"Well…whatever."

Cow groaned from the corner stall and Mr. Arthur shifted his stool and responded with a similar groan before returning to the teats and the rhythmic splash against the side of the metal bucket.

"Mom's different, is what I'm saying…ever since the cellar."

Father pressed the pitchfork into the alfalfa and turned with his one eyebrow raised and after a moment he said, "Women are different, Sport. They're just plain different."

I considered this, my brain twisting it from several angles and I said, "Yer onto somethin else, Dad."

Behind him, hovering near the warmth of the sustaining fire, Mr. Arthur had stirred from his milking stool to stand dwarfed beside his horse, poking at the embers of a fire that cast his face and his long beard with a ghoulish silhouette.

In the corner, Horse stood bored, watching Mr. Arthur, mildly curious of this two-thousand-pound relative that stood twenty hands high who spoke a language Horse didn't understand. Wandering pointlessly and without purpose the chickens and banshees bobbed their brainless heads with each step and overseeing it all, perched along the girders and collar-ties like patrons of the stage, the pigeons and the crows and the innumerable sparrows and swallows and wrens. The air was thick with the scent of animal hides. These were the survivors.

POSSESSING THE SEASONS

Father swung aboard the tractor and pumped the choke and the diesel ignited with a deafening roar. A ripple of movement swept through the barn as a plume of exhaust issued up from the stacks, briefly blacking out the moon overhead. The front bucket shifted with a coarse hydraulic rattle and the stiff carcass of Sow *One* slipped to the back of the scoop. I watched along with Mr. Arthur and all the others as Father leaned down from the seat and raised his voice above the engine, "All your mother needs is a little good news," he said, shortening the throttle. "We all need some good news."

168

TWENTY-SEVEN

In the absence of good news or bad news, there was monotony, the passing of time so nondescript the smallest distractions became noteworthy.

TWENTY-EIGHT

Our visitors, retrospectively speaking, are suspicious, at best. Forged credentials or incredulous titles. Lacking the credibility of an officious footnote. Working for credulous publications or purporting the credence of agencies above reproach. Or perhaps, just as likely, the visitors are imaginary. Figments of this old fool's imagination, assuming, retrospectively, that someone, anyone, actually cared.

"Did your father struggle with the lasting relevance of her little books?"

"I don't think any of us thought about those books in terms of relevance. They were children's books. Personified flowers, that also happened to pay the bills. They weren't a topic of conversation, in other words...if that's what you mean. Her readers, her sales, existed outside of Fall Ridge. Far far beyond our inclusive world."

"Existential, according to some. Existential classics."

"Existential?"

"The last one, the big one, was hardly a children's book."

"It was about flowers. Flowers in love. Like the others. Same characters, same flowers, different story and different illustrations. But more of the same. What she knew would sell. Let's remember, Father's work never translated, at the time, into anything that might be considered financially successful. The barley and alfalfa crops were the default throughout the valley that following year, after the drought, but only that one year and then everyone, including us, returned to corn and soybeans. So, the

subsidy was short-lived. And the west field, well, what we have of that are memories, and photographs of tomatoes like beach balls."

"It was based off an opera. Beyond the scope, I would say, for most children."

"The last book. Well, they came, nevertheless. Now and again. Busloads. Nothing regular, but memorable because so few ever entered the valley from outside the valley. So, it was something you remember. A busload of schoolkids."

"There is an effervescent truth in her garden tales that transcends children's literature. To put it mildly. What astounds me is how no one in her immediate family, and extending to the valley at large, seemed to have had any awareness of that."

"Mother was sickly as a child. While my aunts were off at school, she was kept home for long stretches, alone with Ma and Dad Pond, who by the way were left with five granddaughters with the early deaths of my grandparents from Tuberculosis. She spent her days in the attic, Mother, in her make-believe world, and most afternoons, Dolores would arrive, delivering the day's schoolwork and Dolores, and to a lesser extent, Mother's sisters, were her portal to life beyond the attic. That she was allowed to leave for her one year in Champaign was huge. Her health had returned, but nevertheless, it was rare, back then, that anyone left. When Aunt Harriet, a full eleven years older than Mother, escaped to St. Louis and changed her name from Fortuna, Ma and Dad must have loosened the reins, so to speak. She was so young, Mother. She was only sixteen, I believe. And although Aunt Bim was there, working for the Champaign-Urbana Gazette, she was vulnerable."

"Her health?"

"Maybe, but in general. Vulnerable to the world up north. The world beyond our world. To the charms of my father. He was older. She was his ticket. He must have realized that. And he was her ticket, as well. She, too, must have understood."

"His ticket to continue his work in obscurity."

"His ticket to topsoil ten foot deep and her ticket...well, the farm needed an heir.

TWENTY-NINE

Mother rose from bed late that morning in mid-December, angry to have missed her allotted hours in the attic. The added hours of sleep had served no purpose; too much sleep was wasteful. She washed her face at the sink in the long bath and slipped on a single-piece cotton frock layered with a pull-over woolen sweater and moved to stand facing the dresser mirror at the foot of the bed. A minute passed. Another. Several minutes before she remembered, reaching for the brush to begin counting the one-hundred strokes aloud. Not angry with the loss of any linear progress, but more the loss of those hours each morning when her competence was guaranteed.

From a distance, the tractor's throttle, and from the stairwell, the invariable bickering between myself and Mariah. *Sixty-two, sixty-three,* forestalling life beyond the bedroom door, the complexities of Mr. Arthur's depression, my own boredom and Mariah's impatience with everything and Father's emotional distance so wrapped up in worries those days and only Verdi with her reservoirs and reservoirs of resilience. A surge of sadness with the certainty of Verity's maturity, her little girl so utterly prepared and competent.

172

She sat at the foot of the bed, and in one of those morose moods that would later, from time to time, overcome her, she would recall an urge to burrow beneath the blankets and ignore the day in a state of mind my sisters and I had come to recognize, Mother ignoring one world for another, on the edge of the bed sitting motionless for an hour or more, thinking thoughts not worth thinking—the days to come in this endless winter so sick of the cold cooped up like a groundhog and the Sapps who were the first to sell off, paid in goat sperm by the Javitts-from-Kentucky and probably in their shorts this very morning, plucking fresh Florida oranges, laughing at the high-mindedness of those Salt Fork fools, or Dolores in town now and so horribly far away.

She stood from the bed, too quickly perhaps, bracing one hand on the bedpost for that strange wave of unsteadiness not due to a lack of sleep because she had just awakened from *ten hours in bed!* So, what then? The cold had flared Dee's arthritis something terrible and Marian Snead had been down for more than a week with some kind of flu bug. Dr. Stewart's talk of low blood count, you need more sleep, was silly… Steadfast was old. She loved him for delivering her healthy babies but he was too old and all her life he had been prescribing sleep. She hated sleep.

She missed Hank.

She set the brush onto the dresser and strapped on the apron and entered the library off the bedroom, summoning the strength for another day. Verity sat at the desk facing the wall, reading her book. Mother approached, kissing the back of her neck and called Mariah from the bottom of the stairs and continued on to the kitchen and to the small desk off the laundry where the mail had been accumulating for weeks.

Accumulated mail was not good. *Good* was accomplishing tasks as they were presented but, lately, her efforts seldom lasted for more than a few minutes before she grew frustrated and distracted and left the desk for the short gains of a less intimidating task. The truth, however, was that the sweeping elegance once characterizing her penmanship had become labored and choppy, as if composed in a moving car.

Mariah arrived in the kitchen to stand at the end of the counter, waiting, as if to say, *this better be good.*

"Can you help with the mail this morning?"

"You're kidding, right?"

I arrived, dragging my stocking feet along the kitchen linoleum, simulating an ice skater and Mariah said, *"Go away,"* and I replied, *"You* go away."

"Stop it, you two. Jussie, finish your breakfast. Mariah, I'd like help with the mail, please."

Mariah stood her ground in a posture she had begun to adopt from Mother, hipshot with a hand on her waist but with Mariah, it was more threatening. She resembled Mother in other ways, mimicking her patterns of speech to emphasize certain words or phrases with a subtle intonation in her voice. But often the subtlety was lost and her words were infused with an outspokenness, a firmness that some considered too rough, too intimidating for a young lady. And her appearance, the same hair and facial features and skin tone that defined Mother's unassuming beauty but with an added flair; Mariah could tilt her head and raise one eyebrow and stare down a locomotive with the aplomb of a breeding bull.

Father entered through the side door and a rush of cold air traveled the length of the kitchen. He stomped his Wellingtons and slapped his gloves together and made his way toward the bath as Mother turned her back, fidgeting with the desktop letters.

Mariah, who had skipped the fourth grade and again the ninth grade, approached the desk as a sixteen-year-old on her last leg at Fall Ridge School. She studied the pile of mail and said, "Why can't Verdi do it?"

"I'm not asking Verity. I'm asking you."

"So, it's a question…I have a choice?"

"Of course…in a manner of speaking." Mother sat in the desk chair, resigned to the sort of verbal jousting Mariah seemed to require.

"What type of manner? An existential manner with guilt and stuff, or just a trade-off manner?"

"Oh, for goodness' sake, Mariah."

Mariah waited.

"A trade-off, I guess."

"What for?"

"We'll come to that when we come to that. For now…" and she raised a finger toward the desk.

Mariah considered this for a moment before exchanging seats to begin working her way through the mounds of cards and letters mostly from children but knowing there were those from adults, collectors feigning a child's script with the profiting intention of her mother's signature. She started in:

Thank you for writing.
I'm so pleased you enjoy the books.

Yours truly,
Gracious Meadowsage.

The letters themselves proved a suitable respite and at one point their voices and laughter carried beyond the laundry room. Father returned to pause behind Mother's chair, the seconds passing like hours before he turned away and left through the side door.

My Dear Miss Sage,

I am a forty-five-year-old bachelor of independent means
who has been smitten by a flower. Are you married?

175

*Please forgive my presumptuousness, but it is with the
utmost respect and consideration that I make this inquiry.*

Snapshot enclosed.

Yours truly,
Walter Weathersby
London, England

"He's handsome," Mariah said, holding the photograph.

"Very dignified."

"Do you think it's a joke?" Mariah said. "He sounds shy and sincere and lonely."

Mother shrugged, studying Mariah, her mannerisms and the sound of her voice and the personality so strong that would either serve her or ruin her. How long since they had spent any time together…just the two of them?

"Let's say yes."

"Yes, what?"

"Yes, we'll marry him."

"We?"

"All right…me. I'm writing the letter and I'm not married and, really, he is quite handsome and he's in *Europe,* Mother. Or close enough."

"He sounds older than your father."

"So. All my friends think Daddy's a doll."

"A what?"

"You know…handsome."

"Really, now?"

"Don't act like you don't know, Mom."

"Should I be jealous?"

Mariah smiled and touched her mother's knee, "I don't think so… Daddy adores you."

176

Mother motioned toward the desk, "Just thank Mr. Weathersby for his kind letter and let's move on or we'll never finish."

Mariah returned to her room an hour later, passing me in the dayroom without the usual biting remarks and in fact what to me seemed the hint of a smile. I watched as she disappeared behind the closed door and after some consideration, I stood from the carefully simulated battlefield, lost in thought. It seemed only the other day we used to go fishing or diving off the planks of the bridge or all those afternoons in the dayroom playing out the roles of paper dolls with the dollhouse that had once belonged to Aunt Dee. The great battles with the soldiers on the manure pile behind the silo.

Reluctantly, I had turned to Verity by default but Verity lacked the soldier's character; I missed the bloodletting and the savagery shared with Mariah. I missed Mariah's fearlessness, the swagger in deep summer poised out on the end of the oak diving plank while the rest of us watched, her understudies, as she went airborne with a jackknife and a twist headfirst into a muddled river only five foot deep.

I stood debating Mariah's smile. Or was it a smirk? For a while, during the storm, it was as if she had returned; we played board games and card games and read aloud in a way we hadn't done since…since *The Change*.

I approached the door with the recognizable flutters of standing outside Principal Starr's office. I knocked once.

Mariah's voice came, and I opened the door and set one foot inside the lion's den to see Mariah at her desk, her back to the door, glancing over her shoulder.

"You wanna play with the soldiers…in the dayroom? We could re-enact the battle of Little Round Top…or whatever battle you want."

But I could see by the look in her eyes that I had miscalculated.

"Oh, Jussie...grow up!"
I took a step back, feeling small and childish.

Verity lay awake that night, lulled by my own metered breathing fast asleep against the window overlooking the frosted lawn. Perfectly still with her hands clasped over her stomach and her head cradled carefully within the folds of her pillow, conscious of the curlers she had set herself...the awkward curlers never her thing but as she confessed years later, the following morning's resumed service represented the first social gathering in a month. A calculated opportunity for bumping into who knows who.

THIRTY

In December, lulled by an anesthesia of endless gray, any memories of perfect fall days were as distant and dangerous as the dreams of a spring sky. The weeks were endured one day at a time, anchored on the pettiest mental exercise. The smallest issues provided purpose. A mere ripple of controversy became the fodder for a raging debate. The twins were happy to oblige.

The Fall Ridge Anabaptist congregation held its first worship since the storm and its first service in twenty-eight years without Brother Reeves.

The twins arrived before seven to take possession of the Hill like marauding soldiers. There was to be no debating this; they considered the vacancy theirs to inherit and to the others, well…until a suitable replacement could be found, the two hickory sticks could do as they pleased.

What *pleased* them was wholly unorthodox. To some.

To others, it was nothing short of a blasphemous side show.

The twins had debated for days in a battering crossfire resulting eventually in an agreement to *share* the pulpit. They began with a briefing of their most recent citation in Carbondale, announcing the need for an

179

additional offering contributing to their legal defense fund in the two colorful ceramic bowls on the two nice wrought-iron stands to each side of the front doors.

As their abiding parishioners, we turned as one to assess the new bowls, murmuring some pretense of approval that rippled and rose to collect somewhere among the collarbeams and gussets of the vaulted ceiling cut and set by the master craftsman True Pond while Theodore Roosevelt fished in Vermont and President McKinley was being shot in Buffalo, New York.

"Okay then," Elizabeth said, squaring her shoulders in a practiced gesture.

Silence. From the basement, the coal furnace pulsed through the floorboards with a droning warmth. Verity chanced a glance toward the Fallers' pew while I studied the nailholes in the floorboards under my feet.

"Well then," Madeline said, shifting her weightless frame from one foot to another. She turned a furtive glance to Elizabeth but Elizabeth's eyes were lost and vacant.

Rustling petticoats and sniffling sinuses and the irritating coughs of a winter virus contributed to the lingering silence as I looked up, turning to Verity with wondering eyes and then to Acceptance Davis with a smile and to Clare and Max in their Sunday finery and back to the twins standing like plastic mannequins.

Madeline cleared her throat and ran her hands along the fabric of her dark blue dress and raised her chin slightly.

"So…"

"Oh, any ole thing, Madeline. Anything'll do."

The sound of Givens' voice was a relief. Madeline reacted with a smile and Elizabeth took a few steps to shake the jitters and Vivian slapped Givens' shoulder and the pews rippled with stifled giggles and a general shuffling as Dee's voice rose to travel the distance to the pulpit like an amplified whisper, "There was Cain…"

Her right hand turned lazy circles, prompting more, "And there was Abel..."

"There was..."

Both sisters spoke at once and both silenced, flushed and confused with the mechanics of a double act.

"There was Abel," Madeline began.

"And there was Cain," Elizabeth followed.

"One a shepherd."

They proceeded as an alternating duet closer to the rhythmic cadence of a grade-school poetry recital but with building confidence, they added a strategy of over-rehearsed intonations and mannerisms and even the occasional dramatic accompaniment of Mercy May Jenkins' organ.

They moved out from behind the pulpit to occupy the platform as if it were a stage, throwing their voices over the pews with an imagined posthumous dialogue between brothers that caught, and held, the attention of all of us and when they finished, Mercy May laid into a hymn with such force and drama, the pipes vibrated through the pews.

We sat dumbfounded. Were we expected to applaud? To stand and yell Bravo?

Madeline tapped her heart, settling herself. Elizabeth shifted her weight from one foot to another, as if poised for a bow and curtsy.

The sparkle in their eyes melted away, replaced with a labored breathing that stifled the movement of the muscles required to will themselves off the platform and through the back door at a dead run. So they stood, standing frozen in place with their humiliated hearts racing and their cheeks flushing and the silence lingered like an oppressive criticism.

It was Givens who rose to stand in his wrinkled suit. Givens who had shared every classroom from kindergarten through graduation with those two gals, standing briefly, before Vivian pulled him back by the tail of his jacket and Givens rose again, catapulting to his feet to clap his hands slowly and the sound of each clap carried through the church like a drumming metronome.

Because it was Sunday and we were bored and it was everyone's first social encounter in a month, we too stood up, smiling, clapping, glancing at one another with a rueful solidarity, less in support of the twin sticks than an impatience for the baked goods and gossip waiting in the basement.

As we walked home that Sunday, singing hymns in the brittle air, I thought of how Father didn't understand Fall Ridge Church. That he would never understand what he didn't want to know.

An hour later, the twins occupied the airspace of the dining room with an indefatigable optimism. A surrealist optimism. They sat like coiled springs with their bony little butts poised on the lip of their chairs and then stood with their hands in constant motion and then sat on their hands and really…as Aunt Bim would later say, 'just throw a bag over them both and lock them in a closet.'

"I thought it would never end!" Elizabeth exclaimed.

"On and on and on!" Madeline said.

"What a sweetheart!" they said, together.

Bim stood from her chair and started for the kitchen shaking her head and mumbling to herself and at the hall she turned and said, "Givens is a bigoted old fart."

"You don't know Givvy is all…not like we do," and the twins glanced at one another with twinkling eyes.

"What on *Earth.*" Dee set her coffee down and leaned over the table and when she spoke, the words rolled off her tongue with the sluggish delivery of a reprimand.

"*That was third grade.* Third grade for pity's sake."

"*Standing* applause, Dee," Elizabeth said.

182

"Oh, whatever."

"Ten minutes, at least!" Madeline added.

"Oh, longer...much much longer!" Elizabeth blurted, bouncing from her chair and pressing her hands to her chest and moving around the room with her head tilted toward the ceiling when Mariah entered. She approached Madeline, crossing the room with a presence as affected as the twins, embracing her by the shoulders and kissing first one cheek and then another and rounding the table to where Elizabeth stood waiting with outstretched arms and the game was on.

The collected pig-headedness of Mariah and the twins and Givens was enough to overthrow a small third-world country. Quickly, and in ways no one quite understood, those who opposed that first performance as a mockery found themselves whispering like insurgents, like plotting revolutionists pitted against the strength of a new politburo.

"Big show tomorrow," Father had said one Saturday night, attempting to break the awkward silence that had permeated their bedroom for weeks. The twins' revival, in itself, was of no interest to him; his comment would have been uttered simply to prompt the sound of Mother's voice.

"Show? That what you call it?"

While across the north field, Vivian in bed, alone, the church lights visible from her bedroom window, cursing, surely, the twins and her fool husband.

They established their numbers and vowed solidarity in the aisles of Water's Grocer and along the sidewalks of Fall Ridge and in time came to gather in the back of Dee's shop like a diminishing minority losing strength with each passing performance.

They huddled in the dark near the stove, the sisters of insurgency, along with Dolores, Vivian, and Ruby Morrow, culling over a list of out-

POSSESSING THE SEASONS

of-work preachers mired in controversy or scandal or as Mother later admitted, anyone who bothered to reply to the drafted letters mailed off to a roll of petitioned students in their final year at the Theological Seminary over to Evansville. And in their spare time, to boost morale, they bandied disparaging jokes like: what happens when you breed cross-eyed twin baboons with a steel fencepost?

But the strength of the theater was overwhelming. The following Sunday found Creedance Keating accompanying Mercy May for an orchestral flair as Elizabeth broke from the scripted delivery to engage in a half-spoken half-sung cadence accompanied note-for-note by Creedance's plucking violin. In short order, and without precedent, the twins and their entourage were playing to a standing-room only capacity.

There were mid-week rehearsals grown to week-long rehearsals. A confusion of actors and scripts vibrating off the Hill while Givens, regressing to a third-grade buoyancy, engaged his limited carpentry toward the rickety sets as Mariah and her friends composed a score of rock-a-billy choral accompaniments with a closing coloratura specifically for Verity. Brightly colored backdrops were added, along with matching candy-apple-red robes for the twins. Scooter, Bump, and myself borrowed the flood lights off the back wall of City Hall toward a tangled schematic of wires and colored cellophane. In concert with Creedance Keating's violin, Mercy May Jenkins offered the symphonics of a weeping organ.

The anticipation of Christmas was itself supplanted by the suspense and expectations of a church sermon. A sermon, in the minds of the surviving Resistance, that was better suited to the canopy of a revivalist tent than the sanctity of the church.

Elizabeth and Madeline Pond had elevated themselves to the crest of the Fall Ridge social registry. They scrolled through the invitations for dinner and Sunday gatherings, lavishing in the attention and the respect of their newfound roles like aging princesses finally promoted to the royalty of an abandoned throne. If they seemed changed—a new erectness to their posture and an exalted severity to their manner—it

184

was because they were no longer the *other* Pond sisters, the long-maligned understudies to the Big Three—Bim, Dee, and Fortuna.

The bitterness was a bad fit for Mother, who lacked the art of bullish confrontation once commandeered by Fortuna. To all of them, to Fortuna, Dee, Bim, and even the twins, she was Baby Grace, the runt.

On a chance encounter one afternoon at Water's Grocer, Mother summoned her strength and gestured to the twins' cart brimming with groceries and quipped, "What's all this?"

"The buffet," they answered.

"Buffet?"

"Sundays. In the basement, after the service."

"Oh."

"We have production costs. Sets and props and of course our time. There will be one admission ticket for the service, and another to include the buffet."

"You mean you're charging money?"

"Times are changing, Grace."

"Have you gone mad...both of you?"

The twins tensed. Their eyes hardened with that battle-tough resolve grown from decades of warring with Fortuna and Dee and Bim. It was a look Grace knew all too well, and she felt herself faltering.

"Mad about religion, Grace...unlike others."

"Others?"

"Certain others who never attend church and who tamper with God's creations."

Mother's eye wandered, hoping, perhaps, to find Dee or Bim or Ruby, any of whom were better suited for jousting with the twins and yet it was Scooter standing at the end of the aisle, watching.

"Infecting others," they continued, pressing on, "God-fearing others like Givvy...infecting his crops with sacrilegious errors, Grace."

Errors? Infecting? Mother steadied herself against the spices and spaghetti sauces, the light-headedness flushing the color from her cheeks

POSSESSING THE SEASONS

and she returned suddenly to childhood, with the much older twin vultures destroying her sketches and laughing at her poetry simply to incite the others, trenching in, pressed back-to-back like irrepressible soldiers against the advancing Big Three as Scooter advanced. Strolling to stand beside her like a feral tomcat and when she opened her eyes, the twins were gone. She stood for a moment, steadying herself along the aisle of mustards and sage. The back of her neck was warm and moist and the blur of sauces and spices circled, carrying off the shelves as she followed the tomcat safely outside and up the walk to the *Gazette*.

THIRTY-ONE

So, the winter went on. That stretch of uncompromising months infused with the cruelty of unkindness. If unkindness is the right word. More like inhumane. Merciless barbarity. Cold gray colorless days stacked one after another after another month after month. The relentless droopy canopy so thick it was impossible to remember the rejuvenating powers of an open sky. There were no crops, nor livestock, nor mutant spheres of otherworldly cantaloupe sprouting from the west field to amuse the senses. There was lonely Mr. Arthur who refused to go home, living in the Quarters. There was no hound inhabiting the heaths and heathery of our world for generations. There were no naked swan dives off the bridge, nor painted lead soldiers on the manure pile, nor singsonging octaves from Verity. There were no more Fallers across the road. There was no Ruby who spat with Diligence who spat with his wife Violet and once again Ruby deposed to the high unforgiving brick walls over to Anna and although Scooter was suspected of robbing the depot's unlocked cash drawer and pilfering day-old perishables from the bins of Water's Grocer, the town quietly banked his porch with firewood and fresh edible provisions. There was also this painful awareness that some of us had experienced Florida. Visions of long white powdery-soft

POSSESSING THE SEASONS

beaches, endless groves of palm trees, blue curling swells the temperature of bathwater.

There were no distractions beyond one another, inhabiting the inclemency of winter by turning, naturally, *toward* one another. Battling personages. Bickering adversaries. Hurtful quips slung like poison arrows.

THIRTY-TWO

Mother arose later every morning, missing her early hours for a week, two weeks. She and Dolores had sat holding hands in the kitchen before the holidays, whining like puppies. Dolores professing her reluctance in leaving the farm and the near-hollering proximity to Mother but it was obvious by the lift in her voice that she had no objections to the less laborious life of a small house in town. There would be no dust to permeate the walls and settle over the floors and tabletops of every room; no roosters with cockeyed timetables cockadoodling at two in the morning; no more barnyard stench penetrating the linen closets and bureau drawers so that her sheets and even her own underwear were impregnated with the odor of oats and manure and animal hides; no more worrisome hours watching weak weather fronts fizzling to blue skies along the ridge. And of course there was Florida.

Florida. The very idea seemed as ridiculous as cotton in Illinois. Mother laughed at the thought of Guy in shorts, frolicking in the waves of a sandy beach. Guy had no affinity for leisure; he was not a gadabout or a socializer and he had no business in a pair of shorts, and yet it was no less surprising when they returned ten days later, relaxed and sunburned, to discover that he had signed on for steady work outside the valley. Work with the Edwards County strip mines.

THIRTY-THREE

Late New Year's Day morning we lingered in the library off their bedroom. Out of sorts with the change that had them in bed, behind a closed door, raising their voices like hammers slamming glass.

"So, you want to go to Florida? Is that it? A vacation?"

"They went relaxing…Guy wore shorts."

"*What?*"

"You've never worn shorts. You don't *own* a pair of shorts. You don't know how to relax."

"*What?*"

"Dolores likes town."

"Well, maybe we should sell and live in town, too, with a garden the size of a sink and I'll wear shorts to work. Work in the mines."

"That's not what…"

Verity and I huddled behind Mariah as she knocked softly. A tap, actually. And another.

"Yes," Mother's voice, soft, but strained.

"Can we come in?"

Sounds of shuffling, bed springs, and ruffling bedcovers and Father's voice, "Might as well…might as well come on in."

190

We entered, on this first day of the new year, tiptoeing as if the floor were scattered with thorns.

I peered over to see Mother looking suddenly relaxed and restful, her head against Father's shoulders and Father staring at the ceiling, drumming the bedsheets with his fingers.

"It's nine o'clock or somethin," I said.

"So," Father answered, his eyes still on the ceiling. "What's wrong with nine o'clock? It's a holiday, isn't it?"

"I reckon."

We moved in to fully occupy the room, studying this breach of routine as Verity reached to touch the bed, touch Father's leg.

"You're still in your pajamas."

"I'm leisuring," he said.

It looked more like he was strapped to the mattress.

"We're pretending we're in Florida," he added.

"Huh?"

"You know, Florida."

"I know, Daddy," Verity replied. "I know where Florida is."

"Well, then watch out or you'll burn your feet on the sand. And careful…those crabs are mean as snapping turtles."

Verity glanced at the floor and then back and her face lightened, recognizing, along with Mariah and I, his smiling mischievous face we hadn't seen in weeks when Verity suddenly shrieked and leaped onto the bed. Mariah and I climbed on, not sure what was going on or how to react but ready for whatever sliced through the tensions of the past few weeks.

"Hear that?"

"What?" we answered, all in.

"The ocean. Can't you hear it?"

We listened with chins raised and eyes wide as the tide lapped against the shore. Long lazy lapping waves and the warm languorous breeze rustling the palm fronds and in my mind, I pictured an endless blue, swelling waves cresting like troughs with the beach extending wide and deserted to the grove of palms. Forming the words, building the sentences.

The ocean the beach the grove. Separations like colors on a canvas blue white and green, extending along the land's end for as far as the mind could manage.

It was an infinity without interruption, without the debris and the clutter of the forest floor and the irregular limbs of hickories and cottonwoods and without the punctuations of crops and weeds and cattle and fences and machinery, all the machinery with their endless parts and appendages. Without ice and snow and skies that seemed interminably gray. There was only, for a while, sitting on their bed that morning, the water and the sand and the palms and they were separated like lines on a canvas—blue white green.

Mother was burrowed in close to Father. Her eyes were closed and the sound of her breathing was short and irregular. No one spoke because there was nothing to say.

We left school the following afternoon, Verity and I, to walk beneath the old elms toward downtown. The thriving canopy of songbirds and deranged blue jays were long gone and in the dark gray light of January, the old elms stood naked. The upper boughs were exposed and lonely. Fragile survivors. Slung out over the walk and the street, the stout lowermost limbs like massive outstretched arms.

Beneath all this, we walked silently, pausing at the corner abreast of the Dillman's towering old victorian once white but gone unpainted for too long; the rotting woodwork and the decaying façade announcing an indifferent priority. Approaching up the walk, Aunt Elizabeth crossed the bridge at the creek, detouring up the entry walks of these first homes, these modest original cornerstones just south of the Town Hall, distributing her leaflets for the Sunday service, or show, or circus, or whatever.

"Let's cross over," I leaned a shoulder gently into Verity, nudging her toward the street but she resisted and I nudged a little harder.

"Jussie!"

"I wanna cross, okay?"

"Well, cross then."

I didn't move.

"You can't avoid her, Jussie."

Elizabeth crossed Willow Street and stopped before us, blocking the walkway. She looked at Verity and said, "Oh, Verity, we'll need you and Bump on Thursday, okay?"

Verity nodded, although likely less interested in her role as the sacred voice than the time it allowed with Bump.

Elizabeth turned to me and raised an eyebrow so high it disappeared beneath her bangs.

"Well, my little *tweet*. Appears you're so holy now you can do without the church, without the saving grace of scripture."

I had, for the first time in memory, remained home for the holiday service. A morning where Father and I and Max and Mr. Arthur had settled ourselves on Slave Hill, bundled to the cold, for the idle amusement of firing off rounds. Crouching to steady the barrel over the wooden markers of those poor souls who had long ago fled the deep south for everlasting peace under six feet of free soil. We aimed toward a row of cans aligned atop the west field fence when Mr. Arthur, new to weapons, zinged a hornet's nest from the trunk of a dogwood to release a thousand hornets too drugged from hibernation to know up from down and in the clearing beyond the dogwood an image of what could be Bo sprinted along the riverbank, quickly disappearing into the thicket and we stood, watching a moment more, fixed on the clearing.

Elizabeth stood too close. I looked away, determined not to meet her eyes, studying the Dillman house and its drooping shutters.

"What do you have to say, young man?"

193

POSSESSING THE SEASONS

I turned back, staring at the sidewalk, at Elizabeth's blocky oxfords. "He had to help, Daddy."

Elizabeth looked to Verity and tilted her head just enough to expect an explanation and Verity added, "One of the cows was sick."

Satisfied, Elizabeth turned up the Dillman walk and we continued across Willow Street where the sound of Mercy May's piano and Creedance Keating's struggling registers filtered through the walls of the first of those three cornerstone homes to approach the small bridge spanning the creekwater flowing like a trickling capillary under a sheath of ice.

"You ever think how everything's always moving?"

"Moving?"

"Nothing ever stops."

"What are you talking about, Jussie?"

"I'm talking about moving."

"You mean, like Bump moving to town?"

"I mean like currents...river currents and ocean currents and air currents and time and molecules and how nothing is ever just stopped... perfectly still."

"Well...that's the way it is."

We reached the corner of Main Street alongside the big brick façade of Town Hall weighing against the edge of Town like a flanking ballast. Verity veered up Oak Street toward Dr. Stayer's veterinary office with plans to drop by Bump's new house to help unpack as I made my way up Main Street toward the *Gazette*. I passed beneath the windows of the Café where Acceptance was strapping on her apron and on to the benches outside Water's Grocer, thinking of Bump's grandfather who occupied the benches, weather permitting, along with others from that generation talking stories of a Fall Ridge long gone. Stories pitted with so many endless tangents that they often lapsed into silence, gathered on these benches, searching their brains for the thread of a lost thought triggered by anything, by the smell of mule hide or the smell of a leather

194

harness and how the reins might bite against the calluses in their hands and seeing clear as yesterday the surrounding furrows and the sweep of the land as it looked some fifty years ago.

When Mother would stare out the living room windows with the sort of vacant eyes I could look right through, it reminded me of Bump's grandfather. Or when she lost track of where she was, she reminded me of Granny Davis, and then I thought of Granny's sister dancing among the bodies strewn across the field at Antietam.

I turned into the warmth of the *Gazette* where Bim sat at her layout table. She looked up and her eyes ran to the corner where Scooter sat like a statue, hiding behind the press. She made a face and returned to the copy on the table and I moved to the back, rummaging through the bank of drawers along the wall for a stash of reserve soldiers, dropping them in heaps onto the floor and settling myself down to divide them up, pushing Scooter's share toward him and I tapped the toe of his boot.

"Hey, come on."

I thought how the battles with Scooter were never any good, anyway; he didn't know an artillery soldier from a foot soldier. He didn't know Big Horn from Gettysburg.

"The Battle of Lexington," I said, wasting my breath. "The start of the Revolutionary War. I'm the Colonies and you're the British and you don't have marksmen. It's the first battle ever like this, the Patriots moving around in little groups firing from the trees and you're in the middle but you don't know what to shoot at. You just stand there and get shot."

But it's no use. I pushed the soldiers aside and stood to take hold of him and pull him over to the press where we start with what's familiar, what he knows, the solvents and the brushes, cleaning the plates, and quickly he's absorbed, occupied, and I stepped away to my corner composition table and Bim said over her shoulder, "Watch the modifiers. Every word counts. And remember, you're an entertainer."

A Word More, by Linkum Regards
 The conscience of good and evil
 The balance of Beasts primevil
 Leads us forward, leads us shoreward
 To the banks, ~~with artillery tanks~~
 To the banks of wrong and right
 To the light of ~~the EvilBeast's might~~
 To the light of song over spite

Mother entered with Dee and Dolores and the three of them paused briefly, watching Scooter scrubbing the plates before removing their coats and settling in at the table. Bim set her copy sheet to the side and poured out the tea and slid a container of Pat Davis' morning pastries to the center of the table while I was thinking how there's just too many words; they hover and swirl in the airspace, circling my brain like a swarm of bees and how an entertainer should know his audience, should use the right words for the right audience.

"I 'magine they're upset," Dee said, referring to the Pastors in Carbondale and Marion.

Bim raised both hands. "Well, of course they're upset. Half their congregations are up to Fall Ridge for a couple of un-ordained imposters."

"People are starved for culture. They want entertainment," Dolores said.

"Entertainment?" Dee smoothed the hair from her forehead and repositioned her hairpins with the high-maintenance affectation of swatting flies in the barn. She looked to the soft-spoken Dolores and with pins pursed between her lips, she said, "That what it is…culture? More like a couple 'a psychotic harlots."

Dolores took a breath and held it, as if readying a reply, forming the words, but as always, when in a room with Dee and Bim Pond, her voice was buried beneath the weight of their combined emphatics.

"Mariah's been up every afternoon this week," Mother said.

It was Mariah who was drafting the set for a loose reenactment of the Lord's Supper. Left essentially unchecked by the twins, or anyone, for that matter. Commandeering Buddy and his friends, like tamed kittens, casting and scripting their lines with the Stalinist tactics of closed-door rehearsals that made you wonder.

"If it were just the twins…but that girl's a cannon," Dee said. "I just hope the world's ready for her."

"She thinking of Fortuna's in St. Louis? Washington University, is it?" Bim asked, but Mother was elsewhere. Somewhere distant, or perhaps a skipped nap that was no longer an occasional respite but a biological need.

"Grace?" Bim rested a hand on Mother's arm.

And Mother returned, saying, "She's only sixteen, you know. The other students…they'll all be so much older. The summer session is only a few months away."

"You were sixteen," Dolores said, "Don't you remember?"

Dee straightened herself, planting her hands against the small of her back and stretching, thrusting her chest over the lip of the table like boulders poised for a landslide.

"Seventeen. Gracie was seventeen. Anyway, it's only four hours away. The same as Champaign. It's not paris," Dee said.

"Who said anything about paris?" Bim said. "No one's going to paris."

"We should write Fortuna."

"It's Harriet, Redeemed. *Harriet.* Been Harriet for twenty years now."

"We should write her," Dee repeated. "Let her know what Mariah's thinking."

Gazing through the windows, searching for entertainment, I spotted Sheriff talking to Lester at the depot. He made his way toward the *Gazette* and I went to Scooter who was bent over, brushing the plates as if they were enemy soldiers. "Come on, we need to go in back and get some clean solvent."

The sound of the front door with its groaning hinges opened and closed and a stool dragged across the floor and the conversation shifted to talk of Town's need for ordinances or rules or guidelines governing hunting retreats. Anything short of laws, and following a pause, Sheriff asked after Scooter.

A silence and a moment later the stool dragged across the floor and the front door hinges groaned and Bim called out, "If we see him, we'll let him know, Sam."

Scooter and I reappeared with clean solvent and Mother continued, "Mariah has written Harriet, of course. She's also applied to the school and was accepted and all of it on her own. But…well, what if she doesn't come back? What if she stays there, like Harriet?"

"You came back," Dolores said, resting one hand across Mother's arm.

The others were silent, likely considering a worst-case scenario where Mariah, like Fortuna, returned every two or three years for a short visit, bearing gifts from the big city, while none of the five sisters had ever summoned the courage to make the trip to St. Louis. Leaving the county itself was doable, within reason—the twins with Carbondale and Ruby in Anna and Mother and Bim with their one year in Champaign—but St. Louis was different. St. Louis was a city. It might as well be Chicago.

"Those were the days," Bim took a breath and a deep sigh and straightened herself on her stool. "That little apartment on 6th Street…"

"We all know the story, Bim," Dee interrupted.

"…the *News Gazette*. College graduates. Real journalists."

"One year, Bim."

"Maybe so. My last assignment…interviewing that grad student who had developed his hybrid corn before I introduced that student to you know who."

"Broken record. Senile," Dee mumbled.

Scooter and I moved to the back of the press, greasing the gears and wiping down the black cast iron housing as if it were a precious stone and I said softly, "You know, a jewel like this here baby needs regular maintenance. Someone has to know how to keep it running. Same with those presses over to Carbondale and Marion and Evansville and Paducah. They all could need someone regular for that."

We moved back to the front and started setting the letter blocks and a moment later, with the senile word still hanging in the air, Dee ran her hands over the surface of the counter, smoothing sand in a sandbox, and looked to Bim and Dolores to pick up the conversation but Dolores had closed her eyes, holding Mother's hand, and Bim was still in Champaign, that interview in the Ag lab mentioning to that young man the farm, the Salt Fork Valley, and how the interview had turned to where it was him asking all the questions.

Returning to the safety of Mariah's certain exodus, Dee smiled and turned to Mother and said, "You could be the Carlson's. Ginny Carlson's got her oldest—what is it, Esther? Eleanor? —near thirty and still single and living at home. And from what I hear, there's none too many prospects either."

"That's pure gossip," Bim said. "You don't even *know* their daughter."

"Well, that's true, but…"

"Ever since Sheriff proposed you've taken this high'n mighty view of things. Mariah was five or six 'fore you moved out of the house. You've got no place to criticize Ginny Carlson."

Dee stiffened. "Well, someone had to stay. Ma and Dad were getting on and Fortuna was in St. Louis and you two were off upstate and did you want the place to go to the crows? Or worse, the twins?"

The old clock on the wall clicked with the passing seconds and Dee said, "Who told you that?"

"What?"

"That Sam proposed…that's what."

"I didn't say that."

"You said that. I heard you."

Mother laid a hand on Dee's arm and said, "The Sheriff told Pat

Davis, Dee. Pat told Dilligence who told Listen who told Givens who told Henry who told me, and I told Bim. We've been waiting for you to say something. Is it true?"

"Is what true?"

"Bim raised her hands, leaning toward Dee. *"Did he propose?* Did he?"

"Now lookee here, you two…what Sam and I do is no one's business but ours."

I looked at Scooter and mouthed *Uncle Sheriff* and he smiled and it was the first sign of Scooter returning. I paused, and whispered, "She'll be fine. They take care of her nice over there."

Another long silence from the table, waiting for Dee to say more but Dee wasn't talking. She and Sheriff had a history of setting, and cancelling, wedding dates.

Dee, safely changing the subject, said, "Hank got company?"

"Hank?" Mother said, yawning. She blinked wide.

"Henry…your husband?"

"Yes, Wes is down."

"From school? The schoolboys again?"

Just Wes, and two others. New ones. One from Washington DC, Mr. Harriman, and another from Europe or somewhere. I don't like him. Neither of them. Hank's been nervous. They make him nervous. But Wes is there."

The room turned quiet and following a long silence, Dee and Bim glanced at one another and turned back to Mother and Bim said, "I hear it's raining in Alaska."

For a while, Mother didn't respond. She sat cradling the tea that had managed to postpone the afternoon nap.

"Alaska? Mother said, finally. "Good Lord, Bim…they're in the *barn.*"

I left the press and approached the table. Dolores stood and our eyes met and she said, "I'll drive."

THIRTY-FOUR

The problem with a weekly newspaper is that, it's weekly.

The problem as a columnist with a weekly newspaper is that, it's weekly. Seven long days to pare down the possibilities into a corner of two column inches surrounded by wasted gutters separating something of interest, of merit, from a four-column-inch ad that hasn't changed its copy in decades.

So, the columnist, as a means to stretch his presence, visited the business located in a small nondescript clapboard behind Town Hall, situated alongside the once flooding creek that overflowed into the Town Hall basement, along with the business in question, like foot-deep lap pools for a confusion of water moccasins and wallowing minnows.

I took notes in my reporter's notebook, fraternizing with the enemy whose paid ad-space crowded my column-of-merit to a limiting two column inches while funding the paper itself with the revenue that allowed the column to exist.

POND PERMS

201

POSSESSING THE SEASONS

I licked the lead of my pencil and took a seat in a chair with torn upholstery and to avoid eye contact I faced the owners of the business through a foggy mirror.

"So, you do perms."

"Perms, coloring, waves, braids, blending, bobs, pixies, feathering…"

"I see."

"Oh, and the dutch braid. Your sister and her crowd. It's french. paris french…the dutch braid is."

I closed my notebook and closed the door behind me and ran up the icy walkway to the sanctity of the *Gazette*, distancing myself with each stride.

> *POND PERMS*
> *perms, coloring, and waves*
> *that'll raise the dead from their graves*
> *or the trendy braid that separates the hip from the extinct*
> *for the ingenue who bobbed before she thinked.*

"You've reduced their ad from four column inches to one. They always pay for a four-column-inch ad."

"We'll raise our prices and they pay the same now for one column inch."

"They won't."

"And we charge five cents. You pay to read the *Gazette*."

We set the paper on the table and like two managing partners we reconsidered a new *Fall Ridge Gazette*. Sheriff's two-column-inches concerning a pothole on Sycamore Street and bulletholes in the Tractor Crossing sign along Bonnel Road; Listen Allerton's Farm News listing, in season, beef, hog, and bushel prices like box scores; Church News that formerly previewed Brother Reeves' sermon of the week, and currently in flux; School News by Mr. and Mrs. Hall noting monthly fire drills, piccolo band practice schedules, and, in season, spelling bee finalists;

202

Weather News with assumed highs and lows printed from the broken thermometer nailed to the corner of the bank; Water's Grocer with listed discounts and coupons for the previous week's unsold perishables; and lastly, *Letters-to-the-Editor,* largely fabricated with the likes of *Someone should do something about the racket leaking from church lately. Hard to sleep.*

In the end, *A Word More, by Linkum Regards* grew from two column inches to six.

"Don't offend anyone. And don't scare them. No Beasts. Just something nice, for everyone."

A House for Bo

One morning, out of the blue
Linkum thinks, while tying his shoe.
That he'll build a home, with an elaborate dome,
Where Bo can sleep, and count some sheep,
In a doghouse all his own.

Well Sport, you really wanna pursue it?
Yeah Daddy-o, let's get busy and do it.
We must unpack the box, and count the parts,
We must stack the blocks, before we starts.
We must collect our tools, as if they were jewels,
We'll paint it green, like a jelly bean.

Let's read the instructions, with all their deductions.
Connect A to B with toggled screw, and F to C with dab of glue.
X to Y to Q (see side view), then Z to F to U, and bolt it through.
Turn to the rafter pitch, by and by,
Calculate this n' that, divisible by…

> *And there you have it, just like that*
> *A house for Bo, to hang his hat.*

"Who's Bo?"

"Bo, Aunt Bim. Bo the hound."

She steadied her look and combed a finger through my hair and said, "I see."

THIRTY-FIVE

Physics, by definition: the distance an applied force has moved an object forward. The force that combines defiance with stubbornness and perhaps a blind need to clutch the sameness of a good routine as Mother applied enough force to climb the stairs with a craving for the forward movement of guaranteed results. The very addiction of that guarantee supplanting all else. Moving forward. Pushing forward. Settling not on the uncertainties of something new, something challenging, but the safe bet of more *Miss Meadowsage*. And yet, a twist of complexity. A shift, on the weight of familiar illustrations and a simple story borrowed from a Donizetti opera that ensured the income of her existing audience while tickling the edges of a new audience. Her legs were tired and her grip resisted the handrail and the steep rake of the stairs became an improbable challenge. At the landing, she paused before the dayroom window. The glass was faced with a frost that afforded an obscure view of the station wagon parked in the drive, sectioned like a prismatic puzzle into a geometry of icy triangles. Daylight had already begun to unfurl off the ridge but no sun to strike the ice with that glistening twinkle she loved as a girl. She crossed the dayroom, avoiding my soldiers, and onto the second stairwell winding narrowly to the sanctuary at the top and immediately she was at the drawing board along the window and from her working notes—her increasingly illegible journal kept on the small dayroom desk, read and reread and scrutinized years later—we know there were never any preliminaries or warm-up exercises; her pencils simply went to work, floating across the paper to shade in the fair stem of the personified flower Miss Avery and the voices began circling overhead like a slow ceiling fan and although it was a process she explored in the journals, it was never discussed aloud; there was never talk at the dinner table of her work. Her hours in the attic were more a continuation of what she had been doing since childhood than the immediacy of commissioned expectations. And yet we knew her routine, my sisters and I. The familiarity of the featherbed, the silent patience, the rewards of intimacy.

The libretto itself rested on the small table to her right, stained and dog-eared and memorized. The simplest of simple stories, as I came to understand much later, was originally proposed in a letter to her editor who two years later mentioned the Canadian. A young theatrical producer in Toronto with an interest in a collaborating production. An option, so to speak, by a brash young Canadian named Raleigh Sightsinger.

It seemed odd, at the time, that someone would go to such lengths. The story, the libretto, was openly available to anyone—composed over a century ago. So, it was the Meadowsage twist. The built-in audience. She requested an interview but the young Canadian refused to leave Canada. Their correspondence survives in a trunk against the far corner to the right of my little desk where I write this very sentence.

"Will they sing or speak their lines?"

"Talking sing. Like Broadway. It's opera, right? But not entirely operatic."

"How do you stage a flower, singing?"

"The same way they've been staging Shakespeare for centuries. Poetic license. Artistic interpretation."

"It's a love story."

206

"Yes, opera…well, they're all the same, aren't they? Forbidden love. Wrenching, tragic love. Magic potions and mistaken identities. An opera is an opera is an opera."

The illustrations progressed, gathering against the wall, scene by scene for the past three years. The physics of pushing forward, the need to be occupied, being absorbed, the predictably unpredictable efficiency of earning a living. The Roe family of the Salt Fork Valley needed the money.

Golden Rod, of a brilliant bloom and stiff noble birth, made known his affections for the young and exacting Miss Avery. River Weed, a bloomless lovelorn peasant with the strapping yet hapless lineage of an irregular, presented himself with a similar plea only to be rebuffed. Golden Rod must leave to fight the valiant wars and proposed a quick marriage. Enter the peripatetic quack Mr. Beetle with his magic love potion, etc. etc.

The morning got off to a late start and quickly the light beyond the attic window awakened. She lined in Mr. Beetle's horsecart of potions and placebos, unaware Father had entered to sit on the edge of the featherbed.

"How's it going?" he said, finally, hoping to prompt her downstairs.

She was jolted from a great distance.

"Just thought I'd see how it's going. Our visitors are gone."

"…"

"We're going overseas."

"Overseas?"

"The seeds…they'll be planted this spring upstate and the early harvest will be in Europe by July. A massive aid program that includes the world's first large-scale hybrid harvest."

But she was gone, the scene and all its infestations circling, pulling her back; the poor Weed strapped for the money to afford the expensive potion that was of course nothing more than red wine but the simple Weed was no match for Mr. Beetle's persuasive pitch as Father left

POSSESSING THE SEASONS

unnoticed and a moment later, I arrived and my own voice shattered the airspace, on the edge of the bed twiddling my thumbs, "Hey, Mom... how's it goin?"

The voices repeated themselves, the opera, over and over as she blotted the shading of a seventeenth-century dirt road. They sang to her, poor River Weed so desperate he considered signing up as a rank-and-file in Golden Rod's army for the quick cash for the costly potion for the lovely Avery for the perfect life.

It was late. She knew this. A late start, working when the others were awake and it shouldn't have surprised her that Verity and Mariah now occupied the edge of the bed, for how long?

"Max is here," Mariah said.

"They're setting up some low log fences in the barn," Verity added. "He's on the Javitts' warmblood, with his jodhpurs and crop."

"We wondered if you wanted to come watch," Mariah added, softly. "Max is putting on a show."

208

THIRTY-SIX

Mrs. Hall taught grades one through six, while Mr. Hall taught six through twelve. The younger of us occupied the cafeteria first, punctuated by the loud raucous voices of restless numbskulls. Mrs. Hall would sit alone at a table near the buffet line where she chatted with Elaborate and Reluctance, who, in normal times, would have spent their mornings preparing the organic meals from scratch, drawn from the gardens and fields of the valley but who now, this winter, spent their mornings collating and organizing the boxes of donated cellar preserves and canned goods so…well, so no one would starve to death. Fresh food was a luxury we were living without.

Conversely, Mr. Hall and his older maturing students filed in from their upstairs classrooms to occupy the same cafeteria on the heels of our departure. Mr. Hall occupying the same chair and table as his wife, but with his ever-present palm-slapping ruler to oversee the appearance of a well-behaved maturing student body who spent their lunch hour passing coded lovelorn messages beneath the tables, from table to table, coupled with the furtive glances of silent words driven by hormones bouncing off the cafeteria walls like buckshot.

209

I sat at my desk gazing at the back of Mrs. Hall's recent perm. She stood at the blackboard writing out the times tables as I thought how it was in this very classroom, at one of these same desks, when my aunts all appeared at the door, released from their respective classrooms to retrieve their baby sister on the day their mother succumbed to Tuberculosis. And again, just the following year, when their father gave in to the same hateful malady.

"Mr. Roe...are you with us today?"

I brought the equation on the blackboard into focus and said, "Eighty-one."

"Eighty-one? What does that have to do with anything?"

"I don't know, ma'am."

Mr. Roe, take a seat at the window...your back to the class, while the rest of us continue with the business of learning."

"Now...Mr. Roe."

I shuffled to the dunce's seat by the window, and the classroom, its very existence, faded away like white noise. I stared out through the glass at a day that encouraged daydreams, a day expressing itself with an unimaginable front blown in during the night off the Appalachians to sweep the endless open plains of the Midwest and suddenly, for the first time in five months, there was a blue cloudless ceiling over the valley. The temperature was estimated in the low to high forties and the plates of frozen dew accumulating since November were likely mulling over the idea of a general melt. There had, for three winters running, been no snowfalls, no drifts of powdery buildups gone stiff and icy, possessing the season like an unremitting bully.

And this year, as in the past three years, the meltdown would come in a matter of hours. By lunch, the ground would be exposed to a wet muddy slush that would have some of the farmers convinced, in an emotional show of unfounded optimism sparked by the mud on their boots, that the watertable was brimming and the cold gray days of a wretched winter were behind them.

THIRTY-SEVEN

We have a problem. A rather large problem. Little Mademoiselle stands before the long mirror in the long bath off the bedroom Acceptance and I shared for fifty-two years before I recently retreated to my old twin mattress upstairs with its comforting presence against the window overlooking my heaven on earth.

She's frustrated. She's in tears. Standing in a skirt of some sort, a ballerina's tutu adorned with sparkling glittering pins reflecting off the overhead lighting and a vest of some sort embroidered with sequins also sparkling and glittering in a confusing mesh to collide with the reflecting pins on her skirt. Her hair is host to a series of embellishing bows and ribbons in bright primary colors, almost luminescent, and for a moment, I'm disoriented: the tears and reflections and colliding colors—the magnitude of this overshadowing the immediacy of our problem.

The buttons on her vest don't appear to be cooperating with her efforts and she stomps her foot and yells something and marches away from the mirror toward the door, issuing exhalations and ultimatums and I watch her, my little Buttonhead, and when she calms, I coax her back to the mirror and run my old fingers, ravaged by decades of use, over the sparkling buttons of the vest.

"Everything's backwards in the mirror, Maddy," I say, quietly, calmly, with that most reassuring voice she seems to require.

She ponders this thought for a moment, rolling it through her little mind and suddenly turns around, with her back to the mirror, and quickly buttons her vest and skips out the door, pausing to throw back a "Tank you, Poppa."

There are more of them than I can count. I sometimes lose count. Dust and Sally's boys and their grandkids. Verdi and Bump's, and Mariah and Buddy's. It can't be that hard, keeping track. But I lose my way. Not in and around the house, but with particulars. Reflecting sequins. Names. The thread of any but the shortest conversations. I spend time with thoughts drawn from seventy-five years ago, as clear and unremitting as a photograph while stumbling over who currently occupies the White House or that Mademoiselle's nickname is a nickname and I sometimes forget what her actual name is.

I cry. Without warning. Not because I'm sad, or because I've stubbed my toe, but because the once taut tendons controlling my tear ducts have slackened, loosening their grip.

THIRTY-EIGHT

They return, my league of officials, intent on my company, my recollections. Their disguises don't fool me. The waxed nylon mustaches and corn tassel hairpieces and lips of melting molded clay and plastic shoulder holsters with little revolvers carved from prison soap, painted black. Black as a gun. Do they know I was raised on paint fumes, solvents, oils?

"Relax. We're not conducting a criminal investigation, Mr. Roe."

"..."

"Nothing like that."

"..."

"There was a movement, a vanguard of futurists who long ago sought to tackle a population explosion, feeding a global population that was growing exponentially."

"..."

"Your father, well, everything leads back to him. To his tenure in graduate school at Champaign and of course the ensuing developments here, on this farm. Ground zero."

"..."

"Can I help, Mr. Roe? With your buttons?"

"..."

"There. All good."

213

POSSESSING THE SEASONS

"…"

"So, as I was saying, your father held the patents. The stakes were high."

"Patents. Yes…patents were important."

"They served their purpose. They were successful. The original hybrid crops and the ensuing genetically modified foods that fed the world. That, unfortunately, continue to feed the world."

"…?"

"On a global scale, there are consequences. Long-term consequences that have proven to be nearly impossible to reverse."

"…"

"It's complicated. If we begin with the grain production, modified with chemical additives and hormones to boost the harvest and repel the normal insect infestations. The grain that in turn feeds the beef, poultry, pork, and lamb productions worldwide, as well as the grain itself—what cereals and breads we eat. The DNA of those grains was changed, altered, and while it undoubtedly increased production, it also robbed the grain of its inherent nutrients, reducing the nutrients of the beef, poultry, pork, and lamb markets that were in turn robbed even further with the infusion of additional hormones and chemical additives. The same is true with the fruit and vegetables, his original modified genetics from his famous West Field Experiments.

"So, convincing those who feed themselves from a drive-up window or from the aisles of processed foods in the supermarket how they are starving themselves of the nutrients a body needs, has become a focus of the World Health Organization, where we're also confronted with an alarming spike over seventy years of how those same additives have led to a myriad of ensuing diseases such as cancer…the price we've paid. The price we're all still paying."

"…"

"Can I help, Mr. Roe? Do you need a tissue?"

"…"

"There. All good."

"As I was saying…there's more. The altered genetics of that grain in the field suspends the normal photosynthesis of a plant that no longer releases carbon monoxide

CHARLES PROWELL

into the atmosphere, that in turn reduces the very oxygen we breathe. This impacts the atmosphere, the ozone layer, and it's the ozone layer that impacts our climate.

"The fields of grain, millions and millions of acres across the globe harvesting hybrid and genetically modified crops, draining those chemicals and additives into the creeks and rivers with every rainfall—the erosion of the soil with rainfalls. This then impacts not only the ecosystems of our rivers and lakes, the fish we eat, but the watertables beneath the bedrock. It connects us all, like an airborne infectious disease, spilling into the oceans from continent to continent. The WHO, as you can imagine, is between a rock and a hard place, so to speak. How to reverse a phenomenon your father started seventy years ago. How to even contemplate such a task."

"I see."

"So, what interests us is how he convinced one of the few truly organic farming communities at the time…an insulated, unique community in itself…to have gone down this road. Even briefly."

"Would you like some lunch?"

"Lunch?"

"It's lunchtime."

"All we really have is you, and of course, your own logs. The science is spelled out clearly in his logs, or those that survived, but yours, well…they've provided us with a cultural glimpse into that world. A broader perspective. A narrative, really."

"…"

"But, honestly, your logs…it's sometimes hard to separate fact from fiction. Which leaves us with you. Face to face. There's only you. Not what you've written, but you yourself. Only you can separate the facts. Do you understand?"

"Is lunch ready?"

"Lunch?"

"Lunch."

"One last thing. Do you know what happened to his missing logs? There's a gap. A rather large gap of multiple volumes from what is archived at the University."

"Lunch ready, Poppa…POPPA!"

215

THIRTY-NINE

Over the years, recollections and memories and conflicting fabrications trickled into conversations that quickly became common fodder among us all until there were no secrets left. Until, as always, we all knew what everyone else knew.

That afternoon, as opposed to any other afternoon, with the light short on the horizon, Verity, Bump, Acceptance, and I made our way along Pond Road to straddle its width in a march toward the Arthurs' empty house. Less a march, actually, than a casual stroll in the sun-bouyed air of a surprisingly forgiving sky.

Within view, beyond our front lawn where the riverfront pasture fell away to a floodplain and the roadbed rose to an elevated overlook, Father and Mother walked hand in hand along the fenced lawn toward where Clare and Max stood waiting on Slave Hill, all of them appearing delighted with the mild temperatures of an agreeable southerly.

Never before had Clare known a man so caring and gracious and gentle as her Max. Never before—as she had always made so very very clear, repeatedly, and in the event we weren't listening, amplified with the cupped hand of a megaphone—never had she felt the way she felt in this man's presence. A wholeness. The pieces of her existence falling into place with a sense of belonging that was, well...whole. She slipped her hand through his arm and tugged him playfully[10].

Ahead, beyond the bridge, Buddy's family sedan sauntered through Snead's Corner, cruising with the windows down and Mariah's hair lifting in wisps, flushed like tall grass in a breeze. They sat *close*, she would later recall, when among adults and after that glass or two of wine. Her head *close* against his shoulder.

Coming from town in their aging Plymouth, the twins putted along Bonnel Road with Elizabeth bent over the steering wheel so intent on not leaving the road for the gullied washes and Madeline's sinewy hands braced against the dash and I've allowed myself the comeuppance of a distanced license with my twin aunts because, well...history becomes creditable only when written. So, the insurgent pastors were on a mission in light of the recent and rising opposition from neighboring congregations and the letter from the national chapter regarding their unorthodox misinterpretations and this, this annoying little thing with ordainment. The old Arthur place had been empty for months now and perhaps with a little fussing...and a delicate appeal to Mr. Arthur's devoutness...whatever that was. Really, neither of them had a clue what the Amish believed but could it be that different? Wasn't everything pretty much born from the truest denomination? Well, the sun was out and the air was warm and in her mind Elizabeth pictured a sprawling profitable campus with out-buildings and garden altars and guest dignitaries like pious headliners for these longish retreats booked years in advance with the two of them gliding about their grounds like praying prima donnas.

And from the south, with our country roads fast approaching a congested vortex, Ruby piloted her smoking MG along Deere Road one

---

10. *Decades later, Clare's daughter registered for an online DNA site to discover her father Max was drawn not from austrian heritage or australian heritage or french heritage but, surprisingly, from Moingwena or Shawnee heritage. The high cheekbones and Cherokee-red coloring the result of certain and expected cross-breeding among the early hands migrating up from Mississippi. Hence the horsemanship. The statuesque bearing. It all made sense. Her mother, Clare, was pleased with the revelation.*

day exactly from a short fix and electrifying zap within those crumbling brick walls over in Anna. The top was down, her hair was a tangled mess, the air was fresh, and the sun was gloriously recuperative. Not far behind but close enough, Diligence Wiseman could be on a call from someone, anyone, requiring his widgets and augers.

I moved ahead of the others, stripping off my sweatshirt and standing to my hands to walk along the roadbed with my palms feeling the composite of the cold tamped grade and when I returned to my feet it was with a slight bounce, a lift, as if to usher in the changing air. As if to claim my inherited heaven with a sovereignty beyond question. Or perhaps just showing off for Acceptance.

Mariah ran her hand along Buddy's sleeve. He piloted the sedan at the pace of a slow walk, turning to Mariah and getting lost in her eyes.

Stay calm, Ruby Doll. Don't lose him. Don't go overboard. Don't scare'm off.

Diligence closed the gap and tapped the rear bumper, unable to restrain himself and Ruby Doll tilted her head back, the yellow scarf whipping like a wind sock and she laughed aloud, throwing up an arm, beckoning him on.

"*Buy it?* We're not *buying* anything," Elizabeth said, taking the turn onto Deere Road as if delivering a load of fresh eggs. She straightened the wheel like cranking a stiff valve, squaring to the road and shuffling herself to get comfortable with the narrow paving, the potholes and holidays that bobbed the plastic Jesus on the dash.

"Well, what then?"

"We'll charm him."

"*Charm* him?"

"For heaven's sake, Madeline…were you born yesterday? Two attractive single women. And Givens not the only one…there are others who find us attractive."

"There are?"

"Mr. Arthur's old and his wife has been gone now for several months and Amish men, they must have needs, too."

"So, we'll charm him into giving us his farm? Is that your plan?"

A partnership, I was thinking. An Amish/Anabaptist retreat. The Pond/Arthur Colony of Prayer and…and, something."

Elizabeth spread her open palms to frame the envisioned logo and nearly ran off the road.

Clare and Max and Father and Mother strolled down off the Hill and along the subsidy field to approach the river. From the thicket, Harlan's voice and a low howling bass note floated and lingered with an ecclesiastical timbre.

On the bridge, leaning against the iron railing overlooking the thicket below, Verity issued a responding note that drifted down to the ice with a resonance that bounced and ricocheted toward the harmonizing chorus upriver.

Ruby slowed for the bridge and passed beneath the overhead trellis with its shadowing lines running up and along the MG, waving to us pressed to the railing and I looked to see if it was the good Ruby or the not-so-good Ruby. Diligence threw out a lazy wave but not a smile or a hint of recognition and as they finished the bridge, Ruby accelerated and Diligence throttled and in a moment they were gone, disappearing into the depression of the road.

The old barn still held that rich odor peculiar to draft horses. An empty cavern now, a big open cave penetrated by the Faller sedan like one century infiltrating another. Buddy killed the engine and stepped out of the car to close off the big barn doors. He returned to Mariah and for a moment they sat, wrapped in a hidden silence.

Just beyond the planks of the barn, the MG sputtered and purred to the Wiseman's idling truck that parked behind the outer grain barn. They walked together across the deserted barnyard toward the house with the prancing gaiety of a mad ritual.

Moments later, the Plymouth rolled abreast of the unpainted and unadorned two-story house and for a moment they stared upon its façade like a couple of carpetbaggers sizing up the big score. Paint. Curtains. Flowers. Charming meandering pathways threaded with marigolds and cattails punctuated with those adorable Jesus statuaries flanked by prayer benches and wailing pergolas draped in pigtails of cannas and morning glories. They turned into the drive and onto the front lawn and around the side of the house as if circling an opponent as Acceptance and I approached the dirt driveway. Thirty yards back, Verity walked laced to Bump's arm softly singing and humming the remnants of a duet started on the bridge and when they reached us, the four of us walked together, passing the Arthur house with complete indifference, just as the lower bedroom door would have closed and just as Mr. Arthur would have finished up the day's work packing up more of his wife's belongings to descend the stairs and leave the house, just as the twins would have entered off the side kitchen door.

Mr. Arthur traversed the fallow field toward the river, unaware that his empty house and barn were at the center of a convoluted whirlpool as he treaded along the crest of the furrows, avoiding the muddied dales. He crossed the river at the felled sycamore, as wide as a sidewalk, and joined the others, Mother and Father and Clare and Max, and together they climbed the rise off the lower pasture toward the house.

It was a sunny day in the neighborhood. The first sunny day in five months.

FORTY

We gathered on a late afternoon at Aunt Dee's. The weather holding through the week, drawn to that porch in the heart of the heart of a socializing swirl centered in the center of a Fall Ridge brimming with survivors. There were passersby, strollers, the Boughmans from their own porch across the street, the Widow Drew with her chattering grandson next door, and there was the sunset, gazed upon every few minutes as if it were a rare and magical phenomenon. The gray veil of winter beaten off with the blessed authority of what was suddenly everyone's favorite color, a bluest of blue feathered along the horizon just above the Boughmans' roofline with a harmless wisp of character, a windwhipped thread of clouds stranded over the naked hickory limbs. The wet defrosting lawns up and down the street gleamed with that iridescence of a fragile March.

Sheriff wore an odd floral-patterned vest and smoked a cigar he quickly set aside as a failed experiment and I fingered it, this wet bulbous sausage until he set his copy of the Gazette on his lap and waved me away and brought out the coin, dancing it across his knuckles.

Aunt Dee sat smiling with the officially unofficial news of the wedding made unofficially public as she negotiated a paying apprenticeship with Mariah who pushed the negotiations toward her own pattern table and

221

a subsidiary division of Pond Alterations that divided and demarcated *(her word)* the current aging constituency *(her word)* from a newer younger clientele *(her word).*

Bim sat beside me on the swing, her fingers still smeared in printer's ink, listening for Sheriff's comments on the new layout following Dee's quip how the new Gazette is bordering on becoming a sideshow while I wondered why those passing along the walk or the Boughmans' across the street or the Widow on her porch or anyone, anywhere, hadn't made a mention of Bo's House. *A House for Bo.*

Verity grilled Max on Thoroughbreds and Arabians and Morgans and Tennessee Walkers and the idea of a show, an equestrian trial with jumps and vaulting while Clare and Mother stood to wave the newest townies Guy and Dolores off the walk and onto the porch and quickly Father had an audience in Guy regarding the seeds in Europe and as Max moved to sit in on their conversation, Verity hummed a familiar melody, floating through the porch and across the street in a mezzo octave to dance along the bars as Clare and Mother and Dolores sang along, which presented an opportunity for the twins to try their recent vocal rehearsals held, so far, in the privacy of their shared kitchen and the discordance of that harmony returned the porch to a momentary pause. A brief silence.

Eventually, Dee's voice, "I hear the weather over to Evansville is nice. Holding sunny," she referred without directly referring to the late Dr. Steadfast Stewart's replacement and Mother nodded. Father nodded. Everyone nodded, and the silence returned.

Eventually, turning to the twins, Dee's voice, "Now youse two've been to Ind'ana, haven't you?"

"Ind'ana?" Madeline asked, looking at Elizabeth and then back to Dee. "No…no, I don't believe the good Lord has ever led us in that direction. Not so pretty as Salt Fork, I hear."

"No," Elizabeth said. "Salt Fork is prettier, they say."

"Well, I've heard it is flatter in Ind'ana," Dee said, turning now to Bim.

CHARLES PROWELL

"Is that what you've heard?" Bim said, flatly.

"I had an order from French Lick once," Dee said.

"French what?"

"French Lick. French Lick, Ind'ana."

"French Lick," Bim repeated, slowly. "Sounds like a shanty along the Ohio. But it's a town, you say…and flat?"

"Flat as your…"

FORTY-ONE

Because we had clear skies and mild temperatures that held, all that separated the seasons had come down to the ice on the river. For days running, we paused on the walk home from Eart's bus stop, studying the icepack. In the near distance were the sounds of machinery, of tractors being tuned with the optimism of an early start, of Givens and Liberty Snead jump-starting everyone with the scent of fresh-tilled earth that carried up the road like a drug. But seed was expensive, traditional seed, bought by the bushel from Allerton Feed at the risk of a blindsiding late freeze, or a spring without rain.

And yet not everyone was on board with Allerton Feed. In a rousing debate at Davis' Café, over a limited menu of potatoes and eggs, they debated aloud as if we weren't present. Father and Guy and Bump and myself occupied our booth by the window as they argued, bandying the tiresome hocus pocus talk against what worked. Quicker more robust harvests of drought-resistant barley and alfalfa, and the seed was free. Roe there was offering his seed for free.

The gold doubloons. The seeds of fortune.

"But either everone's in, or no one."

They nodded. Everyone nodded but Listen Allerton, whose seed sales hung in the balance.

224

"There's that drift," Liberty Snead said, glancing at Givens and then over to the booth, to Guy. "We saw what it does to an organic crop. So, it's all Roe's seed, or..."

"I ain't touch'n it," Givens Marsh's voice rose loud, and settled gradually as the Café went silent.

And from Liberty, "So you're willing to risk it, Givens? A fourth year without weather?"

"How bout the soil?" It was Listen, speaking for the first time. He turned to look at Father, raising an eyebrow while waiting for an answer. Everyone waited.

"What will it do to our topsoil, Hank?"

Father made a face and shrugged and said, quietly, "I don't know, for sure. There's only been the one half-season crop, this last year. I don't have data on successive harvests. There's residue, detectable traces in our north and east field soil horizons, but that may be good thing. It's having an impact on our insect population. A sort of built-in defense against weevils, locusts, generally the insect ecosystem."

"Data...is that *information?*"

"Correct."

Wisps of pipe smoke lingered like high clouds, layers of smoke in a room with no current, dangling like clouds.

"We go down this road, Henry Roe, and..."

The sentence was left unfinished, left to linger with the clouds.

"So, what about me?" It was Listen Allerton, whose fifth generation Seed and Feed had, in the course of a conversation, been decimated.

"You took care of us, Listen. We'll take care of you."

We paused on the bridge. A mid-week afternoon. I set my books down and grabbed a stone and slung it thirty yards upriver.

"What are you doing?"

"I'm throwin, Verdi. What's it looks like?"

"Well, don't throw it. Drop it, like always. Just drop it."

It was Mariah's system, from years past and to be played out when it was neither winter nor spring. Control the variables. Standardize the size of the stones and the distance of the fall every afternoon. You could judge the thickness of the ice by the sound of the stone on impact. Just a game, something to do, dropping stones and listening as they clink the ice with a pitch that grew hollower with each passing day. The anticipation of that changing clink.

I set a larger stone the size of my fist on the oak plank cantilevered out over the river, our summer diving board, and gently pushed it off the edge and Verity said, "I could hardly hear it. Try again."

I tried again. And again, but the sound of Givens' tractor overwhelmed the variables of our test.

We stood listening, watching Givens, thinking how everything would soon change; the gray idle days of winter were gone and before long, the valley would be brimming with an activity that extended clear to mid-September.

I turned to Verity and as a single long word slurred together as a single sentence, I said, "You and Bump are always together."

She looked at me with a face that said nothing.

"It's true. You are."

"So what, Jussie? He's my friend, too."

I glanced at the ice, wondering if I was supposed to spend time with Acceptance the way Bump was spending time with Verity. She was fourteen now. Bump was thirteen. Me, well, technically, I was barely twelve.

We lingered, in no hurry to go anywhere.

"So, what do you talk about?"

"With Bump? Stuff. Just stuff."

"What kind of stuff?"

"Regular stuff, Jussie…like always."

"I don't know what *regular stuff* is. Sometimes I don't know what to say."

"Just say regular stuff."

"Do you always hold hands?"

She shrugged and looked away and said, "Sometimes."

"Well, do you kiss?"

"Maybe we do and maybe we don't. It's none of your business."

"So, you kiss?"

"It's none of your business, Jussie. You're just a kid."

The word *kid* was like drawing from her scabbard a long sharp sword. The walls went up and my tone changed and I said, "So, you hold hands *while* you're kissing?"

"Shut up, Jussie."

I puckered my lips and she shot back, "You don't understand, Jussie. You're just a kid. You still play with toy soldiers."

The problem with sisters. The problem with sisters according to the *Manual of Battleground Maneuvers,* is how one is forever opening oneself to the fatal jab. They alone know where and when to strike. So, one must always be prepared. Know your enemy's position and their strengths and when to raise the drawbridge. By this single thrust from Verity, I was felled to the canvas, dropped like those bodies scattered across Antietam. Ashamed, suddenly ashamed of my toy soldiers.

A long silence and I suddenly stood and said, "I think it's ready."

"What?"

"The ice…it's ready to go."

She looked at the river and to me and because she had the same sense of order and routine as Father, the calculating patience of a scientist, I expected resistance. Verity was procedure; the clothes in her bureau were folded and separated as neatly as dinner napkins; the horses displayed along the shelf above her bed were arranged like items in a museum; the bedsheets were folded back every morning, tucked into place and the wrinkles smoothed away.

"We should wait. Mariah's not even here."

I stood to my feet. "Who cares?"

"Mariah's not here and Bump's not here and we need to wait for them. Saturday. We'll do it on Saturday."

I turned away toward the end of the bridge. Verity wasn't Mariah and it was possible, at times, to summon the strength to overcome the pecking order between us.

Off the road was a rock the size of a pumpkin we had spent more than an hour maneuvering up from the gully a week earlier. A boulder, really. The great emancipator. I began rolling it from the gravel onto the bridgeplanks, panting. I stopped and looked up at Verity standing, blocking my progress.

"Are you helping, or what?"

"I told you to wait!"

"I'm not *waiting*, Verdi."

"I'm not *moving*, Jussie."

She stood with her feet spread and her hands on her hips and I yelled, "Fine!"

To give in now was unthinkable; I rolled it a full revolution, an oblong boulder that came to my knees and with each full turn it teetered, before thundering against the flatter edge with an impact that shook the bridge.

"I'm not *moo*-ving, Justus Charles."

"I'm not *stop*-ping, Verdi Lee."

She stood planted, within distance of one more turn, and I understood the real issue had gone beyond dropping rocks from the bridge, beyond the passing of winter into spring. It was Verity, defending her birthplace and her hierarchy of power and my own determination to advance my ranking with whatever means were necessary.

I heaved the boulder another turn and stopped at her feet, balancing it on the crest of the flat edge, breathing so heavily I could no longer hear Givens' tractor.

"Get away."

"No chance."

And it was then she slapped me with an open hand across the face and I let go. The boulder rolled forward onto her foot and against her shinbone and she fell to the planks. There was a short whimpering cry, like a muskrat caught in a springtrap and for a moment, I hesitated, watching her as if to say, *You okay?*

But the moment was brief. She stared up at me angrily, panting and wheezing as I braced my weight and hoisted the boulder forward, digging in, stepping over Verity and another turn and a third turn and she was on her feet, throwing her cobbled weight against the opposite side of the boulder, resisting, leaning parallel to the bridge when the boulder took an awkward turn and I lost my footing, grasping for a hold but it was too late. The boulder dropped, and I followed.

What I remember is how time stopped. For what seemed an eternity, I watched Verity up on the diving plank, her face and the explosion of the boulder on the ice and then me on the ice and hanging to the edge of the ice as my legs dangled about in the cold current. And then I was under.

Darkness. There was that darkness. And the current. And the fleeting thought of death and what Meek Faller must have been thinking as he slipped through the log jam with a last parting glance at a blue sky. I'd rather not think about it, even more so write about it, as writing thoughts longhand is to wallow in slow motion. So often it's returned, my own fall, forced to relive it in the middle of an otherwise restful sleep. How the decades haven't diminished the pounding heartbeat and the adrenalin of touching the bottom, the sludge that gathered around my boots and the force of the current. I pushed off, but it wasn't like the diving plank, thrusting off the bottom of the river in the summer. In the summer, you could linger on the bottom, wallowing nearly naked in the tepid water and push off anywhere, with raised arms, triumphant.

My wet jeans and jacket clung to my skin, and the weight of my boots as I coiled and thrust and felt the ice bump the top of my head. I opened my eyes to almost total darkness, scanning for the light of the hole and began working against the current, through the sludge like climbing a sand dune in a windstorm but the jacket was heavy and the boots were heavy and my jeans were like wet plaster.

At the hole, I could hear the sound of ice cracking, moving and shifting like a log jam and I thought how I was possibly not God's special little boy, that I was no different than the crows and the muskrats or Mrs. Arthur.

I straddled a riverbottom boulder with my knees, running short of breath, holding my position, gripping it, resisting the current, glancing up to find the light and shoving off yet again and suddenly I was clinging to the edge of the ice, gasping for air.

Verity was there, splayed out on her stomach to balance her weight from the shifting ice.

I grabbed a hand and thought how her entire sleeve was wet to the shoulders. I shimmied up, carefully, slowly, rolling onto the ice numb and frozen and shaking from exhaustion and thinking I had cheated death.

On the bank, collapsing against the slope of the mud, we lay for a full minute without a word before I sat up, still dizzy, when I noticed her sock, her lower leg, smeared in blood.

"I'll go get Dad."

She grabbed my sleeve and said, "No. No, I want to watch it."

"I should get Dad."

"I thought you were dead, Jussie."

I stood beside her for a while, peeling away my jacket and my boots and for twenty minutes, as I jogged in place, swinging my arms and legs, shivering, still flushed with adrenalin, we watched with the last of the sunlit warmth bearing down off the ridge as the ice heaved and separated into a series of huge floes, divorced from the hold of winter. Within minutes, it seemed, the river was a traffic jam of ice chunks moving and colliding like bumper cars.

The sound of the truck carried from off the house, leaving the drive, hurtling toward the bridge. There would be trouble to pay. I glanced at Verity, at her bloody ankle. But you never knew with Verity; her eyes were hard and dry and we watched, without speaking, as one season passed into another.

A week later, the ice was nearly gone, reduced to fragments. The current reasserted itself to pass through the gorge in Kickapoo Ridge and beyond Salt Fork to Gallatin County. Our most precious resource belonged to the great Ohio, just south of its confluence with the Wabash and ultimately empty into the Mississippi and there would be no getting it back. By then it belonged to the hardscrabble farms of Tennessee and Missouri, to the cotton fields of Arkansas and Louisiana before eventually emptying into the Mississippi Delta. From the Delta, it was as gone as gone can be.

It was the end of March. The valley would soon be crawling with the field hands up from Cairo, lining the morning roadsides, waiting for work, hoping to be housed and fed in any one of the historical safe houses appointed along the higher bluffs for easy sighting. Laney and Septimus had already arrived, claiming the best cots near the two windows along opposite walls for the deep summer cross-breeze as Mr. Arthur promptly moved from the Quarters into Aunt Dee's old bedroom off the upstairs dayroom. From my own bedside window, I would soon wake to the sight of the first campfires flickering from under the bridge.

FORTY-TWO

Mother's work continued. The illustrations grew more complex and she would raise back from the board and wonder aloud, mumbling to herself, if the built-in audience of eight-year-olds was being left behind. What seemed a simple story, a stolen story, had grown over the past three years to encompass the intricacy of rivalry, of simple love mired in a convolution of mishaps and misunderstandings and mistaken assumptions. 'Eight-year-olds. *Eight-year-olds, Gracie,*' she reminded herself. Why was it taking so long? Abridging Donizetti's story without the complexity of its hypocrisy and false promises and she was left with no story. No story, no illustrations, no book. Three years into this. A bedrock of routine and the discipline of work that found her in the attic where the dopey River Weed was now enlisted in Golden Rod's army but the scheming was rampant, the conspiring stacked by layers as the enlistment pay went to Mr. Beetle for more magic love potion, more elixir, and Mr. Beetle sang the elixir's guarantee in a voice so low and graveled, spilling out rapidly in a charlatan's spiel against Weed's accompanying sweet innocent tenor, the voice of a young man in love.

Her pencil was an extension of the drifting music she had of course learned by heart. It floated with a practiced obedience. The music lingered and buoyed. She shaded and hummed, moving further and further away from her devoted readership.

She straightened, considering the perspective, as Miss Avery gave in with a conflicting acquiescence to the dashing soldier, the braggadocio of a steam-rolling Golden Rod who filled one corner of the sprawling attic with the measure of his conquest and from another corner, Avery's longings for the hapless suitor River Weed with the gift of *true* love. A dinner feast had been set to formalize the announcement and Weed raced the clock to administer more potion…but wait! The maidens of the village heard word of an uncle's death leaving poor Weed as heir and in their sudden kindness and pointed flirtations, he mistook the effects of the love potion, as Mother suddenly paused, leaning away from the drawing board, catching her breath. For a moment, she lost track of time, decades of time, and became herself as an eight-year-old in the same attic where she long ago wrote her little poems and drew her little drawings, waiting for Dolores to arrive from the bus stop and those days when she couldn't breathe, when breathing itself was a mountainous effort. Lungs clustered with shattered glass, waiting for Dolores, or her sisters, or her grandmother laboring up the winding stairs on the hour, encouraging the more accessible daybed in the lower dayroom with the windows overlooking the gardens and the fields.

She stood from her chair, carefully. The chair fell back. It struck the floor with a clap. Where was Dolores? Wasn't school out by now? Where were her sisters? Where was Ma? She scraped her slippered feet across the floorboards and let herself onto the featherbed, an invertebrate rolling into the cloud. Closing her eyes as I left to fetch Father or Clare.

Outside, beyond the attic window, the universe was awakening from a long nap. Forty-four of the forty-seven farms were breaking ground with the synchronicity of a choreographed dance, the synchronicity of a farmer's intuition as their tractor disks were hitched and rotating, arrowheads resurfacing to glitter the fields like sequins, all of it a clattering racket nothing short of a symphony.

Mariah pleaded sick and remained home from school, not leaving her room for the entire day. Clare had her suspicions, providing soup and an attentive disposition. On two occasions, Clare knocked and entered to sit on the edge of the bed, testing for a fever and inquiring toward symptoms but there was no getting anything beyond grunts and a distant look. Mariah seemed fine…except Mariah *didn't* seem fine.

The twins arrived with new linens for Mr. Arthur's new arrangement in Dee's long vacant bedroom. Fresh new linens tucked tight as a drumskin and a thin bedside bouquet of early mustard flowers and a platter of slightly burnt crumb cake left like a calling card on the small spartan table against the west window overlooking the barnyard. They lingered, chatting with Verity, waiting, but Mr. Arthur had lately found an interest in not only the house gardens, tilling immaculate furrows with a hand hoe, but the knowing business of keeping the peach grove pruned. The twins scuttled away, disappointed, but as they made their way out onto the long drive as I passed through the barnyard, Madeline peered toward the grove, unnoticed by Elizabeth as she caught and held Mr. Arthur's returning gaze through the leafless foliage.

From the barn I watched them pulling away from the drive as Mr. Arthur coincidently reappeared from the coverage of the grove and I turned to Father, shadowing him, matching his steps.

"Hey Dad, you got any heroes?"

"Heroes. What do you mean, *heroes?*"

"I reckon I mean *hee*-ros."

A March southerly carried up from the lowlands, careening off the tableland and whipping against the side of the barn to penetrate the missing planks.

I stood braced to the west wall and said, "We gotta get some repairs, Dad."

"We will, and I always admired that Thomas Jefferson."

"Good one. Our third president and an honorable man...with slaves."

"Well, no one's perfect."

"That's a big one, Dad. Slaves. You might want to think about it."

"I like him all the same, Sport."

"It's a problem, Dad...cause mine's Linkum and he was against slavery."

"That's *Lincoln*, son. Not *Linkum*, and haven't we been over this ground?"

"You can't get over owning someone. It's bondage, Dad. That's all about the Quarters, and the old graves on Slave Hill. The Safe House... ole True Pond and the others staked off with their yellow flags."

I could see he was lost in thought, reminded of how he wasn't linked to True Pond. I changed the subject.

"Jefferson wrote a good bible."

He was still away and I thought how he was a part of us, but never a part of us.

"All the right stuff but none of the silly stuff," I added.

He nodded.

I waited and waited some more and finally asked, "How come you're not religious, Dad?"

He looked at me, from somewhere far far away.

"Religious?"

"How come?"

"How come, what?"

"You know, Dad. How come you don't come to church?"

"Because...just because."

"No, really…"

He stood, studying the gaps in the barn wall, as if pondering Whalen Badger's big bandsaw over to Carrier Mills.

"Religion…religion is about faith, son…moral faith."

"Moral…right."

"We all have that. We're born with that. Going to church shouldn't be what keeps any of us from losing our moral footing…from being bad instead of good."

"Sure."

"So, church is okay. Just not necessarily necessary."

"Church is *necessarily*, Dad. It helps remind us."

He tapped a loose plank with his boot and said, "We'll have Whalen mill up the missing planks and get Septimus to put the barn back together."

"Septimus. He's a good hand…and he knows carpentry."

We made our way from the barn to pause at the sliding doors and he turned to me and said, "Well then, maybe I'll come along one of these days. Would you like that?"

"I'd like that, Dad."

FORTY-THREE

Because Mrs. Hall was sick, Mr. Hall assigned a lesson in the upstairs classroom and then walked down the stairs to spend thirty minutes in our classroom and then back upstairs and then back downstairs all day long back and forth.

He stood at the blackboard, catching his breath, tapping the slate with his menacing ruler on our subject this morning of economics.

"Our economy is based on a balance of trade. Goods for commodities. Money, in itself, is just a medium. But when the balance falters, continues to falter over an extended period, and currency, this token of exchange, begins to disappear…what are we left with? Mr. Roe?"

I sat silent, waiting. It was a game. Mr. Hall's inappropriate little game.

"Mr. Roe…we're waiting."

A stupid game by a stupid man wagging his stupid ruler who didn't understand the protocols, who didn't understand how today of all days, there was only optimism.

An impasse that lasted thirty seconds before I straightened and brought my hands down onto the desktop with a slap and said, "RAIN! We're left with rain, Mr. Hall. Lots of it."

POSSESSING THE SEASONS

A few nervous giggles rippled through the classroom but I held my ground, staring into Mr. Hall's eyes, refusing to explain how there would be no going to Florida or buying a nice house in town. It would be a buyer's market with farms going for twenty cents on the dollar and nothing would ever be the same. It was Father's seeds, or nothing.

But no one was saying as much. It was a subject reserved for prayers, not open discussion, and Mr. Hall's flirtations with doom were simply not allowed. Not now, not in March, nor April, nor even June. Not this year.

FORTY-FOUR

The twins went out on a limb and announced future productions would assemble at the old Arthur place. What they failed to mention was the recent ruling from the National Anabaptist Coalition.

New collection bowls were set just inside the church front doors occupying the center of the aisle, forcing the congregation to maneuver the obstruction like an obstacle course. Stiffing the donation was now a public act, no longer obscured by the protection of a pew. Bright floral colors in a ceramic-fired medium, covered by a black fabric screen with an open slot to accept deposits as if it were a ticket window. Because of the screen, only the twins were privy to the profit margins of what was beginning to seem more business than religion.

We waited in pews that had been striped and numbered like bleachers in a ballpark. Specific rows marked by red crosses along those aisles reserved for parishioners, with the remaining pews and side aisles and the back of the church for those visiting from outside the county line, foreigners invading our private sanctum as nothing less than a blatant intrusion. A standing room crowd, pressed with the idly curious, or the identifiable land speculators posing as something else, suffering through a sermonic narrative that ultimately settled into a production overseen from stage left by the magisterial Mariah to include a seven-member choir belting out a boogie woogie melody closer to an off-broadway musical than a service.

It ended with an announcement that a forthcoming announcement would be made to announce the premiere of the Pond Arthur Center for Religious Theatrics. And as we began spilling out, making toward the basement buffet, it was Pat Davis, from the Café, who approached the pulpit in his spring seersucker, the girth of his thick neck spilling over his collar.

"Does old Arthur know bout this?"

From the steps outside the doors, heading for the buffet, Verity and I turned back to see Mr. Hall waving his raised arm as if in class, "Has there been any news with the new preacher?"

And from somewhere amongst a crowd still shuffling in place, reluctant to leave, Aunt Dee and Aunt Bim called out, raising their voices like camouflaged snipers.

"No more boogie woogie!"

"We want preachin!"

"Good ole time preachin!"

Marian Snead took the pulpit and as Chairman of the Deacon Wives' Committee, she raised her hands and restored order and spoke, "Our Pastor Search Committee is currently interviewing through the Seminary at Carbondale and hope to call a resolution by the end of the month."

Bim scuttled along the back wall and from a crouch, called out "Godspeed!" before moving unnoticed out the side door and into Dee's awaiting car and in their break-away, we watched them laughing so hard that when Dee braked and swerved at the cemetery to avoid a slithering copperhead, she nearly ran the sedan into the ditch.

Inside the church, Mariah hadn't moved. Sitting off to one side of the stage, she appeared immune to the turning tide. Her time was short and what did she care? An audience of farmers, after all.

240

CHARLES PROWELL

With an entire month of April Sundays looming vacant, the church emptied in a sea of questioning voices and conversations not unlike the sound of August crickets and mating bullfrogs, maneuvering around the new collection bowls positioned like the tax depositories of a third-world monarchy, making their way gradually down the steps and along the graveled lot beneath the blue chrysalis of an appallingly clear sky.

FORTY-FIVE

With his wife's belongings packed and stored in the loft of the auxiliary barn, Mr. Arthur released his grief with a prayer, kneeling at the foot of the bed where for forty-three years they had shared the kindred bond of childless Amish lovers in a valley of family Anabaptists. He released her hold on him, as I believe Madeline worded it in her diary entry she so thoughtfully bequeathed to me of all people. He smiled at the prospect of new horizons, at the very idea of a man his age comforted by the optimism of another day. Lives change; they move backward, they move sideways, they move upside down, and they sometimes move forward.

Madeline entered the room wielding a broom in one hand and a box of belongings in the other and about her there is the glow of a self-sustaining source of energy. Not the Madeline anyone would have recognized. Not the twin Madeline, linked since birth to the older twin with her two-and-a-half-minute head start. She set the box on the dresser and moved to stand beside him chest height at the window overlooking the barnyard and the fields and they watched as Max led the two draft horses like tamed pets from the barn to the horse trailer parked in the barnyard as Guy Faller, Givens, and Henry Roe sat their tractors, idling, poised in conversation and a moment later they separated with their hitched disks toward the north field. Intent on conquering that vast expanse in just two days.

FORTY-SIX

Later, in the Faller sedan, I sat with my head out the open window, sharing the backseat with Clare as Dolores turned from the Arthur drive out onto Pond Road toward the bridge and as we approached the bridge I heard Hound, I heard Bo sounding off from beneath the bridge. His long sustained howling mantras floating up and down the riverbanks and spilling over onto the Arthurs' north field. His Royal Highness, Lord to the Kingdom Above, and I yelled out the window, hollering, and when I was through hollering, Dolores and Madeline turned to look back at me as if I'd lost my mind. Clare rested a hand on my knee, patting my knee as if I were a pet.

I grinned and Clare grinned and from the front seat, Dolores and Madeline shook their heads and Dolores continued, "…Now Guy will be there. And Vivian and I will get over to help with the gardens and Clare down to help get the house…"

Madeline sat quietly, smiling.

"And we'll get a phone in."

"Phones ain't no good for Mr. Arthur," I said.

"Isn't," Clare said. *"Isn't* no good."

"Any. Isn't *any* good," Dolores said, and catching Clare in the

244

rearview mirror she added, "I guess it doesn't matter so much *how* things are said, does it? It's *what* we say that matters," and to Madeline, "The house needs a phone."

Madeline nodded. "Elmer understands. He needs a phone."

I rolled that around. *Elmer. Elmer.* Mr. Arthur was suddenly Elmer.

"Guy will need help. He'll need to hire hands." And again, Dolores caught Clare in the mirror and added, "Can you find someone to cook? They'll need to be fed."

"To hire?"

"If you can. There might be another Clare among them," she added, smiling. "You can't feed them *and* the Roes' hands."

I could see Clare's head reeling, picturing herself as the hiring boss, plucking from the ranks already arriving, a worthy understudy. An apprentice.

We dipped into the depression beyond the bridge and Dolores rolled to a stop at the foot of our drive. Clare and I left the sedan and Dolores stepped from the driver's seat, waving Madeline over as she said, "You'll need to drive. You need to learn to drive."

The sound of Dolores' voice. The same voice, but different. The Dolores-in-charge voice.

245

FORTY-SEVEN

Guy never spoke of his brief duration in the strip mines. It never came up. One day he was commuting forty minutes to scrape coal from the ground and then on another day he was commuting ten minutes to those fields adjoining our east field. It was Mr. Arthur, or *Elmer*, who must have outgrown Dee's old bedroom when he gave over his fields for a manageable percent of the profits and the house management to Madeline to help enable her Great Escape and for a few days it was *Elmer* this and *Elmer* that.

"So, *Elmer*," I said, as we walked down off the bridge, pulling the little wagon. "You've heard of the Great Kickapoo Raid, no doubt."

"…"

"You know…the tongue raid?"

"…"

"Hey *Elmer*, how come you never shaved?"

"…"

"Here's my thinkin, *Elmer*…"

And what he said, to *me*, was stuff like, "You the boy who went to town with his pants upside down?"

"I'm not thinkin pants, *Elmer*. I'm thinkin…"

246

FORTY-EIGHT

Following the first night of her entire life spent alone, I can imagine Elizabeth slamming the palm of her hand against the steering wheel as she rounded Snead's Corner and hit the gas to send gravel spewing in her wake as she hurtled up Pond Road to make the turn into the Arthur farm with a sharp bank that braked the Plymouth in a cloud of dust and gravel and Madeline making for the outhouse off the other side of the house. Not hard to imagine. She watched, Madeline, peering through the cracks in the closed door. Elizabeth's voice carrying, and Elmer's soft voice, and a moment later the Plymouth heading back down Pond Road to the sound of scattering gravel and spooked crows as Madeline left the sanctity of the outhouse for the sanctity of her newhouse.

FORTY-NINE

A concert of diesel cams and sputtering valves established their rightful place along the valley floor. A glorious orchestra, crooning away in the heart of everyone straddling a tractor seat. Back in the saddle, inhaling the rich-whipped scent of the earth under the open sky doing what they did best. Beautiful farmers.

From Elmer Arthur's fresh tilled east field to our own north field, set between the house gardens and the modest but stable architecture of the Marsh house, Father and I could wave to Givens several hundred yards to the north or look to Liberty Snead a mile to the east or Diligence Wiseman to the west just beyond the blackgum saplings. I could wave, if so moved, to Acceptance Davis who flailed her arms from the passenger seat of her mother's car or to Scooter climbing the trelliswork for an overview spanning the bridge while Ruby stood with Dee leaning against Sheriff's truck parked roadside, eating sandwiches like spectators at a parade.

Somewhere in the north field not far from the gardens, my mind wandered without purpose, lulled by the comforting redundancy of a plowing schematic that seemed endless, when Father set the clutch and cut the engine. Jarred back into reality, the sudden silence, I followed his eyes toward the house.

CHARLES PROWELL

"What's that on the roof?"

"Roof? What roof...where?"

"*Our* roof," he said, raising his arm toward the house.

Straddling the wheel-well, I yanked the hydraulic to raise the disks and bent down close to fill myself with the scent of sweat and soil and the rich whiffs of lubricating oil and as we stared back across the field, the chant of a barn owl drifted lazily up from the river.

"I don't know, Daddyo...it's something, though."

"Daddyo?"

"Larry calls his dad Diligence *Popsicle*. You know, Pop...*Pop*sicle?"

Father stared at me as if studying a rock, or fencepost.

"Well then, *Sonnyo,* can't you see what's on the roof?"

"I can see it's something, that's for sure."

"Where are your glasses? Why don't you wear your glasses?"

I considered my weak left eye and how the right eye was better unless you were trying to stab a pea with the end of your fork and then both eyes somehow got confused.

"In the house, I guess," knowing they were in the drawer beside my bed where they had been pretty much since the prescription was first issued.

"Why don't you wear them?"

"Cause they're clunky, Dad."

"No, Sport, clunky is walking into a tree, or the side of the house. That's clunky. Why you're blind as a bat, boy."

"Dad, I see fine...really."

"And my name's Jumpin Jahossafat."

"What?"

"Never mind...just wear your glasses."

I looked back to the house. "So, what is it? Whataya figure it is?"

"What's what?"

"The roof," I threw a hand out toward the house, as if swatting a bee. "Whataya be figure'ns up there?"

249

POSSESSING THE SEASONS

"Be figure'n?" Where are you from…Mississippi?"

"Illinois, Dad. Good ole Illinois. Same place I be reckon'n you're from."

"They're books. There's book on the roof."

It *could* be books, piled on the porch roof outside the dayroom dormer window and wedged against the eaves of the main gable, hidden from view unless you happened to be sitting atop a tractor and watching on a clear day—with good eyes—from the middle of the north field.

"What sort of books?" I drew down close to his face, studying my reflection in the roundness of his eyes and he blinked, pulling away.

"Well, I can't read the titles, Jussie. They're just books…poetry, I imagine. S'what your mother reads."

"Poetry?"

Givens' tractor had gone quiet. The air was crisp, but no wind to rustle the hickories along the road or churn the squeaking windmill out behind the peach grove. The owl was still hooting like a metronome.

"The bookshelf I reckon's full, eh, Dad?"

Sheriff had left the roadbed, crossing the field on foot, assuming a problem, perhaps an engine failure explaining the extended pause as Father turned back to me with his eyes suddenly watery and I went back in close with the reflection now wavy and distorted.

Sheriff approached smiling, appreciating like anyone the blend of earth and diesel oil as he handed up Aunt Dee's sandwiches to stand with one boot hiked onto the running board. He lifted his chin and raised an eyebrow in a substitute for words and I motioned him aboard the marvelous mechanical beast. He settled against the opposite wheel-well and Father engaged the clutch and pushed the starter to a shot of exhaust and the iron horse roared back to life.

Sheriff leaped free at the turn, throwing out an arm behind him while crossing the ditch to rejoin Dee and Ruby as we made the turn for another length, pulling up to the clink of a stone dredged up from the soil with Father wincing at the thought of hammering out the tines and we continued to pull up now and again for an occasional arrowhead or shards of jeweled Moingwena and Shawnee stones and it was after dark when we turned off toward the house.

FIFTY

Mother entered our bedroom on Wednesday morning to sit on the edge of my bed, running her fingers through my hair. I opened my eyes to a dim light, glancing at the clock on the windowsill. She moved to Verity's bed and repeated her ceremony as I sat up on one elbow and peered out the window to the sound of tractors, to the sight of Father walking from the lower pasture to the barnyard, followed by two new hands who would have been hired before dawn, culled from the dozen or so still camped under the bridge.

Verity stirred as Mother massaged her calf muscle just above the top of the cast when I turned from the window and said, "Mom, it's only six-thirty."

Verity jerked and Mother removed her hands.

"Does it hurt?"

Verity nodded, sleepily.

"How on earth anyone could do this just walking on the bridge is beyond me."

"Mom, it's only six-thirty," I repeated.

"Six-thirty? Why I could've sworn…"

She moved to lean over my bed and inspected the clock on the sill as if to challenge the error. She straightened and for a moment stared out the window, as if troubled by the idea of a lost hour.

Mariah appeared, dressed in her bright robe and with her hair still set in the curlers that had loosened during the night. She stood with her arms folded, "It's early. Anything wrong?"

Mother turned to Mariah and with the not-so-good eyes and the hesitancy of a small white lie, she said, "Jussie thinks it's early but I think his clock is wrong."

Mariah studied Mother's not-so-good eyes and glanced toward the clock in the dayroom and then back to me and then to Verity as I grabbed my pants from the bedpost and said, "Dad's hired some hands from the bridge."

Mariah left and Mother followed, settling into the small auxiliary desk in the dayroom. I sat on the edge of the bed, half-dressed.

"Where are you going?" Verity asked.

I turned and watched as she maneuvered her ankle cast off the edge of her bed. With her birthday only two weeks away, Verity would soon be moving into Aunt Dee's old room. A few weeks earlier that would have been fine, but since the afternoon on the bridge, Verity and I had grown closer."

"Nowhere," I said. "I'm not goin nowhere."

"Then why are you getting dressed? It's early."

"Maybe I'll go down to the fence…check the new hands."

"I'll go, too."

I helped her to her feet in a move having less to do with her need for help than to acknowledge our alliance. In the dayroom, in a near collision at the head of the stairs, we met Mariah leaving her own room and for a moment the three of us stood as motionless as the newel post.

"Would you move?" Mariah said, raising her hands to her hips.

"Why? I ain't goin anywhere."

"You're going downstairs, aren't you?"

"Maybe…maybe not."

POSSESSING THE SEASONS

Two weeks earlier I might simply have stepped around Mariah and that would've been that. But I had beaten death in a fair battle (scolded by Father for the stupidity while praised for a clear-headed victory). I now relished the confrontation and with the smallest provocation, I would strike with absolute resolve. Confident I could overcome the seven-inch height disadvantage. Perhaps too confident.

From the bottom of the stairs, Father arrived to pause at the landing, roadblocked by Mariah.

"What's this?" his buoyant voice, carrying through the dayroom as Mariah moved aside. "Everyone up and dressed already?"

Quickly assessing the stand-off, his bright eyes were lost to a frown of disapproval.

He moved between Mariah and me and crossed the room and in his wake an odor of diesel oil. Mother sat at the small desk along the opposite wall. With papers scattered across the surface of the seldom-used desk, she hunched so close that the end of the pen brushed against her ear.

"Good morning, my darling."

There was no response.

"Aren't you a little close?" he added. "You'll ruin your eyes that way."

He laid his hands over her shoulders, massaging lightly, and she suddenly rose back as if startled from a dream. Her eyes fell on him and for a second or two they were locked in one another's gaze. They kissed, slowly, and she rested her head back so that her cheek nestled against his arm.

"The clocks are wrong," she whispered.

"How's that?"

"The clock," she added, motioning to the desk. She ran her hand over the papers, searching, one must assume, for the clock. "It's an hour off…somewhere."

Henry nodded. "A good hour, I hope."

I moved over to stand beside Father and said, "We hire hands this morning?"

CHARLES PROWELL

But there was no reply and my eyes drifted to the pages scattered across the small desk. The script was large and illegible, a scrawl allowing only three or four words per line and six or seven lines per page. I reached to peel back a random page from the stack and found the same loosely scripted handwriting. Lifting a few more pages, moving back in time, and the handwriting was a little tighter, a few more words per page. Her work journals, outlines and thoughts on each day's progress. The deeper I rummaged, the cleaner and more compressed the script. My mother's script, composed by the hand of an artist.

Father kissed her again and moved over to open the windows along the daybed. The morning air was brittle and the scent of early spring drifted through the room. I remained at the window for a moment, leaning out through the open casements with my head extended beyond the jamb, studying the roof, the books piled against the sidewall. Mother left the desk to stand near the daybed. The look on her face was blank and unrevealing as first Mariah, then Verity, joined Father at the window. He turned and looked at Mother and was about to speak, searching for the words when he suddenly clasped his hands and moved to the stairs and several steps down, he paused, turned back to the dayroom, peering through the balustrades.

"Vivian will be here shortly."

We listened to the sound of his boots carry down the hall through the dining room and Mariah moved to stand at the windows, studying the roof outside the windows.

"They're jes books," I say. "They're not *your* books."

Mariah looked at me with glaring eyes and flushed cheeks and I chanced a tiny mocking smile, furthering my composed offensive while calculating a means of escape up the attic stairs or circling the dayroom but Mariah didn't move.

Mother stepped between us, as if in passing, and said, "Stop it, you two."

The old voice. *Her* voice, disarming the tension like the slap of a judge's gavel.

255

She stood straight-shouldered, tightening her robe as she turned for the stairs and paused, waving us on, "Now how about some breakfast? It's getting late."

We fell in line, not caring if she was back for hours, or minutes.

For hours or minutes or even the better part of an entire day. Questioning us tirelessly, eager for news of anything from school to the forecast of rain to where was Mr. Arthur?

And we responded, as if to the queries from a distant relative, knowing that at any moment she might withdraw from the conversation with empty eyes.

The hard part...not knowing how long she would be gone and when she might return and where on earth was this place stealing her away so convincingly, leaving us alone and abandoned in a world inhabited by everyone but her? Was it painless? Was it a vast and empty dimension indifferent to passing time?

Or a living hell, fully conscious yet imprisoned away from everything and everyone she loved?

Nothing from her. Nothing from that quarter whatsoever.

At breakfast she sat watching me sitting beside her, fidgeting excitedly on my stool while Mariah set out the bowls and Verity brought down the box of cereal and together we read the note on the counter: *'Setting up the new hands. XOXO.'*

Verity brought out the bottle of milk fresh from the barn and sat down at the counter, gleaming as if it were Christmas morning.

"Dr. Stayer's coming to the Javitts this week...you know, the vet?"

"Have you talked to him yet?" Mother asked. "About this summer?"

"I will."

I stood, as if in Mrs. Hall's classroom, and said, "Can I stay over down to Elmer's sometimes?"

"Elmer?"

"Elmer. Mr. Arthur. If Aunt Madeline's living there and Clare's teaching the new cook, well, it'd be sort of our place too…wouldn't it?"

"Clare's at Mr. Arthur's?"

"Just a little bit, Mom."

Mariah turned from the sink and Mother's arm found its way along her waist. Mariah allowed this, lingering at the counter, sponging the spilled milk surrounding my bowl like a flooded moat while seemingly savoring Mother's touch.

"Can we talk, Mom?"

"Sure, honey. What is it?"

"I mean later…in private."

Mother's eyes had fallen on the china cabinet, where the small black cast iron skillet was set, perched among the family silver like a crow in a finch nest. Her arm fell away from Mariah's waist and she went over to the cabinet, opening the glass doors and retrieving the skillet and turning to set it on the counter.

"Since when does the skillet belong in the china cabinet?"

We looked up but no one answered. A car had pulled into the drive and for a moment we listened to the sound of its tires slowly crunching the gravel. We could have mentioned the books on the roof and she would have been shocked. We could have shown her the dinner plates in with the dry goods or the knives and forks in with the spatulas, despite Clare's constant corrections. But why? Why waste precious time when it would serve no real purpose?

The car door opened and closed and we turned to the window at the end of the kitchen, watching Vivian approach the house. The start of a new routine: Vivian, Dolores, Dee, and Bim adopting a rotation of coincidental weekday visits. Mariah and Verity went to get the door

POSSESSING THE SEASONS

and I turned to find Mother in the living room, standing before the long picture windows with her open hands pressed against the glass. She was watching the lower field, the clouds of dust kicked up by the tractors.

FIFTY-ONE

On some evenings I take a drive with little Henry, Mister Whister. We take the truck to rumble along the old tractor trails through the far edge of the north field and down the back dale to come upon the blossoming west field and we might pause, idling at the Point before risking the canopy of tupelos, where the Beast lives.

"Poppa. Hey, Poppa. I'm sitting too low. I can't see. You got the heater on? Poppa? Poppa, you got the heater on?"

"Yes, it's on."

"Good, Poppa, cause I'm freezing. Hey Poppa, you know what? I know where hot air comes from. You know where, Poppa?"

"Where?"

"From dirt, Poppa. No. From mud. Hot air comes from mud."

"From mud?"

"Yeah."

"It comes from the heater. The engine warms it up."

"Oh. Hey Poppa, what are all those buttons there?"

"They're for the heater. One is for the cold air. And this one sends the hot air out either to the bottom or the top near the window."

"Poppa, you know what? Now I know all about trucks. Is it past my bedtime? Poppa, is it past my bedtime yet?"

"Yes. Maybe. We stayed out driving late tonight. You think your mom will be awake when we get home?"

"Yeah, I think she will. Hey Poppa, on this day we're going to that place to play. That park, okay? Okay, Poppa? Poppa? Pop-pa!"

And on some evenings, I read to little Maddy, who has graduated to chapter books. She likes to take over herself, reading only from the bottom of those pages where the sentence continues onto the overleaf page. A quirk of hers, fascinated by how seamlessly she can continue the sentence, turning the page, without pausing. Anyway, her reading is getting better. While mine is getting worse.

I want to tell them, but they're too young. Little Mademoiselle and Henry and their cousins...I want to tell them how to live a good life.

FIFTY-TWO

S. Averill Harriman arrived on the ravaged post war continent with troves of American currency; the complexity of a hammered-out Marshal Plan; and, more immediately, ships whose hulls listed with the weighty containers of a magical hybrid grain intent on feeding a starving continent while Father, within the protective custody of Voodoo Valley, examined and reexamined his logs in search of drifting data. The inconclusive chemical drift.

FIFTY-THREE

While Mother drifted in and out of present-tense awareness and Father had begun spring seeding, Dolores and Mariah drove to St. Louis under the guise of summer-term orientation at Washington University, and a visit with Aunt Harriet. They left early, and returned late the following afternoon. When grilled by Verity and myself, Mariah shrugged, as if St. Louis were no different than Karber's Ridge. As if it were nothing special.

FIFTY-FOUR

From the kitchen door off the side of the Arthur house, there appeared a young woman in a simple one-piece cotton shift layered with a waist-apron. She stood in a pair of worn men's black oxfords too big for her feet, cradling a mixing bowl close to her chest and a long wooden spoon working the bowl. She seemed slightly anxious, confused, possibly, by the scope of her new job—if you believed Clare, who had no cause to be judgmental; her memory of the young protégé never wavered. Clare motioned her over and the woman approached with her eyes cast to the ground, the timid subordination of a woman not yet twenty, a little overwhelmed, perhaps, in the misconstrued presence of a landowner.

"I dunno the stove, Miss Clare."

Clare stood with Madeline and the just-arrived Vivian, who was making her first appearance on the property over the course of some sixty-three years. Vivian bore seeds for the new garden.

"This here's Lavette," Clare said to them both.

Lavette offered a slight nod and an almost imperceptible curtsy.

Vivian moved to rest a hand on Lavette's shoulder, "Let's have a look, hon. What kind of stove is it?"

Clare and Madeline carried on to the gardens where Lavette's younger brother stood, awaiting instructions from whomever was in

263

POSSESSING THE SEASONS

charge, while along the farthest reaches of the south field, Guy piloted his familiar machine back and forth along the fresh furrows as Elmer, out for a joy ride, leaned unsteadily against the wheel-well astride his first tractor, gripping the wheel-well with white knuckles, if you believed Guy and Guy had no cause to be judgmental; his memory of Elmer's first ride never wavered.

FIFTY-FIVE

In April, the valley leaned into the changing season, distancing itself, with each passing day, from the months of immobilizing nor'easterlies. Every day, this bracing air of a new spring deepened its foothold, warmed by a young and tentative sunlight to nourish and encourage the new foliage in a photosynthetic accord that brims with a visibility stretching clear to the horizon.

Rehearsing a May Day ritual still days away, Verity and I doubled up on Horse and rode out Pond Road carrying bunches of early bluebells and spiked lobelia. At the Marshes, we deposited the flowers on the front doorstep, rapped on the door, and rode off across the south field fully exposed, throwing our arms up in the air and laughing hysterically to the sound of Vivian's clanging dinner bell.

Not yet sullied with the humidity of summer, a thin cloud of dust rose over the subsidy field to the southwest. We continued, Horse's coat dappling against the afternoon sun to come around the windmill and onto the bluff above the west grazing field where we ultimately sat Horse at the edge of the Tupelos.

A full crew of hands, hired until there were no more campfires under the bridge, clearing the stones and arrowheads. Without them and the diskblades would be gouged and dulled and useless.

265

POSSESSING THE SEASONS

Father had been gone from before dawn to well after dark and the twelve-hour days he had expected had been stretched to sixteen- and seventeen-hour days in a race to seed. From the Ohio Valley there had been reports of rain on the twenty-eighth. On the twenty-ninth, there was measurable precipitation along the Kentucky side of the state line, both Union and Crittenden counties, and by the thirtieth, the front had spread to as far south as the Cumberland River area. The sky was traveling southeast in a thin cirrus canopy as dry as smoke. The weather was forty miles to the southeast and running parallel yet it wasn't so improbable that the wind could shift ninety degrees and bring the rain no one wanted. Not just yet. Not for the next few days.

If it held, if the morning and evening horizons continued to be charged with the golden orange pigments of the past few days, everyone's mystical seeds could be safely planted and tamped in dry soil. If it rained too soon, and too heavily, there was the risk of not only early erosion but the difficult if not impossible task of working muddy topsoil that clung like glue to the tractor treads. Once the fields were seeded, it could rain all it wanted. Not a heavy rain, not a downpour, but a light steady rain that would be received as nothing less than a Godsend, an omen of virtue.

Verity remounted, swinging the cast on her foot over the back of Horse as if it were nothing more than a heavy boot. I skipped off across the weeded groundcover that gave way to the fresher furrows and a moment later I was straddling the tractor's axle, watching the disks for arrowheads and bright stones.

It was nine before I returned to the house, layered with enough dust to consider showing up in class the following morning, unbathed, as proof I had been in the fields until after dark.

In the morning, it was Dolores who arrived at eight. 'In the neighborhood,' as she put it...all of them, Dee and Bim and Vivian, just 'in the neighborhood.'

Later, Verity and I rode out beneath clouds shelved off the horizon with the body and mass you couldn't ignore. We rode along the cow trail off the back of the barn through the thicket of brambles and then along an understory of blooming mimosa to sight the tractordust rising over the east field. Carrying on by and by, Verity sang to Horse and Horse treaded the open plain with the presence of something celestial. We climbed the roadbed and trodded beneath a sheltering nimbus sky and down the embankment to skirt the gully to canter across the faint vestiges of the old Indian foot trail and on up the shallow draw to the Arthur line. The Elmer Arthur/Madeline Pond/Lavette/Guy Faller/and sometimes Clare line. A regular commune. At the new gardens, Clare turned and called to the kitchen.

"L'vetty! "

Horse pranced in place, sidling the tamped groundcover with Verity handling the bridlereins high and sitting Horse like an appendage as he started off through the barnyard from one end to the other, highstepping to clear the watertrough and pivoting to sling out like a shot with everyone watching.

Lavette appeared from the kitchen door, shuffling her over-sized shoes along the dirt path with the bag of sandwiches and homemade oatmeal cookies looking relaxed; the apprenticing competence of a cook whose sweet-toothed creations were noted and appreciated.

Horse settled against the gardens, pausing like a train at a depot as I re-mounted and situated myself against the flank and reached to accept the bag of sandwiches and cookies.

"Look like to me," said Lavette, "you born on that horse, Miss Verdi."

I wedged the bag against Verity's back, nodding to Clare who glanced to the sky and added, "It 'pears some weather's a'comin."

For three-quarters of a mile, we negotiated the grove of sycamores along the water. Above, perched thick in the upper reaches, a chorus of muted birdsongs reacted to the breeze and the anticipation of what a breeze could mean as Horse cleared the grove to breach the tangled riverweed along the Point before striking the clearing of the east field with the full gait of an open track.

As a former encampment of the Illiniwek and Moingwena, the east field was a treasury of arrowheads and jeweled stones and fragments of painted pottery pushed to the surface from centuries of flooding, exposed by the blade of the plow. It was shaped like a shallow self-draining dish, flanked by the river and the beginning slopes of Moingwena Rise to create soil so fertile it would support anything from wheat to sunflowers to…to a drought-resistant barley.

We pulled up over the knoll to sight Father atop the Chalmers, completing his turn at the river and progressing toward us with only the last quarter section of the field left unplanted. The workers were shoulder to shoulder, stretching from the river to Elmer's south field, sifting the dirt for the stones weighting down their shouldered gunnysacks and now and again a priceless arrowhead or fragmented pottery shard, its painted markings dropped in with the peasantry stones like unappreciated royalty. Father waved and we sat Horse, waiting for the eventual turn and a chance to pass on the sandwiches and cookies when I noticed the Farmall parked in the middle of the field. There was someone beneath the chassis, on his back with only his knees exposed, at work on the front axle assembly. Farther down, parked along the road fence, was the truck from Dubois Implementry.

Father cut the engine twenty yards away and instantly the workers and their harmonizing voices were silent. They found relief sitting where they were standing, some stretching out onto their backs, sore from the long days bent over at the waist. Verity and I dismounted and walked between the furrows to where the workers lay exhausted, dispensing the sandwiches and cookies down a line spanning the width of the field.

"I knowed it. I knowed it when I first seen you comin…more Lavetty's cookies."

"Oatmeal raisin," I said.

"Bless dat girl."

We moved along. I handled the food and Verity the water drawn from the large vat strapped to the tractor, pouring it into the tin cups strung to their waistbands…cups held out by arms wetted with sweat and coated with a film of dust.

"He be along soon?"

Verity shrugged her shoulders.

A few furtive glances to the riverbank, the tupelo wood where the foot-trail disappeared into the thicket…where, from the Compound, you could cross the felled sycamore bridge and emerge onto the east field.

Back at the tractor, I handed Father a sandwich and in his eyes, I could see the look of disappointment.

"What's with the Farmall?"

Father climbed slowly off the tractor and turned to look back across the field. The mechanic was leaving the Farmall, walking toward the truck parked along the access. Father turned back to Verity and me with the face of a coal miner, blackened with dirt and dust all but for the eyes; the eyes were like bright wet stones.

"It's broken, son."

I said nothing, studying his face the way you studied something you don't want to forget. Lately, Father had been leaving the house before we were awake and returning after we were asleep and if not for our rides out to the fields following school, we would not see him at all. He looked older, and I thought how it had been weeks since I had heard him whistling, or joking…since I had heard the sound of his laughter.

"Well, Lankard can fix it, right?"

Father took the cup of water from Verity and raised it to his lips until it was gone. I watched his neck, his head cocked back and his Adam's Apple working that throat like a dumbwaiter with water spilling through the corners of his mouth running in rivulets down his chin and throat and on under his shirt. He pushed back his cap with the heel of his hand and poured a little over that tangled weed-patch scalp and the water trickled over his forehead and down his cheeks in wild dark lines, like war paint.

"Maybe."

He pulled a kerchief from his pocket and ran it over his eyes and then across his cheeks; the dirt and the water smeared to resemble a finger painting.

"Well, can't we get anothern?" I said. "Dubois has tractors for sale," knowing that with only one tractor, there was no hope of finishing. It was already late in the day and tomorrow was the third and then it was the fourth and Evansville was looming. There was just no way he could get it done. "Can't you borrow one…or rent one…or why don't we just buy a new one, Dad? Just buy one."

"It's April, Jussie. There are no extra tractors."

Father seemed estranged, different. The chunky sky that had blown in yesterday had taken on some color and now it was the sort of sky that could surprise you, that could go black in just a few hours and start dumping buckets.

Father walked in tiny circles, stretching his legs and pressing his fingers against the small of his back, watching the truck as it backed along the fence, moving toward them in reverse, and he turned to Verity, "So, how's your mother?"

"Oh, she's okay," Verity said, stroking Horse with one hand. "She and Dolores are packing. Mom keeps putting things in she won't need and Dolores keeps sneaking them out. Mom packed it the first time with nothing but books and a toothbrush. It's going pretty slow, Daddy."

He made a face and turned away and I said, "So what about it, Dad…let's just get another tractor," and he turned to me, looking impatient and tired.

"Because there are no tractors, Justus. They're in the fields, where they belong. You don't just go out and buy a new one at the drop of a hat. We got three tractors already."

"No, Dad...we got one tractor. Other two are broke."

His eyes narrowed and I could see he was in no mood for a debate with a twelve-year-old.

Lankard had left the truck, crossing the field on foot. Father started toward him and I followed, thinking how Lankard was a graduate from the one-year tractor-mechanic's course at Carbondale's Vocational Technical Institute. He was already three years working for Ben Dubois. This was Buddy's dream, a bit of college to impress Mariah, but Buddy would be lucky to finish high school and even luckier to land Mariah and if he knew something about engines, tractor engines, it was like a toddler's knowledge compared to Lankard Calder.

"Whataya got, Lankard?"

"Sorry, Mr. Roe. She's got a busted vertical link...clean through."

"A what?"

"S'what holds up your front end...an iron housing that ties the chassis to the wheel hub. Ain't no bigger than the end of my finger, but without it, you're ride'n on the dirt. 'Fraid I cain't do much without the part."

Father rubbed his jaw and kicked his boot against the dirt and he looked at Lankard and said, "You got that part in the shop?"

"No, sir...no way. Cain't weld one up either...it'll jes snap. Have to order it from up to Urbana. Dillavou Implementary. Be a few days, I imagine."

Father kicked the dirt again, a wide, sweeping kick that sent the dust lifting to the breeze. He turned on Lankard and with a hard voice, he said, "Boy, I don't have a few days! You get over to the shop and get them on the phone...talk to Chuck up there...tell him who it's for and to have someone meet you in Effingham. Today...s'afternoon. You can be back by dark and we'll pull up the truck...give you some light."

"You want me to drive to Effingham...now?"

"I want you to drive to Effingham. Now."

I took a step back, watching the muscles twitching across Father's cheek.

Lankard stood like a bewildered child. "But Mr. Roe..."

Father chopped his fist through the air and said, "You tell Dillavou I need that part. You tell him I need it today! Go on, now. Go on...you're wasting time."

Lankard stood for a moment, and suddenly turned and started running toward his truck. Father turned back toward the tractor and motioned the workers up, sweeping his hand through the air as if he were trapping drifting pollen in his palm.

Later that evening, he returned briefly to the house. Dolores had stayed on to help Clare cook a late dinner and it was while they were in the kitchen, cleaning the dishes, when the screen door slapped and the sound of his footsteps carried in from the hall. He passed beyond the kitchen and turned through the dining room without so much as a hello. I followed him back through the library and into the bedroom and watched as he pulled a wad of bills from the top drawer of his bureau. He counted off a few and shoved them into his back pocket and I said, "What's up, Dad? How's it going down there?"

He said nothing. He returned the wad to the drawer and left the bedroom with that same hard manner, stepping around me as if I were a house pet. I followed him back through the library and the dining room and down the hall and from the screen door, I watched the truck pulling away from the drive, spewing gravel in its wake.

I hurried upstairs and from my bedroom window and through the telescope, I followed the headlights back over the bridge. I watched them turn off the road, the lights bobbing along the access path, flickering through the cottonwoods that flanked the embankment to pull up short of the field. The workers were leaving, making their way up the gully and onto Pond Road because everyone knows they don't work at night. Father had stepped out of the truck and appeared to be addressing them, his arms out wide. But a moment later, they continued on because nothing would change how the copperheads and the water moccasins leave the riverbank at night to feed on the mice and the rodents and anything that happened along.

There would be no chance…working alone. The seeds he had created and nurtured like offspring were now worthless. They were no good with a late planting.

It was almost ten when Dolores left. I listened to the sound of her car backing out the drive and then slipped from bed and for the umpteenth time, I went to the window on the opposite wall to look for the lights in the east field. Still no headlights, no Lankard.

I had been feeling lost and empty, plagued by the recurring sound of Father's cold voice that afternoon in the fields, the strange, heartless look in his eyes then and again on his short return to the house. I understood the timetable and the stress of racing against this fixed timetable but I also understood that without Father's composure and his defining optimism, the good life was edged with an unsettling rawness. It was hard to gauge the slow subtle decline in Mother's condition largely because Father refused to change and it became suddenly very clear how our lives had always hinged on this optimism, our father's unfailing optimism. The look in his eyes had been a look of panic and pessimism and I had been suffering all evening from a sense of doom, concerned with unseeded fields and early downpours and yet another summer of continued drought and a mother whose mind was languishing and lazy. I pictured Father alone and abandoned, stubbornly working the field and fighting a timetable that was useless, knowing that even if Lankard returned and managed to make the repairs, the one hand trained to man the Farmall was back sleeping in the Quarters.

The phone rang and I left the bedroom to cross the dayroom to skip down the stairs to find Mother leaning over the kitchen counter in her robe, cradling the phone to one ear. Verity sat at the opposite end, reading. Mariah casually returning misplaced dishware to its proper cupboards...no one willing to turn in until the Optimist had returned safely to the nest.

Mother returned the phone and ran a hand through my hair, marking her presence with this simple gesture.

"That was Madeline."

Mariah turned from the cupboard along the opposite counter and said, "Madeline? What's she want?"

"She said there's singing in the field, from the Tupelos."

Verity looked up from her book.

Mother nodded.

Verity left her stool and went out to the front porch and through the screen door to stand in the sprawling lawn with the cool grass beneath her bare feet and she released an incanting rhythm drawn up and harbored by the evening breeze. She waited, the night sounds parting, the insects allowing a respectful pause...but nothing. Just the tractor, the hum of the diesel purring up from beyond the river. She moved a few steps to the right and then to the left as if to summon her strength before another call, much longer and from a much greater depth carrying most certainly beyond the neighboring acres and again a parted silence from the barnyard and from the insects and the river critters, all of them poised, waiting, and when it came, it was like a distant horn floating over this terrain, all linked like an extended family.

Verity leapt, unable to contain herself.

Inside, the phone rang again and Mother answered it and a moment later turned to Mariah, "Mr. Arthur just left."

"Mr. Arthur? What can he do?"

Mother shrugged and tightened her robe and went to stand at the living room windows, gazing out beyond Verity to find the tractor lights, to watch them through the treetops bobbing and flickering like fireflies.

Upstairs at the bedroom window, I took a measure on the cow trail, adjusting the lens to a focused distance and finding Harlan, the whiteness of Harlan in shirtsleeves exposed against the partial darkness of a three-quarter moon making his way along the low-growth plain of the trail, disappearing into the trees, returning beyond the sycamore bridge to pass over the east field furrows like a small glittering pearl. He fell in behind the tractor gathering stones and singing, no doubt, to the serpents, soothing their temperament.

It was nearly eleven-thirty. Verity arrived in the room and after a moment at the telescope, she readied herself for bed, reminding me that tomorrow was a school day. I remained at the eyepiece, sighting Mr. Arthur slowly crossing the field.

I turned to Verity but Verity was already in bed, lying stiff as a well-preserved mummy. She had said little on the ride back from the east field, and at the dinner table, and she rested now with her hands clasped over her chest and her eyes fixed on the photograph pinned to the ceiling over her bed, lost in the landscape of a Kentucky horse farm.

I changed and slipped between the covers and with a last parting look before sleep, I made out several of the hands straggling back across the field, mingling with little distinction between the sky and the dirt.

I woke early the next morning, immediately at the eyepiece to find the east field deserted; the Farmall was stationed near the embankment like a forgotten relic. From the dayroom dormer, with Mother along the opposite wall hunched over the small desk in a focused oblivion, I spotted the Allis-Chalmers. It was parked near the road just adjacent to the gardens, waiting, it would seem, for the capable Septimus to arrive. Several hands were already scattered along the fenceline parallel to Pond Road, languishing under the early light.

I ran down the stairs to find Father asleep on the couch in the library. He had not changed nor showered nor even unlaced his boots.

It was Bim who showed up at seven, setting her typewriter down on the small desk off the kitchen where she would have to work, she said, if the paper was to get out on time.

POSSESSING THE SEASONS

A self-serve breakfast, Father sleeping, Mother upstairs, and Aunt Bim pecking on her tool. Mariah, Verity, and me at the counter all in a row, silently spooning our cereal swimming in Cow-milk, Mariah with a book of plays opened alongside her bowl, Verity with her book of equestrian anatomy, and me with the Southern Illinoisan folded into fourths, focused on early-season box scores.

Mariah turned the page as if actually focusing on a playwright's use of staging while Verity pretended to enunciate the labeled parts of the knee upon which everything hinges while I re-folded the paper thinking how I would have volunteered to clean the stalls this morning rather than go to school but Bim was hearing nothing of it. "Your father doesn't need a young'n under foot," she had said. "Not today."

I had staged a minor fuss, sulking and fuming until it was so late, I had to run most of the way to the bus, catching up with Mariah and Verity at the rise abreast of the Marsh house where I paused long enough to take in the north field and the idle tractor and consider precious time wasting.

Every minute now. Every minute of every hour.

276

FIFTY-SIX

Pat Davis stood leaning over the idle griddle of the kitchen pass-through reading the Fall Ridge Gazette while smoking a cigar in the pervasive vacancy of an empty Café.

Elizabeth Pond unlocked the lonely Pond Salon to sweep the floor and arrange the bottled toiletries and to align the stacked edges of the gossip magazines and finally gathering the bevy of scissors all in a pile to be cleaned and stropped one at time. When she was finished, she sat in an empty salon chair and stared at the wall.

Fall Ridge School opened the doors to its incoming charges—an uncommonly mannered lot of mostly girls and a few town-boys; missing now for the third straight day was that definable ingredient, that rowdy presence of their farm boys.

And Dee stood alone at the front windows of her shop with her bolts of fabric waiting to be worked, gazing out onto an empty Main Street and praying for a restrained Godsend, praying for her beautiful farmers with their narrowing timetable pitted to the patience of a threatening sky and if you were Lord of the Kingdom Above looking down with that evanescent presence upon the citizenry of our droopy drowsy little town, encompassing every raised eyebrow and every nervous twitch, sensing

277

every palpable heartbeat and anticipatory edge, you would understand how a mere mortal could live a lifetime, a dozen lifetimes and stack them up and not in a thousand years would you ever again need something called a Vertical Link. Never again would you discover the engine block of your third-string tractor frozen and cracked during the coldest winter storm in history, and the second-string tractor with a part snapped clean as a twig leaving it listing in the middle of the huge east field because of a part no one stocked.

Chicago. That was what Chuck Dillavou told Ben Dubois who told Lankard who told Bim in a call to the house that morning. "No, nothing in Urbana or Springfield or Evansville or Owensboro or even St. Louis."

"Chicago. And it was too far," Ben Dubois had said. "No one could drive up and back in one day. The part would be shipped out next week and tell Henry I'm sorry. It's the best we can do."

That afternoon, I left the bus and took off running up Pond Road. The air was clear and crisp and tinged with the moisture of a southerly front. I filled myself with chestfulls of sacred spring oxygen, blowing exhales and swinging my arms side to side unburdened with textbooks, climbing the Marsh rise to throw a wave off to Givens who was making his turn and as I reached the crest of Pond Road, pausing: the instant disappointment as I sighted the Allis-Chalmers with the trained Septimus at the helm, still working the north field. Reaching the house, I learned of the call from Ben Dubois and I understood there was no hope, not judging from the slow progress in the north field. Both the south Annex and the subsidy field would have to wait until Father returned from Evansville…or Diligence or Givens or Liberty Snead had finished their own planting.

It was more than just a two-week delay. It was a horse race where the gun had sounded and the others were nearly around the first turn before our own mount had left the starting gate. It was a split harvest, a nightmarish scenario that would have half the crops harvested the last week of September and the other half, the late half, exposed to the whims of an October freeze. And a freeze in October was nothing to bet against.

I entered the house through the hall slamming the door behind me to pass up the length of the hall and through the dining room breathing heavy and on into the library where I pulled up to catch my breath before tiptoeing to take a seat beside the couch surrounded by ten-thousand books. I sat perched on the ottoman beside the couch where Father was sleeping when Bim appeared in the doorway with her finger to her lips and I nodded and when she closed the door behind her, I leaned in close. For close to an hour, I timed his inhales against the exhales, wondering if there was a correlation similar to the counts between lightning and thunder. I could sense the awakening with the shorter span between breaths and when he roused from a far-off dream, I was waiting, poised nose to nose, waiting for those eyes, those big brown mirrors.

"Hey, Dad."

He blinked. I was so close, our lashes brushed. But he didn't flinch, my own nose against the side of his nose like studying a bug in the grass. He wrapped his arms around me and pulled me close, lifting me onto the couch, thinking probably how anytime now I would be too old for anything but a hand on the shoulder and then...and then just a handshake. From then on, nothing more than a handshake.

He stretched his brows and rubbed his eyes awake and I saw how the hard look from the day before was gone. Had he given up? Had he understood the futility of fighting overwhelming odds?

"Hey, Sport."

"So, how was your nap?" I asked.

He raised an eyebrow and I could see he wasn't fully awake. I could see he needed more sleep.

"Were you watching?"

I nodded.

"Well, how'd I look?"

"You looked fine, Dad. You were dreamin…your eyes were moving. What about?"

"Baseball. I was dreaming about baseball."

I considered this and said, "Now, were you watchin…or playin?"

"Playing."

"At college, then. So, you were in college."

"I dreamt your mother was watching…a few feet away, clapping and jumping up and down and yelling."

"She wouldn't of been there, Dad. Mom didn't get to school until you were through playin."

"Dreams are what you want them to be, Whisty."

"So, you were on second? Yer on second base beatin your fist into your mitt and Mom's distractin you but you gotta stay on the ball, Dad. Watch the ball."

"I'm watching your mother."

"Oh no."

"She's pretty, I can't help it, Sport."

"Oh no, Dad."

He yawned and raised himself and said, "Just a dream, Whisty."

He stood up and walked through the bedroom and into the long bath and I followed like a mid-day shadow. I sat on the lip of the counter, the tub water running with Father at the sink lathering his hands and I studied the motion of the stroking razor. There was a knock on the door and Bim's voice, "Come eat, Hank…while it's hot."

I called out, "We'll be right there!"

Mother entered the bath from the bedroom, dressed in her bluejeans and one of Father's oversized shirts. She had been in the garden all afternoon, planting the white averys and golden rods and river weeds and bluebells and spring lilies that would circle the meadow sage Father would eventually supply from the greenhouse.

She had on her wide-brimmed bonnet because the clouded skies of the past several days had disappeared and the sun had returned, bright and clear. She pushed the brim away from her forehead to reveal shadowed eyes and pale cheeks. She came to stand beside the sink, watching the last strokes of his razor and with the corner of a towel, she reached to wipe the lather from his cheek and around his neck and then she dropped the towel to the floor and gripped the back of his neck with both hands. He gathered her up, lifting the heel of her sneakers to stand poised on her tiptoes. They held one another. Mother burrowed in beneath his jaw, grazing her cheek against the skin, extracting from his neck the essence of an addiction…the available Henryness of a long-standing compulsion.

All of this as if I weren't there, sitting unnoticed, watching, my legs dangling over the edge of the counter beside the sink…watching, learning how this is done and committing it to a memory that will last a lifetime, and beyond. From generation to generation to generation.

There was a strength in Mother's embrace. A clearheaded lucid intimacy and I could see from the look on Father's face that he'd forgotten about the fields and the certainty of a split harvest. The embrace of a dappling rainfall on a dry crop.

What followed was a quiet dinner, a casserole with cream corn. The tension of the day before was gone, reconciled to a lost deadline and a seeming acceptance to play the cards dealt. A relief, almost.

Father managed a short bath and in less than an hour we were in the north field. The hands returned from Lavetty's and Clare's dinners, moseying up Pond Road, smoking and talking and laughing. Bim waited at the drive and when the road was clear, she turned up toward town with a honk and a wave and I waved from the platform behind the tractor seat, thinking for some reason how Givens' new tractor had an enclosed cab and a radio.

Later, on a pass near the gardens, I waved to the house where Mother and the girls sat watching from the back porch. A few rows on, I tracked a flock of Canadian geese, flying overhead in perfect formation and silhouetted against the deep red sky along the horizon and I thought how the entire sky would be blocked out by the roof of Givens' cab, that it was too sterile and confining and what was the point of being in the fields if you couldn't smell the air and taste the dirt in your teeth? Before you knew it, they would have tractors like robots and a farmer could sit on the porch and plant his fields with the levers of a remote control. But then Givens was sixty-three and a sixty-three-year-old man might think differently.

I thought how it was too bad about the weather, how yesterday's thick clouded sky had disappeared and the rain along the Cumberland had turned south into Kentucky and how there was probably no chance of more rain when what we needed was a light soaking the first week after the planting. I tried to remember what it was like with a hard rain. I was maybe seven when the last good storm came through and what I recalled was the river spilling over onto the lower pasture and when it receded, the pasture was left littered with tree limbs and split logs and a few old whisky bottles that made for good target shooting. One thing was the look of healthy corn, endless rows of tall stout corn spread out over the fields and when the sun came back out and the wind picked up, the fields were a deeper green, shimmering like pond water. A clear dustless green that was pierced by black rainsoaked soil. That I remember.

I leaned down close to Father's ear, "I guess Lankard'll be by next week...with that vertical link."

Father nodded and a few minutes later leaned back to speak over the engine noise, "Be sure you milk Cow every morning and you might want to keep an eye on the new well. If it gets to looking too silty, then call Diligence. Shut the pump off first...you don't want silty water filling the tank. And no more of this trouble between you and Mariah. Dee's got enough without you two bickering."

He turned to look me in the eye. "Okay?"

I gave him a face like I didn't know what he meant and I said, "Sure...sure, Dad."

For a time, we didn't say anything, moving from one end of the field to the other in a mindless redundancy; the clean divisions on either side of the tractor represented our progress and in between there was nothing but daydreams. I imagined Scooter breaking in with the Cardinals as a twelve-year-old and seeing him on the cover of all the baseball magazines and having front-row seats anytime I wanted. And then Buddy racing at the Evansville track and winning all the big purses and he and Mariah living in a mansion up in Indianapolis and sending me pit-passes every year for the Indy 500.

It was after ten when we finished the last row. We came back along the fenceline to pull up beside the gardens. The hands stood gathered quietly behind the tractor, standing tired and quiet, hoping, surely, to be released for the night. I jumped from the platform and staggered to find my land legs. Father leaned over, raising his voice over the engine, "Get yourself a good night's sleep, son. I'll see you in the morning."

"Ain't you comin?"

He shook his head and waved me off and before I could react, the tractor was in motion, heading toward the peach grove. The hands followed up, lumbering tired but without complaint and I stood watching them move along the fence to the edge of the barnyard, rounding the windmill and disappearing beyond the silo and up the west field fence toward the subsidy field until there were only the headlight beams, bobbing shafts of light.

I went inside, sensing Mother and the girls were already in bed. I walked through the kitchen into the living room and through the dining room and into the library, absorbing the odd silence of what seemed an empty house and trying to imagine how it would be with both of them in Evansville.

When the telephone rang, it was like a dinner bell, shattering the silence.

I hurried to the receiver on the kitchen wall. It was Vivian, wanting to know why there were tractor lights in the subsidy field and I told her how Father was still working.

"At this hour?"

"Yes, ma'am."

"Is he about finished?"

"No, ma'am. I reckon not…there's only the one tractor."

There was a pause and she asked how Mother was and I told her she was doing fine all day.

There was another pause and she said, "You go on to bed, honey. It's late…school tomorrow."

I hung up the phone and stood for a moment in the darkness of the kitchen until Clare eventually appeared from her room off the laundry. In her robe and slippers, she sleepily worked up a sandwich while I wandered into the dining room, absorbing the rare emptiness, and on to the stillness of the library where my eyes slowly adjusted to the shadowed configurations of the shelves that lined the walls. When I was younger, much younger, Mother used to tell me that it was during the night when the books breathed, that a good story lived forever and when the bindings expanded and crackled on hot summer nights that it was the sound of the books breathing.

Clare appeared, took my hand and led me back to the kitchen as if I were a blind schoolboy. I sat at the counter, nibbling her sandwich before wandering into the living room and over to the piano, lifting the fallboard, running my fingertips along the keyslip and then lightly over the keyboard, slick with dust. I walked through the living room and back into the kitchen where Clare stood waiting.

"Go to bed."

"I ain't sleepy."

"Go to bed."

I shuffled through the dining room and stood for a moment, stalling, before turning up the stairs to pause at the dormer window. The lights were on at the Marsh house and I thought that was odd considering how Givens and Vivian always turned in early and how Givens had no reason to be working late; no one in that house going to Evansville. I crossed the room to stand over the small desk. The scattered papers had been cleared away. I ran my finger across the wood surface. It seemed unacceptably naked, as bare and disassociated as the furniture in the attic.

I went into the bedroom and looked off toward the fields but it was too dark to see anything. If they were in the east field, I could watch from bed. I could follow the progress of the tractor beams. But they were out of view, beyond the rise of Slave Hill. For a moment, I considered getting dressed and making my way out to the subsidy field. Would Father be glad to see me? Or would it be the cold look he had worn all day yesterday?

I couldn't sleep. I tossed and rolled and stared at the ceiling, wishing Verity was awake, or Mariah, or anyone when I thought I heard a tractor, the Allis-Chalmers. I sat up, listening, feeling certain that it was the Chalmers and that it was approaching the barnyard from...where? The west field? I left the bed and crossed the dayroom and from the long window, I spotted three pairs of narrow high-set beams moving slowly down Pond Road toward the house. I unlatched the window and the sound carried into the dayroom like a glorious symphony. There was Givens' Allis-Chalmers and Liberty Snead's John Deere and what had to be Givens' second-string John Deere and I wanted to call out, to empty my lungs screaming, shouting that I had seen them.

I ran to Verity's window and watched them bobbing across the bridge, their headlights flickering like strobes against the trelliswork and then down the slope to manage the embankment, setting them onto the open plain of the east field. I went to my own window, kneeling on the bed to watch them skirting the far bank of the river until they were beyond the sycamores and deep into the stand of cottonwoods buffering the west field and then gone from view. A light at the Arthurs' went on and I knew Madeline was awake now and probably at the kitchen window on the new phone with Vivian and Marian Snead and who knows who else and I wondered if they would call here, risk waking Mother. Call me.

It was several minutes before I slipped between the bedsheets, opening the window and succumbing to the pillow, listening until the fading hum of the engines was beyond range and there was only the darkness and the silence. It was well after midnight before I finally gave in to sleep.

Seven hours later, I woke to find Mother in the dayroom, studying the clean surface of her desk. I dressed and ran down the stairs and through the house and onto the lawn, hurdling the short fence and to the barnyard to scatter the chickens like feathers in a windstorm. I entered the barn, spooking Sow One and startling Cow with a handslap to her flank before scaling the ladder quick and crossing the loft to reach the far hatch to catch my breath, scanning the fields until I found them, all four of them off the far side of the north field, working the last unseeded acreage.

I slopped Sow One and scattered feed to the Banshees and while milking Cow, I tapped my feet to an imaginary melody. At eight, Marian Snead arrived and a few minutes later, making our way up Pond Road toward the bus stop, Mariah and Verity and I sighted Vivian behind the wheel of their truck, shortcutting along the north field fenceline heading toward the others with breakfast and fresh coffee, no doubt.

We were late returning home. Aunt Dee and I had waited on the porch of Dr. Leemore's house as Verity's cast was removed and delayed again at Bim's to load Dee's trunk with platters of food and a new dress for Mother before arriving at the Fallers where Mariah was sitting in silence, occupying one end of the porch with her back to Buddy who occupied the other end of the porch and Dolores between them, like a referee at a wrestling match. From the Fallers, we stopped at the Salon for Aunt Elizabeth and finally up Sycamore where Ruby and Scooter were idling the MG, falling in line up Main Street as a caravan to turn off Deere Road and parade down Pond Road, kicking up dust like it was deep summer.

At the house, the others mounted the table leaves and smoothed out the tablecloths and arranged the settings with platters and when they were satisfied, they retired with their shawls to the chairs situated along the front edge of the lawn as Scooter and I scattered croquet balls across the grass.

Amidst the chatter and the swinging mallets, we glanced to the changing colors of a sunset bleeding bright pink to violet and eventually, by twilight, the stubborn-red ribbon off the crest of Kickapoo Ridge as Givens sounded off his new horn, something like Carl's train whistle, and we pressed against the fencerails as they arrived, throttling up the embankment and along the barnyard to a row of crazy women waving their arms like children, like spectators at a parade. Being silly.

Dinner for twelve, and if the talk touched on Evansville, it was with the same optimism as the talk of a strong harvest and a drought-busting rain and throughout the following day, from the moment Mother and Father pulled away from the drive, the sounds of that night lingered in the airspace of a house that seemed empty as an old barn.

FIFTY-SEVEN

"We want to thank you, Mr. Roe, for the courtesy of your time. As I've mentioned, you're a resource of invaluable proportions."

"You're welcome."

"The Marshal Plan, as you know, as we all know, was a measure of rehabilitation, aimed to fortify a weakened Europe. To feed them, of course, to prevent widespread starvation, as well as an economic package to rebuild those infrastructures decimated by the war."

"Decimated. Yes."

"The package, however, was not extended to the Russians, our allies on the eastern front, whose casualties exceeded the wildest imaginations. Mr. Harriman was very specific in his allowances. Sanctions, essentially. Preventing your father's contribution from reaching the Russians."

"Yes, confusion."

"There was no confusion. Harriman acted without oversight. He withheld that grain to weaken a potential adversary from rising to control Europe."

"Would you want some tea?"

"Tea? Hmmm, thank you. I have tea already."

"So, at the WHO, we are concerned, among other things, with world hunger. With the history of those with agricultural resources and their monopolizing platforms

288

CHARLES PROWELL

toward those without resources. Your father met with Averill Harriman, according to Harriman's papers and state department records. Here, on this very farm. Just months before Harriman arrived in Britain. They signed an accord. Your father's signature is on that accord."

"Father's signature...on baseballs, mostly."

"Baseballs?"

"Mostly."

FIFTY-EIGHT

Little Maddy and Whisty are learning to play chess. We lie splayed out on the featherbed, Maddy's legs twirling and the board teetering unsteadily. To little Henry, I say, "Move your big men. Move them out so they can capture my men."

"But I don't have a plan, Poppa."

"But you can't win if you don't take a chance. You can't capture my men if you don't move your Rook and your Bishop."

"But I don't have a plan. Do you have a plan, Poppa?"

I shake my head as Maddy gives the Rook and the Bishop their own voices. Little tinny voices. Singing voices. And then out of nowhere, without warning, the board overturns and chessmen go flying, clattering across the attic floor and what follows, what always follows, is a wrestling match. Roughhousing until we're lost in the soft folds of that big featherbed.

FIFTY-NINE

At daybreak, we're awakened to stand gathered in our pajamas watching from the end of the drive as the family stationwagon passed beyond the Marsh house to top the rise and disappear from view in a half-lit haze of reddish dust.

Half a minute passed and Mariah, with the hint of an adultish frown, planted her hands on her hips to strike the early silence with, "Can we go back to bed now?"

But there was no response. We stood squinting into the clear fragile sky drawing off the east field horizon, hypnotized by the quality of the light born off the ridgeline: pink to purple to the threatening blue of a looming June.

The dust settled back onto the roadbed and the colors of the spring sky continued to spill over the fields with that changing phosphorous light good for another two or three weeks before summer arrived like a hammerblow—the whitish blue skies from dawn to dusk without the character or the integrity or the depth of a spring sky.

Mariah folded her arms and rubbed her sleeve against the morning chill.

Verity turned her back to the road, and to Mariah.

291

POSSESSING THE SEASONS

I moved my feet, shuffling my weight back and forth.

We occupied this place at the end of the drive as if isolated, awaiting instructions. Mariah began shifting her stance while running one slipper lightly along the gravel as the whip-poor-wills awakened with something Verity responded to and the whip-poor-wills replied, in unison, and Mariah said, "Are you talking to them?"

Verity shrugged and I said, out of the blue, "I wish they were going to St. Louis. Taking us along."

A hint. A prompt directed perhaps at Mariah. But neither Mariah nor Dolores had offered anything reminiscent of a reaction regarding their St. Louis trip and the prompt went unanswered. To the rest of us, it remained a city of the imagination; Aunt Harriet's house in the center of the city sandwiched, we imagined, between identical houses so close you couldn't wedge a finger between them. Rooms perfectly arranged and immaculate and decorated with expensive odd-looking furniture with everything but comfort in mind. Restaurants and movie theaters and stage shows with elaborate sets and museums you could get lost in. Big sprawling parks with bronzed statues. Sidewalk cafés. The Mississippi River. The mammoth barges maneuvering the harbor. The St. Louis Cardinals.

Back in the house, breakfast was waiting. Dee's breakfast, which is not to be compared to Clare's breakfast.

"They off, then?" Dee said.

We nodded and Dee confirmed her conspiring promise of no school but there was little reaction.

"Why don't you all go down to Madeline and Elmer's? Clare went early. She and Lavette are becoming best friends. I think it'd be good... the three of you together today."

No response.

"Or you can go to school..."

Onto Pond Road, we walked in silence with nothing more in common than the thread of our layered surroundings and the rich depths of our combined genealogies. Lately, with Mariah and Verity embedded in adolescence and me on the cusp of change, our time together—beyond the trek to and from the bus stop—had suffered a fate similar to those afternoons with the toy soldiers and the doll house and the legions of plastic horses. Gone, now...withered away like passing time. Too gradual for any of us to know exactly when we had stopped spending time together.

We walked in an awkward silence, pulling in the spring air, but quickly I dropped off to the side of the road and squatted on my heels to observe a long row of red ants, moving in a systematic march along the edge of the gravel. An army. To my right, a nest of physically larger black ants in a state of red alert. Clearly, a state of panic.

"Hey, look here," I called out, but Mariah and Verity maintained the center of the road. To Verity, Mariah said, "You know, nobody else does that."

"Does what?"

"Singing talk."

Verity shrugged and said, "Did you save the pattern for those black pants?"

"I think so. Do you want another pair?"

"Maybe. Can the waist be brought in, just a little?"

"Sure. That's easy."

Beyond the bridge, Clare and Lavette turned off the drive and headed up on foot, holding hands, singing, and Lavette might have been thinking how things change. How Rufus, her younger brother, had developed an interest in landscaping, given free rein to exercise that interest, and how she was learning to cook, to feed so many hands and how cooking for Miss Pond and Mr. Arthur was different and seeing how Clare lived, with her beau and how things could change. They could.

Behind them, Madeline and Elmer followed. Not holding hands, but companionably communicating, sharing something neither had ever known. Verbal companionship.

A car approached from behind. We stepped aside as Elizabeth rolled past with a slight wave, and from the side of the road, kneeling over the battle site, I glanced at the passing car and made to shiver. I turned back to the anthill, where the red ants were marching a thousand strong.

"So, how's Bump?"

"Bump? He's fine."

"So, you're going out?"

"Going out? What's that mean?"

"It means you're dating."

"Bump doesn't drive, Mariah."

I scored a line in the dirt with my finger. A trench.

Mariah and Verity stepped toward the siege but their thoughts were elsewhere.

"Why don't we double date?"

"You mean, with you and Buddy?"

"Sure. We could go to Golconda for a pizza."

"Is that what you do? Does Mom know?"

"Sometimes. And no, she doesn't know."

Clare and Lavette reached the bridge and their singing paused as Elizabeth passed and as the Plymouth dropped down to the lower roadbed, Madeline stopped and Elmer waited, confused as Madeline glanced at the low fence on the right and the low fence on the left and back toward the house, the distance to the outhouse, but the Plymouth was upon them, rolling to a stop as Elmer reached back to take Madeline's hand and carry forth between her and the sister who spoke from the open window, the Plymouth in reverse, rolling backward as Elmer and Madeline continued walking, approaching the bridge.

The sacking army fell into confusion, piling on top of one another at the trench as Mariah said, "Hey, I just thought of something. What if you married Bump and I married Buddy and we were sisters-in-law? The Bump and Buddy Girls."

CHARLES PROWELL

She laughed aloud and Verity said, "So you'll marry Buddy, then? What about college?"

"I was just kidding, Verdi. Jeeze. Buddy's an idiot."

"So, why do you…"

Clare and Lavette arrived, glancing over their shoulders as the Plymouth negotiated the bridge, in reverse.

I marked off yet another blockade in the dirt and the tide turned as Lavette kneeled beside me as Clare glanced toward the bridge and to Mariah and Verity she said, "They's battl'n…those two's."

Close enough now that Elizabeth's voice carried when suddenly the Plymouth's rear bumper crumpled against the century-old iron trellis. Elizabeth worked the steering wheel, cranking it one way and another but lodged in place as Elmer and Madeline continued on, clearing the bridge and a moment later standing with the rest of us, a gathering of nomads going nowhere in particular.

Mariah leaned to kiss Madeline on both cheeks and kiss Clare on both cheeks and paused to consider Lavette, kneeling at the anthill. Lavette stood and wiped her knees and offered her cheeks as if to an heiress, a grand dame of noble blood as Givens' truck rolled slowly by, coming to a stop short of the bridge and from the window of the Plymouth, "Why Givey, what brings you out this way?"

295

SIXTY

The days moved along.

The house like a mausoleum and the rooms at times too quiet, longing for the sound of the piano and the hymns carrying up the stairs. I took to spending more time in the barn, rising for an earlier start on the morning chores and lingering in the evenings, consumed with tending my idle duties and overseeing the new well slowly going dry until Sheriff was sent to fetch me and occasionally, we lingered behind the barn in the last light of day running off rounds with the 20-gauge and calling it target-shooting but it was more like carpet-bombing, blowing up tin cans aligned like bowling pins along the top fencerail.

Purpose requires structure and structure requires purpose and without them, together, time was marked by nothing more than the rising and setting sun.

The girls worked the long garden until the light was gone and they could no longer see to separate the edge of the hoe from the delicate spring stems while Dee sat positioned outside the kitchen door, overlooking the garden, polishing the family silver. On several evenings, we ate dinner on the screen porch, our folding trays arranged to face the cottonwoods silhouetted against the light of the rising moon.

Ben Dubois announced that Dubois Implementry was going out of business and within hours, it was learned he would sell a portion of his inventory to Dillavou Implementry upstate and a portion back to the manufacturers at a slight loss. The business itself would simply close its doors because no buyer in his right mind would take on the debited accounts of nearly every farmer in the valley. The building, the empty shell that had for fifty-six years housed one of the most stable businesses in Fall Ridge, would be offered up in late May.

The news was initially shocking but when the shock wore off, there was a consensus of sympathy and shaking heads and muttering the way we did when mourning the dead and how the mourning gave way to the collective guilt of all those whose accounts with Ben Dubois were open and outstanding. Ben's loss was everyone's loss and it struck a blow to the community that might easily have prompted an avalanche: sell off before it's too late, before the sum of rising debts overwhelms the value of weakening equities.

But of course, it was already too late. Land prices had been dropping for two months and that Ben had found a more salvageable closure by selling inventory back to the manufacturers than as an auctioned open-market offering was testament enough. Ten days into May. Anyone who hadn't already liquidated was by now committed to waiting, to gambling everything on the Roe seed. On a heavenly graceful rain.

The Arthur farm was developing into a compound. A center of activity populated by the field hands who had stayed on following the seeding to fashion dormitory style quarters in Barn One. A small lawn of Kentucky bluegrass had been seeded by Rufus with a new cinder path cut and tamped in a meandering route that appeared to go

POSSESSING THE SEASONS

nowhere, or everywhere. Those with skills taught those without, to the sound of handsaws and hammers, repairing sideboards and corbels and fencelines bordering nothing, or everything, set and appointed with an invented preoccupation, a purpose that gradually took its form from the structure of an Amish industrialism. Not to be confused with an Amish doctrine, there were no services or prayer gatherings. There was Elmer Arthur who was discovering a craving for noise and commotion, for the company of others while Madeline was discovering her own cravings toward indiscriminate acquaintances.

And gradually the productive purposes took hold throughout the valley. Mending posts and stretching wire. Spring cleaning and reorganized pantries and cellars. Forty-seven farms with their ten-thousand acres of clean symmetrical furrows all seeded. Waiting. Waiting now for what no one dared mention. The mornings all a breathless blue stacked up clear to New Orleans and the afternoons with the hints of a strong June; the precious timidity of a perfect spring infected now with the sallow skies of a changing season. As a prescription for saneness, it was a week for the light-minded occupation of mending perimeters.

Dee deep-cleaned the house and returned the books left on the dayroom dormer to their rightful shelves and assured us how 'no matter what, we would always have her,' and Mariah, Verity, and I, confused, replied with, "What's that mean?"

"Jes means no matter what."

"Well then, no matter what, you'll always have us."

"Good."

"Good."

"Fine."

"Fine."

298

SIXTY-ONE

We bounced down the hall out the big oak schoolhouse doors waltzing like princes through the playground and across the field to trample the newborn grass. Onto the Elm Street sidewalk, we jabbered and hollered and jostled our way to the old field beyond the dead Dr. Steadfast Stewart's house. A new season with no coach and scraps of wood for bases and with a range in ages from nine to eighteen. Just enough for a two-team league.

But it was all for Scooter. The whole thing formed more or less for Scooter, who played the game at a level the rest of us could only imagine and with no league, he had no chance and everyone knew baseball was Scooter's only chance.

Strutting and skipping beneath the leafing elms, we passed the cornerstone homes, covering our ears to Mercy May's redundant scales and over the creek bridge, juggling our mitts in the air and along the Town Hall banging and pushing and shoving like puppies to pull up at the corner of Main Street as if reaching the edge of a precipice.

We stood for a moment, staring, fingering our mitts and shifting our weight from one leg to another like poised rabbits glancing at Scooter and then up toward his mom, occupying the center of the road and then

299

down Elm toward the beckoning ballfield. Scooter stepped off the curb, dropping one arm to motion us back. Pat Davis appeared out front of the Café and farther up, Elizabeth Pond emerged from the Salon as Bim appear on the steps of the Gazette with Scooter approaching, waving them all off as he arrived to peel his mom's fingers off the rim of the open cab window and drew her arms down to her side with a bear-hug as we gingerly crossed Main Street, where Acceptance stood beside her father.

"You should help, Jussie."

"He don't want it."

"He's your best friend."

"Whoever told you that?"

But I lingered, drawn not by an allegiance or romance to Acceptance but more a need to replace the Mariah who once shared my soldier games and the Verity who now belonged to Bump and a mother gone distant.

By the time Bump continued, alone, passing Town Hall, anyone along Sycamore would have noted the kick in his step was lost to a weakening bravado, slapping his mitt to the rhythm of a lethargic stride, interrupted by the convalescing pace of Mr. and Mrs. Dawson leaving Doc Leemore's to negotiate the curb like wobbly toddlers as Buddy pulled alongside with one arm slung out the window, motioning his brother toward the curb. Bump approached to see Mariah, and in the back, Verity.

"Hop in…we'll give you a ride."

"It's only a block."

"Hop in, Numbnuts."

He slid in the backseat and according to Verity, whose lack of dramatic modality only enhanced her very credibility, Bump was uneasy. He glanced furtively in her direction as Mariah moved her left arm along Buddy's shoulders and leaned in to kiss his neck and with a matchmaker's smile, Mariah turned back to where Bump and Verity sat as if sharing a church pew.

"Hey, let's drive out to Cave-In-Rock."

"Too far, baby. We got ball."

Buddy jumped the throttle and the car lurched and he looked to Mariah chuckling and again punched the throttle and the car jerked and lurched and from the backseat, "Dad said not to do that."

Buddy reached his arm back, gripping Bump's collar and Bump wrenched it free, teetering to where Verity caught him with a hand on his shoulder. He froze, one elbow on the seat beside her as she smoothed out his wrinkled collar and looked to the front seat saying, "Hands off my Bumpie!"

Buddy threw his head back and laughed aloud. "Yes, ma'am!"

Mariah ran her fingers along the back of Buddy's neck and said, "So, we going for a ride or what?"

Buddy raised his mitt up, in lieu of words, and Mariah removed her arm as Scooter and Ruby were making their way up the walk. I followed, at some distance. Passing the Davis house, Granny Davis leaned forward from her porch rocker, turning her good ear to matching the sound of footsteps to the identity of the passersby. At the little Queen Anne with its blistering paint and filmy windowpanes, its weedy lawn and listing screen door, we left the magnificent spring air for a front room choked with the scent of tobacco and overflowing ashtrays. Ruby sat herself in the armchair pocked with burnholes and lit a rolled cigarette and adopted her pose—her right leg crossed and woven around her left leg with her elbow on the armrest holding the cigarette near her lips with her head bent low and her chin resting against her breastbone, staring at nothing. Utter nothingness.

We waited a moment, Scooter tapping the bat against the toe of his shoe, before we turned out the front door, practically colliding with Doc Leemore negotiating the porch steps. Doc raised an eyebrow and Scooter answered with a shrug and as we started across the lawn, Doc stood at the screen door and called out, "Hit'em good, boy!"

Hit'em good. But what else can he say? Can anyone say?

POSSESSING THE SEASONS

We rounded the neighbor's house and through the century-old boxleaf to the makeshift outfield where little Bing Bing Larsen was bent over, his mitt on his head, peering between his nine-year-old legs as the God of all Gods approached the infield to come up behind home plate, joining those on the bench with a flurry of banging and jostling and puppylove shoves. Scooter, and his sidekick, had arrived.

There are varying accounts of that afternoon, culled mostly from surviving descendants of those actually present. Those verbal histories where a poignant noun goes missing and then a pivotal sentence gets rearranged until all we're really left with is the one-column-inch wrap-up in that week's Gazette, penned by roving reporter, Linkum Regards:

Opening Day results and stats
Hurled insults and swinging bats
Black eyes and home run flies
A swinging fist and a knockout brawl
A Morrow home run over the wall.
Team #1: 52 Team #2: 53

302

SIXTY-TWO

Decades later, when Lewelyn *Scooter* Morrow died, nearly everyone in Fall Ridge showed up for his funeral. Including Rose and Emily, two half-sisters whose relation neither the diseased nor the two sisters were ever aware of. He was buried alongside the decomposed remains of the town's founders up in the Fall Ridge Cemetery, overlooking the river and the fields and many of the same farmhouses he had robbed over the course of his foreshortened forty-two years of life.

We came because Scooter was a native son. Because he was everyone's son, passing among us all in an act of collective upbringing that left everyone, and no one, fully responsible.

SIXTY-THREE

Mariah, Verity, and I made our way down Sycamore, a step behind the umpire, behind Sheriff, to arrive at Pond Alterations. A moment later, Dee and the girls left in her car. Sheriff and I crossed Bonnel Road in his truck with the window open and the wind rushing against the exposed flesh of a scraped cheek and the Sheriff asked, "Why do you figure you can't hit that ball?"

I looked to the Sheriff and back through the window at the passing countryside, playing the fight through my mind, Scooter and I back-to-back, pulverizing the beanball-pitching Buddy and I said, "Hard to see it, Sheriff. It's blurry."

"Blurry…you mean, as in blurry?"

Sheriff didn't know there were glasses, prescription spectacles buried in the top drawer beside my bed.

We passed Snead's Corner and rolled to a stop at the Arthur Compound's new gate, honking as Lavetty called to Madeline who called to Clare who appeared through the kitchen door. She arrived at the truck to set a few items in the bed and climbed in beside me, studying my cheek.

"What you done?"

"S'nothin."

"Fight'n. With who?"

I shrugged and Clare closed the door and shook her head and as we neared the bridge, I said, "When'll they be back?"

With his left wrist slung over the steering wheel, Sheriff leaned to one side, pulling out his pocket watch and snapping the crystal closed and said, "Any time now."

We waited. Standing at the end of the drive, waiting under the brittle skies of late afternoon while meandering from one side of the drive to another and into the center of the road, watching the rise at the Marsh house as the light feathered from a blue to a darker blue and flooded the fields with an eveningsoft brilliance spilling violently off the ridgeline like buckets of blood.

We waited until the light was gone. Until the nightsky took shape with the twinkling doubts of some unexplained delay when off the crest of Pond Road, a pair of headlights bobbed into view, distant flashlights careening over the rise in a haze of shadowy dust, honking, honking the horn and honking the horn and suddenly we were hollering, laughing out loud to where the sparrows were chased from the twin cherry trees, swooping and fluttering against the light of a thriving moon.

Following them up the drive and gathering at the passenger door like charter members of an exclusive fan club, we registered our impressions with an honesty known only to the privacy of one's thoughts.

Mariah opened the door and Mother swung her legs around the seat and the glow of the porchlight caught her face to expose a change. She smiled and looked at us and for a moment, we stood recording the changes as if itemizing an inventory. She seemed older. She appeared, well...pausing on the edge of the car seat as if summoning a second wind. Her hair had lost some of its luster, replaced with a thinner texture pulled into a tight bun accentuating a hollowness in her cheeks...a dry pallor to her cheeks.

POSSESSING THE SEASONS

Later, with Mother resting and Dee and the girls lingering at the foot of the bed, Father studied the pump gauge while I stood to the side, all business, ready for the questions to which I had the answers—farmer to farmer.

Crouched beside the well, he made a few calculations on a notepad, looking older...moving, it seemed, with a more measured rhythm. Sow caught his scent and lumbered over to nuzzle her snout against his pantlegs while Cow loitered at the saltlick off the corner of the barn, making sounds like she hadn't been milked in two weeks and sensing, somehow, that in the morning she would be returning to the gentler and more practiced stroke she was used to.

Each evening, as instructed, I had carefully doled out portions of last season's baled barley and alfalfa, dropping it through the feedhole in the loft to supplement the grazing. On a good year, the loft would have been stacked to the rafters with enough feed put aside in October to nurse the stock through the winter and, under usual grazing conditions, clear through to September. But this year, not only had everyone sold off their winter livestock—the calves and young hogs—as a harbor against available grain, but the known certainty of grain on credit when grain prices had doubled and credit was no longer an option. There was a meager two dozen bales of barley and alfalfa salvaged from a paltry September harvest, stacked in a loft so empty your voice echoed off the rake of the roof. Two dozen bales more than any other loft in the valley.

There had been no precipitation during Father's absence. The fields, everyone's fields, held the same turned-earth appearance since the rush to seed. No newborn sprouts breaking ground with the excitable green stubble separating providence from failure. Aside from the gardens—and the flourishing Arthur Cooperative gardens in particular, irrigated by a sprinkling of new wells and graywater residue pumped from the new lines—the valley's landscape exposed the contemplation of a waiting game that was trying the nerves of the stoutest resolve. A decision had been made that afternoon in the Café weeks ago. Everyone or no one,

306

opting for the devil-seed that would shift the methodologies of the past one-hundred-fifty years toward an unknown future that banked on an unknown science by an outsider who admitted to a shortage of conclusive data—information.

I told all this to Father, summarizing things as I saw them in a speech I had been rehearsing for days. Father stood listening, studying me, his son with the curious mind, all of it so logically and carefully understood and for a moment, he might have considered himself at the same age. But there was no comparison. I was his wonder boy, privileged, born and raised deep in the heart of the heart of heaven-on-earth, capable of calculating grain to beef prices. But in time, his eyes returned from the distractions of Mother and the stay in Evansville while I continued my rehearsed speech as the slightly pretentious monologue of a kid who understood he was, after all, just a kid.

It was complicated; I thought I understood as well as anyone but there was so much I didn't know and it was an overwhelming relief to have Father hear me out, to have him standing over the well and back on the farm where he belonged.

"It's down to a gallon a minute, Dad."

There was no response and I wondered if his mind was still in Evansville, still at the hospital, watching Mother probed like a rat in a laboratory.

Had I said too much? Should I have waited? Measured out the news over the course of a few hours and then later, much later, mentioned that the well happened to be going dry? That in his absence, Fall Fork's request for federal aid had been denied while breaking a one-hundred-ten-year-old record for the most consecutive days without measurable precipitation. 'Oh, Dad, by the way, in another week or two, we won't be able to water the garden which means we won't have a table harvest to be canned for the cellar which means if it wasn't for Mom's books, we'd have to maybe move to town which means...'

POSSESSING THE SEASONS

The sound of my voice, I realized, had been bordering on the dramatic. I was worried and I was concerned and I needed to hear the sound of his voice. I needed it the way I needed the sound of the piano returning to carry through the rooms of a house that had seemed too quiet for too long.

Father shifted his weight from one foot to another and ran his hand down over his cheek to cup his chin before turning to walk over to the corner of the barn. I followed, stretching my stride to match the imprint, puffs of dust like ground chalk settling over the toes of Father's leather town shoes until the shine of the buffed cordovan had the same dull colorless film that marked the entire valley.

At the edge of the barn, he stopped and rested an arm over Cow's hindquarters. Her tail flipped up to leave a brush of dust against his white shirt as he stroked the back of my neck as if I were the dog, as if I were the hound. For close to a minute, he stared out over the hardened furrows of the lower field and beyond the river, through the clearing in the cottonwoods to where a corner of the fertile east field was exposed like a dry and lifeless photograph.

He turned to me and held the look before the hint of a smile marked his expression and he said, "Good job."

That was all I needed. I didn't want him going on about how or why it was a good job. I needed only to hear what I had just heard and then I wanted to hear the plan.

"So, what's the plan, Dad? Do we have a plan?"

He smiled and his smile grew wider until he was chuckling and I thought he'd lost his mind. Left it back in Indiana.

"What's so funny, Dad?"

"You are, Sport. Sometimes I hear you and I can't believe my ears. Sometimes I look at you and I see a full-grown man, not the boy who's only twelve."

I considered this for a moment, this sharp departure from business. Man-to-man business.

CHARLES PROWELL

"It don't make a matter I'm twelve or not, Dad."

"Make a matter? Good Lord, boy."

"Well, it don't. I see it like everyone else…and we need some plan."

"Some plan?"

"Come on, Dad…what's the plan?"

"You're too serious, son. Life's too short. You shouldn't worry so much. So, how's the ball playing? You getting some hits?"

I stood confused, watching his eyes and wondering if he had been away from the farm too long? Something had happened in Evansville. Something was different.

"Not really, Dad. I don't have any hits, actually. The ball…it's never where I'm swingin."

"Well then, you're thinking too much. It's just like everything else: you study the fundamentals and once you've got the mechanics figured out, after you've worked in all the variables—the chance of rain or the beef market come September or whether he's coming in with a curve inside and up or just a straight fastball…well then, you forget it all and swing with your instincts."

"Huh?"

"Come on."

He started toward the front of the barn and I followed. He grabbed the bat leaning against the sliding doors and the three balls off the shelf and disappeared around the front, flicking on the barnyard floodlight and juggling the three balls in his one hand, tossing them like a slow Ferris wheel. I came through the barn and out the doors where he stood waiting a few feet off the barn sidewall. He held the bat out and I studied it as if it were a violin.

"What?"

"Take it."

"Why?"

"Just take it, Buddyboy."

309

POSSESSING THE SEASONS

I reached for the bat and rested it along my shoulder to adopt a lazy stance and Father faced me, cradling the three balls. He tossed one with an easy arc and it bounced off my chest to strike the ground with a puff of dust.

"You're supposed to swing."

He tossed another and I carried through with a sluggish motion five or six inches below the arc of the ball.

"Come on, Sport…put your heart into it."

"Kinda stupid, Dad. Hardly like what Buddy throws."

He tossed another, then another, and I was swinging with a slightly better effort but nowhere close to the ball.

"Shouldn't we be thinkin of the alfalfa, Dad? There jes ain't enough of it and…"

"Run on up and get those spectacles of yours. I'll wait here."

"I don't do 'em, Dad."

"You don't do 'em? What's that mean?"

"Means I hate'm. They're clunky. I see fine."

"Well go get them, anyway…for me."

"For you?"

"Just get them…please?"

I dropped the bat and turned grudgingly toward the house and ten minutes later, I returned, walking, squishing my face to accommodate the frames resting off my nose like a diseased appendage.

"Okay."

"I think they go over your eyes, son…not down on the end of your nose."

"They won't stay there."

He stepped in and positioned the glasses where they belonged and fingered the stems behind my ears and stepped back.

"How's that?"

"Better, I reckon."

He held out the bat handle and I took it, frowning, planting my feet and tightening my grip and with the first toss, I swung and tapped the

310

ball to glance off the barn behind me and as I stood considering the effort, another ball bounced off my chest.

"Hey, I wasn't ready."

"I can see that."

Another ball arching softly and another swing with partial contact and as I readied my bat, the ball bounced off my chest.

"Hey."

"What?"

"Cut it out, Dad."

Another toss and swing and another and another in quick succession and with each pitch, I was quicker to ready myself with no time to think, no time to do anything but pull the bat quickly back over my shoulder as the next ball left Father's hand and the pitches started clapping off the side of the barn and with each clapping impact, I swung harder until there was the rhythm of a repeating form, a mechanical reflex drawn from instinct and physical attributes and a lack of mental interference.

Ten minutes later, Father stopped. He rubbed his hand against a lower back still sore from the drive home and I held the bat out and said, "How bout it, Dad?"

"How about what?"

"Hit'n one."

He shook his head and said, "That's your thing, kiddo."

"Not really, Dad. It's not really my thing at all."

He took the bat and tossed a ball into the air and casually swung to send the ball sailing somewhere deep into the darkness of the lower pasture and I said, "I meant against the barn, Dad. We'll never find that'n."

"It's just a ball."

"I only had three…now I got two."

"So, why do you say baseball isn't your thing?"

"Oh, I'll play and all, but I'm writin up the games now and the column and I get paid some. It's a job. I get paid some."

"Like your mother. The writer."

We passed the Annex when Father stopped and I quickly maneuvered to avoid a collision. He stepped over to the door and fingered the open boltshackle and turned to his shadow, to me.

"You been in here, son?"

"No way, Dad."

He removed the lock and we entered the humidity of the sanctuary, moving among the flats of germinating seedlings. He scanned the room to settle on the one logbook splayed out on the table, and beside it the gas-oiled lamp with a blackened chimney, and on the dirt below the lamp a checkered bandana. He reached to pick it up and ran it through his fingers and I said, "Ain't that Wes' bandana, Dad?"

Outside, Father locked the boltshackle and moved across the barnyard in long quick steps too quick and too broad for me to match. We rounded the house and reached the cellar and he swung the door open as if it were a sheet of paper, disappearing down the steps and to the back wall. I followed as far as the bottom step, tentatively, negotiating the phobia of the cellar as a tomb as Father slid a row of jars with the back of one hand, exposing the stack of seventeen logs. He returned the jars to their former position and a moment later, at the top of the steps, he closed the cellar door, and said, "We should have a lock on these."

I imagined the threat of being robbed. Of Scooter extending his spree to the canned preserves of farmhouse cellars and said, "A lock?"

"Why not? Some of those jars are from your grandmother's time. Why, they're probably antiques."

Returning to the house, Father said, "We'll simply wait. We'll wait it out. A little weather is all we need. And if we have to, we'll truck it down from Lake Michigan or whatever. Whatever we have to do, we'll do."

"Good deal, Dad. We have a plan."

Inside, with Dee gathering her things to return to town, I migrated toward the downstairs bedroom to join Mariah and Verity while, as

CHARLES PROWELL

Clare always claimed, Father secured the back porch door and drew the curtains on the front plate windows and said goodnight to Dee and as she pulled from the drive there followed the click of the back door lock, when to Clare's recollection, and ours, we had never locked our doors nor drawn our curtains. After my sisters and I had gone to bed and Mother was sound asleep, Clare lay in bed to the sound of his breathing as he stood in his pajamas at the laundry room window peering through a thin sliver in the curtain. Watching the road, one now assumes. Watching for Santa Anna's invincible army.

313

SIXTY-FOUR

He must have known. Exposing the west field to the garden sales and the alfalfa and barley to the subsidy review. A calculated gamble for the needed subsidy income against the sudden exposure after seventeen years undercover that they would come knocking. Whoever they were. The original patent, the flawed hybrid, was ubiquitous, stuffing the University's coffers twelve-fold over any alumni endowments. Profits in large part from the U.S. Department of Agriculture, who seemingly believed all subsequent research results fell under the pre-war patent. Father's recent paperwork in Champaign was just paperwork, legalese, easily challenged by a stacked system.

If you were looking, paying attention, there were imperceptible shifts beginning as far back as the garden sales and furthered with Evansville that effectively marked the beginning of the end of his long isolation from that world beyond Salt Fork. That life before my life. That affiliation with those he'd begun to reaffiliate himself with as an affiliation with the devil. The pressure and coercion and shoulder-holstered bodyguards of that last year in the school lab.

A few days later, I watched from the barn loft as a black sedan pulled into the drive. As if they were expected, Father met them at the gates and

CHARLES PROWELL

they moved through the barnyard to disappear into the Annex. Some time passed, enough time that I left my chores and left the barn to enter the Annex where they sat in the suffocating air with the one logbook opened as I took a seat on the bench, wishing Guy Faller was present or Sheriff or Max but it was just me, too small to make a difference, but thinking nonetheless that it was not Father against four but Father and me against four and what would Lincoln do, young Lincoln the wrestler, back to back, pulverizing them with full nelsons and headlocks when they closed the log and left the Annex and crossed the barnyard like an honor guard of men in black suits with Father in the middle as they rounded the house and disappeared again, down into the cellar. I stood back, at the head of the drive off the peach grove and a moment or two later, they reappeared, bearing their treasure, and then they were gone, disappearing up Pond Road.

315

SIXTY-FIVE

That following Sunday, Father attended church. A visiting pastor from Paducah delivered a monotonous but serviceable scripture to a parish of native-borns. Our parish, our congregation, freed from the standing-room crowds of the past several weeks. He sang, Father, studying the hymn book Mother held before him, tentatively singing the words to the hymns the rest of us knew by heart and somewhere during that chorus of voices was another voice, drawn from the ancient markers across the road.

Later, in the graveled parking lot, with the folding tables and food buffets, we stood visiting. Which is what we did. Talk of the ongoing search for a new pastor and the new members, the Arthur coop, with their peculiar but learned sense of garden rotations and how vegetables, like people, have preferences. There was talk of horse trials at the Javitts' and talk of recreational hunters at the Fallers' and at no time did anyone mention Evansville or the weather or the crops. Nor how, for the first time in seventeen years, Henry Roe was present. At some point, Verity crossed the road and stood on the ridge of the Fall Ridge Cemetery and sent her voice floating down off the ridge over the vast woods of the Shawnee, extending clear to the Ohio River.

SIXTY-SIX

I have every right to write the life of a life no longer living. Less a right, perhaps, than a privilege.

From the bedroom window overlooking the side-yard elm, the light of the moon struck the upper leafage and worked its way through the muscled limbs and tangled foliage like navigating a maze. The lawn beneath the canopy was sprinkled with deposits of moonlight and when the breeze ruffled the elmleaves, the light danced and twinkled and flickered like a pinwheel. In his pajama bottoms, bare-chested, absorbing the nightsounds and hypnotized by the light playing through the elm, Father stood in the shadows of a nearly intolerable loneliness. *I know those moon nights. Acceptance sleeping, finding some measure of comfort, while I once stood at that same window hypnotized by the horror of going it alone and if I transport myself into his shoes, or slippers, it's because in so many ways, I am my father.*

She breathed with an effort, Mother, the bedsheets lifting and lowering to that slow metered pulse. He wanted to discuss me. Their Wonder Boy. And to talk of Verity who was changing before their very eyes, and Mariah, caught in that abyss, that cusp of womanhood, and the trip to St. Louis, and he wanted to do it whispering. So close to her they whisper. He wanted to whisper his silly-talk that made her smile.

317

He crossed the room with the light and easy motion of a fielder, a sure-footed fielding poet to enter the long bathroom and two minutes later, returned with his bare feet stepping softly and silently across the plank floor. He climbed into bed and carefully shuffled beneath the linens until he was close and for a moment, he rested, and pretended. Pretending was all that was left.

"Hmmm?"

He imagined she was awake.

"Hmmm, what?"

"Hmmm."

She moved a finger to graze his leg and he nuzzled in close against her back and burrowed his head in against the nape of her neck and issued a low raspy whispering sound sustained like the A-string of a cello. A cello, on a clear night, late, this plaintive measure encompassing ten-thousand acres rolling from farmhouse to farmhouse, easing the incalculable vacancy of uncertainty.

"Silly boy."

She smiled. He can't see but he knew she was smiling and maybe stroking her hand against his leg to pause with a gentle grip as the back of his fingers ran lightly down her shoulder and with his nose nestled in behind her ear, he vibrated his lips and she trembled with a silent laughter and it is from this place, this private existence, where they gathered and collected and nourished this resource that once ushered in the days and weeks and months and years with the relish of yet more days and weeks and months and years to come.

But the pretense was only a memory, and the loneliness was nearly intolerable.

SIXTY-SEVEN

In the morning, long before daybreak, Mother awakened from the deepest sleep to slip on her robe and make her way up the stairs one tread at a time. At the landing, she rested, summoning her strength before crossing the dayroom and starting up the attic stairs for the first time in almost two weeks, relying heavily on the spiraling handrail and a compulsion to work, to be drawn again into the fantasies of a Meadow Sage opera.

This world. Belonging to her but to all of us, her routines and working methodologies and the disciplined insistence of completion. To Father and Mariah and Verity and myself all separately occupying that featherbed, witnessing the reliable returns waiting in the far corner near the window overlooking the lawn and the lower pasture, encompassed by the surrounding artifacts and the conditioned reflex of so many years. They wait, those sketches, surprised perhaps, confused by the long absence, but quickly awakened and within minutes, the music filled her, the arias resonating down her arm and the length of the pencil and onto the paper and from the drawingboard, it carried through the attic, lifting to the girders and quickly she was absorbed within the mechanics of an instrument that seemed to glide across the paper of its own will. It

319

no longer mattered whether she was idling with her Saturday morning canvas and oils, or earning a living with her pencils; each stroke was pulled with the purpose of a stockpiled agenda working deliberately and methodically, working quickly, bringing to life her interpretation of the dinner scene celebrating the pending marriage of Miss Avery to the dashing Captain Golden Rod with the gay chorus of the maidens and it was astonishing how quickly decisions were made; there was no leaning away from the drawing board, twirling a lock of hair between her fingers as a contemplative measure, but quickly working the baroque Italian architecture surrounding a more detailed pavilion shaded to upstage the backdrop structures and carefully rendering River Weed encircled by the town's maidens swooning over the news of his inheritance and River Weed, unaware of this inheritance, is convinced the love potion has worked when from the corner of the attic an interference, a resounding racket as Father pushed a heavy bureau, scraping it across the plank floor.

Pulled from the spell, she watched him, as Father liked to recall, tugging and pulling furnishings as if aligning building blocks. Stacking and abutting the bureaus and tables and shelving toward some purpose, some grand design as he stood over the featherbed occupying the center of the sprawling attic, contemplating, deliberating its sheer size and weight all in a newfound need to occupy himself. To fill the void of a neglected Annex, an inexplicable void accompanied by an ensuing plan to devote himself, perhaps, toward making her workspace roomier? More spacious? More organized?

"Hen-ry."

He looked up.

"What on earth are you doing?"

He raised an arm, motioning to the arrangements, the furnishings. "I thought I'd…"

Downstairs, at the kitchen counter, I sat with a glass of milk and a stack of cookies, listening to the floor-joists shuddering from the attic when the phone rang. Ringing and ringing until I grudgingly left the stool to lift the receiver and hold it to my ear as if it were an innovation beyond the scope of my needs.

A man's voice.

No, Mother isn't available and Father isn't available and Verity is working at the Javitts' and if he wanted to speak with Mariah, he'd have to call back, let it ring.'

Ten minutes later, the phone rang again and it rang and rang and rang but I don't budge because Mariah and I were approaching a record forty-two hours without exchanging a single word. She was upstairs with the door to her room shut tight and when the phone rang its twelfth ring, I could hear her marching across the floorboards of the dayroom. I listened as she hurried down the stairs and through the hall to come stomping into the kitchen as I sat on my stool at the counter holding up a note that said I AM NOT YOUR SERVANT. She snatched it from my hand and crumpled it in her fist and answered the phone, listening just long enough to know it wasn't Buddy or one of her friends before responding into the mouthpiece with a voice that would scatter the crows from Dee's sycamore.

"Grow up…you little jerk!"

She dropped the receiver on the pile of Mother's unanswered mail and I watched, smiling, as she stalked out of the kitchen…disappointed she hadn't lost her temper or that she hadn't turned to me, screaming, breaking our silence.

I lifted the phone from the stack of mail, smiling.

"Good job, Scoots."

"Scoots?"

"Hello?"

"Hello?"

Three times since lunch, as instructed, Scooter had called in a disguised voice and each time, I had let it ring, knowing she wouldn't chance missing a call from dopey Buddy and each time the chance she might lose control and be the first to break their silence.

321

Bonswha, this is the University of paris francwha calling to say we do not accept madhatters and that you might try the mental hospital, over in Anna-wha.

But it was not Scooter. It was the voice that had called earlier.

"Oh, sorry, I thought you were someone else."

"I'm beginning to wish I was someone else. Was that Mariah?"

"Yeah."

"She's something."

"I reckon."

"You must be the boy, Justus."

"Who's this?"

"Robert Rausch. Your mother's editor. I've been trying to reach her."

"I'll tell her you called."

"Tell her I'm in Fall Fork…I have the Canadian."

"Huh?"

"At the Lincoln Hotel, in Fall Fork. We're waiting."

"Sure."

Father occupied the middle of the dayroom, shuffling, scanning this room that had no purpose. A large room at the top of the stairs that was, in his current state of mind, nothing more than a room without purpose. He dragged our long project table away from the window and considered the vacancy while I sat on the floor in the far corner, setting the last of my lead-melting soldier-molds onto a shelf in an act of final withdrawal before scaling the attic stairs.

Mother leaned back from the board with a clear-headedness, a recaptured focus seemingly separated from her lack of focus by the winding stairs to the attic. She shuffled through a backlog of mail someone had stacked on the small table beside the drawing board. Several letters from her editor, Rausch, and several more from the brash

CHARLES PROWELL

Canadian demanding updates but unwilling to venture over the border into the uncharted wilderness of America for fear of cowboys, or indians, or gangsters, or perhaps the braggadocio of the American psyche. She set them aside and returned to work, the final scenes within sight now, the pencils in high-performance mode, leading her forward at pace with the composition, the lucidity of something from nothing, while I sat occupied at the far opposite corner of the attic as an escape from Father's redistribution in the dayroom. Sitting at what I later learned was True Pond's walnut desk, with its purfling inlays and smooth-carved wood hinges, coated under a century of dust. Mother was likely unaware I was even there, our backs to one another, separated by a good twenty yards as I considered the allowable fabrications of a debut venture beyond news and sports.

Dear Editor,

You know that brick on Elm that sticks up? The one down near the Café? Is it just me or has that one brick on Elm been sticking up for about forever? I figure there's about 200,000 bricks there along the three blocks of Elm and theys all even but for this one and it's been sticking up for about forever.

I leaned back, hemmed in by ancient bureaus and assorted Pond relics and licked my pencil, picturing the brick and all about this brick while Mother delved deeper into her own fantasy. Sweet Avery buying back poor River Weed's freedom from the conscripts of the captain's army, singing her perfect duet with Dr. Beetle in an undulating exchange from bass to soprano and by now, she was no longer the puppeteer. She no longer existed outside the work, monitoring the composition from arm's length but, rather, from within, smelling the smells of her Italian village while witnessing her components from a seat on the lip of the ancient fountain, hearing their melodious voices rising and falling and rising and falling, all within the ineffable tranquility of another century as I pictured the act of tripping over an errant brick. The humor, or comedic timing, of personifying a brick and were my readers ready for that? Ultimately, the lack of an actual lamp and the residue of century-old dust sent me tiptoeing down to the kitchen counter as Clare arrived through the back door with a hurried immediacy, stretched lately between Elmer's, where all the action was, and her real job, her paying job, back and forth, up and down Pond Road, as she manhandled the laundry through the ringer and then over to the sink, chopping and dicing vegetables, humming and singing.

"Clare!"

She turned, looking over her shoulder with the axe poised in mid-air.

"I'm a little busy here."

She raised an arm, motioning to the vegetables and toward the laundry at the end of the kitchen. "Oh, you's a lit-tle busy, are you…?"

In my mind, I pictured Aunt Elizabeth:

Now I'm a good Christian woman who walks with her head high and every morning I cross to the Café, I trip over that brick and I've been tripping over that brick since I was seven years old. How come all the years nobody ever fixed this brick? Fall Ridge is falling apart. Nothing ever getting fixed anymore.

Yours, Loose Brick

In my mind, I also pictured Aunt Bim standing over my shoulder, 'So, how does the editor respond? Something funny, maybe? Make them laugh?

'He could tell her to go jump in the lake cause nobody cares what she thinks anyway.'

Dear L. Brick,

We know that brick. Most the rest of town knows that brick when they trip over it ONCE, and don't keep doin it for 50 years.

Clare cranked the noisy ringer a quarter turn, squeezing the soaked trouser through the roller inch by slow inch, overly conscious of not disturbing His Holiness, Mr. Shakespeare, managing this on her tiptoes as if to accentuate the whole process as something clandestine as the sound of Father's bootsteps made their way down the stairs and through the dining room to enter the kitchen where he stood at the far end of the counter, glancing at me in one direction and Clare in the other as if he had lost his way, forgotten his purpose. He moved to stand opposite Clare, catching the trouser legs as they were released from each quarter turn, holding them from the water as Clare put her finger to her lips and motioned behind her where I, the blind boy, sat bent so close to my composition pad my nose brushed the paper. And Father nodded, and when I stabbed the period of my entertaining response to Aunt Elizabeth's fabricated complaint, both Clare and Father were halfway down Pond Road toward the Arthur Compound. Where all the action was.

SIXTY-EIGHT

What we learned, firsthand, is when thirteen native-borns from Cairo, and beyond, each know thirteen others, who in turn know thirteen others, etc., the scope of their network was staggering. And among those degrees of separation was an acquaintance of Simp Laughton's third cousin once removed, a noted garden theorist named Brianna Blanche. Author of *The Companionable Garden*; frequent lecturer at Northwestern University in Chicago; invited guest of honor at upscale garden clubs throughout greater Chicago and…a voice from the shared ancestry of those at that downstate commune at the heart of so many interesting rumors.

She was given an upstairs bedroom as a weekend stay that stretched to a week of discussions and evening lecturers situated around Rufus' new firepit to the settling hum of Simp Laughton's new water feature cascading over and under carefully stacked layers of antiquated arrowheads and polished gemstones while Madeline, in a simple almost feminized cotton frock, took notes and Elmer sat listening, stroking fistfuls of Bo's mystical jowls.

Vegetables have friends. And enemies. Friends and enemies don't mix.

The house gardens had expanded to encompass most of the former barnyard, while venturing to the eastern hectare of the north field, abutting the river in a decision to supplant Father's seeds, or a portion of those seeds, which had yet to break ground. A decision that marginalized Guy Faller's agreement to lease the north and west fields with a loss that found him returning to the mines one day a week.

When queried that evening at dinner, Father's voice had a buoyant lilt to it, describing how he and Clare had mingled that afternoon at the Compound, and later how he and Elmer had watched Simp, the one who spoke with his hands in constant motion, explaining what was drawn from the two wells for household use was reprocessed to irrigate the gardens, while Clare and Lavetty were off listening to Damien, Lavetty's second cousin from Armory or Amory or somewhere in Mississippi, the one who spoke with a stutter and a drawl drawn from the depths of history, talk of eventual production baskets, delivered to homes or open-air markets within deliverable range.

He broke loose, Father, leaving Clare and the others to make his way into the Arthur field, stepping carefully through the fresh furrows toward the river, as he put it, toward our own house in the distance when this Brianna Blanche appeared, or as she wrote in a chapter of her follow-up book years later, 'he' appeared. 'She sensed his approach,' she wrote. 'The murmuring voices of those around her, on their knees, all of them, burying their seedlings according to the sequence of friends and enemies and then his voice, small talk, and someone's response, 'Yessir, we wok evvy day but Sunday."

When he came closer, close enough to hear his breathing, she stood and turned, brushing her pantlegs and nodding and caught herself on the verge of an inexplicable curtsey. She brushed her hands and recovered with a slapping puff of dust.

He had smiled and offered a hand and said, "Henry Roe…at your service."

POSSESSING THE SEASONS

'Two colleagues,' she had written, 'conspiring toward a new world order.'

When in truth, technically, on that day, they came from opposite sides of the universe.

SIXTY-NINE

Little Whisty has homework. He must have said it a half dozen times as Mademoiselle and I picked him up in the truck and drove back from his first day at Violet Snead's Preschool. We did it the minute we got home, clearing off the upstairs dayroom table and arranging three chairs side by side as he pasted four parts of a yellow school bus together. Coloring them. Maddy and I watched.

Their mother has volunteered once a week to organize what she calls Books and Beyond at the Fall Ridge School. She tracks the number of books the younger grades read and distributes little award booklets. She seems to love the responsibility. Once a month, on awards day, Whisty and Maddy go along to the Big School to pass out the prized booklets.

Mister Whister spends a weekend with his cousins in town. On the drive home, he sits between his father and myself and says he knows how to get $100. As Conquer turns up Deere Road, I ask, "How?"

"It's simple, Poppa...just go to the bank whenever you need $100. Just go to the bank. That's how Aunt Sally does it."

I stay to the old cow trails, the Moingwena, Illiniwek, Shawnee, and Kickapoo foot paths worn wide early on with the grooved ruts of wagon wheels replaced with tractor wheels that weave and wind like a confounding maze. If it's summer and the weeds or the corn dwarf the truck, I can forget where I am. How to get home.

Conquer marked the route with painted-red stakes up the north field to the edge of the old Marsh place and down along the west field behind Max and Clare's little house to the little girder bridge that crosses the river at The Point to traverse the old Arthur Coop and down the east edge to come upon the Snead's barnyard and Violet's little Preschool. Avoiding paved Pond Road, where they drive too fast.

SEVENTY

Father was at the Compound every afternoon that week. A means of passing the time, of strolling down Pond Road at a pace considered leisurely while resurrecting a boyhood gift for whistling puckered notes falling far short of actual melodies. Down there, down at the Compound, a trend was shaping up that placed less if any value on the size and color of a tomato than the guaranteed assurance of its harvesting history. On a production scale.

That Saturday, Father and I sat in the dirt of the coop's expansion garden, his arms wrapping his bent knees and rocking in place, like a preschooler. Between the edge of the new garden and the edge of the Arthur/Faller barley seeding was a hand-tilled protective buffer of fifty yards. A precaution against drifting rumors and fifty yards was anyone's guess.

'It took only an hour of my last afternoon in the valley,' she wrote. 'Honestly, the invitation to the downstate valley was in itself intriguing. How often is anyone invited inside that world, that long-standing organic community with no history of insecticidal farming? No poisoned soil horizons. Because I followed agricultural trending and was well aware of the original hybrid studies in Champaign and the recent articles of

331

POSSESSING THE SEASONS

his reemergence with cantaloupes like beach balls and barley bred to succulents and the cringing assessment of hormones and additives and when I had lowered myself to sit beside him on that last afternoon, in the dirt, it felt as if we were colleagues, old pals. And yet a trickling residue of fraternizing with the enemy.

'I had made a name for myself. A horticultural layman, yes, but a best-selling author and a speaker championing an ideal that was wholly opposite to what this seemingly friendly, approachable man was solely responsible for. It was already too late, I had thought at the time. Within a year, most of the entire midwestern fertile valley would be flourishing with his hybrid crop. A solution to so many problems that it would be impossible to reverse the trend. Fleets of it already sailing for the harbors of Europe.

'Would he say something, please? Just us, the two of us, sitting in the dirt. He was so unassuming. Nothing of what I had imagined. It was hard to grasp, sharing the dirt. In his dusty boots and unruly hair, so close I could smell the scent of his skin, the skin of the man who had quietly changed the world.

'One of the others had appeared, dragging lengths of graywater piping, laying them along the far furrows, joined by more like him, stooping with coupling connectors and one talking with his hands in constant motion, talking and gesticulating as my mind wandered to the embarrassing high-mindedness of my own premise, preached to my garden club audiences who had never faced starvation. To all those children around the world who would be spared from the certainty of starving to death with the doubling of a global grain production. A hybrid grain. Genetically tampered. Made a reality from the brain of a single man who had been forced to disappear, to find this refuge of a good life in an insulated world. I took a chance, that day. Not a romantic act, but the conciliatory offering of resting my hand lightly on his shirtsleeve, for all the children everywhere.'

Father and I walked back up Pond Road together. Not talking. Small steps, Father scraping his boots through the gravel. He was in no hurry. At the bridge, we paused, leaning into the trellis to study the hunters making their way back from the gorge, their shotguns breeched into the crooks of their forearms. Camouflaged trousers and hats and bright orange vests and hunting pockets bulging with young pheasant, chattering among themselves when they suddenly stopped, halfway between the river and the house, or lodge. One of them raised his arm, pointing, and Father's eyes followed to see Mother, standing alone.

Double-timing it up Pond Road as Mariah appeared, running, from the foot of our own drive up the road and into the Faller drive and by the time Father arrived, well ahead of me, Mariah was at the side-yard fence, calling out.

Mother approached the side door of Dolores' former farmhouse and knocked. Knocking harder, pounding against the door with the meat of her hand. The back of her nightgown was powdered with dust. She turned to the side yard, pacing along the new short fence separating the yard from the barnyard as the hunters appeared, standing off the rise, transfixed, and in recounting the incident it was one of the hunters—Mr. Romero, an architect, who would ultimately own and renovate and raise his family in the old Faller place—and Mariah, who always collectively agreed on how Mother stood with her hands buried in the pockets of her apron, singing Sweet By and By while pushing her hip against a section of the new fence as if searching for the gate that was no longer there. She ran her hands across the tops of the pickets while moving with a kind of frantic logic toward the far corner of the yard, searching, seemingly, for a gate that no longer existed.

Mariah remained short of the barnyard as Father continued to the same rail fence where he had stood eight months before bidding against his wife for a tractor neither of them needed nor even wanted.

333

He crossed into the barnyard and approached the house as if drawing in on a spooked horse.

He called out softly, "Grace. Grace, it's me, Henry."

She turned and backed away and he stopped and a few seconds later, he added, "Is Dolores home?"

She shook her head from side to side and he took a step forward and she took a step back and the hunters set their weapons to lean against the fence. She watched them, and then Father, while tugging against the pickets until the new fence wobbled like a rope.

"Darling, the gate's over here."

He pointed to a section of the pickets marked by nothing more than a small latch. He took a few steps forward.

"Why don't I open it for you?"

She stepped back and stopped and turned to Mariah nearing the house and then to Father leaning against the near fence and then to the hunters, strangers, creeping closer, trying to help by creating a second front on the pasture side of the fence. Father waved them off and she began shaking the fence, again, shaking it vigorously back and forth with a racket that flushed from the elm a dark gust of sparrows swooping up and then down in a tight mass as she screamed and threw her hands up, waving them off, crouching to her knees, hugging the pickets.

Father hopped the fence. The swallows disappeared over the house gable. He moved closer, quickly, and she stood to her feet running, running first left then right then toward the back of the house, toward the startled hunters, flailing and flapping her arms to disappear around the back of the house as Father ran in the opposite direction, past the immobilized Mariah, to where they collided, husband and wife, off the back corner. Caught, snared in his folding arms, softening, until his hold loosened and by the time they made their way home, the three of them shuffling down Pond Road to where I had remained at the foot of our own driveway; the hunters had gathered on the back porch with cold beers, overlooking the lower woods, likely discussing the strange sounds earlier that afternoon reverberating off the limestone walls of the gorge. "Since when do pheasant and grouse growl?" they quipped, sipping their beers, laughing, while wondering if they had the appropriate weapons, ammunition.

SEVENTY-ONE

The afternoon passed, filtering in through the dormer window near the drawingboard, coloring the attic with a golden tint as she studied the timbers in the ceiling and when enough time had passed—months, even years, when everyone would always agree on how the attic was the appropriate refuge. Enclosed in the safety of that silence, in the presence of ancestors and all their combined histories and ancient belongings. Safely harbored by the familiar folds of the featherbed, she lay perfectly still, convinced the light spilling over the floorboards was the light of daybreak, that it was early morning and if she made the slightest sound, her mother would look up from the drawingboard, level her eyes with the hint of a smile and say, 'And how long have you been here?'

That was before she stopped hovering like a child. Clinging to her mother's proximity the way children do.

Sometime later, much later, when the light had withdrawn and the timbers had meshed with the darkness that the starlings and swallows could be heard scampering across the roof, in what Mariah afterward always claimed was a dream, with brightly colored beetles scratching the floorboards, surrounding the bed, morphing into the sound of her mother's pencil scratching across the drawing board, when the voices carried up from the dayroom and the dream, the trance, was supplanted by the sound of their footsteps, moving through the lower bedrooms, calling her name, Aunt Dee's voice and then Aunt Bim and then the sound of their footsteps climbing the attic stairs. She closed her eyes and pictured her mother at the drawingboard, humming that silly opera.

"So there you are."

Verity's voice, carrying through the darkness.

"She's up here!"

Verity moved cautiously from the top of the stairs to the foot of the featherbed and said, "You were supposed to watch Mom."

"I know."

"It was your turn. Daddy's really mad. Everyone's been looking for you."

"I know."

Dee and Bim arrived at the top of the attic steps, breathing heavily. Dee moved to the window and pulled the chain of the small lamp. The light was pale, little more than candlelight, contained by the shade to fall on the drawingboard and nothing more.

Mariah sat up, engulfed in the folds of this bed for children. "Where's Mom?"

"In bed," Verity answered. "Asleep. Vivian's with her. Dr. Leemore just left. He said somebody has to be with her all the time now. Bim made up a chart."

"A chart?"

"A schedule."

Dee and Bim sat on the edge of the bed, on opposite sides of this bed, testing it's give as if remembering their own childhoods.

"We're supposed to come home on the bus," Verity continued. "We've got from four to nine. Daddy has the nights."

Dee leaned back, slowly, easing herself into the cloud. Bim followed, playing along.

"Everybody's been worried," Verity said. "We couldn't find you."

"Sorry."

"Did you hear Granny Davis died?"

"She died? When?"

"Just a few hours ago. She was on the porch and Acceptance went to get her some cocoa and when she came back she was, you know…dead. And Mom's publisher was here…from New York! With someone else. Some crazy guy."

"Her publisher?"

"You missed a lot, Mariah."

Bim and Dee patted the fluffs in the mattress and then folded their hands behind their heads, rediscovering something special. Dee depressed the goose feathers with a sudden but slight effort and Bim did the same in an alternating remembered sequence, giggling as Mariah was jostled.

"He said he called the house," Verity continued, watching her aunts. "He waited at the station in Fall Fork and they finally took a taxi…clear from Fall Fork! They came right when everything was happening. He said you called him a jerk!"

Mariah was giggling. Jostled up and down like a child as Father arrived at the landing, pausing to adjust his eyes to the near darkness. Mariah lost her smile and Dee and Bim stopped their child's play and looked away, scanning the overhead girders and the room fell to an awkward silence. Dee and Bim and Verity left the attic and Father's voice, drifting through the stillness, "What are you doing up here?"

Mariah shrugged.

Father moved over to sit on the edge of the mattress and Mariah left the bed and walked across the room. She stood at the window with her back to the bed, staring out into the darkness, imagining the early morning, long before daybreak.

"You been up here the whole time?"

She moved from the window and sat in her mother's chair and pulled it close to the drawingboard and ran her hand over a clean pad of paper. What was always so striking about that afterward, she remembered, was how she had closed her eyes and held the pencil over the paper like a wand, knowing it could be done, knowing how her mother would sit in that chair and not hear anything else but what was in her head…the sound of her drawing.

"I didn't know where you were."

She began with swirls along the top of the page. She smoothed the heel of her left hand over the paper and created more swirls followed by curlicues. She heard his voice but she wasn't listening. She leaned in closer; she had seen it done, braiding her legs and weaving her finger through her hair and humming, softly, mimicking the gestures she knew by heart.

Throughout that afternoon and most of that evening, I remained at the foot of our driveway. I, at times, wandered onto Pond Road and then back to the drive and along the garden furrows and out onto the front lawn to cross the barnyard and then back to the foot of the drive. I could not enter the house, as I had not followed Father and Mariah up the Fallers' driveway. I simply couldn't.

SEVENTY-TWO

Of course, there was time for the county seat in Fall Fork. What else was there if not time? The others, at the Café and in passing, had begun to avoid Father's eyes and as the days passed without that precipitation, that part of the gamble unto which nearly everything else hinged, well… the tension was hidden beneath a strained civility.

I packed a small day bag, having no idea how, but intrigued by the sheer idea of it. A leather bag, with Max's initials that may have been the same bag he packed in austria, or australia.

We left early, Father and I, up Pond Road onto Deere Road to flush up a covey of quail and at the Bonnel turn we braked for a copperhead slowed by a lump in its belly the size of two or three field mice. Farther along Bonnel Road, we spent a quarter-hour running the Dearborns' wandering herd from the center of the road back through the toppled fenceline and fashioning a makeshift repair and by the time we reached the glade of cottonwoods marking uncharted territory, the junction of Route 10, it was close to eight.

Everything was new. Climbing from the valley floor and along the rim of the higher ground and veering west to lose sight of the valley altogether. I had uttered only a few words—at the sight of the fat copperhead—

340

preferring to lean out the window since leaving our driveway, silently filling my cheeks with the rush of air, facing into the wind until my eyes watered. Lulled by the dips and holidays in a road flanked by fields as lifeless as January. An occasional farmhouse, surrounded by stands of hickories and elms and between the farms were a few decaying barns, standing empty and listing in the cropless fields like ships in a headwind.

With my head slung out the window, avoiding conversation, I considered ideas for Letters-to-the-Editor, or the horse show Verity and Max were considering in the open lot behind Town Hall which led to the summer movies, the sheet strapped to the back brick wall and everyone with their blankets and dishes of food to watch the sheet under a sky studded with stars.

"I thought we'd build a gate this week."

I pulled in from the window.

"I said, I thought we might build a gate...for the driveway."

We passed fields and farmhouses I'd never seen before.

"With summer, they'll be coming again for the gardens and your mother...we can't have people showing up at the house...strangers."

I ground my teeth to the rhythm of the tires clipping the road-joints and in my mind, I imagined her expression, shaking the Fallers' picket fence. I knew the gate idea had nothing to do with keeping strangers from the house.

"Did you call Acceptance?"

Gazing through the windshield into an out-of-focus sky, I shook my head and sensed his eyes and turned away to the open window and the monotony of the passing countryside.

"You might call her. She and Granny were close."

There was a new champion. The oldest person in the valley who was probably too old to know it.

Father laid an arm across the back of the seat.

"So, what's wrong?"

I shrugged.

"Nothin. Nothin's wrong."

The countryside changed. Shorter trees. Shorter bushes. The air was thinner and the sky was bluer.

"It's about the other day? At the Fallers'?"

I turned to him. I could barely hear my own voice, "Mariah says you scared her, Dad."

He pulled his arm off the back of the seat and gripped the wheel with both hands as we leaned into the long turn abreast of the tracks, coming 180 degrees to approach the switchback. He said nothing, but I knew he heard. I knew because his knuckles were white and his eyes were wet and because he braked hard at the crossing.

We had reserved the small conference room off the main lobby of the Lincoln Hotel. A room furnished with a long table with elaborately carved legs and six leather-seated, ladderbacked chairs and an oversized red-leathered chair in the corner where I sat like a dwarf, browsing through a stack of magazines. The table was scattered with Mother's sheaths of drawings and texts and coffee cups and a plate of rolls and beside each chair a small serving table with a polished brass spittoon. With no one chewing, the staff moved the tables against the far wall. The room was thick with her editor's pipe and the stench of the chain-smoking Canadian[11].

"It's not complete! There's scenes missing!"

He stood, the young one. He stubbed his cigarette into the ashtray and lit another one and turned back to Father and said, "We had an agreement, a timeline. I have a Toronto venue to pay, rehearsals scheduled...why isn't she here? Where is she?"

Father said nothing, exchanging looks with Mr. Rausch and I left the room, escaping to wander through the old halls of a hotel that had

---

11. *Manufactured cigarettes, with filters, issuing a stale odor unlike the fresh tobacco leaves culled from the curing barns in Kentucky. An addiction, or pastime, throughout the valley in the form of pipes and chewing twists and occasionally, albeit rarely, in the form of Ruby Morrow's self-rolled cigarettes. No one in Salt Fork smoked manufactured cigarettes, with filters, which were rumored to taste like fresh road tar.*

been built in the 1870s. Technically within the county line, but never associated with county culture. The ceilings had gone dull and discolored and the wainscoting was worn and scarred and in places the wallpaper drooped and curled off the plaster. The maids still stamped the sand in the ashtrays, however, with the imprint of the letter L and folded the ends of the paper in the bathroom stalls into points.

I wandered up toward the billiard room at the end of the third-floor hall, pausing to study a photograph of President Grant on the hotel veranda, smoking a cigar. I knocked the balls around but the room was empty and haunted and the green felt was torn in several places. I went down to the lobby and found the door to the reading room locked and took the elevator to the basement, where the walls were thick with the smell of sweat. I took a few strokes on the rowing machine and threw a few punches into the bag and walked down the row of lockers and around the corner toward the steam room where someone was standing in the far corner, wrapped in a towel and facing the long mirror.

He looked through the reflection in the mirror and turned to me with thin hollowed cheeks lathered in shaving cream. In the open locker beside the sink, partially exposed behind a pair of black trousers and black jacket was a shoulder holster hanging from the hook. He pushed the locker door closed with his foot and rinsed his razor and resumed shaving and through the mirror he took in the whole of me and said, "Move along, kid."

I wandered away, exploring the barbells and a door that opened onto a tiled swimming pool in a room with tiled walls and tiled ceilings and thick musty air[12]. I left the basement by the back stairs and returned to the lobby to find Father in the dining room, seated at the corner table saddled between a bobcat and a boar mounted to the wall. He glanced at his pocket watch and said, "One more meeting. It won't take long."

We returned to the conference room that had been bussed and

---

12.   *Swimming pools. Existing for the sole purpose of swimming. Clean filtered water, as opposed to the murky muddy Salt Fork River with its hidden surprises.*

cleaned of cigarette butts and doused with air freshener. The man from the basement sat alone, waiting. He glanced in my direction without a hint of recognition. I took the same seat in the corner and opened the same magazine, balancing the magazine on my lap, listening to the silence, while stealing a look for the bulge of a holster under his jacket. The afternoon light filtered in through the blinds, thrown over the table. I watched the floating dust, trapped in the sunlight as it drifted to settle on the table and the lip of the wainscoting. The smell of honeyscented beeswax claimed the air.

Understanding the silence, I left the room to wander outside, along the storefronts to come upon a public library[13]. A building with books. Intimidated, not understanding, I wandered farther to stop at the theater and studied the posters of coming attractions and imagined the inside of a theater[14]. A couple appeared through the doors, holding hands, glancing my way and holding their look long enough that as they moved down the walkway, I was left to consider the boots I had shined the night before and the trousers Clare had washed and pressed. I returned to the hotel where Father stood leaning against the car, waiting.

We carried the higher country to wind along the ridgeline road in silence. The fresh thin air rushing through the open windows grew thicker and warmer with every switchback turn. We passed the turnoff to Karber's Ridge; a narrow dirt road where a brake of roadside blueberries and blackberries flourished until they flanked the road like hedges and continued to flourish until the ridgeline access to the hunting groves was choked off to everyone who didn't want the thorns pulling the paint from the sides of their trucks.

But it was still May and the passage remained open and Father rolled

---

13. *Public libraries. Brimming with books. Tens of thousands of books. Arranged randomly? In some order? I wanted desperately to wander inside, meander among the shelves. Were there restrictions? Fall Fork members only? Would they ask my name? Glance at my boots? Raise their eyebrows? I would show them, if given a chance, that I could read. I could read as good as anyone.*

14. *Indoor cinemas, with padded seats and refreshments and screens the size of boxcars, as opposed to the white wrinkled sheet stretched and strapped to the back brick wall of Town Hall.*

to a stop along a shoulder constricted by low brush and shoots of stunted junipers, the engine idling as he pondered the paved road down to the valley against the back country variables to Karber's Ridge.

"Whataya think?"

"We'll never make it by dark, Dad."

"Probably not. So, whataya think?"

It would be along this road where Father and Max and Verity would have parked the horse trailer and packed in to disappear for an entire week. The .22-caliber for hunting rabbit and for protection against bobcats and boars; the flyrods for Peters Creek; the telescope for perfect night skies; the boltcutters for disarming illegal traps; and the harmonica to accompany Verity who sang to a gathering entourage so that they seldom traveled alone. I wasn't the horseman for a week in the high country and it was simply a road along the ridge down to the Shawnee Forest and through Karber's Ridge going either north for Garden of the Gods or east for the border, the river. I considered the river, how you might cross the bridge at either Cave-in-Rock or up at Old Shawneetown and touch down hurriedly into Kentucky, quick, before the bridge collapsed or the river flooded and you were trapped among foreigners. Trapped in Kentucky.

We rolled back onto the pavement and began the descent and I asked, "You think the Herefords knew they left Illinois?"

He looked at me, confused. "What kind of a question is that?"

"It's a question about the Herefords knowing the difference between Illinois and Missoura. You think they knew?"

"Maybe. Maybe not."

A jackrabbit the size of a small fox appeared against the high groundcover that thrived along the roadside, a thicket that seemed to survive without water or irrigation or anything but sunshine and the clean thin air.

"Who was that man? I saw him in the basement."

Father shrugged.

"A friend or something?"

POSSESSING THE SEASONS

He made a face I couldn't read and I added, "He had a shoulder holster hung in his locker."

Father shrugged again, as if shoulder holsters were as common as overalls and we carried along the east rake of Moingwena Rise to approach the valley floor and from this perspective it was clear how May was a goner and that spring was being chokeholded by the inevitable and the pleasant weather of the past few weeks wouldn't return until summer gave way to fall.

"You think Granny Davis knows she's left Illinois?"

"Why would I be thinking that?"

"Cause that's what I'm thinkin."

"Why would she leave Illinois?"

"Unless Heaven's in Illinois, she's left."

"Maybe Heaven is in Illinois. Maybe it's heaven-on-earth."

"Be a little crowded, wouldn't it? Everybody from everywhere comin here for Heaven."

We reached the junction at Route 10 and pulled out onto the open pavement and picked up speed on that stretch of road not much wider than a wagon. The air was thick and sultry and I could taste the dust coming off the dirt fields spread off to either side of the road. We drove in silence, banking the turn down toward Deere Road and I asked, "You like Mr. Rausch?"

"Of course."

"What was wrong with the other one?"

"Nervous. A nervous sort."

"You think he loves Mom?"

"Who?"

"Mr. Rausch."

"In a way, sure. They've known one another a long time now."

"That man in the basement of the Lincoln. He's one of them, isn't he?"

"..."

346

"What I think, son, is that I like what Madeline and Elmer are doing."

"They're on to something, Dad. But we're farmers, not gardeners."

From Deere Road onto the graveled Bonnel Road and I said, "I reckon when the new book comes, there'll be more folks comin to the house."

"Maybe."

"We'll be buildin a gate, right?"

"That's right. A nice gate, too."

It was close to five and the house was only a few minutes away when I turned and for close to a minute, I studied his one wrist resting along the wheel and his elbow slung out the window and the side of his face profiled against the Dearborns' grazing field.

"You figure Mom'll be all right? Or go to Heaven with the others? With Granny and Dr. Stewart and Brother Reeves and Mrs. Arthur?"

He turned to me and then back to the road. His hand moved from the wheel to along the seat and slipped down to the back of my neck, working his fingers gently against the skin.

"Your mother's not going anywhere, Sport. Not for a long time."

"But what if you're wrong?"

"You worry too much, Jussie. You're always worrying."

"There's a difference, Dad, with worryin and thinkin."

"Well then, you think too much."

"So?"

"So, nothing. You think too much is all."

"So?"

"So, you need to get that out of your mind, son."

"I can't get it out of my mind, Dad. It won't go out."

We turned onto Pond Road, crawling along at a pace no quicker than a brisk walk. Father squeezed the back of my neck and as we cleared the Marsh rise to oversee the house and the garden, he said, "Me neither, Justus Charles. Me neither."

SEVENTY-THREE

It was a good day and Father coaxed Mother out of the house for the ritual spring picnic down at the Point. Clare and Max joined them. Madeline and Elmer had already arrived; a bright cotton drop was spread across the grassy flange beneath a clearing in the canopy where the current broke north from the gorge. A warm southerly trade, typical to late May, drew off the horizon. It hauled up the scent of barren fields and the residues of a starving turf to breach the glade of tupelos and gather a little moisture off the river. A gift to the picnickers, a reminder to the now-passing perfections of spring.

Madeline distributed Lavetty's lunch menu and Clare added her lunch menu, a carousel of delights set just so, fanning out like a pinwheel. Madeline reset the tomatoes with the peppers and the melon with the squash and the peas with the cucumbers, as if positioning chess men along the spokes of a companionable wheel. Clare repositioned a cupcake beside a cucumber and a slice of fudge beside a beet and Madeline giggled while considering her move when Elmer reached in and the tomato was captured, eaten, with Madeline wiping the juice from a beard that had been trimmed to half its former length.

On his back with one arm tucked behind his head, Father ran his fingers lightly along Mother's forearm and as Madeline recalled, there were the birds. Everywhere. The songbirds back from their wintering havens, singing from the upper reaches of the canopy with the sheer joy of being back home while in competition with the hammerblows and light machinery drawing off the Faller place across the road and the Lofton farm beyond Snead's Corner.

"I don't know what they thinkin," Clare said, lowering herself to one elbow.

The others listened, acknowledging the sounds of change. Duck blinds had been built, stationed along the far edge of the Fallers' lower pasture just across the road, carpeted, it was rumored, and furnished with cushioned chairs, and how the pheasant were being bred and stocked like fish ponds. But it was shallow humor—good bottomland going to waste.

Clare and Max had decided on a high riverfront corner of the west field for the house Septimus would build and Rufus would landscape. A walkable setting, and someday, it was decided, someone would build a small foot bridge, replacing the current felled sycamore too narrow for even Max's trick steed to consider.

They discussed recipes and gardens and the horse show against the interference of a noise like crashing cymbals. The powersaws rising off the Faller place were met, from the opposite direction, beyond Snead's Corner, with a simulating echo. The Lofton foreclosure had been picked up by a childless couple from California. Arriving with their own team of out-of-state carpenters, the old place was being altered beyond recognition; one day, leaving the Cooperative for a mid-day walk, Madeline mentioned she had witnessed the new owners having their breakfast on a recently constructed platform off the north wing—in their robes—and it was understood how, to their new neighbors, farming would be little more than a gentleman's hobby.

It was an assault. That spring haven, that peninsula of shaded tranquility projecting off The Point beneath the tent of cottonwoods and sycamores, bounded on three sides by the mesmerizing drone of a sluggish current, assaulted from the south and from the northwest by a din of generators and striking hammers and it seemed a hopeless notion, those Sunday picnics.

Behind them, to their backs, Harlan stood amongst those working the sprawling Arthur gardens. He began with a high C and without the warm-up of an approaching scale, he danced along this staff with a soft pianissimo voice, carrying with the modesty of a brittle suggestion. He dropped a stave to shade his voice with a fuller dimension and then back to the high coloratura and back and forth in a soft flexibility so frail it dissipated into an airspace suddenly gone silent. The hammerblows and the machinery displaced, momentarily, by a colorless frame towering off the furrows, positioned more as an apparition than molecules in motion.

Two hunters appeared on the elevated roadbed, standing in their camouflage trousers and vests, their hands raised to visor the sunlight as they stood scanning the gardens and the picnickers as Madeline stretched her legs out onto the blanket and tucked her arms behind her head while Max fingered the brass buttons on his vest and Mother closed her eyes and rested her head on Father's shoulder and the voice lowered, gathering muscle, expanding its depth-of-field to a fuller broader quality, carrying beyond the leafy tents of the tupelo wood as Elmer pondered Guy's sacrifice, his Mondays at the mines, and Clare envisioned the little house, with no shortage of windows and Father's mind as blank as the sky with the voice dropping another stave, rounded and rich and lifting to a fortissimo migrating now over our pasture and traveling up our lawn and from this distance, standing off the back porch, Verity responded, piggybacking the breeze over the pasture and penetrating the margin of riverbank thicket with a light lyrical quality that allowed the two voices to pass without colliding.

The innocence of spring was giving way, weakening against a summer heat soon to come lumbering over Kickapoo Ridge. Settling across the valley like a coat of paint.

SEVENTY-FOUR

The Daniel and the Dearborn places went on the market at an asking price Dad Pond would've considered cheap. The Eddings farm to the northern end of the valley and the Clark farm just beyond Bonnel Corner foreclosed and as word spread how the vault at First National was as empty as Merrimack Cave, Mother clung to her attic like the last standing soldier and slept away the days and our house buckled and shifted, bracing itself.

The decades of crackling thunderstorms and flourishing crops and good beef markets gone away. The empty posturing and pumped-up confidence of April and May succumbed to a fear that spread like a disease, spreading and penetrating and worn like an exposed wound.

She never left the house. Dr. Leemore coordinated his visits to the lunch or dinner hour.

How disconcerting to know we were being watched. From beyond the circumference of the drought, those curious countrymen watched the valley like well-fed spectators witnessing a slow slaughter. They arrived as vultures in shiny cars, prowling for bargains, touring the graveled roads of the valley like shoppers at an exclusive flea market. Not to be called men, nor even farmers. Predators. Looters. No sense of anything but the scent of misfortune…lions drawn to the kill.

351

She descended the winding stairs, with help, and settled into the daybed arranged before the dormer window. From here, she could overlook the north field in a room flushed with light and the activity of my sisters and I coming and going and it had been a week now since she last visited the kitchen or the library, even her own bedroom. From here, she could see those arriving like a procession to usher themselves through the gate and into the house and up the stairs, gathering around the daybed, gossiping and chattering as she dozed in and out of a drugged sleep.

When the first offers were made on the Daniel and Dearborn farms, everyone laughed.

'Why, that's ridiculous. Who do they think they are?'

And at Davis' Café, they said to Pride Daniel, 'Tell'em fools go to Hades. It's a gott-darned insult.'

But the laughing stopped when both farms accepted the insults and it became desperately clear how neither Pride Daniel nor Pardon Dearborn were in a position to bargain. They were leaving, the Daniels to Owensboro with a job in the dry-cleaning business and the Dearborns to upstate Bloomington for a job as the equipment manager for the school's athletic department. With them, the carryovers of a second and third mortgage.

Seldom more than an hour now, before the brushes and paints were returned to the tray and Mother and Dolores turned for the stairs and later, from what can only be described as the Salt Fork Social Club, they heard how Sheriff had confiscated Dee's scattergun for blowing the spark arrester off the Widow Drew's chimney. Bim related the story in a reliable account that unraveled over a period of several days, how Dee retaliated by hiring Droopy Dix to cut the nesting crow's favorite sycamore clear to the ground and how Droopy knew nothing about felling trees so once again the upper branches fell crashing onto the power lines and once again half of Fall Ridge was without electricity. And once again Sheriff threatened to arrest Dee for felling a tree without a permit and Dee repeated how he wouldn't know a permit from a pothole and he said he couldn't love someone who didn't respect the law and that he might very well arrest her and she stomped off, slamming the screen door behind her to come back stalking across the lawn with another scattergun slung through her arm to tell her unofficial husband she'd shoot his big toe clean the hell off if he tried any such thing.

Services returned to the Fall Ridge Anabaptist Church. The Arthur Compound relegated itself to the worshiping needs of its cooperative members with some attending church and some clinging to the homespun faiths of a semi-evangelical Sunday prayer gathering held in the open fields beneath the skies of heaven as the community-at-large braced ourselves for the young recruit far too handsome for preach'n.

Addressing Marian Snead, chairman of the Deacons' Wives Committee and the Pastor Search Committee, Lavetty asked, "Why you hire sumbody so pretty?"

Marian raised an eyebrow and with a faint smile, she responded, "I have not the faintest notion what you mean. He's qualified. He's young. He doesn't stutter or stammer and he can write sermons."

"He's pretty...all I'm sayin."

We came to church like broken spirits. The church, as a structural centerpiece, a well-appointed monument calling us back beneath the vaulted timbers where we belonged, returning to our designated pews to fan ourselves in that odd morning light peculiar to summer services—a white, neutral light striking the east wall to penetrate the long stained-glass pictorials and wash the sullen spirits in the diffused shades of a watercoloring.

But the Pretty Preacher lacked the inflection for a good sermon; there was a nervous uncertainty to his delivery and a sapling's caliber to his squeaky voice and once again I found myself counting the nailholes in the floorboards.

She sat between Father and I, Mother, running her right hand along Father's arm back and forth trying so hard to follow the sermon and focus on the words and their context but it was easy to see she was elsewhere, her mind wandering like a spent casing, returning with a mild incoherence of swapping one life for another as she and Father once lumbered south, long ago, on Carl's midnight run, whispering nose to nose, half expecting the building momentum of their plan to be thwarted by search parties blocking the tracks. She had done what Dad Pond wanted, what her sisters wanted. She had her man.

Mercy May left the front pew for the organ roll that signaled the start of the closing hymns and Father breathed a sigh of relief; he had not followed the sermon, obviously, not a word of what was said. He sat holding her hand, lost in his own thoughts. I knew he had agreed to come only because Mother had wanted to leave the house, to go to church… adamant about going to church. For him, it was likely an hour's respite from calculating our options and weighing our possibilities and his thoughts, like Mother's, had wandered. The two of them, sitting beside me, present and accounted for but distanced from the new preacher's nearly inaudible delivery, as Father later admitted to images of me trapped under the river-ice and then to Mother running scared behind the Faller house and eventually, with the passing hour, his church-sermon nightmares or daydreams grew less frantic, floating toward a pleasant image with Verity and Max the previous summer in the high country and then the imaginary trip to Florida and by the closing hymns, he was thinking how long it had been since their last party. Out on the lawn, platters of food, croquet, target-shooting, dancing, laughing. Far too long.

Outside, stretching our legs under the warming sun, Dee cornered Marian to question the Board's decision.

"He's just nervous is all."

"Well, what about that one from the Seminary up to Bloomington? Why didn't you hire him?"

"Oh, honey, we tried. But he turned us down."

"Oh, come on. This is Fall Ridge."

"But don't you think he's cute?"

"Who? The one up to Normal, or Bloomington?"

"The one I hired. Don't you think he's cute?"

"Cute? Dearie, no one could hear a word that boy said."

"He's got the most adorable little nose."

"Oh, for pity's sake…"

Groups began to wander and migrate across the parking lot, stalling, taking their time. The convenience of everyone present and everyone present needing desperately to gorge themselves on one another's supporting voices. On Sundays past, it was often the church parking lot doubling as a town-hall meeting and as we waited for someone to get the ball rolling, a shiny sedan cruised by, rolling slowly between the church and the cemetery with its out-of-town shoppers gawking at the natives, wondering if they, too, were for sale and the natives with their indifferent faces representing a sanctity of purebloods breeding amongst themselves.

Verity and I navigated the wheelchair over the gravel and the women gathered in as the talk got going and the men followed along like understudies in the art of conversation. They stood listening, impatient with the pointless chatter until Diligence said, to no one in particular, "I heard Lisa Montgomery was up to Plant's house Friday night."

Lisa being the county records clerk and Pardon Plant the loan officer and general manager of the First National Bank.

The ladies quit their talk and everyone watched Diligence.

"Notarizing the Eddings' foreclosures what I heard." He shrugged his shoulders and added, "And the Clark place…goin to a speculator from Chicago. Only knows what he's got in mind."

Neither the Clarks nor Eddings were present. The Clarks had been away *visiting relatives* in Mt. Vernon for more than a month now, and the Eddings were in East St. Louis, *vacationing.* Diligence's rumor made it clear that neither the Clarks nor the Eddings would be returning.

Liberty Snead scraped his Sunday boots across the gravel and said, "It's about money. The bank is blinded by dirty money…approving everything from hunting retreats to riverfront highrises, I s'pect. I don't blame Jan and Leven Eddings."

"Well, let's do something," Dee said, and we all looked to where she stood with her hands on her hips in that nice floral dress with the wide bonnet shading out the sunlight. The Sheriff stood beside her with forgiving eyes.

But no one spoke.

"It's not really about us, anymore." It was Eart, the bus driver, who seldom offered an opinion on anything but who now motioned to the Roes' car, the group standing off the front fender. Mariah, Buddy, Verity, Bump, myself, Acceptance, half a dozen others drawn closer in recent weeks by the threads of convenience and shared interests. The disparity in ages that once separated Buddy and myself like opposite cliffs of a common canyon were closing. In a manner, due both to the passing of time and the strengths of a collective maturity, we had gone from underlings to heirs and heiresses, representing the equity and the collateral and the hopes of everyone present.

And yet we were only understudies and in no position to reverse the foreclosing Eddings and Clark farms, or to overrule the intrusion of outside speculators. Many of us, linked to the helms of grounded families, were also tutored in the tactful silence practiced by solvent families watching insolvent families slip gracefully away.

"More power to him," Eart said, shrugging his shoulders, and we wondered if he meant the bank manager, David Plant, or the speculator from Chicago, or Leven Eddings.

"Plant's strapped for cash," Liberty said. "No secret there."

"Join the club." A pitiless remark, uttered from someone, speaking for everyone. Nearly everyone, as the shoppers in their shiny sedans idled at a short distance, wielding their cameras and advancing the shutters through its frames, clicking clicking clicking.

SEVENTY-FIVE

When a week passed and Ruby hadn't returned, Marian Snead and Vivian Marsh left the county and drove to Anna in Hamilton County. Diligence himself had insisted on the honor, the privilege, but he was dismissed, rather emphatically. They left the county on the Tunnel Hill Trail down through the forest and just outside Buhcombe they passed Elizabeth's Plymouth heading home, one assumed, from her return to peddling bibles on the streetcorners of Carbondale. They waved but as Vivian later reported, Elizabeth's eyes were glued to the road, creeping along, all alone, at the pace of a loping deer.

Beyond Anna, up Willard's Ferry Road, they parked at the circular driveway of the Southern Hospital for the Insane with its appointed bricks and porticos unchanged since 1869.

At the front Sallyport, they provided identification, checked their purses, signed in, and were ushered along a labyrinth of stone hallways dark as tombs, arriving ultimately at an upper floor Recreation Hall. Ruby sat holding court at a corner table populated by half a dozen gentlemen in mismatched socks and shirt collars drenched in drool, fanning her cards in a game of Crazy Eights with her yellow scarf dangling down the back of her chair and the hem of her skirt resting just above the knee of her crossed legs.

357

POSSESSING THE SEASONS

Their arrival, and the ride home, seemed anticipated. A big show, for the benefit of her entourage, made of her life beyond the hospital.

It was about then, the weeks and months following, when the robberies developed a pattern, a systemic sameness until it seemed easier, more accommodating, to acquiesce the pattern than resist; canned food and vegetables were left surreptitiously outside Water's Grocer; a few coins left in Lester's cash drawer each night at the depot; and a random rotation of just about everyone turning up the Morrow walk on their way here or there as a preferred consolation to the permanence of Anna. A permanence, by the way, Ruby recounted as if it were paris, or austria. An exclusive resort, so exclusive its applicants were handpicked. Registered guests only.

358

SEVENTY-SIX

Costa Rica. Over Mexico, New Mexico, Oklahoma Kansas Missouri came the last of the hummingbirds and songbirds migrating from the tropics drenched in rainfall. They were scarcely aware of the changing topography, paying little note to the lush green peaks of the Sierra Madres or the southwest desert blooms or the early wheat blowing like a vast fertile carpet or the mossy shadowed gullies of the Ozarks. A vast flotilla of wings and scapulars and tail feathers bathed and scented and fluttering lightly as they rode the currents north over the Mississippi and into southern Illinois where we waited, watching their arrival as the last validation to the passing seasons.

They would have considered their landmarks, their instinctive nesting grounds, dropping to scan the treetops along the waterlines to hear that sound they knew, circling back and swooping down over the lower pasture to where he stood, Harlan, calling them in, sweeping within a few feet of him to pass over the tupelo woods and along the west field and back to the treetops beyond the bridge, a mile away, alighting in a stand of tulip poplars. Home again, five-thousand wood thrushes and hummingbirds the last of the lot, fluttering their breastplates and cleansing their wings still fresh from the rains and settling in to discharge their sacred chorus.

He listened, calling to them.

Below, even under the shade of the canopy, the white heat bore down on russet-colored fields marked by a few blooming aberrations along the river; the elderberries and the brown-eyed susans and the puttyroot orchids flowering against all odds. As they had for centuries, while along the road, Liberty Snead's truck raced over the bridge and up the cow trail, bounding and jostling over the clumps and divots of burrowing prairie dogs.

Reports of a front hanging off the western reaches of Kentucky had sent Liberty toward the overlooks off Moingwena Rise to see what his own eyes could see. He didn't bother dodging the venomous snakes emerging from their spring dens to feast on said prairie dogs or to absorb the heat of the baked earth, or the woodchucks smart enough to dash back out of his way, or the turtles crunching like potato chips to gum up the tire treads.

He had retraced this route every day for four straight days and every day, in his reports to Father and the others—their wilderness scout returning from the high-country margins—he stood for an hour perched on Moingwena Rise with his back to the river gorge, staring southwest until on the fourth day, the same day his wife and Vivian left the county on a 'mission of mercy,' the horizon diffused with the soft irregular lines of a definable front.

Culled from the stacks of archival boxes dating from the Rutherford B. Hayes administration, the Gazette carried a front-page photograph of a farmer in overalls, his head tilted up and holding his hat to bare his balding scalp to a drenching downpour. A smiling farmer, from Kentucky, presumably, standing ankle-deep in the sludge of a rain-drenched field.

Radios were tuned to the weather band as if it were broadcasting the Cardinals in a pennant race. There were no conversations or chance meetings that didn't begin with talk of the front hanging stubbornly to the south, hugging the tri-corner borders of Kentucky, Missouri and Illinois.

Finishing up at the Gazette, Scooter, Bump, and I paused at the bench in front of the Grocer, where Bump's grandfather sat with the carpenter Septimus and the stationmaster Lester, finished with Carl's mid-day run.

"Station'ry."

We looked up from where we stood pitching Scooter's pennies against the curb—Lester's pennies, no doubt.

Lester turned to the old farmer and asked, "How's that, Mr. Faller?"

"I said, it's station'ry."

Lester looked to us shaking his head and we smiled as Bump's grandfather leaned forward to send a stream of brown spittle onto the frontage of bricks separating the sidewalk from Main Street.

"Ass what dey'll do…jes sit still."

From the other end of the bench, Septimus shook his head, slowly, occupying the bench in the middle of a work day while the milled barn planks brought in on Carl's run were being loaded into the truck. Septimus the boss, the journeyman carpenter. He looked at the old man and made a face and said, "I have not a idea what on earth youse talk'n about."

Dee stepped from her shop across the street to sweep the walk and glance up into the sky and then over toward where we pitched our pennies. She stepped off the curb and crossed the street with broom in hand, disappearing into the Gazette.

Bump's grandfather pulled a twist of tobacco from his shirt pocket. He bit off a chunk and worked it such that it separated his upper plate from their seated gums and the plate fell clear of his mouth to land on the bench between his legs. He looked up wide-eyed and toothless with one hand patting his lap to locate the teeth and return them to the roof of his mouth and continue working the tobacco against his cheek, lodging it against his cheek like a golf ball and when he had it to his satisfaction, he said, "Sometimes a week. Dey'll sit for a week."

Lester said, "I have not a clue what yer goin on about."

We looked up from our pennies and smiled and I said, "It's the storm, Mr. Faller? The storm being stationary?"

Septimus and Lester returned to the depot where the Roe truck awaited, camouflaged under the weight of enough planks to repair the entire west wall of our barn.

On the twenty-eighth, a light wind rose up from the south and later that same day, reports of a secondary front forming over the grazelands to the south of Cape Girardeau. Beneath the clear and unfettered skies over Fall Ridge, Listen Allerton commented how 'a light wind was good for ruffling chicken feathers but that it takes a full-grown blow to give a storm direction,' while Liberty Snead said, 'A little wind can move a storm farthern you might think.'

I woke on the twenty-ninth, my twelfth birthday, to the filtered light of a thin haze. The wind maintained a nominal presence from the south and with morning passing into early afternoon the haze thickened and matured but it was still just a haze.

From Mother, two gifts: a plain-papered hardbound journal and an anthology of American Verse, both wrapped by Mariah and Verity in white tissue paper. From Father, two gifts: a light beautifully weighted .22-caliber single-shot rifle and a book of Botanical Species with color photographs, wrapped in Christmas paper. From Mariah, two gifts: a new bat wrapped in plain brown paper and a baseball with no wrapping, signed by Father before I was born and inscribed to her, to Mariah. From Verity, two gifts: a pearl-handled knife from Cole Hardware, with its own leather sheath and a saddle blanket with Verity's name embroidered in the corner. There were no gifts having anything to do with the Civil War or any war. Nor a single toy soldier.

Later, my shift beside the daybed, readying to read from the new book while noticing how some of the entries in the anthology were already bookmarked with small strips of torn paper.

"Any one you want," she said. "Make it a surprise."

She was feeling good, good enough to have requested the shade of the elm for much of the afternoon and it was this, along with the reports of sighted storms, that had everyone feeling almost giddy.

I raised the book and leafed through the pages to settle on a short piece. I took a slow breath and smoothed the page with the palm of my hand and began to read.

"Did you ever see a Jack Pine, tall on a deserted field?"

"What's this? Why this one?"

"Because it's marked, Mom. You got a big piece of cardboard marking the page."

I turned back to the book and ran my hand over the page.

"Start again," she said. "From the beginning."

"Did you ever see a Jack Pine, tall on a deserted field?"

"Listen to the meter, Jussie. Can you hear it?"

"I ain't read far enough to hear anything."

"Haven't. You haven't read far enough."

"Exactly."

"Well, go on," she said, lazily raising her hand. "Go on…read."

"Did you ever see a Jack Pine, tall on a deserted field?"

"You can't hear that?"

I shrugged and she said, "You'll never write a good sentence, Justus Charles, without learning your meters. In good prose, the rhythm never stumbles. It's like music…full notes, half notes, quarter notes."

She raised a limp hand, lofting it through the air from left to right, left to right. "Do you understand?"

I understood it had been a long time since we had had a real conversation. I had forgotten how she could be when she wasn't stuttering or talking nonsense or falling off to sleep in the middle of a sentence. I

POSSESSING THE SEASONS

also understood she had quit taking the pesticides from the medicine cabinet.

"So, you want me to read some more?"

"We don't want to insult her."

"Who? Insult who?"

"The poet, of course."

"So, I should read some more?"

"It's her only book. We have it downstairs."

I don't mention that this is the book from downstairs.

"That why you marked it, with cardboard? You wanted me to read it?"

"She wrote about what matters. I write gibberish rhymes. I draw silly pictures."

"She probably doesn't think so."

"She doesn't know who I am."

I stared at her, studying the lines in her face. I was tired of waiting for her to get well, tired of being patient. But it had been a good day, one of the best, and if we were all charged with thoughts of hope and promise, it was due largely to a single good day.

I touched her arm and said, "Course she does, Mom. Everyone knows you."

"Read some more, honey."

I nodded and smoothed the page and cleared my throat and started again.

"And have you ever counted
the limbs it has lost
to the prairie winds,
the storms,
the ice and snow,
the ravages of time?

364

CHARLES PROWELL

Look,
Look real close.
Count, and you will see
the dignity of the tree."

"Now do you hear it?"

"What's that, Mom?"

"Her rhythm. It's so plain and unassuming. Don't you think so?"

"It's nice. I feel sorry for the tree."

"But why?"

"It's all torn up...it's all alone."

"Oh, it's not alone. 'Count and you will see...the dignity of the tree.' Read it again."

"Again?"

"Yes, again."

I took another slow breath and ran my hand over the page and began reading the first stanza when Mariah appeared at the top of the stairs. She leaned over the balustrade. Her eyes were bright and excited.

"Daddy says it's time to set the table," she pointed toward the dormer. "Did you see the sky?"

I glanced at the window and left the chair to stand near the glass, peering out at the north field toward the clouded patchwork of a darkening gray sky, a traveling sky. Along the road, the upper branches of the hickories were being brushed by a slight wind.

Mariah ran back down the stairs. Through the corner of the window, I could see Father standing outside the kitchen door. He had on Clare's apron and there was a spatula dangling from his left hand and he was just standing there, staring at the sky.

I returned and sat on the edge of the chair and closed the book and said, "I have to set the table."

She held my hand and looked me in the eye and said, "Jussie, what were you thinking that day you fell in the river?"

365

I returned suddenly to the dark cold water, as if I were still there, the weight of the jacket and the strength of the current. A surge of adrenalin sweeping through my chest. Goosebumps. Fear.

"I guess I wasn't thinkin anything."

"When you were actually in the water. What was going through your head?"

I considerd the question and after a moment I said, "Mostly I was thinkin how to get out. I kept thinkin how to get out is all. I could see the light of the hole in the ice and I was trying to get to that."

"Promise me you'll be careful. Always be careful."

"Sure, Mom. I will."

The adrenalin drained away, but I knew it would be back at night, sitting up, drenched in sweat, my heart beating like a wild drum, awakened from the same recurring nightmare that had me giving in to the current, the hole in the ice getting smaller and smaller.

"You're growing up so fast."

"I'm the same, Mom."

She smiled and turned to the window and said, "How's the sky?"

"Somethin's blowin in. Somethin big, it looks."

"Your father must be beside himself."

I nodded. My thoughts turning quickly to the weather and how a change in the weather can affect everything. I was suddenly wildly excited and I said, "What if the Cardinals game is rained out? I read Dale's column this morning and he said they don't have the pitching… that it'll never hold up through August and September."

I wondered why, of all things, I had settled on this shattering news. Jackie Dale was the Sports Editor of Carbondale's Southern Illinoisan, and although we read him almost religiously, the very notion of pitching and baseball seemed now utterly and completely meaningless.

"That's nice," she said, "How about you…how's your job coming?"

"Okay, I guess. I cover the league here, the same two teams. The column is better. I make stuff up."

I could see she was growing tired. Her eyes were closing and the sound of her voice trailing off. I sat for a moment longer and when she was asleep, I went downstairs to the others, thinking to myself how things change, how sometimes you have to wait and the changes come with nothing more than the passing time. Well then, Mother was suddenly better and there was suddenly weather and things were shaping up... shaping up nicely.

SEVENTY-SEVEN

The young Mister Whister and little Mademoiselle are setting up the card table and two small chairs at the foot of the driveway. In the cash drawer of the red toy register are a few coins to make change, if needed. The rest of the small table is covered with the select offerings culled from what was discovered in the attic. Boxes upon boxes of mine and my father's baseball cards stashed in the drawers of an antique bureau, some of them dating to the playing days of Honus Wagner and Ty Cobb, some of Joe DiMaggio and Ted Williams. Bundles of five, wrapped and taped in Christmas paper and priced by a committee of three, ranging from 5¢ to 25¢.

From the dayroom dormer, I watch as they occupy the end of the driveway on an uncomfortably warm humid day. Watching as they wait, as they check the cash drawer, as they count the coins-for-change in the drawer, as they inspect the stacks of wrapped offerings, as the sun rises higher and the heat becomes stifling. Their father Conquer and their mother Dominate join me, watching from the upstairs dormer, spying, when their mother has had enough and calls Lavette down the road who appears with her granddaughter making their way up Pond Road and then Lyda, Max, and Clare's daughter who appears shortly with her son, and the childless Goldsteins up at the old Marsh place and the Roveros, who had long ago bought the old hunting retreat, and they all converge at the end of the driveway in a flurry of exchanges, coins for mystery

368

CHARLES PROWELL

cards wrapped in Christmas paper. And then they are gone and Whisty counts and divides the profits, slipping a handful of coins into the pocket of Maddy's blue-pleated dress and they return to the house. The house with central air conditioning.

SEVENTY-EIGHT

Daybreak. A lone whip-poor-will called like an oboe from the side-yard elm. Father stood over my bed with a look to remember…his hair bent and shaped from a fitful sleep to stand off his scalp like shocks of straw and in his eyes an exhausted wild almost ecstatic look. He squeezed my arm through the bedsheets and bent down close.

"We're in for a big one."

I sat up, turning to the window for a sky that was indigo dark and commanding and then back to look into his eyes bright as sunlit pools but tired drawn all used up. His face was shadowed and unshaven.

"I need your help," he said. "It's come up fast and there's a lot to do. Get dressed."

I moved from under the bedsheets to sit upright, to sit erect on the edge of the mattress like a soldier on the morning of a long-coming battle, awaiting my orders from an absurd figure in bare feet and wrinkled pajamas and with tufts of wild, untamed hair shooting off like trampled river weeds. My commander, with the eyes of someone who thrives on the unknown.

"What time is it?"

But there was no response, Father already crossing the dayroom and starting down the stairs. I quickly changed, searching the room for my boots to discover Verity's bed was empty. There were footsteps on the stairs and a moment later, she entered the bedroom in her pajamas and robe and I said, "There's a big'n comin. Where's my boots?"

I kicked through the clothes scattered across the floor like groundcover.

"Where the heck are my boots? I can't find my gott-danged boots!"

No response and I stopped and looked at Verity still standing in the open doorway. I knew the face. Her big-sister face but I ignored it and said, "Why are you up? How long you been up?"

"Jussie, you really have to watch your language. Just because Mom's..."

I knew the tone, that return to our former hierarchy. All the intonations of the old rank and file.

"Didn't Dad tell you?" I said, excitedly. "There's a storm."

I fished the boots out from beneath the bed and strapped them on and turned to Verity. I stepped over the taped-off line separating the cluttered half from the orderly half like snowdrifts against a fenceline and said, "What's the matter? How come you're not gettin dressed?"

"Because some things are more important."

Oh, I knew that tone. Verdi downplaying the excitement of an unusual event. The composed and orderly Verdi lingering in bed on Christmas morning, repressing her anticipation with a maddening patience.

I stood, frantically buttoning my shirt. "Like what? There ain't nothin more important. "

"Didn't you hear anything last night, Jussie?"

I stopped. My fingers still on the button loops, watching her. Confused. Not the big-sister voice, entirely. Something more.

"Hear anything? Like what?"

"Didn't you hear Mom? How could you sleep through that?"

"I didn't hear nothin."

"She had a really bad night. Daddy was up the whole night. He even called Dr. Leemore. Everybody was up but you. I can't believe you, Jussie."

Okay. Back to that voice…the censuring and the posturing voice I hated.

"What did I do? I didn't hear anything at all."

"All you care about is what you care about and you don't care about anything else. You just care about yourself, Jussie."

"Huh?"

"It's true. You don't care about Mom, or about anything but yourself."

"I care about Mom. Why did you say that? What's the matter with you?"

"Then how come you only sit with her when you have to…when it's your turn?"

My head reeling, reduced to an injured eight-year-old. Verity, in an instant, regained the ground I had won and occupied since that afternoon on the bridge and I was stunned by the deftness of her blow. I searched in a panic for the old defenses that had been dismantled and retired with an unbelievable naivety.

"What the heck's wrong with you? What the hell are you talkin about?"

But the sound of my voice was empty and without strength.

"Stop cussing, Jussie. It's really stupid. You sound like Scooter."

"I'll sound any way I want. I don't have to listen to you."

"You don't listen to anybody anymore. You're still just a kid and no one's watching you. You won't listen to me or Mariah and Daddy's too busy and Mom's too sick and everybody's worried about you."

So, she was a traitor. I should have guessed. She had all the tactical, painstaking patience of a cold-blooded traitor and I had been caught with my boots off and I could be months regaining the ground lost in an instant. My eyes settled on the other half of our shared room, many of her belongings already moved into Dee's old bedroom across the dayroom. In a matter of days, everything would be gone, replaced with a void I had no use for. The Verity void.

"I don't need no one watchin me."

My voice was hollow and without conviction, studying the floor, smelling defeat. But when I looked up, her eyes were wet and swollen and suddenly I didn't know up from down.

"Why are you crying? What's wrong?"

"What's wrong? What's wrong? Mom's really sick is what, and Daddy's been trying to call Dr. Leemore but the phone doesn't work and…"

Mariah rounded the top of the stairs and came to stand beside Verity. She looked tired and grumpy and turned to me and said, "Daddy says you're to help him in the barn…now."

She turned to Verity. "We're supposed to get Mom ready for the cellar. They're saying it's a tornado."

I took the stairs three at a time, through the library down the hall and out onto the front porch. A sliver of sunlight threaded through the pass on Moingwena Rise, throwing a deep ancient glow over the fields. I started out across the lawn and quickly the light disappeared to an evening dusk.

The wind was charging up from the south-southeast, a steady bracing wind rich and soupy and thick with moisture. The clouds were in an excited motion traveling and shifting and as I hurdled the fence, they parted to a shaft of light that washed myself and the barnyard with an eerie golden glow and I thought how it wasn't the bloated sluggish sky of a rainstorm. No, it was a charging sky, a violent sky that was advancing with confidence, a fast and powerful sky that was clearing the ridgelines like floodwaters over a levy. Racing headlong into the valley.

Father had Horse by the catchrope, struggling to get him into the barn. But the animal was skittish, rearing back on his hind legs and resisting the pull of the rope. I grabbed hold just behind Father when a sudden blow kicked up a swirl of dust to spook Horse and for a moment, we were crossing the barnyard with the heels of our boots dug into the dirt.

"The end of the rope…strap it off!"

I let go and chased the dangling rope through the dirt, grabbing it, gripping tight as Horse bolted forward and I was sent stumbling into the empty sheep dip, dragged the length of the sheep dip and up the ramp on my stomach to catch the ramppost hard against my right shoulder. Eyes closed, I wrapped the rope to the post and felt the post give, tweaking against the pull.

I stood to a sharp pain running through my shoulder and shoulderblades. I opened my eyes and coughed up a cake of dust and unbuckled my belt and dropped my jeans like a bucket of wet mud.

"You all right?"

I nodded, scooping the dirt from my boxers and pulling up my pants as Father fingered my shoulder, feeling for breaks. Horse moved back and forth, held by the catchrope and prancing like a deranged showhorse and Father turned, spitting dust and wiping his sleeve against his lips and said, "Go get Verdi, for heaven's sake."

I took a wide loop around Horse, setting out across the barnyard to come onto the front porch and through the side door to find Verity and Mariah in the kitchen. They had a laundry basket set up on the counter, packing food and fresh water.

"We need help with Horse!"

I didn't wait for an answer, turning to leave the porch and running back toward the barn, staggering in a windblown course to come around the corn shed and up to the hog pen where Father stood braced against the troughpost, driving Sow into the barn with a length of broken fencerail, slapping her flanks. I rounded the empty pen and secured the door to the chicken coop but the chickens were panicked, scattering through the hatch access and fluttering brainlessly against the wire of the pen. They were goners, anyway. The coop would never hold up.

I came back around the front of the pen to see Verity listing into the wind. She had hold of her shirt collar, blocking the dust from her eyes and walking toward the barn doors with Horse following like a pet poodle.

Continuing beyond the pen and around the corner of the barn, I was conscious of the windmill clattering in the distance, spinning like a loose fan. A pair of muskrats were at the trough, disoriented and skirting through Cow's hind legs. She kicked and the muskrats leapt clear and came back and Cow stood stationed at the trough like a building, slurping from the tank as I leaned into her and slapped her midsection and slowly we lumbered around to the back of the barn with the muskrats running circles.

Entering the barn, the wind died away and I led Cow back to a corner stall and closed and latched the gate.

Verity and I rejoined Father, staggering to close the huge sliding doors to a sudden piercing sound. The shrill of metal tweaking and separating and we stepped away from the barn to watch the windmill giving way, listing toward the buckling hickories along the road. The blades out of balance and wobbling and screeching with a horrible stabbing racket and slowly, the windmill toppled, collapsing like a felled tree with an impact that shook the ground, crushing half a dozen peach trees.

Father moved to draw the sliding door to the empty lab Annex and motioned us toward the house, taking hold of our hands as we zigzagged through the barnyard and along the side yard, dodging planks of loosened fence and lawn chairs propelled across the barnyard like dry leaves. We opened the screen door and the door was hurled from its hinges; it skipped over the lawn clear to the drive, pasting itself against the side of the truck.

Inside, shouldering the door to close out the wind and the howling and for a moment, there was the sanctity of a relative silence. Father glanced at the picture windows running the length of the living room, exposed head-on to the wind. He turned to Mariah.

"You ready?"

She nodded.

He started down the hall and a moment later reappeared with Mother in his arms. Her eyes were wide and frightened, trembling all over.

I opened the back door to a blast of wind. The girls passed through and then Father and Mother and I pulled the door shut and we all moved along the side of the house listing, listing like sailboats, bounced against the siding as Mariah released the hasp to the repaired cellar doors and a moment later, we were under the house. The stolid moist air of the cellar with the doors closed and latched and Mariah lighting the oil lamp and Father positioning Mother on the cot brought down from the attic.

We stood like strangers. No one speaking. Driven once again into the recesses of our protective bunker, our cave, listening to the storm. Mariah was at the small double-paned rectangular window set just above ground level, watching the debris carry over the drive and the gardens, rising and lowering, traversing the north field, hitchhiking the air pockets to reach the side of the Marsh house where Givens and Vivian watched from their own cellar window, watching the Roe house.

"They's in," Givens said. "All of 'em."

"Grace?"

"All of 'em."

Vivian set the small table in the center of their immaculate cellar, readying a lunch of ham sandwiches and fruit juice as if it were a Sunday picnic.

"Have yourself something to eat."

She sat and placed the cloth napkin over her lap and at this point of her telling, she would always vary from the calm and collected thoughts of considering new curtains and a new rug to how the wind and clattering were like a marching band prancing through her brain. She settled on the shelf of board games—the calm and collected version—with her mind returning to all the tornadoes over the past sixty some years. All the ice storms and tornadoes since she was a girl playing checkers with her parents while mother nature wreaked havoc. Marrying the excitable flirtatious Givens, a town boy, and now, as he stood watch at the window, how that marriage was nearing the fifty-year mark and still the longing regret of no little ones to raise. The end of the lineage.

Givens followed three hunters making their way unsteadily up the rise toward the house, leaning into the wind, gripping the fence rails as a lifeline and he wondered aloud if they knew where the Faller cellar was, that it was detached from the house, a bunker off the barn side of the house.

"Come have a sandwich, dear. You'll feel better."

She began without him, her eyes falling on a small stain blotching a corner of the tablecloth and considering various detergents but without knowing what it was…perhaps Dee Pond would know. She would drive in next week, pay a visit to the shop, and bring the soiled cloth along and her mind wandered, as it was prone to doing, again to the early years, the wedding, and how Dee was only fourteen and even Harriet was still a teenager. What a calamity, all those Pond girls yelling and fighting and laughing and singing for all those years and the boys…the boys drawn to that house like flies to a plate of molasses and somehow, somehow little Gracie had survived and look what she had become and now…

Givens turned from the window. He glanced at the sandwich, his eyes like shutters to the soul, so lifeless and unaffectionate.

"There's some hunters over to the Fallers. Lookin for the bunker."

"Don't they know?"

"They's disappeared behind the house, in the wrong direction."

She sipped her fruit juice and said nothing as he made his way to the other side of the cellar and stood staring out this north window with his back to her and her thoughts returned to the stained tablecloth and then the marching band. The hunters were on their own.

The hunters were not prepared. Four of them from four corners of the country for a week of reminiscing their college years while idly engaged in the pursuit of guaranteed game. Buckshot, poker, tall tales, beer, a little whisky, with no mention in the brochure of tornadoes and underground bunkers. They panicked, running and scurrying separately around the circumference of the house, the lodge, searching for a hint of cellar doors and on to the barnyard to be slapped and jolted by loosened barn planks eddying with a discordance that had them all thinking of their wives and their children back home where tornadoes were like tsunamis—something you read about, something that happened elsewhere. In their confusion, one of them separated and made his way down the lane and onto Pond Road with the instincts of home, of San Francisco earthquakes with the threat of being buried alive under the rubble of collapsing buildings. Romero-the-Architect, who would later renovate that house—'up from the rubble,' he aways said, waving his hands if it were all in a day's work as he described staggering past the Roe farmhouse to his left that fateful day, darkened windows and swirling debris clattering and battering everything in its path to eventually reach the river and the twisting deformed steel of the bridge and under that bridge crouching like a newborn, covering his ears to the earsplitting crack of felled trees.

Hot. Not the intense heat of a mid-day sun, but a thick roiling heat that made breathing difficult. Not the same cellar where Mother and I had nearly frozen to death, nor the same cool pleasant cellar where we went to replenish our preserves in deep summer. The air was dense and close and I wondered how long I would last before the air went bad. How long before I chose the tornado over the claustrophobic suffocation of the cellar.

I hated the cellar—a grim clammy dank underground prison cell. I stood with my heart fluttering like a barn swallow, spreading my stance as the color drained from my cheeks and the dizziness arrived like a chokehold. I took a deep breath to fill myself with the bad air and then another and quickly another until I stood in a swerving hyperventilating race for equilibrium when Father's arm slipped over my shoulder and straddled my chest like a grounding harness.

"Take it easy, son."

I stood with my eyes shut and the dizziness gradually subsided. The beating heart slowed and the adrenalin drained away. The sweat rolled off my scalp and along my jaw and when I opened my eyes to focus on nothing, a chill settled in along the back of my neck and down my spine and I stepped away from Father's arm to stand shaking.

I looked at the girls in the low flickering light of the lamp and I could see the sweat already glistening off their cheeks. I wanted out. I could not stay down here. Not for a minute or five minutes. The vast open fields and the deep endless skies narrowed to the cowering existence of a mole. I would take my chances and face dismemberment-by-tornado rather than die like a worm in a tomb. I paced and moved in tiny circles and looked furtively to Father and suddenly I started for the cellar steps, charging toward the steps to push against the underside of the doors and pressing my lips close to the slivers of light, whimpering like a small child.

"Jussie!"

The sound of Father's voice carrying through the buried air like a muffled echo.

I crouched on the steps ramming my back up against the doors and then stopped. I turned toward the voice and began to tremble. I lowered my head and wrapped myself in my own arms, separated from the salvation of my open fields by the stubbornness of a cellar door, sitting on the steps doubled over, clutching my own waist and rocking back and forth. Softly crying.

I could sense Father crossing the cellar and then leaning close and then feeling his breath, feeling his hands around my waist, lifting me as if he were a bucket of mulch. Riding his hip like an infant. Burrowing my head in deep and clutching tight and feeling his hand stroking my sweat-soaked hair and cupping the back of my neck and eventually the trembling stopped and the whimpering cry was quieted.

"You can do this, Sport. Just relax."

Lowered to the dirt, I stood again with my eyes closed, rocking on my heels and listening to the wind and from the corner of the cellar, the short rhythm of Mother breathing. Each breath an abbreviated gasp. The faint petite whispering breath of an injured bird.

Sitting alone and composed, Verity cooled Mother's forehead with a damp cloth.

"Think about other things, Jussie," Verity said.

I moved a few steps, feeling the sweat roll off my forehead and down the side of my chest in trickling rivulets.

"Like what?"

"Something quiet."

She set a jar of peaches on the table, turning it slowly, a full turn, and looked at me, "Like a book…anything quiet and peaceful."

"A book?"

And from along the shelves of canned goods, Father said, "Or of a particular day…a fun day, maybe from last summer."

I closed my eyes and pictured the roadside ant war and the billiard table at the Lincoln Hotel with its torn felt, and the couple leaving the cinema, staring at me, and to swimming in the river and lying on our backs in the weeds, studying the sky and then Scooter and I perched in the cherry trees, watching Buddy's Ford racing through Snead's Corner and when I opened my eyes, it was as if awakening from a meditative dream. The closeness, the thick air and the claustrophobia...all of it somehow less threatening.

I moved to the opposite window, comforted by the sight of the lawn and the riverbank trees and the elm leaves floating like paper airplanes, a fleet of planes swooping over the fenceline and along the lower pasture and over the grove of cottonwoods gliding into the Arthur Compound like an army of angels.

Mr. Arthur dodged and blinked and pulled the angel from his face as he left Barn One, thinking surely how there was only the one cellar.

The others furiously gathered their stores. Madeline and Lavette jogged between the side door and the cellar off the barn, ushering the others toward a bunker the size of a large closet. A cellar dug by hand a century ago. And for a moment, and I think it was Madeline, or maybe Lavette, who always said how they all stood at the top of the steps, frozen in place, more than a dozen of them, clutching their hats and collars, standing buttressed to the wind as if waiting for the wind itself to blow them into what was surely to be their last resting place.

"All us cain't never fit in there!" Lavette said, yelling over the wind.

But within minutes, they did fit, jammed like canned peaches, standing shoulder to shoulder, breathing that secondhand air as Rufus closed and latched the doors and the cellar went black. The paralysis of a dirt-wall grave, made bearable by the nearly indiscernible sound of Clare's soft voice, floating a quiet melody.

POSSESSING THE SEASONS

✳ ✳ ✳

Father tuned in the radio, tracking the tornado's progress through a weakening reception. His eyes grew big, smiling, almost laughing aloud with the news of heavy rains just forty miles south.

But the rains were well behind the tornado. The report plotted its course at the southeastern edge of the valley and moving northwest, dead on for the river. High winds were one thing. Being aligned to the funnel itself was something else altogether.

"Will we see it?" I asked.

Father raised an eyebrow and tilted his head as if to say, Maybe. Perhaps. He sat on top of the freezer, his eyes resting on Mother and the girls, his mind seemingly accepting the rest, the mandatory time-out and when he spoke, the sound of his voice caught everyone by surprise.

"You know what I like about mowing our lawn?"

We looked up, confused, conscience of the lazy tone in his voice.

A moment passed and, "What, Daddy?"

"I like how it smells. It's the best smell of all. I can smell it now."

We contemplated this, this abrupt departure, searching our senses.

"And you know what else?"

"What, Daddy?"

"I like smelling cow poop. I like how it smells."

Mariah responded with a groaning disgust and Verity said, "Me too, Daddy. I actually like it. And horses, too."

"And you know what else? I like it when the wildflowers are up in the spring and walking through the lower pastures, smelling all those purple coneflowers and the mimosa and the purple martins and that one that always grows along the road."

"Compass plant, Daddy."

"Yeah, the hummingbirds like that one."

From the cot, Mother whispered, "Humming...birds."

"That's right, sweetie. And you know what else...what I do sometimes, when no one is looking?"

"What, Daddy?"

He slid off the freezer and stepped to the center of the cellar floor and with the toe of his right boot as an axis, he turned once around followed by a step to the left and a step to the right, humming.

"You're ridiculous, Daddy."

But because Mariah was a wonderful dancer, she left her seat beside the cot and began moving slowly to the sound of his humming rhythm, joined by Verity, holding hands for a slow spinning side pass and Father turning to me with a motion to join them and from the small window I shook my head once and responded, "Nooo way, Dad."

And later, we ate apples and peaches sliced into quarters and drank from the water Mariah had bottled and when we thought we had had enough, Father encouraged us to drink more. Mariah made some instant tea and she and Verity stood watching through the small window as the wind died off and the cellar dropped into a long eerie silence. The cellar air like a precious shared commodity, thick and languorous and filling our lungs like cream. I took my place beside the cot, working the damp cloth over Mother's forehead while Father studied the barometer and fiddled with the radio. I offered Mother a sip of tea, guiding the straw to her lips.

We waited, nibbling nervously on the popsicles found in the freezer, passing the binoculars around and faking an easy manner when the barometer began to fall, dropping like a weighted second hand and quickly, the radio went to static. A stiff wind rustled up and the peach trees bent like river weeds.

From the window, Mariah released a sudden yelp, upsetting the small table to send the apples and peaches pitching across the dirt floor.

We gathered at the window, watching the funnel hovering along the rise off Pond Road, clean as a photograph, gliding effortlessly along the crest of the Marsh field like a spinning top across a polished floor before sweeping off the crest to glance down against the stand of hickories, uprooting them like twigs.

It zigzagged through the field north of the old Faller farm before shifting to bound straight on for the renovated lodge with an explosion of glass and timber, slicing through the new west wing like the cross section of a dollhouse. It carried through the grassy furrows of the lower pasture before crossing the road for the northern reaches of our property. As it drew closer, our visibility grew poorer, the funnel less a perfect spiral than a cloud of whirling dust. The wind rattled the clapboards and then a raging startling blast so loud and deafening, we covered our ears and jumped back from the window, screaming with pantomimed voices lost to the roar.

The girls and I returned to the window to stand atop the repositioned peach crates, watching a telephone pole along the road suddenly snap like kindling; the live wires danced off the ground in a flurry of sparks and fizzles. The fence separating the north field from the barnyard splintered into a thousand pieces and the peach trees uprooted and lifted into the air like tumbleweeds to disappear somewhere over the fallen silo. The new gate disintegrated, tearing apart and sweeping into the air like pickup sticks. The house squealed and shrieked at the joints and any sense of order was now lost to the chaos of a deafening racket that left us screaming and jumping in place like utter lunatics. A series of quick explosions directly overhead; the bedroom floor joists, just inches from our heads, moved with sharp lateral jolts and it seemed any moment the house would lift away, exposing us like worms under a rock. We screamed without constraint, holding one another on our knees in a pandemonium of explosions and loosening timbers.

But the house didn't lift away. It held up, and as the funnel skittered off toward the barnyard, it was a long moment before anyone dared to move.

"Everyone okay?"

Father raised himself away from the cot. The girls on their stomachs, face down on the dirt floor as I glanced at Mother wrapped in the linens with her head propped on the cot, exposed like someone buried in sand.

CHARLES PROWELL

The girls repositioned the crate beneath the small window on the opposite side of the cellar. Crowded by shelves of canned goods and preserved fruits, they pressed their faces to the double-paned glass and peered toward the barnyard to watch the chicken coop disintegrating before their eyes, hens spiraling upward and thrown out over the ground in a sea of feathers.

They watched as the funnel distanced itself over the lower pasture, cutting a swath through the cottonwoods along the river like a mower leveling high weeds, leaving a visible scar that would remain for years to come. They watched as it skated over the landscape, diminished by the distance, skirting the Arthur Compound to climb the grade up Kickapoo Ridge, prancing along the ridgeline and then it was gone. Four minutes. From the first sighting to its disappearance over the ridge, just four minutes.

385

SEVENTY-NINE

Father lifted Mother from the cot like a priceless vase, standing for a moment, cradling her in place, his arms rocking side to side until her eyes closed and we all turned to scale the cellar steps like cowards from a cave. Like survivors.

Outside, beneath the blackened skies, the mark of the intruder had scored the countryside with a massive faultline and in its wake, nothing survived. Not the Californians' house nor the east wing of the Faller house nor the hickories along the road nor the peach trees at the edge of the garden. Even the iron trelliswork of the bridge was left twisted and deformed. The truck had been relocated just beyond the barnyard gate and the station wagon rested upside down, wedged in the roadside gully, buried beneath the rubbish of fencerails and tree limbs. And yet, only a few yards off course, the barn and the corn shed were untouched.

"We're jes cowards, Dad."

"Survivors, Sport. There's a difference."

"Cowards, Dad."

"Well, what would you have us do, Buddy Boy...stand up to a tornado?"

"Yeah…I would. I'd stand up to it any day."

Mariah turned to me and grunted and said, "Gawd, Jussie…you're so full of it."

EIGHTY

Although the house, with its old-world timber framing and interlocking joinery, had held firm, the latter-day accoutrements—glass windows—had not. We tiptoed through a living room with the fragments of glass shifting and crunching beneath us, a beach of diamonds with a limb from the elm drooping lazily through the far window to rest against the heel of the crippled baby-grand piano. The back porch of so many summer evenings was a brick footing with a scattering of naked joists. Through the dining room with Wrestling and Chastity's New England china and silver settings strewn everywhere, on through the library with the missing south window, stepping on piles of books like stones in a pond to scale the stairs to the dayroom, with its elevated view of the approaching storm.

I was dispatched to the attic and returned to report the roof was intact and the attic was preserved, like a still-life, preserved with a curator's care.

There was no one to call, no means of calling anyone. Beyond the north-facing dayroom dormer, the light was the light of an hour past sunset—although it was early afternoon. The Marsh house was a mere shadow in the distance; there were no lights, no lights anywhere but the crackling power lines dancing along the middle of Pond Road.

The linens draping the daybed rose and fell almost imperceptibly, each slight movement followed by a laboring effort that punctuated the stillness of the dayroom but also beyond the dayroom to a resting landscape, seemingly asleep, napping, on the heels of some rousing mayhem while squinting with a wakefulness of what was to come.

Mariah and Verity left for the kitchen and returned with a few edible scraps and a pitcher of iced tea and Mariah asked, "Should we go back to the cellar?"

Father muttered, "A flooding cellar...no. Stay above grade, above ground level."

From the Marsh house, three beams of light. Followed a few minutes later by three more successive beams. We watched, unable to respond; the flashlight and the oil lamp were left in the cellar.

I left for my room and returned with the field glasses. Vivian was holding a sign, shining a light on the sign: OKAY?

From the small desk on the opposite wall, we rolled a sheet of paper. Matches were located. We held the torch against the window until the torch burned itself out and we sat, mesmerized by the changing sky, fat sluggish clouds tiered up in a canvas of masks and shadows.

A gust of wind struck the side of the house and we trembled.

Verity disappeared into the bath at the top of the stairs and returned with a new dampened washcloth she draped carefully over Mother's forehead, pausing to study the linen bedsheet rising like a slow tide and returned to the window, peering out onto a lampblack sky.

Mariah unlatched the casement, pushing it open to a blast of wind that strained the hinges. She quickly pulled it shut and brushed the hair from her eyes and the scent of rich moist air lingered in the room.

The afternoon passed to evening almost unnoticed; the color of the light aging on a gradient from gloomy to gloomier. The sky accepted the definition of an obscured rising moon. Layers upon layers of black tarpaulin clouds rimmed with the lighter shades of a diffused moonlight to create depth, to create the tiered hierarchy of a cruel bluff advancing in over the ridge on a stiff headwind. Swooping off the ridge.

For dinner, the girls put together sandwiches from the kitchen, stepping over and around the twigs and leaves and debris invited in through the exposed living room windows. They walked across floors pebbled with glass, crunching like shelled peanuts.

Upstairs, eating our sandwiches, nibbling like mice, who could have known the lull would last well into evening? We grew restless. Verity brushed Mariah's hair. Father fiddled with the washcloth, adjusting it across Mother's forehead. I mindlessly stacked toy wooden blocks I hadn't played with in years, when the wind began to reestablish itself, shifting in from the east to send the two cherry trees bowing toward the road.

A signal from the Marshes' and another paper torch, responding, gravitating to the window now as we braced ourselves with a ringside view in a mixture of fear and anticipation when the first few sprinkles freckled the glass, and quickly, the far skies over Moingwena Rise opened with a broad spline of light splintering across the horizon to touch the valley floor with a long rumbling drumroll that vibrated through the floorboards. We exchanged looks and gathered in closer and the drumroll escalated to a flurry of crackling interruptions and at once an explosion so long and deafening we backed away from the glass. A second streak and a third sliced across the sky with a thunderous roar that shook the entire house and suddenly, there was rain.

Raindrops the size of blackberries pelted the glass and the sharp clap of a thunderbolt and then a magnificent booming report that trembled the joists and the rafters and we were screaming, backpedaling from the window and screaming but the sound of our voices was lost to a percussion of rolling thunderbolts. To a squall slapping the window and the sideboards like gunfire.

For several minutes, the thunder was continuous and deafening and we screamed in a collective pantomime until our lungs were empty and our cheeks were flushed and then we laughed. We laughed, roaring like idiots, laughing until our eyes watered and our sides ached.

EIGHTY-ONE

The Fall Ridge Gazette, that paper of record, penned by the fact-checking Linkum Regards and his overseeing sidekick, published an archival edition of superlatives and modifiers.

It rained like cats and dogs.

She stood with a hand on my shoulder, thinking. "I've always wondered about that. I mean, really…why cats and dogs?"

"I've heard it, Aunt Bim. People say that about rain."

"Buckets…now that I could see. But cats'n dogs?"

"Buckets? Well then, why not fenceposts or somethin?"

"Buckets of *water.*"

"So, the whole bucket rains? Or just the water that's in the buckets?"

"I couldn't say, exactly."

"Buckets would hurt."

"So would dogs."

"Well, since it ain't rained forever and we don't really know about writin about rain, maybe we should just say it rained."

"Okay. No metaphors or similes."

"No what?"

EIGHTY-TWO

I went to college. Verity went to college. Mariah went to college. We all went to college. I studied metaphors and modifiers toward a lifelong pastime of weekly editorials. Verity, sutures and surgeries toward a notable career in animal behavior. Mariah, silk chiffons and french chenilles, returning to spend forty years speaking francewha to the upscale clientele patronizing Pond's Passion for Fashion.

Speaking of metaphors, of words, or more specifically, letters, little Henry and his cousin Marjorie present the award certificates to Books and Beyond winners-of-the-month. To the first-floor primary grade students who, to Henry and Marjorie, must seem like adults. Someone bandied the phrase straight As.

Mariah's daughter Sally drops them off at the farm and she and Dominate set the dayroom play table with colored pencils and lined composition booklets and colored rulers and pencil sharpeners and Henry and Marjorie spend the afternoon in school, writing the letter A in straight lines.

The Pond Planting Log of present and for some years now is recorded on spreadsheets. Rotations, planting schedules, timetables, bushel values with built-in calculations and simulating bar graphs with PowerPoint presentations and regularly scheduled group video conferences. All of it organized and managed by Dominate at the small desk in the dayroom and backed up onto a cloud server. The data is networked across a coalition of two-hundred-thirty family-owned farms throughout the entire Missouri Valley, thus providing a greater impact on the market values as a whole, while mitigating the imbalance against a wave of larger corporate farms.

  A similar system is employed by Lavette and her husband and Rufus and his wife across the river, coordinating an alliance of garden-to-table produce through the popular Missouri Valley Farmer's Markets and a growing presence of trendy eateries and restaurants from the triangle of Louisville, St. Louis, and Nashville.

  Wedged between these and Henry Roe's unreadable slide rule algorithms[15], are those logs of my own tenure. These pages before you, expanding on those eighteen months and making their way into subsequent printings through the son of my mother's long-time publisher and attributable to a revenue source, along with Mother's perpetual residuals, that is distributed over mine, Verity's and Mariah's families, as well as an annal contribution to The Valley-Wide Fund for Emergency Needs.

---

15. *One of the Rovero daughters left the valley for berkeley, california, across the bay from her ancestral home. She returned five years later as a lawyer with flowers in her hair. She opened a small office, Rainbow Rovero, Attorney at Law, located next door to Mariah's Passion for Fashion shop. Upon learning of our father's missing logs, she became indignant. The industrial complex. The wrinkling white male industrial complex flexing their manifest destiny like spoiled schoolboys vs. the upstart 5'4" leftist female legal whiz, a syntactical sorceress who spent two years taunting the state department with endless briefs, subpoenas, memorandums, proceedings, and appeals until the missing logs were ultimately banked in the archival collections at the University of Illinois. She and Mariah Roe-Faller were best friends.*

EIGHTY-THREE

Six days of continuous pelting rain and on the third day, the day Mother died, the river overflowed to flood every bottomland pasture between the Point and the Kickapoo Gorge and on the fourth it swelled over Pond Road to lap against the bridge planks and on the fifth the twisted ironwork was left exposed like the riggings of a sinking ship.

Two miles upriver, the banks of the narrow gorge were dammed with the bloated carcasses of those Herefords ravaged by the tornado or drowned by the floods, backing the floodplain clear to Deere Road.

We launched the flat-bottom boats as an armada, shoving off the dry rise of the front lawn in a pelting rain, traumatized by a tornado and then five days of prophesying floods to launch our little boats on the strength of adrenalin alone.

Father and myself; Liberty Snead; Givens Marsh; Diligence Wiseman; Guy, Buddy, and Bump Faller; Sheriff Sam Dittmar; our hands Septimus and Laney along with the Compound's Rufus and Simp; Lester from the depot and Carl the engineer; Eart the bus driver and Pat Davis; and Mr. Rovero, Dick Rovero, the one surviving hunter, the

394

CHARLES PROWELL

architect raised sailing in the San Francisco Bay who assumed his place amongst the rest of us as if...as if he were *one* of us[16].

We made our way over the sluggish floodplain east of Pond Road to cross the road that was three feet below the hulls and carried along south, avoiding the groves and the stronger currents as we progressed south-southwest on a course parallel with the river. We stayed to the northern edge, hugging the rises at the watermark to make good time through the domesticated waters of what could be a lake or a lagoon, harbored from the open-water pastures flanking the river. We were tired. All of us, spent clean from sheathing off the sidewalls of exposed homes and gathering livestock and abbreviated funerals and maneuvering whole families to higher ground, lost in our collective thoughts with the sound of flywheels churning underwater and the pitch and hum of single-stroke engines. We sat without talking, struggling to stay awake.

At the old Sapp acreage, we gathered up and cut the engines and gripped one another's gunwales and considered an approach to the gorge. But no one spoke. We bobbed and rolled and stared off to the open waters and beyond to where the river turned nasty and beyond that, well...who could say? Clearly, there was only the one route in and the pause was more to summon our strength and consider our blessings while relishing the calm of the northern watermark.

Liberty swept his arm slowly off the starboard quarter.

"It'll be along there. That far side...we won't get run against the hickories."

He turned to the rest of us but no one had anything left. We sat without a word, willing to go along with whatever it was he had in mind because his was the one place fronting the gorge. He would have

---

16. *Mr. Rovero. Dick Rovero, bunking for that week in Aunt Dee's old bedroom, with Verity reoccupying our former shared bedroom until the families arrived from their four corners of the country to claim the bodies and his own family arrived from the coast, from San Francisco. Months later, the Rovero's bought the ravaged Faller acreage from the Bostonian and, being an architect, he rebuilt the house to replicate the original Faller floorplan and it was in that house where generations of liberal Rovero's took root.*

POSSESSING THE SEASONS

grown up hiking those limestone caverns. But he waited, wanting our reassurance. His eyes traveled to Bump and Buddy and then to myself, thinking surely how the gorge would make no distinction between boys and men. He turned to Father, who was in no shape to handle anything.

"You okay, Hank?"

But Father regarded him without expression and from the forward bow, I sat like a lost soul, focusing on the water clapping the aluminum hull, and beyond, mesmerized by the roll of the waves, the whitecaps. We were present, Father and I, but adrift in a wave of injustice. Hobbling along on a manufactured faith.

We lingered, bobbing, our hulls clattering against one another as Liberty sat on the silence, assessing our chances and the liability of a wrong decision and we all began to wonder if the whole idea wasn't a mistake. If we cleared the gorge, the floodplains receded. If we didn't, half the valley would remain flooded for weeks to come, and rising, until everything within a mile of the river was underwater.

And yet we sat, avoiding one another's looks, heckled by the incessant rain when it carried up from the caverns, as if skimming along the water's surface as something belonging more to mother nature than Mercy May's wailing organ. Something belonging to the rain and the wind and as the first incantation arrived, there was another, like those cool breezes penetrating the back porch all those summer evenings. We all looked up; but for the hunter Rovero, we were all the same, all of us equally susceptible to the objectivity of our heritage, the existence of Beasts and Messiahs. So, we listened, watching the netherworld of the gorge as the sound continued, stacked and tiered in a succession of sustaining spells when Rufus engaged Liberty's outboard and Septimus pushed them off and Liberty turned to us and yelled, "Remember, if you get in trouble, throw your line out to the nearest boat."

We moved into the open water. With an acknowledged history spent navigating the Ohio, Simp Laughton manned the bow of the lead boat as we advanced along the down-current edge of the hickories and

396

through a maze of debris and driftwood, striking the hulls like muted drums. Judging the swollen banks at fifty yards, we left the protective hickories to ride the stronger current and those at the bow worked their paddles against the traveling logs and those at the transom worked their throttle arms in an accelerating, de-accelerating, zigzagging dance. As we approached the Sapp's east line, we broke in for the river and accepted the current. We idled down, negotiating a centerline between the trees that marked the narrowing banks. A chance to catch our breath, the oarsmen to balance their blades over the gunwales and their partners to cool their engines and exchange sidelong looks, the eyes of men humbled with an acquiescent modesty.

But the reprieve was short-lived. The trees gave way to the alluvial substrates that gave way to the bedrock formations of sandstone rising to limestone sheer-walls sculpted by glacial meltwaters into the tectonic gates of the Kickapoo Ridge Gorge. Shielded from the direct force of the blowing rain, we maneuvered the bends and with each bend, we slammed starboard into the leeward canyon walls and against one another and there was just time to ready ourselves before slamming aft into the next bend and for three-hundred yards, we bounced through the gorge. The last blind turn and we were upon the diminutive breakwaters jammed with a medley of carcasses and tree trunks and everything buttressed against the pass-through like a sealed vault.

Impossible to know just how many bloated hides were stacked submerged beneath the waterline. How many fence posts, how many miles of barbed wire, how many kitchen sinks. Impossible to gauge the scope of our work, swinging in broadside and throttling up to stand our ground against the current in a cloud of oily exhaust and screaming driveshafts.

We communicated by gesture, deafened by the engines and the floodwaters echoing off the canyon walls and yet maintaining the sequence rehearsed earlier on the lawn. Those in the bow left their posts to gather the lines amidship and crawl with their knees splayed across

POSSESSING THE SEASONS

the ribs of the hulls to position the grappling hooks off the stern like novices working a lasso. Liberty signaled and the hooks lofted to embed the hides and the bowmen belly-down as the boats moved away from the cataract. At fifty yards, safe from the pull of the vortex, we brought the lines taut and with an accelerating thrust, we dislodged a dozen buoyant carcasses, swept downstream alongside a tattered bed mattress coiled in barbed wire.

There was only the one effort; with the force of the renewed current, it was no longer safe, nor possible, to approach the vortex. We found refuge in a tributary rivulet banked by a limestone precipice twenty feet high, cutting the engines and securing the boats and climbing onto the plateaus of a stone ledge and while some stretched out on their backs, others set up the tents and brought out the equipment to start an early dinner of cold cuts and sliced fruit and here we settled in for the afternoon and the night and the following morning until the floodwaters had ebbed and we could manage our way back downstream through the gorge.

That night, with some harbored under their tents with the flaps open and others under an open tarpaulin, we listened to Simp and his gesticulating hands talk of the mighty Ohio, his years navigating the shifting currents and the hidden sandbars and skirting barges the size of airport hangars and the legendary hideouts along that route for the likes of John Dillinger and Pretty Boy Floyd on the heels of another murdering rampage in Chicago. Retelling his father's and grandfather's stories of bounty hunters hiding in the shoreline weeds for runaways and the verbal histories of the early trade barges on the heels of the Eerie Canal being plundered by pirates who lay in waiting just above Elizabethtown, hunkered down at Cave-In-Rock and fortified with an arsenal suited for nothing short of butchery. Or Rovero, the hunter, who spoke of beam reaches and keeling hulls and regattas in full sail on the San Francisco Bay as a Sunday pastime, a sport; we listened, a captive audience perched on this protected plateau surrounded by floodwaters without fully understanding the language of regattas and sporting Sundays.

398

EIGHTY-FOUR

It was the first week in July, two weeks later, when I regressed to an old habit so far gone, I mentioned it to no one. I woke each night in the middle of the night, changed into dry pajamas, crept down the stairs and stood for a moment listening to the books breathe before I opened the bedroom door and entered this sanctuary of her associated scents and odors, slipping quietly into the bed beside Father and when he woke, as he invariably did, to pace the length of the dining room, I followed, falling in line, matching his footsteps, like a silent shadow, careful lest we collide at the turns.

EIGHTY-FIVE

I work now from the small desk in the dayroom; the winding attic stairs just one added effort beyond what I'm willing to manage. Behind me, arranged in chairs facing the big dormer window, set up to simulate a classroom, little Mademoiselle, Marjorie, Clare and Max's grandson, Lavetty's granddaughter, the Roveros' grandkids, Verity and Mariah's grandkids—the usual gang—sit giggling and fidgeting in their makeshift school as Teacher Henry—Mister Whister—the oldest, attempts to restore order from the other side of the long play table, tapping his ruler against the table.

"Now, class..."

But the more he taps, the louder the giggles, until the dayroom erupts into mayhem and I write another sentence, and then another, more concerned anymore with aligning my letters squarely across the page than the significance of their content. The habit of words has outlived what I have left to say.

400

EIGHTY-SIX

Months later, on the brink of fall, as we gravitated from survival to a foothold on the good life at hand, I awakened as the best man's son from an overnighter at Sheriff's to leave the house Lavetty and Madeline and Dolores had cleaned and scrubbed to make ready for a grand new phase in Sheriff and Dee's life. A house Sheriff was born in and lived his life in, alone…until that stretch of recent months when he and Dee began referring to one another as husband and wife, as honey-pie and sweetie-pie, followed by occupying one house and then another and settling ultimately on what led Lavetty and Madeline and Dolores to spend two days cleaning dustballs. The single deciding factor boiling down to Dee's twenty-year feud with her neighbor, the Widow Drew.

We stepped off the porch and onto the walk, whistling, half-heartedly ducking a brood of giant swallowtails swooping out of the elm and down close overhead to circle up in tight formation and back home to the elm. Along Sheriff's forearm, the new wedding suit slipped forward and I caught it inches from the stains of a lush September lawn and as we straightened from the passing swallowtails, we paused to appreciate the call of an eastern screech owl and to watch the dragonflies hawking the

POSSESSING THE SEASONS

lawn for a suitable breakfast and to draw in a breath of the tall Indian grass flowering half a block away. Idle pauses, I believe, as an effort to salve the Sheriff's nerves and convince ourselves it was just another beautiful day in paradise.

Halfway across town, Aunt Dee was in a state salvaged only by a surprisingly clear-headed Bim, who over the years, tended to extrapolate her portrait of that day from the defined maid-of-honor to the only level-headed soul in all of Fall Fork. She stood at the kitchen phone, Bim, securing last-minute arrangements with caterers from Dixon Springs and florists from Golconda and musicians from Elizabethtown and every five minutes another call from Clare.

"You shore they know it?"

"I'm sure, Clare."

"In the Sweet By and By?"

"I told them, Clare."

"Max wants that'n played."

"I know. I know."

Dee pulled up at the door to the kitchen and paused and stood for a moment like a lost bird and said, *"Dress."*

"The dress is in the car, Dee. Everything but you'n me. So, let's go. Times gettin on."

And back to the receiver, "Clare? Madeline'll be there shortly to drive you up to Hank's. How's the dress?"

"Good. Fits my watermelon belly."

"Preacher Lloyd'll do you and Max first and then Dee and Sam."

"Okay."

Bim hung up and Dee reappeared in the doorway.

"Sam? You talk to Sam?"

"They're just leavin."

"Lorraine?"

"Lorraine? What about Lorraine?"

"Pretty Boy knows what time?"

402

"He's not *Pretty Boy*. It's Preacher Lloyd, and yes...Lorraine's talked to him several times already this morning."

"And I suppose he knows how to do this sort a thing?"

"For goodness sakes, he's a *preacher.*"

"We'll take Bonnel Road. Sam and I aren't s'spose to catch sight 'a one another and they'll be taking Deere Road and..."

Diligence Wiseman settled his aging mother into the cab of the clean truck that afternoon and as they turned off Spruce, he tapped the horn and waved to Sheriff and I as we turned onto Sycamore to pause alongside the Fallers' station wagon with Bump and Scooter in the backseat. Scooter leaned his combed and parted head out the window, wagging his finger and calling out, *"To the church. To the church."*

I threw a thumbs-up and we moved along to watch Violet Wisemen gathering her dress and lowering herself into the backseat of Liberty and Lorraine Snead's sedan and Sheriff tapped the horn as we rolled up Sycamore, where we stopped long enough for me to leave the cab and take the camera from Pat Davis and snap a picture of Acceptance and her parents in their get-up before continuing to where Ruby Morrow sat on her porch looking confused and forgotten. Dr. Leemore stepped out his front door and with a wave to the Sheriff, he slowly crossed the lawn onto the Morrow porch as the groom and the best man's son turned onto Willow Street, passing Town Hall and crossing the creek bridge and along the cornerstone homes where Mercy May stepped off her porch cradling her sheet music and at the sight of us, she threw out a preview of her scheduled performance, a single note from an unenlightened octave and the Sheriff lifted his eyebrows and smiled when Bim's car was sighted off the Dillmans' Victorian at the corner of the school and suddenly Sheriff braked and crouched below the windshield, throwing an arm out the window as Dee hid herself with an open palm held up like a hand-fan, as they swerved onto Alder Street laughing like teenagers.

We crisscrossed the graveled roads through the open countryside of a perfect fall. Scooter and Bump and I were released to head out on foot through the honeysuckles and along the levied rise behind the church, banging and pushing and shoving, and more shoving, and more shoving, until our clean pantlegs were dulled with dust when we paused at the sound of Buddy's new toy.

Back on our feet, we stood with our arms dangling, surrounded by blooming goldenrods and purple martins, centered between that caravan inching onto Pond Road and another, in the opposite direction, along Deere Road. Buddy's blue coupe was returning from the depot in Fall Fork with Mariah home for the weekend, carrying down the straight open way in a backwash of dust headlong toward Madeline and Elmer, Madeline behind the wheel, carefully negotiating the corner, thinking surely, right pedal-gas, middle pedal-brake, left pedal…left pedal…the C word. Crutch, or something. She shifted down, as she later recalled, and forgot the C-pedal and the grinding racket roused a brood of fledgling goldfinches, coming from nowhere in a flight path across her front windshield as she braked the wrong pedal and lurched through Snead's Corner like a leaping toad.

Behind her, Diligence braked and, over the years, depending on the audience, mumbled, "Sheesh, Madeline."

A moment later, he slapped the wheel and groaned and looked into the rearview mirror and then to his mother who hadn't said a single word about Violet riding with the Sneads and he looked back to the road, wishing he were dead.

Dr. Leemore, who committed his account to a written, rather personal diary, slowed to maintain a fair distance from the hot-headed Wiseman, drawn away from his recurring daydream that he'd had a nice practice in El Dorado and had accepted the vacancy in Fall Ridge in a desperate need for change. But it had been six months since the good

404

Lord had taken his wife and he found himself imagining it was her and not Ruby Morrow sharing the front seat. Drawn away from his thoughts, he was forced to consider his patient who seemed suddenly agitated and had he administered fifty, or one-hundred, milligrams?

But it was too late. Ruby was wrestling with the door handle, and although her version of that day changed with every telling over the years, her language was consistently age-inappropriate, and there was, we assume, a desperate need to free herself from the confinement of 'the old fart who hadn't thought to maybe take another route…anything but smack dab behind that bastard's truck…but the goddamned door wouldn't open and what was wrong with the goddamned door?' when she felt the needle in her shoulder and from that point ever-after, her story was scattered with hallucinatory claims she had been kidnapped and wedded against her will.

Dee and Bim looked at one another wide-eyed and then back to Dr. Leemore's rear window and Bim said, "Did you see that?"

Dee covered her face with her hands and mumbled, "Where's good ole Steadfast when we need him?"

"He's dead, dear. Dead and a mold'n in his grave."

"Ah Lord, Ruby…not today."

"That crazy quack."

They sat, stalled in traffic, all bathed and powdered and slowly melting like fresh biscuits frosted in sweat and molasses. Dee gazed off across Liberty Snead's field, tilled like potting soil, re-seeded and harvested and seeded again, for goodness sakes, for yet another quick-to-market Hybrid return toward the assurance of a strong recovery. Beyond the blossoming milkweeds marking the selvedge from one field to another, a flowering copse of early autumnal dogwoods from which two horses emerged. The riders folding low, dodging through the maze in a crisscrossing gait and along the margin of the woods toward the north field.

POSSESSING THE SEASONS

We carried on between the church and the Marsh house, Bump and Scooter and I, chasing lizards and hurling toads and glancing now and again to the approaching coupe and to the backup at Snead's Corner and when we caught sight of the two horses, we stood waving our arms and hollering beneath the mottled skies. We stood atop the small embankment separating the Marsh and Roe fields, jockeying for position with leading shoulders and playful shoves and quickly on our hands and knees wrestling and clambering over one another and from the Marsh lawn, our hollering voices carried like chattering squirrels as Vivian Marsh crossed her lawn and deposited a stack of clean tablecloths in the bed of Sheriff's truck and as Sheriff positioned them against the back of the cab, Vivian later recalled how she had considered the ailing Givens in bed all morning. How it was just another of his manipulations. She knew this. Her Givens at the center of his own universe, demanding her rotating presence in a manipulative con game she could not afford to ignore as Pat Davis rolled to a stop behind Sheriff's truck and for a moment, watching us, Acceptance said all she could think of was tall grass. She said tall grass came to mind, growing wild and then that side of me concentrating so hard on my little sentences for the *Gazette* and for a moment, saddened—the lonely, vulnerable side of me lasting all summer as Liberty and Marian idled behind them with Liberty later claiming how Violet Wiseman in the backseat had positioned both he and Marian on the Violet side of that awkward brouhaha between she and Diligence while Marian gazed off toward the bridge where Lavetty and Rufus and Simp and the others were all crossing the our east field on foot, singing, following that beloved albino. The harmonizing tenor of their voices carried lazily up the road to where Guy and Dolores were snarled behind the Sneads' sedan, Dolores sitting close, lightly touching the muscles in Guy's arm while watching the two horses cross Hank's field into Givens' field and around the backside of the Marsh house toward the church at a full canter.

406

Father and Verity rode low to the pommels, racing, and as they came parallel to the fenceline, Father, Sheriff's best man, threw out an arm to the gridlocked cars and it was then and there Dolores seized on that subtle image, marking it forever in her mind as the end of one era and the beginning of another.

The two horses banked off into the open plain, galloping in a race along the grassy swales and onto the elevated slope in full view of those early arrivals lingering in the church parking lot, drawing in on Bump, Scooter, and myself as we broke off running for the church like gazelles beneath the bluest of blue skies, yelping and hollering like bloodhounds, making for the stand of flowering dogwoods with Father and Verity closing in, seemingly airborne.

More like a frolicking fox hunt than a wedding party.

EIGHTY-SEVEN

On some mornings, I can hear the incantations floating off the river. On others, both voices at once, rising and falling in a medley of dueling octaves. Even now, I can hear them, as I tell you this.

EIGHTY-EIGHT

"We want to thank you for your time…for agreeing to help fill in a few blanks where your father-in-law left off before, before…"

"It's quite all right. How can I help?"

"Is it Dominate? For the record, you know."

"What record?"

"WHO's record."

"…?"

"It's an unusual name. A nickname, perhaps?"

"Dominate Rea Snead by birth. Dominate Rea Roe by marriage."

"Rea Roe, row your boat…ha."

"Could I see some identification?"

"Oh, that's not necessary. Your father-in-law and I were old friends."

"You don't look that old. He never mentioned you, whoever you are."

"Just call me Director."

"Director of what?"

"Of WHO, not what."

"…?"

"So, just a few loose nuts to tighten up."

"…?"

409

POSSESSING THE SEASONS

"Our report indicates no one in your family was aware of Henry Roe's affiliations?"

"Affiliations?"

"Connections."

"With who?"

"Not with WHO. No. No way. I swear we at WHO had nothing to do with it."

"With what?"

"With what?"

"Who, who had nothing to do with what?"

"Is your husband home?"

"He's busy. I'm busy."

"Is that him...his voice from the other room?"

"He's on the phone, running your plates through the Sheriff."

"Sheriff?"

"The Sheriff...he's on his way."

"I want to thank you for your time. It's been most helpful. We at WHO apologize for dominating your time. Good day to you."

"That's the door to the pantry."

ACKNOWLEDGEMENTS

In an act of silence and solitude, the novelist moves through a progression of drafts in a search for what he or she ultimately hopes to say. And yet now and again there emerges a sprinkling of voices weighing in with their own fresh and appreciated perspectives. The author wants to thank J.M. Coetzee for his thoughtful suggestions and input on earlier drafts. And a collection of diversified readers through yet another early draft in a chapter-by-chapter offering: Eric Johnson for his poet's ear, Patricia Francis for her valuable line edits, Sarah Prowell, Guy Beiderman, Laura Close,and Sally Washburn. A special consideration to Irene Moore, of the Frederick Hill Agency, for her early line edits and staunch support. And finally, to the staff at April Gloaming for their outstanding cooperation and not to ever be overlooked, their pervasive southern culture of kindness and courtesy.

ABOUT THE AUTHOR

Charles Prowell and his three sisters were raised on a farm in central Illinois, with frequent stretches on the family heritage farm in southern Illinois. Upon graduation from Southern Illinois University studying Architecture, Design, and Psychology, he relocated to San Francisco and currently lives in Sonoma County, CA. As the founder of Prowell Woodworks, inc, his articles, profiles and features have appeared in Fine Woodworking, Fine Homebuilding, This Old House, Woodwork, and Old House Journal, among others. His short fiction has appeared in Alaska Quarterly and Great River Review (Pushcart nominations), among others. Possessing the Seasons is his first novel.

www.ingramcontent.com/pod-product-compliance
Lightning Source LLC
LaVergne TN
LVHW040734250125
801961LV00026B/434